PRAISE FO

"Malfi constructs a panoramic narrative [illegible] of individuals sharpens the sense of horror overwhelming the town. This smartly written novel succeeds as both an allegory of smalltown life and a tale of visceral horror." *Publishers Weekly*

"Well-drawn characters, horrific creatures, gruesome deaths, plenty of blood . . . a soupcon of mystery and an atmosphere of dread that just oozes from the pages." *Dread Central*

"You hear a lot of talk about 'The next big name' in Horror . . . If there is any justice, Ronald Malfi will be a 'Big Name' . . . I'm looking forward to seeing what he has in store for us in the future." *Horror World*

PRAISE FOR RONALD MALFI

"Malfi is horror's Faulkner." Gabino Iglesias, award-winning author of *The Devil Takes You Home*

"Malfi is a masterful writer, a storyteller who has no interest in pulling punches or playing nice when it comes to his fiction." Philip Fracassi, author of *Boys in the Valley*

"His writing is so strong and so of-the-moment that these horrors and fears tap into horror nostalgia while also feeling brand new. It's some kind of magic trick, which makes Malfi one hell of a magician." Christopher Golden, *New York Times* bestselling author of *The House of Last Resort* and *Road of Bones*

Also by Ronald Malfi and available from Titan Books

Come with Me
Black Mouth
Ghostwritten
They Lurk
Small Town Horror

Also by Ronald Malfi

Bone White
The Night Parade
Little Girls
December Park
Floating Staircase
Cradle Lake
The Ascent
Snow
Shamrock Alley
Passenger
Via Dolorosa
The Nature of Monsters
The Fall of Never
The Space Between

Novellas

Borealis
The Stranger
The Separation
Skullbelly
After the Fade
The Mourning House
A Shrill Keening
Mr. Cables

Collections

We Should Have Left Well Enough Alone: Short Stories

RONALD MALFI

THE NARROWS

TITAN BOOKS

The Narrows
Paperback edition ISBN: 9781835410530
Broken Binding edition ISBN: 9781835411988
E-book edition ISBN: 9781835410813

Published by Titan Books
A division of Titan Publishing Group Ltd
144 Southwark Street, London SE1 0UP
www.titanbooks.com

First edition: October 2024
10 9 8 7 6 5 4 3 2 1

This is a work of fiction. All of the characters, organizations, and events portrayed in this novel are either products of the author's imagination or are used fictitiously. Any resemblance to actual persons, living or dead (except for satirical purposes), is entirely coincidental.

A CIP catalogue record for this title is available from the British Library.

Printed and bound by CPI Group (UK) Ltd, Croydon CR0 4YY.

For Don,
A great editor and one helluva good guy.

COLD-FIRE EYES AND SHOWER-STALL SAUNAS: AN INTRODUCTION TO *THE NARROWS*

"I want to write a vampire novel, only I don't want to put any vampires in it."

This was a statement I made some time in the late spring or early summer of 2011, during a period when Barack Obama was enjoying his first tour of the White House, and I was similarly enjoying a surge of creative profusion that was nearly euphoric. In the span of two years, I had written and published four novels with three different publishing companies—*Snow* with Leisure Books/Dorchester Publishing, *The Ascent* and *Floating Staircase* with Medallion Press, and *Cradle Lake* as a limited-edition hardcover with Delirium Books (also later published in paperback with Medallion). I believe I first uttered these words over a lunch with a former editor who had taken on a new gig and was looking to bring over some of his old clients.

Because I thought he either hadn't heard me or hadn't understood, I repeated the sentiment with a bit more emphasis: "I want to write a *vampire* novel, only I don't want to put any *vampires* in it."

The editor smiled then languidly shook his head. "Yeah? And how does that work?"

"It could work. Of course it could. What I mean is, I like the *tone* of a vampire novel, the *sensibilities* of them. I like the atmosphere, and you know I'm all about atmosphere. I like to get my readers drunk on atmosphere. I just don't want to write about vampires."

"Then what will the book be about?"

"Oh, about four hundred pages, give or take."

"That's it," he said. "I'm cutting you off. No more vodka tonics with lunch."

"Come on, hear me out. What I really want to write about is the death of Small Town U.S.A. presented through the allegory of something . . . horrific . . . that has come to bring about the town's final death blow. It's about blue-collar folks and shuttered storefronts and a storm that has come and ravaged all that remains of this town. It's just teetering there on the brink of existence."

"Go on," said the editor.

I didn't really know where I was going, but I motored on just the same: "But it's not just about the town, right? It's about the *people* in the town, these last vestiges of humanity clinging to whatever is left of the place where they grew up. And the thing, of course, that has come to bring about their demise."

"And what's the thing if it's not a vampire?"

I shrugged then waved the waitress over to order another round of drinks. Once she'd left—and afforded me a sufficient amount of time to formulate a response—I said, "I'll make up my own *thing.* Maybe something that, throughout history, people may have mistaken for a vampire. A myth hiding behind the guise of another myth."

"You shouldn't have ordered that last round," my editor friend said.

"What do you mean *last* round?" I replied, cocking an eyebrow.

I spent the rest of that summer and part of the fall working on the novel that would eventually become *The Narrows.* I owed much of the storyline to an old manuscript I'd written back in high school, an exercise in juvenilia for sure, but it had good bones, and anyway, the story had never really left the back of my mind after all those years. (Easter egg: that high school version of *The Narrows* was originally titled *Dread's Hand.* It was a title I attempted to use several years later for another book but was summarily—and justifiably—roadblocked by my editor at the time. In the end, I settled for using Dread's Hand as the name of the haunted Alaskan town in my 2018 novel *Bone White.*) I had settled on my cast of characters, I could close my eyes and see the fictional town of Stillwater as if it were a true place, and I even understood the dark *thing* that had come to my dying little town—a creature whose mission was to siphon the last vestiges of life and humanity from an already dying world. I could *see* it, even if it continued to try to hide from me whenever I looked.

Warning: you're about to judge me . . .

The final few chapters of the novel were written in a one-room cabin on the edge of a wildlife refuge somewhere in the wilds of West Virginia. It had been my intention to go out there and garner some peace and quiet to finish the novel, but fate seemed intent on disrupting my plans: the cabin was oddly, bitterly cold for so early in the fall, the food was horrendous, and every night I'd hear all manner of nefarious cryptids muscle their way through the thicket outside my cabin's solitary window. Moreover, the accommodations were not ideal for writing—there was no desk in the room, only a small round table that wobbled no matter how many coasters from the bar down the street I managed to wedge beneath the table legs, and I was straining my back muscles trying to type on a laptop while propped uncomfortably in bed. So I did the only logical thing: I went into the bathroom, set the laptop on top of the closed toilet lid, cranked the shower to create a sauna-like effect, and finished the novel cross-legged right there on the bathroom floor.

I remember the moment I finished the novel. I stood from the bathroom floor, my legs aching and wobbly, the laptop monitor glistening with a sheen of wetness from the shower-stall sauna. My reflection in the steamy mirror was part Slender Man, part vaporous revenant. There was a beer bottle jeweled with condensation on the toilet tank and empty Slim Jim wrappers lay scattered about the tiled floor like sloughed snakeskin.

I was trembling.

Every novel has weight, and I carry that weight for the duration of the writing process. It falls off my shoulders and drops to the floor, heavy as chainmail, the moment I write that last sentence. Experience has taught me that the weight does not return during the editorial process—there's a clearheaded athleticism I somehow employ when editing that feels like the polar opposite of the trudging-through-quicksand process of writing.

I moved out of that bathroom, light as a feather, careful not to trip myself up on that chainmail lying in a heap on the bathroom floor. I went to my suitcase and yanked out a set of fresh clothes. I shucked off my damp old clothes and crawled into the new ones. The metaphor of metamorphosis was not lost on me.

It was then that I froze.

A pair of pale blue eyes gleamed luminously from the other side of the cabin window. That corner of the cabin, I knew, was situated on a sloping hillside, which meant that whatever was standing on the other side of that glass in the darkness peering in at me was very, very big.

But this wasn't a horror novel.

I went to the window, expecting the owner of those cold-fire eyes to flee. But the thing held fast, its gaze laser-focused on me. A few more steps (it was a small cabin) and I was at the window, so close my breath was fogging up the glass.

Those eyes . . .

I reached out and tapped a finger on the windowpane—*tink tink tink*.

The owner of those eyes cocked its head at such a precise angle that I first jumped backed, then instantly realized they belonged to an owl—a very large owl—a moment before the massive bird took flight, leaving me breathless and admittedly rattled.

I stood there for a moment longer, until a nervous laugh juddered up the vent of my throat. But then I went silent. My body went still. Because the sight of those eyes made me think of something *else*—something that *should be in the new novel*—and I literally walked backward into the bathroom, my gaze still hinged on the window. The shower was still running, the mirror still fogged. I swiped a hand across the moist screen of the laptop as I hunkered back down before it. And as I began to write, I could feel that heavy chainmail crawl up off the bathroom floor, creep up my back, and drape itself once more over my shoulders.

There is no denying that *The Narrows* was written by an ambitious and somewhat naive author who, to some degree, was still trying to find his footing. It's clearly one of my more "monstery" novels, though, just as *Publishers Weekly* had commented upon the book's release, I think it serves well as an allegory of small-town life in the face of visceral horror. The book was published the following year, in 2012, by a publishing outfit that is now defunct. My editor friend who had purchased the novel read it quickly and had minimal notes. Later, when we discussed the book over the phone, he said, "Well, I guess you pulled it off—a vampire novel with no vampires. But you do realize that people will still think of it as a vampire novel, right? The things in the story are so—"

"Stop," I told him. "It's fine. People will think what people will think."

"People will," he agreed. And he was right.

The prologue to the novel, titled "The Boy in the Lot," was released as a free e-book-only download in an attempt to garner interest in the novel prior to its release; that prologue was never actually included in any print edition of the book until now. So here, for the first time, *The Narrows* is complete.

Stillwater is a small, dying town where a series of terrible things are about to happen. The Narrows have flooded, the people are scared, and something dark and unfathomable has come to roost.

RONALD MALFI
January 16, 2024
Annapolis, Maryland

AUTHOR'S NOTE

This is the part where I ask forgiveness from all the good folks who reside in the western part of Maryland and along the swollen green range of the Allegheny Mountains; for the purposes of this story, I have taken many liberties with your region, to include its topography, history, and its people, and I know how these things can be sacred to some. For the uninitiated, U.S. Route 40 certainly does exist, as do the specific mountains named within this book. The Narrows and Wills Creek exist, as well. But anyone familiar with the area will know I have taken liberty in altering certain details to better suit this author's tale.

However, that's not to say dark things don't hide in real places . . .

RONALD MALFI
April 11, 2011

"I feel a wonderful peace and rest to-night.
It is as if some haunting presence were
removed from me. Perhaps . . ."

—Bram Stoker, *Dracula*

PROLOGUE

THE BOY IN THE LOT

Eleven-year-old Mark Davis took one look at the rundown motel and thought it perfectly suited his mood. It was a crumbling saltbox against the backdrop of a black hillside forest, the windows bleak, lidded with colorless plastic shades, the entranceway about as welcoming and cheerful as the gates of a cemetery. An uneven slip of potholed blacktop—the motel's parking lot—stood as a barrier between the ruinous building and the curve of U.S. Route 40.

As Mark's dad turned the car into the parking lot, the chassis roller-coastering across the irregular blacktop, Mark surveyed the place. Beside him in the backseat, Tim—short for Timbuktu—panted, his hot dog-breath steaming up the car's windows. Mark petted the old dog and watched as a clear rope of saliva depended from the dog's mouth and pattered to the car seat.

"Really, Will?" asked Mark's mother from the passenger seat.

Will Davis pulled the car into a parking space and geared it into Park. "I'm starting to fall asleep at the wheel," he said. "Unless you want to keep driving, we're stopping for the night."

Mark's mother quickly rolled up her window. "It looks like Armageddon came and went."

"Quit being so dramatic."

"We passed a perfectly good Holiday Inn half an hour ago."

"Forget it. I'm not backtracking. This'll be fine for the night." His father turned around in the driver's seat and smiled wearily at Mark. "This work for you, bud?"

Mark shrugged. Compared to his mood, the motel was a brightly lit amusement park.

"I'll go in and grab us a room," his father said, popping open his door. "You guys wait here."

Tim whined as the door slammed shut. Mark continued petting the old dog. He watched his dad hustle across the poorly lit parking lot until he disappeared beneath the entrance portico. Stenciling on the lighted front window said OFFICE.

"You okay?" his mother asked from up front. Unlike his father, she didn't turn around and look at him.

"Whatever," he said.

She sighed. She was normally a pleasant-looking woman, but the stress of the move—and no doubt the stress of dealing with Mark lately—had caused her to look weary and strung-out. "Don't you think you've sulked about this long enough?"

He folded his arms and glanced out the window. Lights were on in some of the rooms, rimming the rectangular shades in milky light. "No," he said.

"Grandpa Mike was in the military," she reminded him, "and I had moved five times by the time I was your age."

Good for you, Mark thought, but didn't dare say aloud.

"You know," his mother continued, "your father and I have been talking. Seeing how you're leaving all your friends behind, we thought it might be okay for you to finally get that cell phone."

Mark brightened. "Really?" He had been asking for a cell phone for the better part of the past year. All his friends had one, yet his parents had been adamant that an eleven-year-old boy didn't need to carry around his own personal cell phone.

"Your dad and I will lay down some ground rules," she said, "but yes, we think that if you can be responsible with it, we're willing to get it for you. Do you think you can be responsible with it?"

"You bet," he said.

His mother sighed contentedly in the passenger seat. "Good boy," she said.

A shape exited the motel's front office and moved like a shadow across the parking lot. As the shape passed beneath an arc sodium light, Mark saw that it was his father. Will Davis opened the driver's door and poked his head inside.

"Everybody out!"

"Lovely," grumbled Mark's mother.

Mark got out of the car and held the door open for Tim, who bounded out after the boy. The dog went immediately to one of the potholes filled with rain and began lapping up the black water.

Holy crap, a cell phone! Wait till I tell the guys! Of course, this excitement was blanketed by the same black pall that had hung above his head like a thundercloud since he had been told by his parents that they would be moving. His father had gotten a new job in a different state, and that meant leaving all of Mark's friends behind. A cell phone was a grand thing—it would be his own little slice of independence—but what good was a cell phone if you couldn't call up your friends and make plans? Sure, he could call them and they could joke over the phone . . . but in the end, he would just have to hang up again and continue being friendless in their new neighborhood.

Timbuktu looked up at him. As was often the case, Mark discerned a deep intelligence in the old dog's eyes.

"You're my friend, aren't you, boy?" he asked the dog, once more stroking the silken gold fur along the dog's back. "You aren't going anywhere."

His father swung a few duffel bags over one shoulder then slammed the car's trunk. He whistled as he joined Mark's mother, who looked up at the sagging motel roof and fizzing neon VACANCY sign with barefaced displeasure. "We're in Room 104," he said cheerily enough.

Inwardly, Mark groaned. His father was always in a good mood when faced with adversity. He wondered if the man actually relished the little daily confrontations—switching jobs, moving from one city to another, spending the night in some horror movie motel in rural Maryland. Not for the first time, Mark secretly wished his dad would get fired, just like what happened to Davey Hannah's dad back in Spring Grove, only without ending in his parents getting a divorce, which is what happened to Davey's parents. Davey was Mark's best friend back in Spring Grove. They had gone all through grade school together, not to mention the Boy Scouts, and had even been on the same Little League team two years in a row. People even said they looked the same—they were both slender, tow-headed, freckled, cheerful—and once, in third grade, they had told everyone they were twin brothers and had even managed to convince a few of their classmates. Mark figured they would have also convinced their teacher, Mrs. Treble, had she not seen their last names on her class roster.

An eighteen-wheeler, all roaring tires and spaceship headlights, blasted along the curl of highway on the far side of the parking lot. Tim barked at the truck while Mark watched it cruise past, its taillights glowing like demonic eyes before being swallowed up by the darkness.

Mark looped two fingers beneath Tim's collar. "Come on, boy. Let's get inside."

He turned and followed his parents along the motel curb, Tim bounding obediently beside him. He passed lighted windows, their shades drawn, and for seemingly the first time noticed the other cars scattered about the parking lot. It truly was a miserable place; his mother had every right to balk at the accommodations, particularly since they had driven past several nice-looking hotels coming out of the last city. To Mark, this looked like the kind of place bank robbers would hole up.

The room was only slightly better than the outside of the place. Drab walls, worn carpeting the color of sawdust, two twin beds laid out like coffins in the center of the claustrophobic little room. There was a TV atop a nicked and scarred dresser, though it wasn't even a flat screen. Similarly, the telephone that sat on the nightstand between the two beds looked like something salvaged from an antiques shop.

Tim emitted a high keening—a sentiment Mark could certainly relate to.

So could Mark's mother, it seemed. She stood with her arms folded while her eyes volleyed from one bed to the other. "They didn't have anything larger than twin beds?"

"Not if we wanted to all stay in the same room," said his father, dumping their duffel bags on top of the bed farthest from the door.

"Terrific." His mother turned and peered at the partially open bathroom door. "I'm afraid to go in there."

"Cut it out, Sharon, will you?"

Tim padded across the room and settled down on the floor between the two beds. The old retriever rested his muzzle down on his front paws while his eyebrows triggered back and forth, back and forth. Mark smiled warmly at the dog then went to the one duffel bag his father had set on the bed that he knew contained his belongings. He unzipped the bag and pulled out a few comic books, along with a plastic baggie that contained a few of Tim's favorite dog treats. Mark opened the bag and withdrew one of the treats. It was a greasy brown pipette that reminded him of a Slim Jim, though they tasted—and Mark knew this from experience, having been bested one afternoon by curiosity—like mint.

Tim's head lifted up off his paws. A beggar's whine filled the small motel room.

"Come get it," Mark said, extending the treat toward the dog.

Tim rose, padded over to Mark, sniffed the greasy thin cylinder pinched between Mark's fingers, then quickly gobbled it up. This made Mark smile, though there was a distant sadness in him now. He recognized that old Timbuktu wasn't the young pup he'd once been—that there was gray in his muzzle and something called arthritis in his joints, which made him move more slowly and cautiously than he had in his earlier years. There would come a time in the not-too-distant future when Tim would no longer be with him. It would be a separation worse than leaving his friends behind in the old neighborhood, Mark knew. But each time he thought of it, the notion struck him with such grief that he forced the thought away before it could fully form. He didn't like to think about a world without Timbuktu.

Mark's mother looked around the bathroom then returned to the room, an unreadable expression on her face. His father was taking off his wristwatch while peering out the singular window that looked out on the parking lot.

"Maybe I should bring the car in closer," his father muttered, more to himself than to them.

"Maybe you should pull that shade so no one can see in here," Mark's mother suggested.

His father pulled the shade down then tossed his wristwatch on the bedspread. He met Mark's eyes and winked. Despite the cheerfulness of his father's demeanor, the old guy looked bushed.

"I'm going to attempt to shower," said his mother, digging some fresh bedclothes and toiletries out of her own duffel bag. "The quicker I get to bed the quicker morning will be here and we can move along."

Mark saw the tired smile on his father's face falter, albeit for just a brief moment. When the bathroom door shut, his father sat down on the edge of the bed and kicked off his shoes.

"I'm gonna hibernate tonight, Mark-o," he said. Then he reclined on the mattress, lacing his hands behind his head.

Tim whined and went to the door.

"I think he's gotta go out, Dad."

"We just came in," his father said, staring at the ceiling.

"I'll take him."

"Don't go far," said his father.

"I won't."

Mark flipped open one of his comic books and found the postcard he'd purchased for seventy-five cents at the last rest stop. The card depicted a grouchy cartoon crab, a pouty frown on its face. The caption read WE'RE ALL A LITTLE CRABBY IN MARYLAND. He promised to send Davey a postcard from the road, and this was the coolest one he could find. A stretch, to be sure, but what could he do about it?

He stuffed the postcard in the back pocket of his jeans then went to the motel room door. He toed Tim aside so he could open the door.

"Be careful," his father admonished from the bed. He sounded like he was halfway asleep already.

"I will," Mark said, snatching Tim up by his collar again. "Come, Tim." He led the dog out onto the curb then shut the motel door behind him. Glancing around, he saw nothing but the parking lot stretched out before him. Beyond that, the little white reflectors along the highway glowed in the moonlight. He looked to the right, where the parking lot concluded in a black plume of foliage, and thought that might be the best bet.

Mark tugged Tim's collar along the curb toward the trees. Overhead, thunder rumbled, causing him to freeze. Even Tim froze. The air was cool. From his years in the Scouts he'd learned to smell a storm in the air. There was definitely a storm coming. A big one.

"Hurry up," Mark said, and gently swatted at Tim's backside.

The dog loped forward then slowed to a concentrative trot. When Tim reached the edge of the curb, he sniffed around while walking in circles, until he hopped down and wended through the underbrush.

Lightning exploded overhead. Mark gasped and looked up in time to see the resonating bluish lights leeching from a bulwark of angry black clouds. The moon looked like a face that was slowly retreating into a darkened room.

"Come on, Tim!" he shouted into the darkness. He waited several seconds but the dog did not reappear from the trees. A scraping sound caught his attention. Mark looked up and saw barren tree branches scudding against the motel roof, blown by the wind.

Stupid dog . . .

He stepped down off the curb and peered through the dark trees. Movement—a whitish blur—caught his eyes.

"Tim!"

But whatever it had been faded back into the darkness. It wasn't like Tim to be disobedient.

What if it's not Tim? Mark thought. *What if it's something else?*

The thought frightened him. Yet it was stupid. What else could it possibly be? He didn't believe in monsters. Bears, maybe . . . or wildcats . . . but not some monster . . .

Then Davey Hannah stepped out from behind a large tree. The boy's pale white face seemed to radiate with an incandescent light. A smile was half-cocked on the boy's face, his wide black eyes shimmering out at Mark.

It took Mark a second to find his voice. "Davey? Is that . . . is that you?"

Almost imperceptibly, Davey's head turned first to the right then to the left.

"What are you doing here?" Mark asked.

Davey's smile widened. He turned and glanced at something behind the tree—the tree from behind which he had come—then looked back at Mark. Yet before Mark could utter another word, Davey stepped back behind the tree, filling his void with absolute darkness.

"Davey, wait," Mark said, and pushed toward his friend through the thicket. When he reached the tree, he peered behind it . . . but Davey was not there.

Something came up behind him. Something larger than Davey Hannah.

Mark turned around and saw it.

Something flashed over Mark's eyes. A moment after that, he felt an unforgiving constriction around his chest, cutting off his airway. He tried to scream but couldn't. When he felt something hot and sharp pierce the flesh at the base of his spine, he tried to thrash and pull himself free, but it was a futile attempt.

" . . . avey . . . "

Mark's vision faded. He gasped for air but could harness none. His body went numb, numb.

Only a few yards away, Timbuktu barked. Then the old dog turned around and ran off through the woods. A motorist would find the dog hours later, wandering up Route 40 in the direction of a rural little Maryland hamlet called Stillwater.

PART ONE

STILLWATER RUNS DEEP

"We all rose early, and I think that sleep did much for each and all of us."

—Bram Stoker, *Dracula*

CHAPTER ONE

1

The students in Miss Sleet's sixth-grade class were reading quietly to themselves when one of the girls in the back of the room screamed. Heads whirled in the girl's direction—it was Cynthia Paterson, sitting stiff as a board in her chair, her head craned back on her neck—and there was the sound of pencils rolling to the floor. Matthew Crawly, whose desk was just two up from Cynthia's, followed Cynthia's eyes toward the bank of windows that looked out upon the football field, a bright green grid mapped with white spray-painted lines. He could see nothing of significance on the field itself or in the parade of champagne-colored trees that lined Schoolhouse Road beyond the field.

Miss Sleet stood sharply from behind her desk. She was a narrow, hardened woman in her sixties whose body—cloaked in garish floral prints with lace cuffs—looked angular and violent. Her hands were like the claws of a rooster.

"What is—" Miss Sleet began . . . but then the rest of her words were replaced by a guttural groan as her own eyes flitted toward the wall of windows.

Toward the back of the room, a few more students cried out. A good number of the girls had already popped out of their desks and stood like pageant contestants at the back of the classroom, their backs against the filing cabinets and the rank of hooks that held their autumn coats. Cynthia Paterson jumped out of her chair as well, her face suddenly pale, her eyes impossibly wide. Soundlessly, she pointed up at the windows.

Matthew looked again, this time at the windows themselves, streaky with dried soap scum and peppered with Halloween decorations made from brown and orange construction paper. Spotty gray shades made of thick vinyl were rolled into tubes at the tops of the windows, wispy with cobwebs. As he looked, he spotted a furtive movement at the top of the window closest to Miss Sleet's desk—a twitching, incongruent thing where the shade met the wall. Something small and black hung from the shade. It was no bigger than the sandwiches his mother packed him for lunch, but even from this distance he could see that it was comprised of coarse brownish-black hair and vibrated with life.

"A bat!" one of the boys shouted. "It's a bat!"

The furry thing stirred and, even over the shouts and whimpers of the students, Matthew heard it emit a high-pitched, tittering sound. Its wings cranked open, its movements as seemingly uncertain as those of a newborn baby. A tiny triangular head capped with pointed ears bobbed as it sniffed the air—up, down, all around. Then it dropped from the shade and, amid a collective cry of fear from the students as well as old Miss Sleet, it zigzagged across the room. Its papery wings flapped frantically.

The students standing at the rear of the room scattered. The sound of their shoes on the linoleum was like an adult's reprimand to remain quiet: *shhh*. Some of them made it to the door but, in their panic, they couldn't seem to get it open. Those still in their seats—Matthew Crawly among them—ducked as the winged critter flitted above their heads. The thing screeched as it drove itself into the chalkboard—Miss Sleet screeched, too—then it cartwheeled up into the ceiling where it beat its wings against the acoustical tiles with a sound disarmingly similar to tree branches whapping against windowpanes in a strong wind.

"Good Lord," Miss Sleet croaked. When the classroom door was finally wrenched open and a stream of kids spilled out into the hall, Miss Sleet shouted at them not to let the bat out of the classroom. Then she staggered backward into one corner, snatching her purse from her desk and clutching it to her chest like some protective idol.

Matthew got out of his chair and walked across the room toward the windows. His eyes did not leave the frightened creature vibrating against the ceiling. He'd seen plenty of bats before—at dusk, the sky above the Crawly house was alive with them—but he'd never seen one in the daytime. And he'd never seen one so afraid.

Dwight Dandridge, Matthew's best friend, was one of the students who'd remained in their seats. The larger boy had his head pressed down on the desktop, his meaty arms hugging his body, a look of petrification on his face. Sweat beaded his reddened brow. As Matthew approached, he gave Dwight a wink that Dwight returned, even in his stupefied state, with a crooked grin.

At the front of the room, Miss Sleet inched her way toward the open door. More kids filed out, though a good number of them remained standing in the doorway, too mesmerized by the thing flitting against the ceiling to look away. Someone pointed at it and murmured nonsense.

Matthew went to the center window, peeled away a grinning jack-o'-lantern made of orange construction paper, and undid the latch.

"What are you doing?" Dwight said, craning his head to watch Matthew but apparently too afraid to lift it off his desk. "You gonna jump out?"

"No." With a grunt, Matthew pushed open the window on squealing hinges.

"Matthew Crawly!" Miss Sleet half barked, half whispered from across the classroom. She was shoving students out the door and into the hallway, her purse still clutched to her chest. Matthew could hear a lot of commotion going on out there in the hall. "Stop that!"

"It's okay," Matthew said evenly.

The bat swung around until it nested in a potted plant atop a large metal filing cabinet at the back of the room. Its movements caused the students out in the hall to shriek shrilly and—almost humorously—caused Miss Sleet to hustle more quickly from the classroom.

"Those things got rabies," Dwight informed Matthew, still slouched down at his desk.

"Not all of them," Matthew said . . . though he was a bit discomfited by the bat having appeared now in the middle of the day. Bats were nocturnal. Of course, it was entirely possible that the thing had gotten trapped in the school during the night and had simply been sleeping here, undisturbed, until chubby little Cynthia Paterson had noticed it. It could have been here for weeks, in fact.

Wild and fuming, Mr. Pulaski staggered into the classroom, his janitorial jumpsuit a palette of stains, his wiry, gray hair a frizzy mat on his head. With the eyes of a hawk, he quickly spotted the bat nesting in the potted plant on the filing cabinet. Mr. Pulaski was chewing hungrily on his lower lip and holding a wrench out before him like a fencing sword. Many of the students in Stillwater Elementary were afraid of Mr. Pulaski, and there was no shortage of stories—each one more frightening and implausible than the next—circulating about the creepy old janitor. Once, Matthew had seen the old fellow dump sawdust on a puddle of pinkish vomit in the cafeteria. When Mr. Pulaski had sensed Matthew's eyes on him, the old janitor had met his gaze—those steel-colored eyes like the burned-out headlights in a Buick—and had held him in it, trancelike. "Might taste a bit different," Mr. Pulaski had said, his voice like the twisting of old leather, "but it still looks the same." Then he had winked, sending Matthew scurrying off down the hallway, his skin gone cold.

Now, Mr. Pulaski struck Matthew as oddly comical. Wielding an oversized wrench and peering across the room at the bat with excessive disdain, he suddenly reminded Matthew of Don Quixote, from the book he'd read over summer break: the confused and improbable hero who battled windmills.

"You boys get out of here," Mr. Pulaski said, referring to Matthew, Dwight, and the smattering of other boys who still lingered in the room, pressed against the tops of their desks.

"Don't hurt it," Matthew said.

If Mr. Pulaski had heard him, he made no acknowledgment. Holding the wrench now in both hands, he crept slowly down one aisle of desks toward the filing cabinet, his eyes trained on the small brown husk of vibrating fur clinging to the leaves of the potted plant. Out in the hallway, someone moaned. Matthew thought it was probably Miss Sleet.

A cool breeze whistled through the open window, blowing papers off desks and rustling the Halloween decorations. Tornadoes of dead leaves whirred to life out on the lawn. On top of the filing cabinet, the bat burst from the plant and carved a clumsy arc across the classroom toward the open window. Mr. Pulaski made a pathetic *gah* sound as he took a swing at the bat with the wrench, and some of the girls out in the hallway cried out in a combination of nervous laughter and abject fear.

"Holy shit," Dwight squeaked then rolled out of his desk chair onto the floor, covering the back of his head with his hands. The bat swerved toward him, executing a fairly commendable loop-the-loop, then pitched out the open window. A second later, it was gone.

Mr. Pulaski, who was still in the process of gaining his balance by leaning on one of the desks, stared blankly at the window then over at Matthew. Again, Matthew thought of the creepy wink the old janitor had given him that day he saw him cleaning up puke in the cafeteria. *Might taste a bit different but it still looks the same.* For whatever reason, eleven-year-old Matthew Crawly was stricken at that moment by an unfounded sense of guilt.

Then the bell rang, signaling the end of the school day, and everyone cried out in surprise.

2

It was mid-October, and the western Maryland town of Stillwater was still drying out from a rainy season that had arrived with the swift and unmitigated vengeance of a Greek god, flooding the Narrows and temporarily darkening the town square. Wills Creek—a slate-colored, serpentine ribbon that forged a valley between two tired mountains and ran along Stillwater's northern border in a semicircular concrete basin, more familiarly known to the locals as the Narrows—had swelled like a cauldron coming to a boil, washing the Highland Street Bridge into the Potomac and casting torrents of black water down the length of the B&O tracks. The town's roads had served as conduits, flushing gallons of water through the neighborhoods and out to the farm roads, while at the center of town, shop owners had watched with mounting horror as the level of the water had risen incrementally against the brick facades and plate-glass windows of their buildings. Some livestock drowned and automobiles that hadn't been repositioned to higher ground flooded. If one were to stand on the circular walkway that circumnavigated the top of the abandoned grain silo on Gracie Street, the destruction would have appeared to be of biblical proportions. It took a full week for the water to retreat completely, leaving behind clumps of reeking, muddy sludge clogged with tree limbs and garbage in the streets. Many houses remained dark for several days more, the power having been snuffed out like a candle in a strong wind. The air stank of diesel exhaust from the litany of gas-powered generators that hummed in open yards. Shop owners were left to contend with flooded storefronts and stockrooms, freezers and refrigerators that were nothing more than coffin-shaped boxes in which goods thawed and rotted. The basement of the elementary school that Matthew Crawly attended had filled with several feet of water that had turned black and oily after mixing with the soot and muck from the school's ancient furnace. Generators were hooked up and a pumping machine was submerged into the swampy mess, trailing a long plastic sleeve up through one of the storm windows, across the playground and the muddied, ruinous baseball diamond, and over the chain-link fence where it vomited fecal-colored water into the woods.

On this rain-swept Friday afternoon, Matthew and Dwight stepped over the train tracks and headed up the slight embankment toward Cemetery Road, their sneakers already blackened with mud. Dwight snapped a branch off a nearby birch tree and began whipping the air. Up ahead, the black iron gates of the Stillwater Cemetery rose up out of the rainy mist like spearheads. As they walked past the gates, Matthew could see the swampy cemetery grounds and the tombstones rising out of shimmering quicksilver puddles. The moss-covered mausoleums beneath the bare limbs of elm trees looked like props in a horror movie. The nearby willow trees hung in wet, loopy garlands, and the sky beyond looked terminally ill. The Crawly house had sustained some damage from the storm, and the electricity had only come back on two nights ago, but that wasn't the worst of it. The worst of it was the smell—a permeating, moldy stink that, when inhaled, felt like it got caught up in your lungs like lint in a dryer vent. Lately, it seemed like the whole town smelled this way.

"I want to see it," Dwight said.

"I can't. I'm not allowed out that far."

"Says who?"

"Says my mom."

"Goddamn it, Crawly. Why are you such a chickenshit?"

"I'm not a chickenshit," Matthew said, shifting his backpack from one shoulder to the other. His sneakers squished in the mud. "What do I want to go all the way out there for, anyway? It's just a stupid deer."

"Billy Leary said it looked like some monster tore it to pieces."

"It's probably gone by now anyway."

"Gone where?" Dwight asked, still swinging at the air with the birch branch. "It just got up and walked away?"

Matthew shrugged. He was still thinking about the bat. After the bell had rung and the hallways had flooded with students anxious to begin their weekend, Matthew had gathered his books from his desk, stuffed them in his backpack, and was about to join Dwight out in the hallway when a heavy hand fell on his shoulder. Startled, he had turned around to see Mr. Pulaski towering over him, the oversized wrench still clenched in one thick-knuckled hand. "Shouldn't be cavalier with bats, son," Mr. Pulaski had warned him. (While Matthew had not known what the word *cavalier* meant, the heart of the statement was not lost on him.) "Sometimes they's dangerous. Sometimes."

"Man, I just *gotta* see this thing," Dwight droned on. "Billy Leary said it might have even been attacked by a bear. Can you believe it?"

No, Matthew couldn't believe it. Billy Leary was a crusty-faced half-wit who spent most of the school day in the remedial classroom by the gymnasium with four or five other students. Matthew did not put much stock in anything Billy Leary said.

"It probably just got hit by a car crossing Route 40."

"Either way, let's *go*," Dwight insisted. Frustrated, he snapped the birch branch in half then tossed both pieces over the cemetery fence. "We'll be home before supper. I promise."

"Okay. But I want to stop by Hogarth's first."

Dwight moaned. Unlike Matthew, whose slight frame and baby-blond hair made him look even younger than he was, Dwight Dandridge was a meaty, solid block of flesh in a striped polo shirt. According to Dwight's father (who was a drunkard, if the one-sided conversations Matthew had overheard when his mother was on the telephone were at all reliable), his son was rapidly on his way to Gutsville. If that meant Dwight was on his way to becoming fat, Matthew surmised that Mr. Dandridge had been living in Gutsville for most of his adult life and could probably run for mayor.

"Hogarth's is on the other side of town, dummy," Dwight groaned. His hands were stuffed into the overly tight pockets of his jeans, and he was kicking rocks as he walked. Matthew glanced at him and found his friend's profile, with his upturned nose and protruding front teeth, piggish and off-putting.

"I'll go with you to the Narrows if you come with me to Hogarth's first," Matthew said.

"It's still there, you know," Dwight assured him. "You don't have to keep checking up on it. No one's buying it."

"Someone might."

"Everyone else has already got their Halloween costumes picked out, dummy. You're the only holdout."

"That's not true."

"Of course it's true. Halloween's two weeks away. What do you think everyone's waiting for?"

"So what are you gonna be?"

"A fuckin' cool space alien." Dwight licked his lips in his excitement. "I got these big rubbery gloves with claws on the ends and this mask, such a freaky mask. You gotta see it! It's got this fishy green skin and eyes like swimming goggles." He was nearly out of breath talking about it.

"Cool," Matthew said.

"Do you even have enough money to buy it yet?"

"No."

"Give it up. You should just be a homicidal serial killer," Dwight suggested. "Wear some ripped-up clothes, put some fake blood all over your face and hands, and walk around with a butcher's knife. It's easy."

"That's stupid."

"You're stupid. Homicidal serial killer's a fuckin' awesome idea."

"Then you can be the stupid serial killer, and I'll wear your alien mask."

"No way, dummy."

They veered off Cemetery Road and headed across town. Even at this hour, the streets were mostly empty, and many of the shops along Hamilton Street, the town's main thoroughfare, were dark and vacant, their plate-glass windows soaped over and their doors boarded up. Matthew imagined that he heard the autumn wind whistling through the ranks of empty storefronts as if through a system of caves. The arcade was gone now, along with the old pizza joint and the video store. The ice cream parlor where Brandy, Matthew's sister, had worked two summers ago was gone as well; all that remained of it was a hollowed-out shell on the corner of Hamilton and Rapunzel, like something out of a movie about nuclear warfare.

Those stores that were still open and thriving had their front stoops ornamented with sandbag barricades. Muddy debris cluttered the sidewalk and, every once in a while, the boys had to step over fallen tree limbs rattling their brown, crunchy leaves in the wind. The last time Stillwater had flooded this badly, Matthew was five years old. His father had shored up the foundation of the house with sandbags and moved all his tools and equipment in the garage to the higher shelves. He had plugged up the exhaust pipes of the pickup truck and the old Dodge with tennis balls and wrapped them over with electrical tape. The water came, simmering at first in the street out in front of the Crawly house, the surface alive with dancing raindrops, the water itself oily and black like ink. Soon enough, the Narrows flooded, and a torrent came gushing down the street and across the opposite field. From the living room windows, Matthew and Brandy had watched as the muddy water rose against the framework of the house. *Things* had been in that water. Brandy had readily pointed them out to him at the time—the bobbing head of a passing snake, the arched and moss-slickened back of an enormous turtle, someone's cat clinging to an iceberg of Styrofoam. Plastic lawn furniture had washed across their backyard. To this day, Matthew could still recall the loud pop just before the power had blown out.

He wondered now if it flooded like that where his father was . . .

The traffic light at the intersection of Hamilton and Susquehanna—which was the only traffic light in Stillwater, unless you counted the blinking-yellow yield lights where Paxton Street merged with Route 40 on the far side of Haystack Mountain—was dark. Both boys darted across the street to Hogarth's, the scalloped edging of the drugstore's green-and-white canvas awning flapping in the wind. There were more sandbags here, along with overturned trash cans and mounds of sodden leaves, glittery and blackish-brown, smashed up against the front of the building. Some of the windows in the nearby shops boasted long spidery cracks, probably from items having been scooped up by the torrent and thrown against the glass. That mildew smell was here, too, just as it was back home, and just as it had been all week at school. It seemed the air was clogged with rot.

Matthew stood before the drugstore's front window in reverential silence. Dwight came up beside him, their mismatched reflections like two ghosts standing side by side in the smoked glass. Scraps of paper whipped against their shins and a single Styrofoam cup cartwheeled down the sidewalk toward them.

"See?" Dwight said.

Matthew stared longingly at the intricately detailed Dracula mask in the window, complete with realistic hair as dark and smooth as raven feathers. The vampire's mouth was a ragged, fang-ringed hole from which exclamations of fake blood streamed in perfect ribbons. Its pallid skin looked as colorless as dough, the blackened pits of its eyes seeming to contain infinite space.

"Yeah. It's still there," Matthew said.

"I told you it would be." Dwight sounded bored. "You can probably get it for cheap after Halloween."

"Yeah," Matthew said, disappointment evident in his voice. It meant nothing, having the Dracula mask *after* Halloween. What good would that do him?

"Hey," said Dwight, suddenly perking up. "You think that was a vampire bat back in Miss Sleet's classroom?"

"No. It was just a fruit bat or something."

"A bat that eats fruit?"

"Or maybe it ate bugs."

"How do you know?"

"I don't know. I just know."

"Vampires," Dwight said . . . and the eyes of his ghostly counterpart suddenly lit up in the reflection of the drugstore window. "Maybe that's what got that hairless boy."

Matthew said nothing. He didn't want to think about the hairless boy. In fact, he'd had nightmares about the boy since some kids in school had told him about it.

"How much are you short, anyway?" Dwight asked.

Matthew did the quick math in his head—he had a Superman lunchbox back in his bedroom where he kept his meager savings—and said, "Only about seven dollars."

"That's not so bad."

"My allowance is three bucks a week."

"Ask for an advance," Dwight said.

"What's that?"

"It's when you get money before you do the work. My dad does it all the time at the shop."

"That sounds like a rip. Who would do that?"

"I just said my dad does it at work."

Matthew did not think his mother would give him an advance. Moreover, the fact that getting an advance was something Dwight's father did confirmed that it sounded like a rip-off. He stared at the mask in the drugstore's window and thought about how cool it would be to have that mask for Halloween, to wear it with a black cape and the star-shaped pendant he'd already made out of cardboard covered in tinfoil, which was also salted away in his Superman lunchbox.

"Okay," Dwight said in a huff. "We came and we saw the stupid mask. Can we go down to the Narrows now? You promised."

The eyeholes in the mask were gaping black pits; the pronged maw of its mouth looked like some sort of trap set deep in the woods to catch bears. Matthew only looked away from it when he felt Dwight tugging at the hem of his shirt.

"Dude," Dwight moaned, "you *promised*."

Matthew sighed. "Okay. Let's go. But we gotta hurry."

"Sure."

They headed back toward Cemetery Road, then crossed into the undisciplined swell of forestry that comprised the foothills of Haystack Mountain. Beyond, the Cumberland landscape, with all its swells and slaloms, looked like there was something enormous just beneath the earth trying to push its way out. In the summer, the trees surrounding the base of the mountain were full and green, obscuring the curving blacktop of Route 40 and the roiling gray water of the Narrows beyond. Now, in autumn, the trees were bare and the curl of asphalt could be glimpsed though the meshwork of ash-colored branches.

Despite his labored respiration, Dwight Dandridge moved quickly ahead of Matthew, crossing through the trees and out onto a plain of sun-bleached reeds like some pioneer straight out of a history textbook. There was a darkened triangle of sweat at the back of Dwight's striped polo shirt, and Matthew could hear his friend's wheezing exhalations—*heee, heee*—as clear as day.

Matthew was still thinking about the Dracula mask as they slowed down to an airy trot at the cusp of Route 40, the winding whip-crack of highway that cut through the mountains. Matthew's mother didn't allow him to travel this far from town, and she had on more than one occasion forbidden him from crossing Route 40. Although it was typically within the boy's nature to adhere to his mother's mandates, Dwight Dandridge's influence over him was greater than any other force in his life, as is customarily the way with young boys and their friends. Often, his mother would employ the old adage, suggesting that, if Dwight jumped off the Highland Street Bridge, she had no doubt her easily manipulated yet good-hearted son would readily follow. This comment always reminded Matthew of the time Dwight had tied a bunch of kites to his back, arms, and legs, and contemplated jumping off the highest point of the bridge to see if he could fly. Somehow Matthew had talked him out of it.

"Come on," Dwight urged, making Matthew aware that he was lagging behind. "Don't chicken out on me now."

"I'm not chickening out."

"Bok bok bok bok bok!"

"Cut it out, jerk."

Dwight waved a hand at him as he crossed the highway. "Come on!"

After checking for traffic, Matthew crossed the highway toward the steep embankment on the other side that led down into the cold, black waters of the Narrows. Dwight was already peering down the embankment, no doubt assessing the tribulations of traversing the rocky decline down toward the flume of water. White stones burst out of the hillside, looking like the tops of skulls rising from their graves, and Matthew could see tentacular tree limbs and nests of brambles sprouting from the earth, ready to snatch them up and trip them down the side of the mountain and into the Narrows. Some random garbage was strewn about as well, remnants of the storm. People's lives had been uprooted and swept away, the leftover bits scattered like flotsam and jetsam throughout the wooded mountainside.

Dwight began descending the hillside, pausing halfway down to peer over his shoulder at Matthew, who remained standing at the cusp of the highway. "You coming?"

"This is stupid," he responded, though he was already testing his footing on one of the large white stones. Slowly he descended the hillside, using the stones when he could to secure his footing; when he couldn't, he crouched low to the ground, hoping that the muddy earth wouldn't betray him and send him tumbling down the rest of the way. At one point, startled by the growl of a heavy engine whipping along Route 40 directly above his head, he nearly lost his balance and tumbled down. Dwight, having seemingly materialized beside him like a guardian angel, managed to snag a handful of Matthew's shirt and prevent the fall.

At the bottom of the valley they crossed over to the concrete lip of the Narrows and peered down. The water level was still very high, the water itself black, swirling, and fast moving. Cattails spun out of rents in the concrete and crickets chirped happily in the tall grass. Dried mud covered everything, further evidence of the flood that had so recently besieged their hometown.

Matthew had heard stories of fishermen pulling three-eyed rockfish from the Narrows, or kids catching uniquely colored frogs with extra appendages. Before his father had left, Matthew had asked him if these stories were true. Hugh Crawly, who had evidently been just months away from leaving his son, daughter, and wife, had told the boy that he couldn't vouch for the stories of others, but that he had once personally witnessed a two-headed turtle sunning itself on one of the footpaths down by the creek. He'd been with some other friends that afternoon and claimed that one of his buddies had suggested they catch the thing and call the Smithsonian in D.C. Someone else volunteered that they should make soup from it, though the notion of eating a creature as so clearly deformed and unnatural as this one did not sit well with the rest of the men. Finally, in the end, no one wanted to touch it. "It's because of the old plastics plant," his father had concluded that afternoon. They had been out by the garage, where his old man had been working on the family pickup truck, wiping down some greasy gadget he'd removed from beneath the pickup's hood. "Before that plant closed down, people would see all sorts of funny-looking critters down in the Narrows. The water there is still polluted with runoff from the plant. You should never swim there."

Matthew never had. Now, he looked across the Narrows and halfway up the neighboring mountain where the old plastics factory, now long defunct and abandoned, squatted low to the ground like an animal lying in wait. Its ranks of tiny barred windows looked like grids on a circuit board and its stone facade was networked with thick cords of ivy. Two slender concrete smokestacks rose up like medieval prison towers at one end of the factory.

"Help me look," Dwight said. He had a big stick now, which he used to thwack the overgrown grass.

Matthew glanced around. "How do you know we're even in the right spot?"

"Billy Leary said it was down by the Narrows, between the Witch Tree and the stone bridge." Dwight pointed to the overpass made of black stones that spanned the Narrows in a tight little arc, then he pointed over to the Witch Tree, a creeping, skeletal horror that clawed up out of a base of brownish nettles, its branches like flailing arms, the suggestion of faces etched into its ashy bark. Matthew knew countless stories and rumors surrounding that tree, the most sinister suggesting that the tree had once been a little boy who had broken into an old witch's house and stolen all her sweets. The boy had thought he'd gotten away with it, but the witch came looking for him later that night, her grotesque face peering right into his bedroom window. She kidnapped the boy and turned him into a tree so he could never steal things from her or anyone else again. Indeed, if you stared at the trunk of the twisted and gnarled tree long enough, there seemed to be a face—or many faces—within the bark.

"How much do you get doing your paper route?" Matthew asked.

"Fifteen bucks a week."

"Wow. That much, huh?"

"Yeah." Dwight wandered over to the stone footbridge, a semicircle of daylight winking out from beneath it. Beyond the bridge, one of the many footpaths described a winding walkway through the thicket. With the tip of his thwacking stick, Dwight chipped away some of the mortar between the stones in the bridge's foundation. "Why?"

"You think maybe I can take it over for a week? Just till I get enough money to pay for the Dracula mask."

"That wasn't Dracula," Dwight said, still searching the ground.

"Yeah it was."

"No it wasn't, dummy."

"Who was it, then?"

"Just a regular old vampire."

"What's the difference?"

"Dracula is a specific vampire. Maybe even the lead vampire. He's one guy, you know? Dracula is his name. It's like saying all monkeys are called King Kong."

"My sister says Dracula's real name was Vlad."

"You know what I mean, dummy," Dwight said.

"And King Kong wasn't a monkey," Matthew said. "He was an ape."

Dwight paused in chipping away the mortar from between the stones, propping the long stick over one shoulder. He winced into the sun as he looked toward Matthew. "What's the difference?"

Matthew admitted that he did not know.

"Have you ever even seen *Dracula*?" Dwight asked, peering beneath the stone footbridge.

"He's not a real person," Matthew said.

"Not in person, dummy. The movie, I mean. Have you seen it?"

"Oh. Yes. I mean, no. I don't know." He couldn't remember now. He'd seen a vampire movie on a cable-access channel late one night over the summer after his mom and his sister had gone to bed. Had that movie been *Dracula*? He couldn't remember now. There had been a vampire who looked strikingly like the mask in Hogarth's window. He'd suffered nightmares for several days after watching that movie.

"It's pretty boring," Dwight said. "And it's so *old.* It's not even in color. The only creepy part is he lives in this big old castle, and there are candles on the walls and shadows everywhere." Dwight pointed across the Narrows to where the old plastics factory appeared superimposed against the cloudy sky. "Sort of looked like that place."

For some inexplicable reason, looking at it now, Matthew felt a chill radiate up his spine.

"Anyway, I can't just have you take over my route, doofus," Dwight continued. "You gotta get up crazy early, before school even, and if you oversleep and miss the route, I'll catch hell."

"I won't oversleep."

"And besides, I'm saving up my money to buy a new dirt bike."

Matthew sighed.

"Oh damn," Dwight said. The tone of his voice ratcheted up a notch with excitement. "Here it is! Take a look!"

Matthew turned away from the view of the abandoned plastics factory and found Dwight crouching in the tall grass, his stick planted like a staff in the ground. Dwight peered at something at his feet, a look of pure awe on his chubby face. From where Matthew stood, he could see there was something big down there in the grass, bending the stalks of the reeds and creating what appeared to be a crater in the earth.

Matthew sidled up beside Dwight . . . then immediately recoiled when he saw what Dwight was looking at.

"That's . . . that's not a deer," Matthew said, his voice small. "Is it?"

The thing no longer resembled whatever it had been when it was alive. Matthew could make out the suggestion of long, muscular legs covered in short tawny hair and hooves like chunks of obsidian. Through what was left of its skull, he could see a whitish zipper of dull teeth along a tapered snout. The skull itself looked like a bowl with some pinkish fluid at its center.

The entire torso of the animal had been demolished, reduced to a bloody, sizzling vomitus that rotted in the heat of midday. White ribs poked like bicycle spokes from a ragged tear in its side, through which Matthew could see its purplish organs and banded, milky pustules of fat. At first glance, he thought he could see the organs behind the ribs working, as if the thing was somehow still alive . . . but on closer inspection, he realized the movement he was seeing was the wriggling of maggots that had infested the carcass. The entire thing hummed with horseflies.

"Sure it is," Dwight said, though Matthew could hear the skepticism in his friend's voice, too. "What else could it be?"

"Whatever it is, it's disgusting," Matthew said.

Dwight cocked his head, as if to examine the thing from a different angle. He pointed to the thing's tattered hindquarters, where the ragged hook of a two-toned tail curled stiffly out of the brown weeds.

"It's a whitetail," said Dwight. Sweat beaded his forehead.

"What do you think happened to it?" Matthew looked up to estimate the distance between the carcass and Route 40 at the top of the hill. "Do you think a car hit it?"

"A car didn't do this. It looks like something ate it," Dwight suggested. He stood and prodded the corpse with his stick. One stiff leg rocked and there was a ripping sound as part of its gore-matted hide tore out of the grass.

Matthew wrinkled his nose. "Gross. Don't do that."

"Why not?"

"Because it's—"

Both boys jumped back, startled by the massive beetle that spilled out of the whitetail's snout and scuttled into the grass, its metallic green carapace glinting sunlight. Nervously, Dwight laughed. Then he tossed the stick onto the ground and withdrew a small boning knife from his backpack.

"What are you doing?" Matthew said. Then, as an afterthought, he added, "You're not supposed to bring knives to school, Dwight."

"You're not supposed to blah blah blah," Dwight parroted. "You're such a sissy. Help me cut the tail off."

"What? No way!"

"Don't be a baby."

"I'm not touching it." Matthew took an unconscious step backward.

"Why do you want that tail, anyway?"

"I'm gonna hang it from my bike." The tone of Dwight's voice suggested that Matthew was an imbecile for not understanding this.

"You do it yourself."

"I need you to help." Dwight stepped over what Matthew estimated to be the ropy, silvered spools of the deer's entrails, then hunkered down again. Sunlight shimmered along the blade of the boning knife. "Either pull the tail straight out or keep the body steady while I cut."

Matthew sucked his lower lip. He couldn't pull his eyes from the dead animal decomposing and crawling with flies in the grass. He could hear their buzzing, an industrial, machinelike drone.

"Okay," he said finally, "but on one condition."

Dwight groaned and peered up at him from beneath his brow. It was the same look he shot Mr. Hodgson at school when asked to come to the blackboard and solve a math problem in front of the class. "What?"

"You let me take over your paper route, just until I have enough money so I can buy the Dracula mask."

"It's not a fucking Dracula mask . . . "

"Vampire mask, then. Deal?"

Dwight's mouth twisted into a knot. He looked down at the dead deer's tail, his longish hair damp with perspiration and curling over his eyes, then back up at Matthew. Before he even opened his mouth, Matthew knew he would agree to it.

"I can't give you the route, Matt. I just can't. But yeah, okay, I'll lend you the money. You can pay me back through your allowance. Okay?"

"Okay."

"But then I get to wear the mask sometimes, too. Deal?"

"Deal."

"Swear on it."

Matthew Crawly spat on the ground then said, "Swear."

This seemed to suffice. Dwight nodded succinctly then jerked his head at the dead animal's tail. Matthew tromped through the underbrush and squatted down beside Dwight. This close to the carcass, he could see with perfect clarity the maggots squirming within the pulpy gruel, fat and white, like overcooked macaroni. There was a sticky web of foam spilling out of the rent in the flesh, pinkish with blood and mucus.

"Come on," Dwight said, prodding the rear of the animal with the point of the boning knife. Agitated flies clotted the air above them.

The tail jutted up at a perfect ninety-degree angle, stiff as a coat hanger. Matthew pinched its tip between his thumb and forefinger then pulled it taut. The fur was incredibly soft, and, beneath the fur, he could feel the tapered, pencil-thin tailbone.

"Just hurry up and do it," Matthew said.

Dwight placed the blade of the boning knife against the tail, at the point where the tail met the creature's hindquarters, and proceeded to saw back and forth with disciplined alacrity. The sound was like twisting a leather wallet, and the sight of the act turned Matthew's stomach. He looked away, back up the opposite hillside where the undulating fields climbed toward the square stone shell of the plastics factory, partially masked behind a network of dead trees. A cool breeze issued down the mountain, rustling the prickly underbrush and causing the tall, yellow grass to blow.

A figure stood within the dark lee of the building, partially shrouded by trees. Matthew discerned the pale flesh of a phantom but could make out no discernible features. Not at first, anyway. As Matthew watched, the figure retreated back into the shadows until it was impossible to distinguish the figure from the weathered stone of the factory walls. It was only after the figure had vanished from view that something clicked over in his head, and he thought, okay, yes, he *had* seen who the person was. But could it be . . . ?

Matthew felt the tail come away from the carcass—he had been unwittingly pulling at it with such force that its liberation caused him to lose his balance—and he fell backward in the dirt to the score of Dwight's laughter. Matthew held the tail up and let it blow like a wind sock in the breeze. There wasn't any blood at all.

"Sweet," Dwight crooned. "Let me have it."

"It's yours," Matthew said, handing the stiff tuft of fur over to his best friend, who snatched it up with a giddy enthusiasm. Then he stood and looked back over at the factory, and to the hollow of shadow where he'd seen the figure.

But the figure was gone.

It's not him. It can't be. Why would he be up there, anyway?

Dwight held the tail up against the sun with both hands, as if trying to determine the authenticity of an artifact, his round, brown face dripping sweat. "Maybe I'll get one of those flagpole things for the back of my bike and hang this thing from it."

Matthew was hardly listening to him. He scanned the factory grounds but could no longer make out the person who had appeared to be watching him from a web of shadows.

"I bet this would make some killer fishing bait," Dwight continued to ramble. Then he looked at Matthew. "What's the matter with you?"

Matthew pointed. "There was somebody standing up there just a second ago, right by the factory. Now he's gone."

"What?" Dwight executed his own quick scan of the area.

"Yeah . . . and he . . . he was . . . "

"What?"

Matthew swallowed an uncomfortable lump and said, "I think it was my dad."

Silence fell over both boys for the length of a single heartbeat. Then Dwight brayed laughter and punched Matthew in the arm. "Cut it out. You're just trying to freak me out, right?"

"I'm being serious." He spat again on the ground. "Swear."

Dwight stood sharply. "So where'd he go?"

"I don't know."

Dwight stuffed the deer tail in his backpack, though he didn't take his eyes from the old factory on the other side of the Narrows. "Why would your dad be up there?"

"I don't know. But it looked like him."

"I think you're just seeing things," Dwight said.

"Let's go check it out."

"Wait—what? I thought you needed to get home."

Matthew felt his left eyelid twitch.

"Come on, Matt. It's just shadows and trees up there."

But Matthew was already walking back up the embankment and crossing onto the stone footbridge that spanned the Narrows. Dwight stared up at him, his big stick over his shoulder, reminding Matthew of Tom Sawyer, and of all the Mark Twain stories he'd read in English class. Dwight was a year older than him, but they were in the same grade. Dwight swore it was because he'd had a talk with his old man—what Dwight called a *sit-down*—where Dwight professed his desire to stay back a year so that he and Matthew could be in the same class. But Matthew wasn't naive and he knew better: Dwight Dandridge just wasn't all that smart. As he saw his best friend climb up the slope and cross onto the stone footbridge after him, Matthew was suddenly overcome by a wealth of emotion for his friend—a feeling that was frighteningly and uncharacteristically adult.

"We should go home," Dwight called to him.

"Come on," Matthew called back, the sound of his voice already trailing away in a sudden and strong wind as he crossed the bridge and headed up the incline of the neighboring hillside toward the old plastics factory. "Just a quick look."

They were halfway up the hill and heading toward the old building,

Dwight whacking tall grass and reeds out of his way with his stick, when Matthew paused. His eyes bore through the interlocking arms of the trees and he saw the bone-colored facade of the factory beyond. Sweat had suddenly sprung out along his skin and there was a cold needling at the base of his spine now. He felt . . . strange.

"Maybe I was wrong," Matthew said. "I mean, maybe there's no one here and I was just seeing things."

"What do you call those visions people see when they're real thirsty in the desert?" Dwight asked.

"A mirage?" Matthew said. He had read a story about mirages in one of his comic books. They were like hallucinations. Sometimes people out wandering in the desert dropped to their knees and downed mouthfuls of sand that their addled minds had fooled them into believing was water.

"Yeah," Dwight said, "a mirage. Maybe that's what it was."

"But I'm not thirsty."

Dwight shrugged. "Maybe you don't gotta always be thirsty to see a mirage."

"Maybe," he said, though he knew it hadn't been a mirage, hadn't been a hallucination. Only people dying in the desert saw mirages and only crazy people had hallucinations. Matthew knew he was neither.

At their backs, thunder rolled as angry-looking clouds filled the sky over the mountaintop. The boys cast wary glances at each other as the sunlight retreated from the long lashes of yellow grass that sprouted up all around them.

The old plastics factory, rotting away in a bowl of weeds and scrubland and hidden behind a fence of trees, looked like the forgotten relic that it was. Matthew had never been this close to the building before—he'd never crossed Route 40 and the Narrows before—and just seeing it caused a cool, unbalanced chill to infiltrate his body. That needling icicle drove deeper into his spine.

"It's bigger up close, huh?" Dwight intoned. He stepped closer to the stone wall and stood on his tiptoes to peer into one of the multicolored windows. The bars on the windows looked rusty and dangerous, foreboding, and Matthew wondered what would happen if someone were to cut their hand open on one of those bars. He'd heard of tetanus and other such infections, and he wondered if touching those angry-looking bars would result in him rotting away in some sterile, white hospital room somewhere, his skin slowly peeling away from his skeleton, his musculature shriveling like paper thrown into a bonfire. What exactly was tetanus, anyway? Tiny microbes that got into your bloodstream and wreaked havoc until your joints disassembled and your limbs fell off? Did it cause you to go blind? Deaf? Would he spend the rest of his miserable life slumped over in a wheelchair?

"Where exactly did you see him?" Dwight asked, moving slowly around the side of the building.

Matthew was frozen and unable to speak. He stared up at the two immense smokestacks that rose up and pierced the gunmetal sky, nearly breaching the low-hanging storm clouds.

"Hey!" Dwight thumped him on the forearm with his stick. "Did you hear me?"

"What?"

"Where did you see him?"

Matthew pointed toward the hollow of shadow against the side of the building, where the trees crowded in and caused spangles of strained sunlight to filter down against the whitish, moss-covered wall of the factory. "There," he said dryly.

Dwight bent down and dipped beneath the overhanging trees. He faded into the shadows, mingling within the space where Matthew had seen the strange figure he believed to have been his father . . . but of course there was no one there now. Dwight stomped around, trampling wildflowers and swatting at gnats.

"There's nobody here," he said, relief evident in his voice.

"That's where he was."

"And then what? Where did he go?"

How could he explain it? "He just sort of . . . backed up and faded into the background," Matthew said.

Dwight laughed sharply. "What background?" He placed one hand against the outer wall of the factory. "Is there a trapdoor or secret passageway or something? There's nowhere else to go, Matt." Then he looked up at the building, a wry grin on his face that showed he did not find the building as imposing as Matthew did. "You think he went inside?"

"I don't know." He looked around but couldn't see a way into the building; the doorways had been filled in with concrete years ago. Similarly, the windows were comprised of tiny gridded panes overlaid with iron bars and wire meshwork. As he looked, he saw—or imagined he saw—shapes swimming in the warped and colored glass of the windows. Anything could be beyond those milky, opaque cataracts of glass, he realized. *Anything.* It was an unsettling thought.

"There's no one here," Dwight said again, emerging from beneath the shade of the overhanging trees. A cloud of mosquitoes orbited his head and he swatted at them, scowling.

"Boost me up so I can have a look in those windows," Matthew said.

"There's nothing to see, Matt. The glass is covered in muck. Anyway, it's pitch-black inside."

"Just boost me."

Grunting, Dwight sidled over, laced his hands together, and held them out for Matthew to utilize as a sling. Placing his hands on Dwight's shoulders, Matthew stepped one foot into Dwight's cupped hands and Dwight, groaning, hoisted him up.

Matthew's eyes rose just above the windowsill. Indeed, the thick glass was cloudy with age, reinforced with industrial meshwork from the inside. With the heel of one hand he attempted to rub away the grime, but it was too caked on. Decades of dirt and filth had become solid as cement.

Then, through the cloudy panes of glass, the breathy twist of an image flickered inside the darkened building. It was like watching a candle flare briefly to life before being snuffed out.

"Hurry," Dwight groaned from below.

"I think I see something."

"You're too *heavy*."

A second later, Dwight's hands gave out. Matthew dropped straight down into the grass, instantly lost his footing, and fell backward on his tailbone. Dwight snorted a laugh and leaned, panting for breath, against the side of the building.

"Do you think we can find a way in?" Matthew said, climbing back onto his feet and brushing the mud and grass from his legs.

"A way in? No way. This building's been locked up forever."

"We need to go in there."

"Dude." Dwight reached out and shook one of Matthew's shoulders. "Hey. What's the matter with you? Your dad ain't here, Matt."

Matthew didn't take his eyes from the bank of milky windows above. "Maybe if we went around back," he muttered, this time more to himself than to Dwight.

"No way. I'm not going in there."

Matthew took a step toward the building, ran one finger down the seam between two of the large stones in the facade. The pad of his fingertip was now white with stone dust. "Then maybe I'll go in without you, Dwight."

He sensed, more than saw, Dwight shuffle uncomfortably around him. After a few moments of silence, Dwight offered a trembling laugh. He clubbed Matthew on the back and the feel of his hand seemed to break the trance that had overtaken Matthew.

"Good one," Dwight said. "But let's quit dicking around."

Matthew nodded and rubbed his eyes. "Yeah. Maybe you were right," Matthew said, just wanting to go home now, too. That icy needling at the base of his spine had vanished. "Maybe it was a mirage."

"Yeah." Dwight sounded satisfied. Relieved, too. Besides, he'd gotten his goddamn deer tail . . .

A vision then accosted Matthew—the figure springing straight out of the shadows, its long, colorless arms extending and wrapping around Dwight, then pulling him backward into the murky, black, sunless place until they disappeared together. In this vision, the figure was no longer Matthew's father, but some indistinct and featureless approximation of a human being. Matthew shivered at the thought.

"Okay," Matthew said. "Let's get out of here."

3

Somehow, the rain managed to hold off until they reached the Crawly house. It was a modest, two-story Cape Cod that looked weather-beaten and exhausted. Shutters hung at awkward angles, and the front porch slouched to the left so severely that Matthew had to remember not to leave his baseball on it for fear that it would roll off, bound down the street, and vanish from his life altogether. The storm had wreaked havoc on the place, shoving mud up against the foundation and knocking down some of the smaller trees. His mother had attempted to sandbag the perimeter of the house, just as his father had done all those years ago when Matthew was five, but her work had been hasty and ineffectual, and there had been some flooding. Many of the sandbags had burst as well, leaving damp mounds of sawdust-colored muck in various places around the yard.

Before continuing down the block to his own house, Dwight outfitted Matthew's hand with a wad of damp dollar bills. "Here. It's the money for the vampire mask. Just don't forget," he told Matthew, staring longingly at the crumpled currency in Matthew's hand, probably regretting his decision immediately. "I get to wear the mask, too."

"I won't forget."

Dwight nodded then licked the sweat off his upper lip with a small, pink, pointed tongue. His arms were tanned and freckled, and his brows knitted together as if in deep concentration.

"What is it?" Matthew asked.

"It's where they found that boy," Dwight said. He brushed his curly hair off his forehead and Matthew could see a finger of snot vibrating in the channel of his left nostril. "Down by the Narrows, I mean. Right down there where we saw the dead deer."

"So?"

"What if. . ." Dwight's eyes flitted furtively around before looking down at his muddy sneakers. "Forget it."

"What?"

Dwight looked up at him. "I hear things outside my window at night."

"What kinds of things?"

"Like someone moving around in the yard. I keep the window open and I wake up in the middle of the night, sometimes to take a piss, but then I hear someone down there. It sounds like someone moving back and forth on the gravel driveway. I look but there's never anybody there."

"Maybe it's an animal," Matthew said. "Like a raccoon or a stray cat or something."

"It's not."

"Then what do you think it is?"

"I thought maybe it was Ricky Codger, or one of his jerk-off friends. But then I think about it and wonder what the hell Ricky Codger would be doing stumbling around in my backyard. One night I left Gideon out there on the porch, tied to the railing." Gideon was Dwight's German shepherd. "He heard the noise, too, and normally he would bark and chase away any trespassers. But that night I only heard him whining. The next morning when I went to get him, he'd bitten through his leash and was hiding under the porch. He'd been really frightened."

"Of what?" Matthew said.

Dwight shook his head. "I don't know. Do you hear things at night?"

"No." It was the truth.

"Okay."

"Are you trying to scare me?" he asked Dwight.

"No."

"You swear it?"

Dwight Dandridge spat on the ground. "I swear. God's honest truth."

"Okay," Matthew said.

Suddenly, Dwight did not look like he wanted to leave. Overhead, thunder rumbled. The boys looked up at the troubled, threatening sky. When Dwight's eyes fell on Matthew again, they were sober and the color of motor oil. "Anyway, I'll see you tomorrow."

"Yeah."

"Later."

"Later."

Dwight took off down the street, and Matthew watched him go. He was overtaken by the very adult realization that his friend was becoming sadly overweight. Not just chunky, as he'd always known Dwight Dandridge to be, but flat-out *fat.*

Gutsville, Matthew thought, then immediately hated himself for thinking it.

He went around to the back of the house and saw his mother's truck in the yard, home early from work. Glancing up at the house to make sure no one was watching, he hurried over to the truck and peered in the driver's window, hoping to spy a discarded pack of cigarettes on the dashboard or in the console between the two front seats. Sometimes his mother was careless and left a pack unattended. Disappointingly, tonight was not one of those nights.

As he climbed the porch steps, a crooked finger of lightning lit up the sky, followed by a clash of thunder so frighteningly close it sounded like it had emanated straight up out of the earth. He accidentally slammed the screen door behind him as he entered the house then winced in anticipation of his mother's reproving voice echoing out from the kitchen.

"Is that you, Mattie?" she called, right on schedule. He could smell the meal she was preparing and could hear things sizzling in cooking oil on the stove. "I've told you a hundred times not to slam that door."

"Sorry."

He padded into the kitchen. His mother was at the sink washing lettuce and Brandy was setting the table. Brandy shot him a disapproving look—since she'd turned sixteen, all of Brandy's looks had become disapproving—then she said, "Mom, he's filthy."

His mother glanced at him over her shoulder. "Oh, Matthew. Your hands are black as tar. What have you been doing?" She dried her own hands on a dish towel then yanked his T-shirt up over his shoulders to expose his frail bird's chest and milk-white skin.

"Just hanging around with Dwight," he said, moving toward the refrigerator, where he grabbed a can of Coke and popped the tab.

His mother balled up the T-shirt then carried it into the adjoining laundry room.

"You come back dumber every time you hang out with that kid," Brandy said.

"Your *face* is dumb."

She rolled her eyes.

Matthew appraised his sister from over the rim of his Coke can. When they were younger they had been close. They had even been friends. They would watch horror movies together and piece together jigsaw puzzles and catch toads down at the mud pit at the end of their street. The past year, however, had brought a change to Brandy Crawly's personality, just as it had gradually brought a change to her appearance. Her legs had lengthened, her hands looked longer, and her whole body seemed to have graduated toward adulthood in one subtle and prolonged breath. Her face had changed, too, though Matthew wasn't sure if that was due to chemistry or the makeup she'd begun applying last year. And while he had needed Dwight Dandridge to point out the fact that she had grown breasts—what Dwight called "lady-tadies"—the evidence of them had become undeniable.

Perhaps these physical changes wouldn't have bothered Matthew all that much had Brandy not also turned into such a bitch.

"Why don't you go wash up?" his mother said, coming back into the kitchen. She opened the oven and peered in at whatever was glowing in there. "We'll be eating in five minutes."

"Okay."

He cut through the living room, where the television was flickering in front of an empty sofa, then bounded up the stairs to the hallway bathroom. Tugging on the water and finagling the bar of Ivory soap from the soap dish, he lathered his face and hands, scrubbed them clean. Then he dipped his head beneath the faucet to wet his hair, raking his fingers along his scalp to get all the dirt and grit out. Cold water sprayed down his back, causing him to shiver. His shorts were grimy, too, so he climbed out of them and scurried like a rabbit into his bedroom where he pulled on a fresh pair of shorts and a *Transformers* T-shirt. Atop his bookcase was his entry in this year's science fair—three plastic cups filled with soil in which various seeds germinated.

An ultraviolet lamp shone directly above the first cup while the second received only natural light from his bedroom windows. The third cup sat prisoner beneath a shoebox, receiving no sunlight at all. He permitted himself to peek under the shoebox just once a day, and he did this now. Unlike the other two cups, there were no greening buds curling up out of the soil, and no spidery roots pressed against the underside of the cup. It had been an experiment he'd read about in one of his father's science and nature books . . .

From his bedroom window, he could see the open door of the detached garage, the multitude of junk heaped within. That had been his father's junk; what purpose it served, Matthew Crawly had no idea. He didn't think his mother had any idea either, though she did not appear to be in much of a hurry to dispose of it. In fact, it looked as though she had relocated the items to the higher shelves in preparation for last week's storm, just as his father used to do when he still lived there. Matthew remembered being young, watching his father from this very window as his old man milled about in the yard, his denim-colored postal uniform dark with sweat, the shirt partially unbuttoned. He had watched his father smoke cigarettes beneath the garage's awning then hurry across the yard to the house for dinner. Hugh Crawly had done this almost every night: smoked on the far side of the garage, where he thought he was hidden from everyone in the house. He'd slam the screen door just like Matthew did, and Matthew's mother would yell at him, and his father would laugh his big-bellied laugh and that would be the end of it.

It was the end, all right, Matthew thought now . . . and there was a part of him that was frightened by the depth of what that meant, and the maturity of the thought. Why had his father left? With all that big-bellied laughter, was he covering up for something? Had he just had too much and decided never to come back? Worse still, had it been something Matthew had done? Had it been his fault that his father had picked up in the middle of the night and disappeared? Matthew didn't know. And quite often, like right now, he felt he didn't *want* to know.

4

The dinner table was the only place the remainder of the Crawly family came together with any sort of regularity. It was a firm rule: no matter what your day and evening plans were, you had to be home for dinner. The only exception was when their mother had to work the dinner shift at the diner or if Brandy had an early babysitting gig. A few times Brandy had tried to weasel out of having dinner with the family so she could instead have dinner at a friend's house or go to an early movie with some girls from school, but their mother had firmly put her foot down without so much as a discussion. "I don't jockey around my shifts at the diner just to come home and have dinner at an empty table," their mother was fond of saying. Matthew was only eleven, but he was not stupid. The dining ritual had been instituted right around the same time Hugh Crawly crept out and left them behind in the night. It was his mother's way of making sure the remaining members of the Crawly household stayed together. Even at his unworldly age, Matthew felt a sense of sad desperation in his mother in knowing this.

With a light rain pattering against the kitchen windows, the three of them sat at the table. A fourth chair remained at the table, loud as an explosion in its emptiness. A few times, when it was Matthew's turn to set the table, he'd accidentally set a place for his father, too. Once, it had made his mother cry. She'd gone out on the porch to do it, but it was summer, and all the windows had been open, and he had heard her sobbing in her muted, embarrassed way. It had hurt

Matthew terribly to hear it, and Brandy had called him an idiot as she cleared away the extra place setting.

Matthew's mother looked at him from across the table. Her face was too thin, her eyes like lusterless stones. She was still in her powder-blue waitress uniform, her name tag on her breast. Matthew could remember a time when he'd thought she was pretty—beautiful, even, in that innocent and giddy way all young boys find their mothers beautiful—but she looked simply tired and drained now. "Why don't you say it, honey?"

"I said it last night," he groaned. "Make Brandy do it."

"I set the table," Brandy countered quickly, "so you have to say it."

"Matthew," his mother said. The exhaustion in her voice informed him that this was not the time to argue over something so trivial.

"Dear God, thank you for the food and for bringing us all together again. Amen." He had considered throwing in a request—namely, that no one would come in and buy the vampire mask from Hogarth's before he was able to get down there early tomorrow morning with his and Dwight's money in tow—but decided to omit it in the end.

His mother shoveled peas onto her plate. "How was everyone's day?"

"Aced my geography test," Brandy said.

"Nice job."

"Then Mrs. Oxland almost got run over by a school bus."

Wendy Crawly gaped at her daughter. "What?"

"She was out in the parking lot after school, yelling at some kid, not watching where she was going, and a school bus nearly ran her over," Brandy said. "She hopped back up on the curb at the last minute."

"Lord," Wendy muttered. Her eyes swung toward her son. "How about you?"

Matthew shrugged. "School was okay."

"Do anything fun after school?"

"Dwight and I went down to the park and played some kickball with some other kids." He could tell his mother was suddenly scrutinizing the grime beneath her son's fingernails. "Dwight kicked a home run and won the game," he added quickly, hoping more detail would make a believer out of his mom.

"Dwight's a big kid," his mother said.

"Fat, you mean," Brandy added.

"Shut up," Matthew barked.

"You guys didn't go anywhere else today?" his mother asked.

"No, ma'am." His face burned.

"Interesting." His mother got up, went to the fridge, and returned to the table with a bottle of Budweiser. Unscrewing the cap, she said, "So I guess David Moore would be lying had he told me he saw you and Dwight crossing Route 40 down by the Narrows this afternoon?"

Matthew felt a sinking in his stomach. "Oh."

"Yeah," said his mother. "Oh." She took a small sip of her beer then set the bottle on the table. Foam bubbled up the neck, reminding Matthew of the fully working model volcano Jimmy Ornswaith had made for science class last year. "You know you're not supposed to play out there," his mother went on. "I've told you not to cross that highway and to stay away from the Narrows."

"I didn't want to go. There was this stupid dead deer Dwight wanted to see. Billy Leary said it had been killed by a bear and we—"

"We've talked about this, Matthew. You could drown in that water. Especially after the storm we've had. That water gets out of control and can be very dangerous."

"We weren't in the water. We never go into it."

"You could have fallen in. It's dangerous. You're too young to be out there."

"It's where they found that boy," Brandy spoke up, and Matthew looked at her, recalling that Dwight had said a similar thing. "The police found him in Wills Creek."

"That's not dinner talk," Wendy Crawly said in a small voice.

Brandy looked quickly down at her plate. "Sorry."

"And I don't want to have this discussion with you again, Matthew. Am I understood?"

"Yes, ma'am."

"I don't appreciate being lied to, either."

"Sorry," he said . . . and felt his sister administer a swift kick to his shin underneath the table.

"All right, then," said Wendy.

They ate the rest of their meal in silence.

5

That evening, as everyone else slept soundly in the Crawly house, young Matthew awoke with a scream ratcheting up his throat. He was tacky with sweat, the ghost-fingers of a retreating nightmare still tickling his spine. He sat up stiffly in bed, the twin windows across the room like eyes, seeming to blaze with moonlight.

In the dream, he had been back in the field staring up at the plastics factory. This time he was alone and it was nighttime—or at least the sky was dark enough to make it seem like nighttime, though he supposed it could have been dark with an oncoming storm. As he stared up at the building, dull flashes of light bled out from the gridded windows. He approached the building and attempted to climb on top of some fallen trees to peer in through the windows. But the windows were too high, and it seemed the higher he climbed, the farther up the side of the building the windows scaled. Then, from all around him, there came the sound of a thousand beating wings, filling his ears like the drumbeat sound of rushing blood, and he was crippled and frozen by a shuddery disquiet.

In the half-light, he listened to the house creak and moan—*house-speak*, his father had called it on the nights when Matthew was younger, afraid to sleep alone in his room with all the noises of the house surrounding him. Just house-speak: talking to the wind, the moon, the stars. Nothing at all to be afraid of. As it often did, this memory caused his face to turn hot and his eyes to sting. Matthew hadn't seen his father in over a year, and he'd spoken with him on the phone less than a half-dozen times. He was living now in some place that had a strange and unfamiliar name. And while no one had ever directly confirmed this bit of information, he had surmised that he was living there with another woman. The few times he had summoned the courage to ask his mother for more details about his father's disappearance, one look at Wendy Crawly's worn and beaten face would cause him to change his mind. He did not want to talk about those things with his mother. She had cried enough on the porch by herself in the beginning, just barely within earshot, and that had been bad enough. Matthew didn't think he could take it if she broke down in front of him. Or *because* of him. So he never asked questions.

He flipped the sweaty sheet off his body then climbed out of bed. Without turning on the bedroom light, he found the mound of his clothes at the foot of his bed. Snatching his shorts up off the floor, he carried them over to his small desk where his Superman lunchbox sat. He felt around in the pockets of his shorts for the money Dwight had given him, his panic rising when he found both pockets empty. He rechecked them, pulling them inside out, but there was no money in there.

He clicked the desk lamp on. Yellow light spilled out across the desk and half of the desk chair. Beneath the cone of light, Matthew again re-examined the pockets of his shorts. Then he went to the heap of clothes at the foot of his bed and sifted through each article of clothing—shirts, balled-up socks, another pair of shorts. There was no money anywhere.

Retrace your steps, said a voice in his head. He thought of the story of Hansel and Gretel, how they'd left behind a trail of breadcrumbs in order to find their way back home. Stupidly, this made him think again of his father, who had left no trail of breadcrumbs and appeared to have no intention of ever coming back home.

Holding his breath, because he thought doing so would stop his heart from beating so loudly, he crept out of his bedroom and onto the second-floor landing. Across the hall, the doors to his mother's and Brandy's bedrooms were closed, the doorknobs a shimmery blue in the moonlight coming in through the high front windows. He proceeded to descend the steps, avoiding from memory the risers that made the most noise. It was like sinking down into the belly of a great ship. Over summer vacation he'd read Jules Verne's *Twenty Thousand Leagues Under the Sea,* and not the dumbed-down version for children, either. This had been the actual, honest-to-God novel. And while he did not fully understand everything he'd read, the glory and trepidation and horror of the adventure resonated with him more than any movie ever had. He thought of that book now, and how the underwater light shining through the portholes of Captain Nemo's submarine, the *Nautilus,* must have looked just like the swampy, blue-gelled moonlight coming through the windows of the front hall right now.

He'd hoped that thinking about this would alleviate his fears.

It hadn't.

Around him, the house sounded alive. As he crossed from the front hall to the kitchen, a gust of wind bullied the house and made popping, groaning sounds within the walls. Matthew froze, his heart thudding with a series of pronounced hammer strikes within the frail wall of his chest. On the kitchen counter, silverware and drinking glasses gleamed in the moonlight coming through the window over the sink. Across the kitchen, the flimsy floral curtain that hung over the panel of glass in the upper section of the porch door seemed to radiate with a cool, lackadaisical light. His bare feet padding on the cold kitchen tiles, he went to the door, unlocked the dead bolt, and slid the slide lock to the unlocked position. It made a sound that echoed loudly in the empty, silent kitchen, causing Matthew to once again hold his breath.

There came a knocking on the other side of the door. Matthew froze, his skin suddenly blistered with gooseflesh. He waited for the silhouette of a head to appear on the other side of the sheer curtain. No one appeared. He waited. Outside, the wind picked back up, angry and unforgiving. The sound of the bare tree branches bullied by the wind was a haunted, creaking one, reminiscent of warped and loose floorboards. That knocking sound came again, slightly more muted this time. Again, Matthew expected the silhouette of a head to appear framed in the curtained panel of light. Again, no one appeared.

The door squealed on its hinges as he slowly opened it, though much of the noise was obscured by the rattling, locomotive sound of the whipping wind. Cold air blasted him, and the flimsy T-shirt and boxer shorts he wore felt no more substantial than cobwebs. The banging sound, he realized, was the screen door banging against the frame. Beyond the screen, he could see the way the wind shook the bushes alongside the detached garage and, beyond, rattled the chain-link fence. Farther out, a sea of cornstalks undulated in the wind. Whirlwinds of dead leaves and scraps of trash danced across the yard.

It occurred to him that if he'd dropped Dwight's money out here, it was long gone by now. In his mind's eye—and not without a sense of utter despair—he imagined the dollar bills flitting like bats through the storm-laden night sky somewhere over the Cumberland Gap. Heck, for all he knew, they could be somewhere over the Atlantic Ocean by now . . .

Nonetheless, he pushed open the screen door and stepped out onto the porch. The rickety boards complained loudly beneath his bare feet. The strong wind chilled his bones, and flecks of icy rain pattered against the side of his face. He hugged himself as he scanned the yard. There were scraps of paper stuck in some of the bushes beside the garage. Could they be Dwight's money?

Matthew took a deep breath, steeling himself for the act . . . then quickly bounded down the porch steps. He hurried out across the yard, the wind icy cold and unrelenting without the confines of the house to serve as a buffer. Bits of flying grit stung his eyes. There was a motion-sensor light above the garage doors; Matthew had completely forgotten about it until it clicked on, blinding and startling him. Like someone caught attempting to escape from a prison yard, he momentarily froze in the spotlight. He knew the light was visible from his own bedroom window, but Brandy's and his mother's bedrooms were at the opposite end of the house, facing the road. They wouldn't be awakened by the light; he was safe for the time being.

Someone moved behind the tall hedgerow. Again, Matthew froze. The hedges stood just over four feet tall and ran the length of the yard to the side of the garage. Matthew blinked and tried to discern through the darkness the movement he had just seen a moment ago—a gliding, whitish blur passing just behind the bushes.

"Is someone there?" His voice was as weak as his knees. It frightened him to address the darkness aloud.

From the periphery of his vision, he caught another glimpse of someone—or something—moving behind the bushes, closer to the garage now. Had the motion-sensor light not come on he might have been able to see more, but the gleaming halogen bulb caused inky pools of shadow to drip from the hedges and puddle around the side of the garage, blinding him if he looked too closely in its approximate direction. A twisting shape seemed to ebb and flow in the darkness just beyond the bushes, and he was reminded of the twisting shape he'd seen earlier that day when peering in the windows of the old plastics factory. He thought then of his nightmare, and of the flashing explosions of light going off behind the grimy windows of the factory in his dream. And of Dwight's voice, now eerily prophetic, saying, *It sounds like someone moving back and forth on the gravel driveway. I look but there's never anybody there.*

As he watched, a figure stepped out from behind the hedgerow and paused, facing him, in the shaft of space between the hedgerow and the garage. The figure was a black blur, as indistinct as a distant memory, but Matthew had no question as to its authenticity. There was someone standing *right there*.

Matthew managed one hesitant step backward.

The figure took one step forward; one bare foot and a slender white shin appeared in the cone of light issuing from the motion sensor. A second foot joined it. As Matthew stared, the whitish legs and feet appeared to waver, and it was like looking at something from behind the distorting waves of rising heat. The legs weren't bare at all. They were clad in grayish-blue denim, the feet encased in hard, black shoes.

Another step forward and the figure's face emerged from the darkness. Matthew could see his father's face, stubble along his cheeks and neck, the crooked part in the man's prematurely graying hair. Still in his postal uniform, his shirt partway unbuttoned just as he used to wear it on those days after work when he went immediately to the garage to tinker around without changing his clothes first.

It took a moment for his father's eyes to focus on him.

The motion-sensor light clicked off.

Matthew Crawly was aware of a rush of wind, a strong embrace of arms . . . and then a piercing sensation at the small of his back. For a moment, he thought he could smell his father's aftershave lotion mingled with the familiar scent of his perspiration. But that was quickly replaced by a sharp, medicinal smell that stung Matthew's nose and caused his eyes to water. When he opened his mouth to scream, no sound came out. It was like trying to scream underwater.

His last conscious thought was of Captain Nemo's submarine coasting soundlessly through the tar-colored waters of a frozen sea, silvery fish flitting by like mirrors of dancing light.

CHAPTER TWO

1

Maggie Quedentock was still shaking when she climbed back into her husband's Pontiac. With one shaking hand, she keyed the ignition and pulled out onto the darkened strip of pavement that was Full Hill Road. The radio was on, John Fogerty straining the speakers, singing about something that had fallen out of the sky. Maggie quickly turned it off. Though they'd owned the car for several years, it now felt completely alien to her: the seat was uncomfortable and too close to the steering wheel, the dashboard controls were in all the wrong places, and when she went to hit the high beams she accidentally flicked on the windshield wipers.

Am I really going to lose my shit right now? After all this?

Once she got far enough down Full Hill Road that the lights of the houses behind her had blinked out of existence, she pulled along the shoulder beneath a lamppost and slid the gearshift to Park. She clicked on the Pontiac's interior light but didn't look at her reflection in the rearview mirror right away. Instead, she sat in the uncomfortable driver's seat and faced forward, staring blankly at the curve of roadway and the dense black trees that loomed up on either side. Already her mind was replaying snapshot scenes from the night's escapades, accusatory in all their vividness. She couldn't blink them away. Finally, she confronted the creature in the rearview mirror.

Muddy eyes, blotchy complexion, hair askew, she was instantly reminded of those self-deprecating little moments back in high school, so many years ago now, when she had surrendered countless times to boyfriends' lustful desires. They used to paw at her mercilessly in the backseats of their parents' cars. She was forty-five years old now and married, with high school a distant, if not smeary and indistinct, memory, and the blotchy skin and wild nest of hair suddenly struck her as vulgar. A deep, personal resentment briefly rumbled around inside her chest, thick as a blood clot.

She had never had an affair before—had never even considered cheating on Evan—and now, less than an hour after the deed had been done, she wondered what the hell she was doing. Was it possible she had been a completely different person just a couple of hours ago, sitting at Crossroads and nursing a Heineken at the bar?

From her purse, which she'd tossed haphazardly onto the passenger seat in an effort to leave Tom Schuler's house as quickly as possible, she produced a small black makeup bag. She dropped the bag in her lap then fumbled with the zipper until the contents spilled into her lap and onto the floor.

"Fuck."

Get it under control, lady. You're vibrating like a guitar string.

She leaned forward, the side of her face resting against the steering wheel, and scrounged around in the footwell. When her fingers brushed along the thin, square packets of moist towelettes, she snatched them up and hastily peeled one open, her eyes volleying furtively between her unsteady fingers and the blotchy mask of her face in the rearview mirror. She was attractive and she kept in good shape, exercising several times a week and watching what she ate, yet the visage staring back at her was horrific.

She exhaled nervously then began wiping the streaks of mascara that had leaked from her eyes to the tops of her cheeks. The smell of ammonia burned her nostrils.

Fifteen years of marriage and this is what I do. Again, she unleashed a shaky breath, this time certain she could smell Tom Schuler on her. Her mouth was full of him. His perspiration was commingled with hers, too, clinging guiltily to her body like an illness. Moreover, she could still feel him inside her—a tender, vacant sensation nestled between her thighs that, even now, simultaneously nauseated and excited her. *Fifteen years of marriage.*

She and Evan had dated on and off throughout high school, and even for a while after graduation. They'd fumbled through their fair shares of other relationships—Evan had even gotten engaged to a woman from Delaware, though it had never culminated in marriage—before reconnecting. At that point she had been thirty, and although she did not feel the motherly desire to have children, she knew that a woman in her forties had a better chance of being killed by terrorists than getting married. Or so she'd heard. Whatever the case, forty had only been a scant decade away at that point, and the notion that she might be doomed to spend her life unmarried and alone terrified her.

She confessed her desire to Evan on more than just a few occasions, but Evan Quedentock, high school football star and the life of the party (as long as the party was in a bar with his lifelong friends), was not the type of man to be easily persuaded. They lived together, took care of each other. What more did she want? *Marriage,* she'd informed him. *Commitment.* To this, Evan would always chuckle and ask what more commitment there was than a man forking over his paycheck every two weeks. It was then that she realized this approach wasn't going to get her anywhere with him.

Like a sailor tacking for new wind, she decided on a different approach: she lied and told him she was pregnant. *You really want to be responsible for bringing a bastard kid into the world?* That did the trick. They went down to the courthouse the following week and got hitched. It seemed Evan Quedentock could be caught after all; she just had to put the right bait in the right trap.

A week or so after they got married, she had summoned some tears by spraying perfume in her face. She thought she'd done an admirable job telling him she had lost the baby. At the news, Evan had seemed both relieved and a bit disappointed (the latter emotion a surprising revelation to Maggie since she knew Evan, much like her, had no great desire to have children). He had comforted her in his clumsy, brutish way, and that had been the end of it. Fifteen years later, they were still married.

Fifteen years . . .

Tom was one of Evan's friends and had been over to the house countless times. The flirtatiousness between them had always been of the innocuous variety, or so Maggie had thought. She had flirted with men in the past but never adulterously. So how had the situation with Tom gotten so goddamn out of hand? Tom had been over at the house one night, drinking too much with Evan. Under the pretense of using the bathroom, he'd followed her into the house while Evan remained on the back porch. Yet he hadn't used the bathroom; he'd followed her into the kitchen, his shirt partially unbuttoned, and leaned against the refrigerator while they talked in quick, glib, declarative sentences. It wasn't that he was drop-dead gorgeous or even roguishly handsome—Tom Schuler was a bit too skinny, and his face was patchy with old acne scars—but that did not seem to matter to Maggie. For whatever reason, she felt a flutter of uneasiness while he talked to her, his eyes drinking her in. And she found that she *liked* this uneasiness.

Tom had left their house that evening with Maggie's cell phone number, along with some indistinct promise in his eyes. Later that evening, she had lain awake in bed, staring at the misaligned panels of moonlight playing across the ceiling as Evan snored like an old hunting dog beside her. She wondered what Evan would think if he knew she'd given Tom Schuler her cell phone number. Moreover—and this was the forbidden part, yet at the same time, the part that elicited some childlike glee within her—she wondered what Evan would do if she were to have an affair with Tom Schuler and he found out.

That childlike glee was gone now. Sitting behind the wheel of her husband's car, cleaning up the smeared streamers of makeup from her face, she felt as obvious as a beacon of light on a darkened coast. Terror enveloped her when she realized that there would be no way to hide the smell of sex from her husband once she got home. Would he leave her? Would he hit her? On both counts, she thought maybe he would.

Tonight's rendezvous at Crossroads was the culmination of a month-long game of cat and mouse. Tom had pursued her with regularity, calling her whenever he knew Evan was at work, trying to convince her to meet him for a drink. A few times she promised she would but later backed out, sending him vague texts that suggested conflicting schedules and last-minute chores. If Tom was ever dissuaded by her continual misdirection, he never let on.

Finally, when he proposed they have a few drinks at Crossroads while Evan was on the late shift—strictly platonic, he had assured her—she had agreed. Of course, she did not put any stock in his promise of chastity, and while she was uncertain what her intentions were up until she was taking her clothes off in the downstairs hallway of his house, she had showered, shaved, groomed with meticulous dedication, and spritzed herself with expensive perfume. She had selected her tightest pair of jeans and a loose-fitting blouse that revealed her tanned and freckled cleavage. Just one drink, she'd promised herself, knowing damn well she was a liar before she ever got in the car and drove out to Crossroads on Melville Street.

Maggie reapplied her makeup then ran a brush through her hair. She spied a bottle of perfume on the floor beneath the accelerator, which she scooped up and administered liberally to her neck, hair, shoulders, and breasts. When she finished, she dug her cell phone out of her purse and deleted the call log. To her knowledge, Evan had never snooped through her phone, but she wasn't about to leave it up to chance.

After she replaced all her fallen cosmetics back in her purse, fixed her hair, and sat behind the wheel staring blankly off into the darkness for some undisclosed amount of time, a warm serenity seemed to overtake her. After a few more minutes, she felt calm enough to drive. Her plan was to get back to the house, take a shower, and crawl into bed before Evan got home from the night shift. With any luck, she could pull it off as though the affair had never happened.

She dropped the gearshift to Drive, readjusted the rearview mirror, then pulled slowly back out onto Full Hill Road. She drove slowly, the car's headlights cleaving through the muddy darkness. She hated this stretch of Full Hill Road—hated, as a matter of fact, all the wooded roadways that snaked out of downtown and wound up into the rocky foothills of the mountains. Maggie Quedentock did not like to feel like she was alone.

Pressing the accelerator closer to the floor, the Pontiac advanced to a rough gallop, the black woods on either side of the road a smudgy blur. More calmly now, Maggie switched the radio back on and surfed through the stations until she found an old Beach Boys number. It soothed her. When she glanced up at her reflection again in the rearview mirror, she was pleasantly surprised to find a timorous smile on her face.

Something darted out into the road. Maggie saw it only peripherally—the slight, colorless approximation of a person—before she struck it with the car. Simultaneously slamming on the brakes and spinning the steering wheel, the car shuddered then fishtailed. The acrid stench of burning rubber filled her nose.

The car finally came to a stop in the middle of the road. Having achieved a complete 180-degree spin, the vehicle's headlights now illuminated the road in the direction that she had come. The reek of scorched rubber was hot and suffocating. Shaking, Maggie looked over one shoulder and peered out the dark rectangle of the Pontiac's rear window. Aside from the few feet of asphalt illuminated in the blood-red glow of the brake lights, the world beyond was pitch-black. For all Maggie knew, she could have been staring off into space.

My God, I felt the fucking impact. If I live to be one hundred, I will never forget what that felt like . . . what it sounded like . . .

She fumbled with her seat belt and managed to get it undone. Her heart strumming like a banjo, she opened the car door and staggered dazedly out onto the roadway. She braced herself for the horror of what must surely lay several feet or yards down the road, though she was too terrified to move away from the pool of warm light that issued out of the open car door.

"Hello?" Her voice held the paper-thin quality of an AM radio broadcast.

Something moved in the center of the roadway. Maggie's body went cold. As her eyes adjusted to the lightlessness, she could see the crumbled form of a small human body, a pair of bare legs folded up into a fetal position. The figure was whitish-blue beneath the glow of the moon, though the tapered swell of its thighs radiated with the sickly red light of the Pontiac's taillights.

As she watched, the figure's legs parted. She heard—or thought she heard—a wet, guttural clicking coming from the shape. Even now, with its undeniably human form, Maggie was struggling to convince herself that what she had hit had been a deer or a dog or any such careless, brainless animal that had wandered stupidly out onto the road in the middle of the night . . .

It's not a person, it can't be, that is a fucking whitetail deer, a goddamn stray dog, that is not a person, it isn't, it's too fucking small to even . . .

It was small because it was a *child.* There would be no convincing herself otherwise.

The figure dragged itself across the pavement toward the cusp of the trees, retreating from out of the taillights' glow. Maggie saw one tiny white foot—five distinct toes splayed—scrabble for purchase on the roadway. The child was injured, probably severely, and she wanted to go to it and attend to it and make sure there wasn't something she could do to help it, but fear rooted her firmly in place. She was powerless to move.

The bleating of a car horn followed by the blinding dazzle of high beams caused Maggie to scream. She spun around to see a pair of headlights engulfed in a cloud of exhaust barreling toward her. She heard the approaching vehicle's brakes squeal. The headlights jounced as the vehicle jerked to a sudden stop.

"Help me!" she screamed, frightened by the fear and panic she heard in her voice. She raced toward the driver's side of the vehicle just as the door popped open. "Please! I need help!"

"Calm down, calm down." Even in her hysterical state, she could see that the driver was Cal Cordrick. He had a John Deere cap tugged down low on his scalp with a large brass fishhook clipped to the brim and a few days' growth at his chin. He reached out and placed one hand on Maggie's shoulder. "That you, Maggie? Maggie Quedentock?"

"Jesus, Cal! Thank God you're here! I hit—"

"You all right?"

"I hit someone! He's in the road!"

Cal peered over her shoulder, presumably to examine the queer positioning of the Pontiac in the center of the road. Then he looked back at her, his eyes small and pink and wet, like the leaky yet soulful eyes of a hound. Nervously, he rubbed one thumb up and down his prickly chin. "Stay here," he said, shoving past her.

She turned and watched him walk slowly past the Pontiac. He paused only for a moment to peer into the open door then kept going. To the darkness, Maggie heard him call out, "Is anyone out there? Hello? Anyone need help?" When no answer came, he kicked into a slight jog, his footfalls hollow-sounding on the pavement, until he disappeared into the blackness. Only the sound of his boot heels assured Maggie of his existence.

Cal Cordrick's footfalls stopped.

Maggie felt something leap in her chest. Silently to herself she counted to ten . . . or at least planned to; by the time she reached six, she could no longer control her fear. Too easily she could imagine the darkness as an actual living creature, a creature that had just devoured poor Cal Cordrick whole, just as it had seemingly devoured the child she'd hit.

"Cal!" she shrieked, the timbre of her voice shattering the silence. "Cal! Cal Cordrick!"

Nothing . . . nothing . . .

"Cal!"

Cal's shape reemerged from the darkness, though for one horrific second she thought the figure was that of the person she'd struck with her car. Maybe it wasn't the darkness that was alive after all. Maybe it was the thing she'd hit that had devoured Cal and was now coming back for her.

Thing, she thought.

But it was Cal, only Cal. His John Deere cap was off and he was running one hand through the stubble at his scalp. She didn't like the look on his face.

"Ain't no one out there," he told her evenly.

"Cal, I *saw*—"

"Ain't no one out there, Maggie." He stopped beside the front grille of the Pontiac and looked at it. There was a dent in the hood and the plastic grille was cracked in two places. "You been drinking some, hon?"

"No," she blurted.

"Maybe a little?"

"Well, I mean, yes. I was. Earlier." She felt confused and foolish. Was she dreaming all this? "I'm not drunk, Cal."

"Could be you just imagined you'd hit someone . . ."

"No."

"Or maybe it was a deer. Maybe it just kept running off into the woods. They can do that, you know. My brother once hit a twelve-point buck up on 40 with his Durango and the thing hardly batted an eye at—"

"No. It wasn't a deer, Cal." She felt a strange relief about having to convince him of what, only moments ago, she hadn't been so sure of herself. Even more peculiar was the laugh she felt threatening to burst from her throat. Was she out here losing her goddamn mind?

"Well, Maggie, there ain't nobody out there."

"Did you look in the woods?"

"I did. It's dark and I don't got a flashlight but I didn't see nothing. Didn't hear nothing, either."

"The person . . . was still alive," she said. Closing her eyes, she could see the split-second glimpse of the face, white as the moon with small, dark eyes. "He crawled over there into the trees." She pointed.

With his hands on his hips and the John Deere cap now stuffed in the rear pocket of his dungarees, Cal turned back around and surveyed the dark and vacant roadway. "Out here?"

She clutched at one of his forearms with both hands. "What do you mean?"

"Who'd be walking all the way out here at this hour?"

She didn't care if it didn't make sense or if Cal fucking Cordrick thought she was out of her mind. She closed her eyes and could clearly see the accident over and over, vivid as a film projected onto a screen.

In a small voice, she added, "I think it was a child."

Cal sighed and turned back around. He was maybe just a few years older than Maggie, but in the false light of crisscrossing vehicular headlamps he looked ghastly and no younger than a mummy exhumed from an ancient tomb. Again, he raked one thumb along his bristling chin. Car exhaust veiled him like mist.

"Christ," Maggie moaned. Her knees gave out and she felt herself go down, the world becoming a pixelated grid of smeary light, like looking at the world below from the window of an airliner. "Jesus Christ, Cal."

Cal Cordrick grabbed her and held her upright. He smelled of camphor and Old Spice. Faintly of bourbon, too, she thought. *That kid in the road . . .*

"Hang on there, Maggie. I'm sure Evan can—"

"He's on the night shift tonight," she whimpered into Cal's flannel shirt. She was gripping him as if letting go would cast her off the face of the planet.

"Okay," Cal said. There was an exhausted gruffness in his voice. His breath settled sourly against her face but she hardly noticed. "Do you think you can drive? I can follow you back to your—"

Trembling, Maggie Quedentock released her two-handed grip on Cal's shirt. Her body numb and her bones as reliable and sturdy as rubber bands, she sank slowly to the pavement. A high-pitched whine began trilling from her throat.

"I think maybe we need to call the police," Cal said.

2

It was midnight. Sergeant Benjamin Journell of the Stillwater Police Department stood in Porter Conroy's field beneath a moon that looked like a skull cracked in half. What had been mild weather earlier that afternoon had turned frigidly cold in the wake of the day's thunderstorm, and he wished he'd brought his parka from his cruiser.

Ben was thirty-five, unmarried, and he possessed a smooth, clean face and youthful eyes that made him look more like an Ivy League fraternity boy than a police officer. Ben had joined the department the day after his twenty-third birthday, when it became clear to him that, having spent his entire life living in the rural western Maryland town of Stillwater, his career choices were cripplingly limited: he could either join the police department or toil away at one of the various factories around town. And while he certainly possessed an affinity for the job, it sometimes seemed like he had just opened his eyes one morning and found himself in uniform. The department had been larger back then and he had found the anonymity of the khaki uniform with the numbered badge at the breast comforting and, sometimes, even freeing. He'd grown up in Stillwater, knew pretty much everyone straight out to the Cumberland Gap (which made the job easier), and he had always considered himself to be one of those rare individuals who found contentment in mediocrity.

He'd gone to college just outside of Baltimore, in Towson, where he'd been an average student. Debt piled up, but it had been Ben's father who had paid the bills, and the old man never said boo about it. Ben had majored in criminal justice and minored in English literature, a combination that granted him a wealth of diverse friends, and he had been groomed for lofty aspirations upon graduation—aspirations he most likely would have followed had his mother not passed away immediately thereafter.

So he had returned home to Stillwater and to the Journell family farm. Ah, Stillwater! The town existed only because a foolish man named Jeremiah Barnsworth had stumbled upon its crooked valley bookended by two grand mountains back in 1829, arriving just in time to witness a vista of black, stagnant water after one of the great floods had drowned the land. Why Barnsworth had thought this land would be the perfect location to establish some semblance of civilization, one can only wonder. Who proudly plants a flag at the center of decimation? Yet, still waters run deep, as they say, and Barnsworth—who had been a drunkard, a gambler, and a career adulterer, according to some of the descendants of families who had actually known the man—had created a town.

Nearly two centuries after Barnsworth's usurping of the land, twenty-one-year-old Ben Journell had returned from college to bury his dead mother and attend to his heartbroken father. Four years spent at Towson, and returning to Stillwater had been like returning to youthful memories—the type of memories that are so distant that they might have never happened to begin with. Yet he'd returned, and the hot summer dust rolled up off the roads as he drove back into town, the dust settling at the back of his throat and the smells of the land—the farms with their pig shit and chicken coops and tractor fumes, mingled with the brackish stink of the Narrows—practically clawing at his lungs. *Remember me, remember me!* Stillwater cried, as if to forget where he came from was to lose some important part of himself. *Remember me, remember me!* Indeed, how could he forget?

Like a good son, he remained until he felt that his father had moved beyond the grief of losing his wife, Ben's mother. Ben moved beyond that, too, feeling that the grief had been replaced by some unspoken allegiance between the two remaining members of the

Journell family, father and son. They had their roots already firmly planted in Stillwater; where else did he need to go? Back then, there were jobs to be had in Stillwater. With a college degree in hand, Ben already had a leg up on ninety percent of the workforce in town. Hell, he could do whatever he wanted. So what did he want to do? As it turned out, what he wanted to do was put his criminal justice degree to work and join the police department.

He had only been on the force for five years when his father, William Journell, a retired sustenance farmer who still lived in Ben's childhood home off Sideling Road in Stillwater, began seeing and speaking with Ben's dead mother. Bill would speak of seeing his dead wife out in the field behind the house, which had once been lush with crops but had slowly become overgrown as the soil hardened and the town dried up all around it. It was usually around dusk, just as the sun melted behind the mountains and Bill was out on the back porch smoking a pipe and drinking a glass of tea. Often, he would wander out into the field where they would engage in long conversations. Other times, she would continue walking clear across the property until she vanished into the curtain of trees at the far end of the farm. On these occasions, Bill Journell would call to his dead wife and attempt to follow her, but he moved too slowly and she seemed determined to remain elusive.

That was how the dementia started for Ben's father—in momentary bursts of unreality that were quickly forgotten the moment they were over. Ben had witnessed his father standing in the middle of the field one afternoon, talking to someone who was not there. When he went over to his father and took him gently by the forearm, Bill Journell smiled wearily at his son and told him to say hello to his mother. "Doesn't she look beautiful?" the old man had asked, simultaneously frightening Ben and breaking his heart. He took the old man to Cumberland to see a cadre of doctors who all diagnosed him with dementia.

That was when Ben moved back into his childhood home to take care of his father. He would remain there for the next year, through the worsening dementia and the onset of Alzheimer's, until Bill Journell inevitably passed the previous year. Ben had never moved out of his childhood home and, in the days following his father's funeral, he thought he could still hear the old man treading the tired old floorboards of the farmhouse. Some evenings, he was afraid to look out the windows and into the rear fields for fear that he would see both his parents out there, reunited in death but just as lively as they had been in life. He began to wonder, not without some sense of irony, if the Alzheimer's had needed someplace to go now that his father was dead, and since Ben was the only creature still living in the farmhouse, it had invaded him. Was that possible? Could the disease be working him over, worming its virulent fingers through the gray knots of his brain while he slept in the night? This notion made him uneasy. Instead of losing his mind, he took a brief vacation. When he returned, he no longer heard his father's footsteps creaking up and down the halls, and he no longer feared the sight of his dead parents standing out in the rear fields.

After his father died, and for the first time in Ben Journell's life, he had begun to second-guess his own life choices. The plants and factories had all dried up as work was farmed out more cheaply overseas. Similarly, the mom-and-pop stores along Hamilton were being systematically replaced over in Cumberland by massive department stores, bookstores that doubled as cafés and toy stores, and corporate chain restaurants with gimmicky menus and salvaged bric-a-brac on the walls. Here he was, Benjamin Journell, only son of the great William and Helen Journell, presiding like Charon over a town that, like a shallow swimming hole in the middle of summer, was slowly drying up beneath his feet. He could go out to Baltimore or Washington, D.C.—or any of the myriad metropolises throughout the East Coast—and live among the living. Hell, why did it have to stop there? He could pick up and go anywhere in the whole country . . . anywhere in the *world*, if he wanted to. For the first time in his life, he felt truly free . . . and also guilty that it had taken his father's death for him to feel this way.

However, the dying town of Stillwater and the Stillwater Police Department had different plans for him. Just when he was about to make the leap, he was promoted to sergeant. The last mortgage payment on the farm was handed over to the bank and now Ben owned his childhood home free and clear. And because complacency is the demise of momentum, he had stayed. Meanwhile, the shallow swimming hole had become nothing but a pit of dust.

Now, standing in Porter Conroy's east field in the middle of the night, Ben once more questioned the choices that had caused him to remain in Stillwater, presiding over some farmer's dead livestock. Sighing, he unhooked the flashlight from his Sam Browne belt and clicked it on. A few steps behind him, he could hear the labored respiration of Porter Conroy and Officer Eddie La Pointe. At the crest of the hill, Ben paused and ran the beam of the flashlight along the expansive field. He could see nothing but black piles of cow shit and swampy pools of rainwater, each one reflecting the stars. Against the horizon, brought into stark relief only when lightning struck, Porter Conroy's barn loomed like Noah's ark, the white-shingled cupola like the dome of a space shuttle. Ben cursed silently.

Porter sidled up beside him, reeking of booze and days-old sweat. He was an anemic fellow with a nose like the periscope of a submarine and skin as roughly textured as burlap. At least Porter had been forward-thinking enough to slip into a fleece-lined dungaree jacket.

"Where?" Ben said.

Porter pointed beyond the crest of the hill. In a voice that sounded very much like a sinner confessing to a priest, Porter said, "Just over the hill. I first came across 'em less than an hour ago. I figure it's some kind of animal did it."

Ben scratched one ear. "Did you hear any noises, any commotion?"

"Not a sound," Porter told him. "For an animal to do something like that, you'd think you'd hear something, right?"

"You'd think," Ben agreed.

Eddie La Pointe appeared beside Ben's other elbow. The officer had the green, sallow skin of someone chronically seasick. He glanced at Ben with large, beseeching eyes. He looked tired and very young. "Do you smell that?"

Ben nodded. "I do."

"What *is* that?"

Without responding, Ben Journell walked to the top of the hill then swiped the beam of his flashlight back and forth across Porter's east field. Whitish lumps appeared in the searchlight's beam, humping out of the grass like great mounds of sand. Ben counted eight of them before Porter and Eddie joined him at the top of the hill, their combined respiration forming clouds of vapor in the frigid air.

"There they are," Porter said, disgust evident in his voice.

"How many in all?"

"Christ," said Porter. "All of 'em."

"I mean, how many is that?"

"Thirteen."

Scanning the field again, Ben quickly recounted. "Where are the others?"

"In the barn."

Ben frowned. "Whatever did this got into the barn, too?"

"Yeah, Ben," Porter said. "Bold little cuss, whatever it was."

Ben went over to the first whitish heap rising out of the field, Eddie and Porter following close at his heels. The whitish heap was one of Porter Conroy's Holsteins, keeled over dead on its side. Its mottled white hide looked incongruous lying in the black, wet grass. Ben's flashlight illuminated the massive piebald flank first. He was surprised to find no wounds along the cow's body that would have been common in an animal attack. A muddy, congealed jelly that at first looked like it could be blood coated the Holstein's rear, but on closer inspection—and getting a whiff of the stuff—Ben realized it was feces. He traced the flashlight's beam along the flank to the neck and saw that the white hair of its throat was fully exposed. Thin red crescents, like a series of curved puncture wounds, scaled the length of its throat, the depth and severity of which could not have been fatal.

Finally shining the light onto the cow's head, Ben saw that it had been twisted in such a fashion that allowed him to see the open mouth ringed in foam, the snot-webbed portals of its cavernous nostrils, and one glazed, soupy, tar-colored eye rolled back in its socket. A pencil-thin rivulet of dark blood snaked out of one ear.

Ben frowned and said, "I don't see any type of wound that could be—"

"Back of the head," Porter interrupted.

Ben and the others stepped around to the other side of the cow, Ben's flashlight beam now training on the top of the cow's head.

Eddie pulled a face. "Jesus, Ben, the goddamn thing's skull has been busted open. What the hell does something like that to a cow?"

Ben squatted and took a closer look at the wound. The top of the cow's skull had been smashed open like a gourd, the concave bowl of its cranium glistening with black blood punctuated by tiny pinkish-white fragments of tissue and brain matter. The stench was beyond brutal.

"Its goddamn brain is gone," Ben muttered.

"A wolf, maybe?" Eddie suggested, kneeling down beside Ben. Behind them, Porter Conroy stood like a scarecrow waiting to be scooped up and carried away by the next strong gust of wind.

"Coyote, is what I think," Porter opined.

"Wolves and coyotes don't do this," Ben said.

"Been rumors of a mountain lion over in the next county, Ben," Eddie added.

Ben brought the flashlight closer to the gaping wound, the shadows shifting within the bloody chasm. He held the beam tightly on the bones of the skull that poked up like serrated teeth through the torn flesh, whitish-yellow and marbled with grayish striations. Spongy, brownish marrow was visible around the circumference. The flesh at the edge of the wound looked like it had been burned away, not torn. There were parts along the side of the cow's head where hair had been completely shorn away.

Without taking his eyes from the wound, Ben pointed beyond Eddie to where a large branch lay in the wet grass. "Hand me that, will you, Eddie?"

"Uh . . ." The officer snatched up the stick and handed it over to Ben. At this proximity, Ben could hear one of Eddie's nostrils whistling.

With the branch, Ben gently prodded a clump of greenish sludge that clung to the serrated edge of the skull.

"What the hell," Porter said somewhere above Ben's head.

Ben pushed harder. The sludge quivered and appeared to be as malleable as taffy. For one instant, Ben thought of marshmallows roasting over a bonfire, melting and dripping into the flames.

"What *is* that?" Eddie asked.

Ben withdrew the stick and tossed it into the grass. "I don't know," he said. It looked like moss clinging to the bone. There was a webbing of the stuff caught in the cow's eyelashes too, Ben noted. "What are you feeding these things, Porter?"

"London broil. The hell you think I'm feeding them?"

Shaking his head, Eddie said, "What kind of animal does something like that?"

"I have no idea," Ben said.

"I know what it is," Porter barked, shattering the quiet. Apparently something had just dawned on him.

Both Ben and Eddie turned their heads toward the older man.

"Ted Minsky," said Porter.

"Ted Minsky did this," Ben said. He jerked his chin due north, in the direction of the Minsky farm. "That's what you're saying?"

"The son of a bitch has been skinning deer and leaving them dangling from his porch. Damn things attract buzzards and then the buzzards shit all over the place and tear the hell out of the bedding in my barn." He jabbed a knotted finger at the dead milk cow. "Buzzards did this."

"Buzzards don't go after living animals," Ben told him.

"Don't tell me." Porter was obstinate. "I've seen those filthy birds all over the goddamn property. They got claws like industrial machinery."

Ignoring Porter, Eddie looked back at Ben and shrugged his shoulders. "What about a bear?"

Deep in thought, Ben didn't answer. It wasn't unusual for black bears to come down from the mountains and make their way into the surrounding towns. He had seen them loitering around trash cans and at the cusp of Wills Creek on more than just a few occasions. When he was a boy, he'd had friends who'd crossed their paths—unharmed, thankfully—while hiking through the woods no more than a mile or so away from civilization. However, he had never heard of a bear attacking a field of livestock before. And such a precise wound as this? To crack open the back of the skull and presumably eat the contents? Ben couldn't think of any indigenous animal capable of doing such a thing.

Ben stood up. In the beam of his flashlight he could make out all the other slumped forms dead in the field. They appeared to glow beneath the light of the moon. "They all look the same?" he asked Porter.

"What do you mean?"

"The other cows. Their bodies all look like this one?"

"More or less," said Porter. "Except maybe for the ones in the barn."

Ben asked about the ones in the barn.

"Their heads," said Porter. "Goddamn buzzards tore their heads clean off."

3

With Ben's assistance, Porter pulled open the large double doors of the barn, the squealing hinges like the shrieks of pterodactyls. From within—and almost instantaneously—a pungent, almost medicinal odor accosted them. Eddie said, "Ah, phew," then pulled a face and waved his hand back and forth in front of his nose.

That's not the smell of cow shit, Ben thought, following his flashlight's beam into the barn.

The barn was spacious and wide, with a ceiling that yawned to nearly three stories. The floor was scattered with hay and there were great bales of the stuff stacked like oversized building blocks beneath a roost. In the beam of his flashlight, Ben made out farming tools hanging from pegs driven into support beams and tools hanging from a pegboard against one wall. The smell of the place caused his eyes to water.

Porter took down a kerosene lamp from a nail that protruded from the doorframe and lit it. Soft, orange light pulsed ahead of them, making the shadows dance. "Storm knocked out the power to the barn," Porter said, addressing the electrical outlets gridded about the high beams in the ceiling with a crooked, arthritic finger.

"Where are the cows?" Ben asked.

"I'll show you." Porter cut around Ben and headed for the shadows deep in the belly of the barn. The lantern's light cast a halo around his stooped old frame. Ben and Eddie followed, stopping only when they arrived at a wall of three segregated stalls. Each Dutch door stood ajar. There was more straw here as well, heaped in mounds and scattered with what Ben assessed to be oats and grain. And something else, too. Spotlighting a specific mound of hay, he bent down and immediately recognized the third substance as blood.

Ben looked up and peered into the first stall. Inside lay the patchwork hull of another large cow. It was on its side, hooves out toward the open Dutch door, exposing a quill of tender-looking white udders for Ben's scrutiny.

"There's two more just like that one," Porter said, jabbing his gnarled finger at the other two stalls where similar humped shapes rose up out of the darkness.

Just as Porter Conroy had promised, the cows' heads looked to have been practically sheared off their bodies, leaving nothing behind, save for a pulpy tangle of tendons surrounding the jagged protrusion of a backbone jutting up through the mess like the tapered and pointy head of a spear. There were slashes of bright red blood on the wooden walls of each stall and in the hay surrounding the stalls.

"Where are the heads?" Ben asked after he'd examined each carcass.

"Beats me," Porter said.

Ben rubbed his upper lip while Eddie, still peering down at the massacre in one of the stalls, kept muttering over and over to himself, "Sweet Mary."

Ben jerked a thumb over his shoulder in the direction of the barn's double doors. "You typically keep those locked?"

"No, sir. I don't." There was an undeniable pride in the old man's voice. Like many of the old farmers out in this part of the country, Porter Conroy was adamant about not changing his ways. The only way someone like Porter would put a lock on his barn doors was when cows figured out how to work door handles.

"Mr. Conroy, have you had any . . . disagreements . . . with anyone lately?" Humorlessly, he added, "Aside from Ted Minsky, I mean."

"Disagreements?" Porter said, as if he did not understand the word. The old man's eyes reflected the dancing flame contained in the glass housing of the lantern, which he'd set on the half wall of the nearest stall.

"Arguments," Ben clarified. "Fights. Anything like that."

Porter laughed. "What kind of fights you fellas think I'm getting into at my age?"

Eddie was looking at Ben with wide eyes, his face narrow and slack and nearly translucent in the firelight.

"What are you getting at, Ben?" Porter asked evenly. "I'm not following."

Ben had raked a set of fingers slowly up and down his chin before mumbling something about just being curious. *Animals don't do this,* he thought. *Someone broke in here and took these cows' heads, mutilated these poor animals.* It would have had to have been someone—or a group of someones—who possessed more than just a mean streak and had some bone to pick with Porter; it would have had to have been someone evil.

A papery, rustling sound from above caused the three of them to jump. Ben looked up. In the glow of the lantern, it looked like the underside of the hayloft, which was directly above their heads, was moving. Ben clicked his flashlight back on and directed the beam upward.

The underside of the hayloft was teeming with bats, dozens of them, dangling upside down by their tiny, clawed feet, their piggish heads bobbing and jerking while the thin membrane of their wings quivered.

"Oh, yeah," Porter said conversationally. "Been having a bat problem lately, too."

4

On the car ride back to the station, Eddie said, "You know what eats brains, don't you, Ben?"

"What's that?"

"Zombies."

"Ah. Of course. Zombie cows."

"You joke, but strange stuff like that happens all the time."

"Is that right?"

"Quit humoring me. You ever hear about those exploding sheep over in Ireland?"

Ben clicked off the cruiser's high beams as another vehicle approached him on the wooded road. "What are you talkin' about?"

"I read this news article on the computer once, about a farmer in Ireland. A bolt of lightning hit one of his sheep while it was out grazing on a hill. The static in the wool or something caused some kind of electrical chain reaction, and the lightning zigzagged from sheep to sheep—*blam, blam, blam!*—and fried every single one of the buggers right there on the spot."

Ben laughed. "That sounds like bullshit."

"Next day, there were thirty, forty of the sons of bitches sizzling in the field, looking like chicken legs that had been burned to charcoal on a barbecue."

"Yeah, well, I don't think lightning was the culprit this time." He was thinking about the dead cows in the barn. *What instrument would someone use to take off a cow's head like that? Those didn't look like cuts at all. And how would someone get a goddamn cow to stay put for the amount of time it would take to do something like that?*

There was a ratcheting sound as Eddie reclined his seat. He took a cigarette out of the breast pocket of his khaki uniform, poked it between his lips, but out of respect for Ben's rule about not smoking in the police cars, he did not light it. "Well, don't sell that mountain lion business short," he said, the cigarette bouncing. "Paulie Davenport over in Garrett said they had one been coming into the neighborhoods at night, knocking over trash cans and eating house cats or whatever. A bunch of guys saw it slinking away into the hills one night behind Torry's Tavern, and one of them took some shots at it with a handgun but missed."

"Just what I like to hear. A bunch of rogue drunks firing guns out behind a bar."

"One of the other guys snapped a photo of it on his phone. Can you believe that?"

"Sure." He knew the Potomac Highlands was no stranger to the creatures, though he had never seen one in person nor heard of them attacking livestock, especially not an entire field of grazing cattle. Not that it was impossible, of course. Recalling the crescent-shaped wounds at the throat of the first cow, Ben could acknowledge that they resembled the type of attack wound generated by a set of claws . . .

Even if it was a rogue mountain lion, Ben thought, *that doesn't explain the state of the carcasses. Mountain lions attack the head, sure . . . but what mountain lion eats only the brains and leaves the rest of the meat behind?* That part troubled him the most.

"Davenport called someone at Fish and Wildlife, and they told him that it wasn't unusual for a particular mountain lion to migrate halfway across the country," Eddie said. "I mean, they said it's rare, but they've seen it happen before."

"How do they know?"

"They dig through its shit, see where it's been and what it's eaten. Also, I heard they do DNA tests on them, too. See, mountain lions out here have slightly different DNA than, say, mountain lions from Arizona or wherever."

"I don't think there are mountain lions in Arizona," Ben said.

"Or wherever they're from. The son of a bitch could've been from Colorado or Montana or the goddamn Pacific Northwest."

"How do you know so much about mountain lions?"

Absently, Eddie said, "It's just what I heard from Davenport."

"This wasn't a mountain lion," Ben assured him.

"I'm just saying." Eddie sucked his tongue along his teeth. "What you were asking Porter back in his barn about having been in an argument with anyone lately?"

"Yeah?"

"You think a *person* could have done that?"

The radio crackled. Ben hit the CB and said, "Go ahead, Shirley."

"Possible 71 on Full Hill Road, between mile-markers ten and eleven," Shirley said, her voice laced with static.

Eddie sat up straight. "Well, shit." A 71 was a pedestrian struck by a vehicle.

Into the transmitter, Ben said, "Go ahead, Shirley."

"Just got a call from Cal Cordrick. Says Maggie Quedentock was in a car accident over on Full Hill. She told him she hit somebody out in the road but Cal, he says he checked the area but couldn't see nothing. He thought maybe she was just shaken up."

"We're on our way back from Porter Conroy's farm now," Ben said. "We can be there in two minutes, Shirley. You call for an ambulance?"

"It's on the way."

"Thanks, Shirl."

"Well, goddamn," said Eddie, sticking his cigarette behind his ear.

Ben switched on the cruiser's bar lights, washing the world around them in alternating blue and red. He pressed down on the accelerator and felt the raw power beneath the hood of the cruiser burst to life. Ben executed a graceful U-turn in the middle of the street then continued along in the direction he had come from.

"There," Eddie said, pointing through the darkness at the turnoff onto Full Hill Road. Not that Ben needed him to do so. Ben Journell could walk the circumference of Stillwater blindfolded and tell you the name of every tree he bumped into along the way.

Ben took the turn at a quick clip, the dark, swampy trees bowing over the roof of the cruiser and closing in around them.

"Who the hell would she hit?" Eddie said. "I mean, who's out here walking after midnight?"

"There they are." Ben slowed down as he spotted the headlights up ahead, smoky in the buildup of exhaust fumes that hung in thick clouds above the roadway. A figure moved in front of one pair of headlights, long-limbed and slump-shouldered. Ben brought the cruiser to a stop at the side of the road. He reached beneath his seat and grabbed his spare Maglite, then quickly stepped out.

Cal Cordrick waved both arms over his head as Ben and Eddie approached.

"Is everyone okay?" Ben asked, already surveying the situation. Cal's Buick was facing Evan Quedentock's Pontiac, and one of the Pontiac's fog lamps was out. He could see that the cheap plastic grille was cracked and there was a nice little ding in the hood. "Where's Maggie?"

Cal jerked a thumb over his shoulder. "She's sitting on the side of the road. She wouldn't get back in her car and she didn't want to wait in mine."

"Go check her out," he said to Eddie, who hustled down the road while lighting a flare. A moment later, a bright spark of purple magnesium illuminated the darkness. The fog seemed to coalesce.

"She seems okay, aside from being pretty well shaken up," Cal said. He gulped audibly. "She thinks she hit somebody. I walked around but couldn't—"

"Let's take a look," Ben said, handing Cal his spare Maglite.

They walked down the center of the road, the asphalt glowing with an unnatural pink-purple hue from the road flare, their flashlights piercing the heavy foliage of the underbrush at the shoulders of the road. A cursory review of the surrounding area showed no evidence of a struck pedestrian.

"When did you get on the scene?" Ben asked Cal.

"Just after it happened, I guess. Ten minutes ago? I was coming down the road and saw her headlights facing me, so I slowed down—you know how the road narrows and you need to slow down if there's a car passing, Ben—but when I got closer I could see that her car door was open and that the car was in the middle of the road. Then I saw her standing out there, looking off into the dark."

"You said you looked around for the pedestrian?"

"Yeah, but I didn't have a light on me and I just did it real quick, in case there really was someone hurt out here." The tone of Cal's voice suggested he did not believe Maggie had hit anyone.

When they'd walked far enough away from the vehicles, Ben paused and looked around. It seemed implausible that someone could be thrown this far. Without saying a word to Cal, he turned around and headed back to the Pontiac. Maggie was perched on a large stone at the shoulder of the road, her skin pale, her hair an unkempt nest of bristling auburn wires. From this distance, and in the poor lighting, her eyes looked like hollow black sockets. Eddie stood above her, asking questions in his soft, placating voice.

Ben bent down and examined the skid marks on the pavement. To even call them "skid marks" was hyperbole; Ben spotted two smudgy exclamations of melted rubber on the surface of the road, hardly noticeable. It meant Maggie Quedentock hadn't been going all that fast when she'd slammed on the brakes and spun the wheel.

Ben stood up, popping the tendons in his back. Out of nowhere, he felt ridiculously old, despite his thirty-five years. He looked over to Eddie who appeared engrossed in his little notepad, where he was jotting some notes. Ben went over to them.

"Hey, Maggie," he said. "How're you doing, hon? You okay?"

"Jesus. Yeah, Ben. Hi. Sorry." Her voice had the squeaky, broken quality of a badly dented trumpet.

"Nothing to be sorry about." He looked to Eddie, who shrugged his shoulders. "What happened here, Maggie?"

She told him—she'd been coming down the road when, in a split second, someone jumped out in front of her car. "I think . . ." She stuttered and quickly averted her eyes. Her whole body trembled. Then she met his eyes again. "Whoever it was just came right out of the woods. I tried to stop, but then the car started spinning." Her voice hitched. "Did you find anyone out there?"

Ben shook his head. He could hear sirens in the distance. "You have a few drinks tonight?"

"Earlier I had a few."

"How much earlier?"

"I don't remember. Maybe around seven o'clock? I was down at Crossroads."

"Were you alone?"

Her brow furrowed. "At Crossroads?" Her voice was paper thin. She appeared to chew over the answer to his question. "Yes," she said finally.

"Okay. Any chance what you hit was a deer?"

She looked directly at him then. Those eyeless pits in her skull stared straight through him, chilling his blood to ice water. It was only after he realized she had mascara smeared around her eyes that he released a slow and weary breath.

"It looked like a person," she said in a low voice then immediately dropped her head again. "I mean, I saw . . . I *think* . . . it was a little boy, Ben. I mean, I think it was."

A wave of heat radiated through Ben's body. "You think?"

"I'm almost positive . . . but . . ."

"But what?"

"No hair," she said. "The kid didn't have any hair."

Without missing a beat, Ben thought about how he had fished a hairless boy out of the cold waters of Wills Creek last week. The boy had been in the water for an unknown period of time, the color leached from his flesh and the hair shorn from his scalp. Thinking about it now made Ben Journell uneasy.

"When the ambulance gets here, have 'em give Maggie a once-over, then have them wait around until I can do a better search of the surrounding woods," Ben told Eddie.

"You got it," Eddie said, stuffing his notebook back into the breast pocket of his shirt.

Ben got back into his cruiser just as the whirling lights of the ambulance approached in his rearview mirror. He pulled around the Pontiac then slowly coasted up the shoulder of the road, shining the windshield-mounted searchlight into the trees. He clicked on the high beams too, though all that seemed to accomplish was to give substance to the clouds of exhaust clogging the air. Fat, white moths swirled in the funnel of light. He was looking for anything—busted tree limbs, trampled underbrush, perhaps some blood on the bark of a tree. But he could see nothing.

Eventually he brought the car to a stop and put it in Park. When he stepped out, he first thought that the temperature had dropped another ten degrees, but then realized he had been sweating to death in the cruiser. Beneath his uniform, his Kevlar vest seemed to weigh a thousand pounds.

Clicking on his flashlight again, he stepped off the road and into the tangled underbrush at the cusp of the woods. Each exhalation clouded before his face, and he could feel the sweat on his forehead and at the back of his neck freezing in the night. He crossed several yards into the trees, the network of bare branches crisscrossing the moon above his head. Beneath his heavy boots, dead leaves and fallen tree limbs crunched like potato chips. He paused, scanning the area with the flashlight's beam. Everything moved—the trees, the twiggy shrubs, the shadows. The world was alive with the chorus of countless insects.

The longer he stared at a spot of darkness, the more he could convince himself that things were moving within. At one point, Ben thought he could hear a high-pitched keening coming from somewhere far back in the woods—a distant falcon screeching from a branch.

"Ben?" Eddie said, coming up behind him.

"Christ. Don't sneak up on me like that."

"The EMTs want to know what they should do. They checked over Mrs. Quedentock and said she looks fine, she's just a little freaked out, you know? She doesn't want to go with them, says she doesn't need an ambulance and just wants to go home. The EMTs are just sitting there, waiting. What should I tell them?"

"Tell them I got some extra flashlights in the trunk of my car," Ben said. "They can go home after we check the other side of the road."

5

They searched the woods off Full Hill Road for nearly two hours but found no evidence of a person having been struck by Maggie Quedentock's car. The EMTs became quickly annoyed and said they had more important things to do than traipse around the woods for what would probably amount to an injured deer, and they soon left. Ben didn't blame them. He was just relieved that no victim had been found.

It was after three in the morning when the cruiser pulled into the empty parking lot of the police station. At this hour, even Shirley was gone. Any emergency calls would be rerouted to a dispatcher in Cumberland. With the exception of the floodlight that cast an unwavering beam on the American flag in the front yard, the entire building was dark.

Ben parked in a spot right up front then elbowed Eddie awake. Jerking up awkwardly from where he'd been slouched, snoring, against the passenger window, Eddie La Pointe looked around, temporarily disoriented.

"Go home," Ben told him.

"You going, too?" Eddie already had the passenger door open. The sound of crickets infiltrated the vehicle.

"In a few minutes."

"Crazy night, huh?"

"You got it. Goodnight, Eddie."

"Goodnight, Ben."

Eddie slammed the door and padded across the parking lot to his car with his head down. Ben watched him drive away and turn onto Belfast Avenue before he shut the cruiser down and climbed out. Ben could tell it would be a cold winter up here in the mountains. The trees were already whispering about it and the air smelled smoky and cool. He unlocked the station doors and pushed them open on hinges that shrieked like banshees. Green-and-black checkerboard tile floors, oatmeal-colored walls, fizzy sodium fixtures in the ceiling that didn't always work—he had become so used to this place that it felt like crawling back into the womb each time he walked through the doors.

In the dispatcher's cubicle, he fed Shirley's goldfish, Abbott and Costello, muttering to them as he did so. Then he went into what the guys called the "Batter's Box," the spacious room segregated into four cubicles where the officers sat when they weren't out on the road. Ben unbuttoned his shirt and pulled his vest off, his undershirt matted with sweat. He hung the vest on one of the cubicle walls, directly over a stack of Eddie's *Fangoria* magazines and the very slim case file on the unidentified boy whose nude body had washed up on the shores of Wills Creek early last week. To date, the boy had not been identified or claimed by anyone and, as far as Ben was aware, the pallid, hairless body still sat in a stainless-steel drawer at the county morgue over in Cumberland.

Ben continued down the hall to the kitchen, where he retrieved an apple from the foul-smelling communal refrigerator. There were photographs of some of the officers' kids stuck to the outside of the fridge with magnets. Taking a knife from his belt, he began cutting the apple into wedges as he headed toward the two-car sally port at the far end of the station. He opened the door to the sally port and felt along the wall for the light switch while popping one of the apple wedges into his mouth. Dim yellow light poured down from an industrial spotlight in the center of the ceiling housed in a wire casing that reminded Ben of a catcher's mask. The port was empty—all of the officers took their vehicles home with them—and the room was as cold and as silent as a cave.

That was why he'd put the bat back here.

It was a tiny thing with short brown hair and ears like little radar dishes. It had the fuzzy face of a pig with moist, black eyes. As Ben approached the bell-shaped birdcage that sat on a shelf among paint cans and plastic quarts of motor oil, the creature inside began to twitter and chirp. It hung upside down from the perch, its tiny head bobbing and its piggish little snout sniffing the cool air.

"Hey, bud. You hanging in there?" Two days ago, the thing had gotten trapped in the sally port. He had wanted to let it go but the other guys thought it would be cool to keep the bat as a mascot of sorts, at least for a little while. Mike Keller had gone home and returned with the bell-shaped birdcage. When Chief Harris had simply grunted his indifference, more interested in his upcoming vacation with his wife than any police business, Ben had acquiesced.

So here I am now, three o'clock in the goddamn morning, sticking apple wedges into a birdcage.

He couldn't help but smile to himself.

"There you go, buddy." He dropped the final wedge into the cage.

The bat chirped and fluttered its wings.

Both of us trapped here in this town, he thought, surprised by the depth of his comparison. Suddenly, he wanted to release the bat into the night, but he fought off this urge at the last minute.

"Two peas in a pod," he told the bat before shutting off the light and going home.

CHAPTER THREE

1

From the sky, the rural western Maryland hamlet of Stillwater might appear to be a ghost town. It sits at the bottom of a river valley, bookended to the east and west by the tree-studded swell of the Allegheny Mountains. The town itself is bisected by Wills Creek, which traverses the concrete slalom of the Narrows before emptying into the Potomac River east of town. The roadways twist and wind and turn to dirt the farther out into the foothills they go. The only testament to the town's connection with the outside world is the two-lane concrete ribbon that is U.S. Route 40, which clings like bunting to the side of Wills Mountain. This cut of asphalt runs for over two hundred miles across the state, from Garrett County straight out to Elkton, where it continues on into Delaware before it disappears completely like the vaporous contrail of a jetliner.

In the predawn hours this Saturday, the streets of Stillwater are empty and dark. Many of the streetlights along Hamilton and Susquehanna are still out due to damage from the recent storm and its subsequent flooding. The stone-fronted shops along Hamilton resemble mausoleums. The bell tower of the Methodist church on Poplar Ridge Road rises before a backdrop of stirring vermilion light that has just barely begun to bleed into the sky. A low susurration whispers through the trees as eddies of autumn wind work their magic along the empty streets.

The old folks rise earliest. These are generations of farmers and blue-collar workers who have eked out an existence for themselves—much as their forefathers had done before them—applying their brawn and discipline toward hard manual labor. Sully Goodwin rises to the horned leaves of the holly bushes scraping against his bedroom window. Since Hugh Crawly split town, Sully has taken over Stillwater's mail delivery. Without showering, he dresses silently in the dark, his eyes still partially lidded and crusted with sleep, his mouth tasting of the foul cigars and stale beer he had the night before over in Cumberland. His mail truck sits out front of his ranch house—an old Ford station wagon with a detachable orange bubble light that adheres to the roof with magnets. When he's done with today's run, he'll drop the bubble light off at Bobby Furnell's place, since Bobby uses that same light on the cab of his F-150 when he works construction over in the Gap.

Old Porter Conroy rises early as well, despite having been up late last night dealing with the police and fretting over his livestock. He has a long day ahead of him. The mutilated livestock will need to be incinerated and their remains either buried in the western field or trucked out to the dump. Undoubtedly, he will have to call the Kowalski brothers, those unreliable knucklehead alcoholics, to lend him a hand. Five bucks apiece and he'll have them doing manual labor all day. He will have to replace the locks on the barn doors, too. For the first time in all his life, he considers getting one of those Yale padlocks Dean Cropsy keeps on his boathouse. Who would have thought it would come to this? He's got an old remedy for getting rid of the bats as well, but it will take him much of the afternoon to prepare it—a fetid stew that goes on like apple butter but stings the eyes something fierce. Then it's off to his brother's place in Charles Town for a few days. He's decided to lose himself in a sea of slot machines and watered-down cocktails. He knows his problems will still be waiting for him here in Stillwater, but damn if the temporary relief doesn't do a world of good for his old soul.

Out on Full Hill Road, old Melba Codger sits in her recliner and stares out at a set of blackened windows. In her senility, she believes she can see many shapes capering in the darkness just beyond the glass.

In a two-story A-frame on Susquehanna, seventy-year-old Cordell Jones creeps out of bed, careful not to disturb his wife, and slinks downstairs to the kitchen without turning on a single light. There, he indulges in a sandwich piled high with sliced deli meats and cheeses, mayo, and purple spirals of onion. May his acid indigestion and high cholesterol be damned.

Sarah Kamish has not slept well for quite a while now. She leaves her husband in bed—his snoring like the pulverization of granite in a crusher—and wends ghostlike about the rambling old farmhouse. Her son, twenty-two-year-old Michael Kamish, was killed last summer in Iraq . . . and while she has been haunted by his death every moment since it happened, she has been troubled for the past week by what she assumes to be her own slipping sanity. Late last week, just as she drove back from Cumberland along Route 40 and as the sun set behind the western mountains, she thought she saw Michael standing on the mud-caked embankment of the Narrows. He was still in his military uniform, with a white satchel slung over his right shoulder. As she drove by, his head turned slowly and mechanically and followed her progress along the highway. Sarah slammed on the brakes and got out of the car. She went back around the bend of the highway and crept down the sloping hillside of the embankment that led to the overflowing waters of the Narrows. Of course, it was all just a hallucination; Michael was not there. There in the tall grass, she cried for twenty minutes before returning to her car and driving back into town. Now, Sarah cries silently to herself as she stands in the darkened living room of the old farmhouse—a farmhouse where her parents once lived and where she grew up. It is hers now—hers and her husband's—and they will be the last of their meager lineage to reside there.

Joe Flip, better known to the patrons of Crossroads as "Flip the Drip," finds himself jarred awake from a dream that has left him in quite an impressive state of arousal. The details of the dream are lost the moment he opens his eyes, but he knows it had something to do with Wendy Crawly, the attractive, middle-aged waitress who works down at the Belly Barn. Even if she is quite a few years his junior, she continues to be awfully flirty with him whenever he stops into the Barn for lunch. She has a nice smile and nicer tits and—not for the first time—old Flip the Drip wonders if she's just been *aching* for it ever since her husband split town with a younger broad. Recalling the way Wendy Crawly's breasts fill out her waitress uniform, Flip the Drip fumbles his meaty cock from the fly of his boxer shorts and proceeds to masturbate with the discipline of a millworker.

On the outskirts of town, where Wills Creek empties into the steady, black drink that is the Potomac, a woman named Hazel McIntosh is already making coffee in her kitchen. It is still dark outside, and she can see nothing beyond the blackened panel of glass above the kitchen sink as she rinses her coffeepot save for the twinkling of moonlit diamonds glittering along the surface of the river. The flooding had been bad, and the river had rushed up to greet the old house where she lives alone with her seven calico cats, and it swept her lawn furniture away. Nights earlier, she had been staring out this very window when she saw a section of the Highland Street Bridge go cruising by. One of its stanchions poked up out of the water like the smokestack of a ship. She guessed that it had been washed straight out into the Chesapeake . . . or, for that matter, the Atlantic Ocean. Stranger things have happened in her lifetime.

Small towns are secrets kept by the elderly. The old keep watch, and while they don't quite realize it—not on any conscious level, that is—there is a certain primal part of their makeup, perhaps ingrained in their earthly DNA, that keeps them up and alert and continually rising early to beat the sun at its own game. And it would be a lie to say that, on occasion, one or more of these individuals doesn't feel a tingling sense of stewardship during these dark, predawn moments—a sense that they have been selected to keep watch over a town that, for years now, has been slowly dying beneath their feet.

The people of the Narrows keep watch.

2

Brandy Crawly awoke early, just as she did every Saturday, and winced at the slivers of sunlight that speared through the blinds. She remained in bed for several more minutes, watching motes of dust swim in the shafts of light, and considering the possibilities for the day ahead. The daylight hours were hers, to do with as she pleased after her chores around the house were done. Later that evening, she was babysitting Tabby Olson for some extra spending money. The Harvest Dance was only a week away—Jim Talbot had asked her to go with him—and there was an off-the-shoulder black dress at Macy's over in Garrett that she wanted to buy. The babysitting money should put her in the black.

When she heard her mother's bedroom door open and the old shower pipes clank and shudder in the bathroom, Brandy climbed out of bed. She combed her hair in the beveled glass then pulled it back into a ponytail. Then she bladed her body, sucked in her belly, and flattened her nightshirt against her chest to examine her profile. Her breasts were too small, her hair too frizzy, her nose just a vague, upturned nub between eyes that, in just the past year or so, had grown too widely spaced apart. She thought her legs looked funny, too. They were too wide in the upper thighs and too narrow at the calf. She lifted one foot and flexed the calf muscle, pointing her toes down like a ballerina. Had she continued with the track team through last year, her legs might have had a more even, tapered look.

Girls on the track team don't get asked to the Harvest Dance by boys like Jim Talbot, she thought. *And boys don't like girls who run faster than they do.*

She pulled on a pair of lacrosse shorts and glanced one last time with some dismay at her reflection in the beveled glass. Then she went downstairs to prepare breakfast.

She heard the screen door banging against the frame from the hallway. Entering the kitchen, she froze. The porch door stood wide open while the screen beyond banged and clattered in the breeze. Matted wet leaves lay in clumps on the tile and there was grit and debris like sprinkles of pepper on the kitchen counter.

Her initial conclusion was that someone had broken into the house at night while the three of them slept, and a cold dread overtook her. Suddenly, the rattling water pipes upstairs sounded as insubstantial as noise coming through a television set. Brandy went to the door and examined the lock and, to her immediate relief, she found that the lock had not been busted. This had not been done by any intruder. This had been the work of her stupid, careless brother.

Upstairs, she stormed into Matthew's room, her brother's name already on her tongue, but caught herself when she saw that his room was empty. The place was also a pigsty. Why the little brat couldn't take his dirty clothes down to the laundry room, she'd never understand.

She was back down in the kitchen scrambling egg whites when her mother came down in her waitress uniform. Wendy pinned up her hair, went to the coffee machine on the counter, and poured herself a steaming mug.

"Got time for some eggs?" Brandy said, scraping the eggs from the pan into a plate.

Her mother sipped the coffee loudly. "What is this mess?" She was looking at the muddy leaves and dirt on the kitchen floor.

"Matthew left the door open when he went out this morning."

"That kid," Wendy sighed.

Brandy took the plate to the table and set it down beside a glass of grapefruit juice. "Can I have the truck for the day if I drive you?" she asked her mother, thinking it might be a good idea to head into Garrett and put the dress on layaway before someone else grabbed it.

"You know I don't like you driving around when I'm not home." Wendy went into the laundry room and reappeared a second later with a whisk broom. She opened the porch door and propped open the screen then proceeded to sweep the dead leaves and dirt out onto the porch.

"What's the difference if you're home or at work?"

"If I'm home I can come get you if something happens."

"What would happen?"

"Brandy, you're sixteen. You just got your license three months ago. Anything could happen."

Brandy scraped her fork along her plate and said, "You know I'm careful. I'm a good driver."

"You're an *inexperienced* driver," her mother said. "What if you blow a tire?"

"I'll change it."

"We don't even have a spare," Wendy said, sweeping the last of the filth out the door.

"Then I'll leave the car on the side of the road and walk home, just like you would have to do if *you* blew a tire." She set her fork down, her eggs only half-eaten. "It's not fair that we have to share the one stupid truck."

"That's the thing that's not fair, huh?" said her mother, lingering in the open doorway. A slight breeze caused her apron to flap. She was looking out at something in the yard.

"We can't keep using Dad as an excuse for why we don't have shit around here," Brandy said.

In a small voice, her mother said, "Watch your mouth." Then she stepped quickly out onto the porch.

"Mom." Brandy felt instantly horrible. She turned around at the table and, from the kitchen windows, saw her mother cross down into the yard. She was still clutching the broom.

Brandy got up and stood at the back door. The pickup's keys still hung from the pegboard on the wall by the door, so she knew her mother wasn't just going to climb into the truck and drive away. Instead, Wendy Crawly went over to the line of hedges beside the garage, where she crouched down, the broom poking out from under one arm like a jousting pole. For one heartbreaking moment, Brandy thought her mother had broken down, fatally injured by her daughter's careless comment.

When Wendy stood back up and turned around, Brandy could see her mother clutching something in one hand.

Heading back toward the porch, her mother asked her if she had actually seen Matthew leave the house this morning.

Brandy shook her head. "No. What is that?"

Her mother mounted the porch steps and set the broom against the railing. The thing she held looked like an article of clothing, wet and speckled with mud. "It's one of your brother's shirts." Water dripped from it onto the porch.

The look that swam briefly across her mother's face made Brandy uncomfortable.

Wendy Crawly looked over her shoulder and back out into the yard. She said, "I guess it could've fallen from the clothesline without anyone noticing."

Brandy followed her mother's gaze to the length of rubber cord that ran from the porch to the side of the garage, about four-and-a-half feet off the ground. It drooped slightly in the middle. Then she turned back to her mother, who was fingering a series of holes in the T-shirt. "That kid," Wendy muttered then stomped past her daughter back into the house.

Brandy turned back toward the yard. Something flapping against the low chain-link fence caught her eye. She stepped into a pair of her mother's sandals that had been left on the porch and crossed down into the yard and over to the fence. Bending down, she saw a dollar bill caught in the diamond-shaped lattice of the fence.

Back in the kitchen, with the dollar bill tucked securely in the waistband of her lacrosse shorts, Brandy dumped the remainder of her breakfast into the trash then washed off the plate at the sink. She could hear her mother in the living room, searching for her purse and cursing quietly to herself.

"Your purse is in the laundry room, Mom."

Looking distraught and glancing at the slender gold wristwatch she wore, Wendy hurried across the kitchen and into the laundry room. She began to say she didn't see it but cut herself off midsentence. She reappeared in the kitchen, peering down into the opened compartment of her handbag.

"Okay," Wendy said, zipping the bag closed and winding the strap over one shoulder. "What time do you have to be at the Olsons' tonight?"

"Six."

"Then I'll stay late and pick up some extra tables at the diner."

"You sure I can't drive you?"

"No. You can take your bike or walk. And you can throw in a load of laundry for me, too." Wendy snatched the pickup's keys off the pegboard on the wall. "If you see your brother, tell him I want him home before dark. There are leftovers in the fridge."

Her mother went out the door, careful not to let the screen door slam, and a moment later Brandy could hear the stubborn growl of the pickup's engine rumbling to life. From the kitchen windows, she watched as the truck pulled around the dirt turnabout then pulled out into the street.

After she straightened up the kitchen (and took a sip from the open bottle of Budweiser that stood on the bottom shelf of the fridge), Brandy went upstairs and took a long shower then pulled on some fresh clothes. Grumbling to herself about her brother, she went into his room and collected his dirty clothes off the floor—they were filthy and they stank—and kicked his muddy shoes under the bed. She gathered up her clothes from the bathroom, along with some blouses that were strewn about in her mother's room, then she carried the whole bundle in a laundry basket downstairs. There was already a load in the washing machine and another jumble of colored garments in the dryer. She pulled a shirt and a pair of slacks out of the dryer, found them terribly wrinkled—they must have been sitting in the dryer for too long—then dropped them back in, along with a damp bandana, and restarted the cycle. She exchanged the unwashed clothes in the laundry basket for the damp ones in the washer and was about to carry them outside to the clothesline when she saw Matthew's T-shirt—the one her mother had found outside in the yard—balled up on a shelf next to a tub of detergent and a box of fabric softener sheets.

She took the shirt down, held it out, and looked it over. It was speckled with mud and smelled of her little brother's perspiration. The armpits were yellowed and the cuffs of the sleeves were frayed.

She turned the shirt around and examined the line of small holes running vertically down the back. Frowning, she poked a finger through one of the holes.

Outside, she was halfway across the lawn with the laundry basket in tow when she stopped. Matthew's bike was leaning against the side of the garage. The pickup had been parked in front of it, so neither Brandy nor her mother had seen it. The bike—a red-and-black contraption their father had gotten him from a yard sale a few years ago—had grown too small for Matthew but he still rode it, cherished it. The chrome gleamed in the sun and there were waterproof stickers on the handlebars. The handgrips looked worn and the plastic seat was cracked.

She didn't like the way the bike sat there. The single reflector at the front of the handlebars was a single eye staring at her.

Weekends, Matthew spent the entire day on his bike, usually with his dumb friend Dwight Dandridge. She didn't like seeing it here now, with Matthew gone, having left it behind.

Brandy hung the laundry on the line quickly, her mind only half on the task. Sunlight glinting off the bicycle's chrome and the single reflector kept catching her in the periphery of her vision.

It bothered her.

3

After she finished with the laundry, Brandy laced up a pair of sneakers, took another swig from her mother's beer bottle in the fridge, then went back outside. The Dandridge house was just a few blocks up the road. With the air still cool and breezy from the previous night's storm, the walk was pleasant enough despite her urgency.

The Dandridge house appeared over the next hill. It was a Cape Cod in the style of the Crawly home, but that was where the similarities stopped. Splintered, sun-bleached siding, crumbling porch steps, a roof that sloughed mossy green shingles like a reptile shedding old skin, the Dandridge house looked like the residence of a family of hillbilly cannibals in a horror movie. She had gone to the house only a handful of times in her life—typically to fetch her brother when he had forgotten to return home by curfew—though she had never been inside. Two of Dwight's older brothers were in Brandy's grade, Kyler and Fulton, and even though they weren't twins she could never tell them apart. Equally long-haired and grimy, the Dandridge boys always smelled of cigarettes and spouted vulgarities with the unpremeditated casualness of sailors. There had been sisters, too, even older than Kyler and Fulton, but they no longer lived in Stillwater and Brandy could not recall their names. Mrs. Dandridge, whom Brandy had spied only a handful of times despite having lived a few blocks from the Dandridges her whole life, surfaced in Brandy's head as a waiflike chain-smoker with sunken jowls, jaundiced skin, and the wide, gaping eyes of a curious owl.

As she approached the house, Brandy found herself thinking mostly of Mr. Dandridge, the father. He was a vulgar, overweight drunk who worked odd jobs around town. Often, his metallic-gold Ford pickup could be seen parked across the street from Brandy's school, which was within walking distance of Crossroads, the local watering hole. On more than one occasion, she had read in the local blotter about Dwight's father getting arrested for drunken misconduct, fighting, and a DUI. Now, as she stepped off the road and onto the flagstone path that led up to the front of the Dandridge house, it was Dwight's father she was hoping would not answer the door. She couldn't see the metallic-gold pickup at the side of the house, so she held out hope.

Brandy took the porch steps cautiously, fearful of their unsteadiness. Dragonfly wind chimes hung from the porch and tinkled in the breeze.

A few wicker chairs stood around like uncomfortable strangers. Beside the front door, stacks of plastic flowerpots stood in curved towers. Her nose caught a faint but undeniable whiff of dog shit. Casually, she checked the soles of her sneakers then knocked on the door.

Some time went by before she heard commotion on the other side of the door. Someone shouted at someone else. A dog barked sharply several times then whimpered when a man's equally sharp voice silenced it.

Damn, she thought. *It's him.*

The door opened to reveal Mr. Dandridge's bulldog face with receding hair. His cheeks were full and pockmarked, his lips a deep purplish hue. A perfectly round belly protruded from the sleeveless T-shirt he wore and hung over the waistband of paint-splattered chinos. His bare feet looked short and stumpy and threaded with coarse hair, like the feet of a hobbit.

"Hi, Mr. Dandridge. I was looking for Matthew. Is he here?"

His eyes appraised her. Brandy was suddenly very aware of her bare legs and the tightness of her shirt.

"Hey, Dwight!" he shouted into the house, though he didn't take his eyes off Brandy. Behind Mr. Dandridge, Brandy was aware of a dog pacing anxiously back and forth in the hallway. A television blared from somewhere inside that horrible place. "Dwight! Get your ass over here, boy!"

Brandy shifted uncomfortably on the porch. Mr. Dandridge's lecherous stare was like a hot spike being driven into her chest. Inside the house, the sound of rapid and heavy footfalls prompted Mr. Dandridge to waddle unceremoniously out onto the porch—Brandy shifted sideways, giving him a wide berth—and over to the assemblage of wicker chairs.

Dwight appeared in the doorway, a frown creasing his tanned and round face at the sight of her. "What do you want?" Dwight asked.

His voice was squeaky, like an old cellar door.

"I'm looking for my brother," she said just as Mr. Dandridge lowered himself into one of the wicker chairs. The chair made a rustling sound and Brandy was certain it would collapse under the large man's weight. It didn't.

"He's not here," Dwight said.

"Have you seen him at all today?"

"No. Last time I saw him was yesterday."

"Do you know where he could've gone?"

Dwight rolled his meaty shoulders. He was wearing a Marilyn Manson T-shirt that was too small for him; the sleeves squeezed his thick forearms.

"Maybe someplace he wouldn't have taken his bike?" she pressed.

"Oh." Dwight's eyebrows arched. "He might have gone to Hogarth's."

"The drugstore?"

"Yeah. There was a vampire mask in the window he wanted to buy." His eyes darted furtively toward his father then back at Brandy. "He had enough money yesterday and he said he wanted to buy it before someone else did."

But why wouldn't he take his bike? she wondered.

"Okay," she said, already taking a step back from the door. Behind Dwight, the shapeless dog paced tirelessly back and forth, back and forth. "If you see him, tell him to come on home."

Dwight nodded and shot another look at his father, who had lit a cigarette and now stared vacuously out at the road. Then he shut the door, leaving Brandy alone with Mr. Dandridge.

"Good-bye," she said quickly, moving toward the stairs.

"Brandy, right?"

She froze. "Yes, sir."

"Your daddy ever come back?"

It was like being slapped across the face by a stranger. "No."

Mr. Dandridge grimaced, as if the cigarette suddenly tasted bad. A clot of bluish smoke wafted about his balding head. Eyes the color of oil continued to scrutinize her.

"Your mom at home?"

"She's working," she said curtly.

"She seeing anyone?"

Her first instinct was to pretend she didn't know what he was talking about, even though she knew damn well what he was talking about. Then she thought she might lie and say yes, her mother had been seeing someone lately. Either way, she did not want to have this conversation with Dwight's father. She did not want to stand there and look into his hungry eyes a moment longer.

Either he sensed her discomfort or he simply grew tired of her silence. "Forget it," he said, dismissing her with a wave of his hand. "Just get on home."

She hurried down the steps and moved quickly down the flagstone path toward the road. She felt his eyes on her until she crossed the hill and disappeared from his sight.

4

No matter the season, nighttime always came early to Stillwater. The mountains were to blame, prematurely blotting out the sun and casting a dark pall over the sleepy little town. Livestock were ushered back into their pens after a day of grazing. Out along some of the more remote roadways where power had yet to be restored, generators kicked back on, one after another, until a sustained deep-bellied growl gently shook the earth. The old grain silo in the field off Gracie Street, which served as a fairly reliable if overlarge sundial throughout the afternoon, was now shrouded in the deep, black shadow of Haystack Mountain.

Come five-thirty, Brandy had already contemplated calling her mother at the diner, twice. Both times, however, she fought off the urge, knowing damn well that the second she had her mother on the phone, Matthew would come bounding through the back door, his knees skinned, his hands grimy, his hair damp with sweat. But at five-thirty she could no longer pace around the house deliberating about phoning her mom; she had to get over to the Olson place by six.

She changed into jeans and a long-sleeved, loose-fitting blouse then left a note for Matthew on the kitchen counter, telling him there were leftovers in the fridge and to stay home until their mom got back from work. Then she locked up the house and walked up the road until she reached the grid of manicured streets where the Olsons lived. By the time she got there, the sky was a cool lavender color and a chilly October wind shuttled down from the mountains and bullied the trees.

"We won't be late, hon," Mrs. Olson promised as she ushered her husband out the front door.

Their daughter, Tabby Olson, was five. She was a timid little thing with pigtails, and she never gave Brandy a hard time, so Brandy didn't mind babysitting the girl. They watched a Pixar cartoon on DVD and Brandy made popcorn. By the end of the movie, Tabby had fallen asleep on the sofa, her head cocked at an awkward angle, one leg dangling over the sofa cushion. Gently, Brandy slipped her arms around the girl and carried her down the hall to the girl's bedroom. The walls were the color of Pepto-Bismol and pink stuffed animals kept watch over the room from every available perch.

Brandy rolled the girl into bed. Tabby stirred and her eyes blinked open.

"Go to sleep," Brandy told her soothingly.

"Can you leave the door open a crack?"

"Yes."

She shut the light and closed the door only halfway before returning to the living room. Popping the Pixar DVD from the player, she replaced it in its case then surveyed the collection of DVDs on the higher shelves. Most of the movies looked boring—by her own observations, she figured the Olsons to be a relatively boring couple—but she finally selected a film that had a blood-drenched bride on the cover. It looked old and was probably less titillating than the box art promised, but she figured *what the hell* and dropped the disc into the DVD player.

Before the opening credits had ended, Tabby Olson appeared in the living room doorway clutching a tattered panda bear to her chest.

Brandy paused the DVD. "What is it, honey?"

"There's a boy outside my window."

"Come show me."

She followed the little girl back down the hall and into her bedroom. The stuffed animals were rearranged and the curtains at the window had been pulled aside. She told Tabby to get into bed then went straight to the window and peered out. Tabby's bedroom window looked out onto the Olsons' side yard, which was as black as the interior of a cave. The sky was moonless. Beneath the window, holly bushes scraped along the siding of the house.

"There's no one out there," Brandy told the girl, who had crawled back into bed and pulled the covers up nearly to her neck. The tattered panda bear was propped on one pillow.

"He's out there," Tabby said.

"It's the bushes making noise in the wind."

"Brandy, I *saw* him."

Brandy sucked her lower lip. She looked back at the window, that rectangle of infinite blackness. "Okay. Come here and show me."

Tabby flung the blankets off and hopped down from the bed. The little girl padded across the room and stopped at the window, both her tiny pink hands perched on the sill. A look of intense concentration came across her face as she surveyed the darkened yard.

"Well?" said Brandy.

"He's not there anymore."

"Okay. Good. Now you can go to sleep."

Tabby didn't immediately let go of the windowsill.

"Come on," Brandy said, playfully tugging on one of the girl's pigtails. "Back into bed with you."

Looking disappointed, Tabby left the window and climbed back into bed. Brandy tucked the blankets in all around her. "Good night, squirt."

"Don't forget the door," Tabby warned.

"I won't," she said, leaving the door partway open again when she left.

In the kitchen, she filled up a glass with ice cubes and Coke then reclaimed her seat on the sofa. She restarted the DVD and watched about twenty minutes of the movie—as she'd suspected, it was a bit slow and boring—before she thought she saw someone or something pass by one of the living room windows. The sight caused her to jump and her skin quickly prickled with sweat. Again she paused the movie then got up and went to the window and looked out. She could see no more from here than she could from Tabby's bedroom.

An indistinct rattling sound came from the kitchen. Brandy froze. The rattling stopped. Her mouth suddenly dry, she licked her lips before saying, "Tabby? Honey, is that you?"

The girl did not answer.

Peeling herself away from the window, Brandy crossed the living room into the kitchen. The only light came from the single bulb over the sink. She glanced around the kitchen, finding it empty, and realized that Tabby would have had to cross through the living room to get into the kitchen. Brandy would have seen her.

When she looked toward the door that led from the kitchen out to the side of the house, Brandy suddenly realized what that rattling sound had been—the doorknob. She suddenly felt vulnerable, standing there in the middle of the kitchen in the dark.

There's a boy outside my window, Brandy thought, her eyes locked on the oval of pebbled glass in the center of the door. Beyond, black shapes were distorted and bled into one another. Brandy held her breath and waited for a figure to materialize beyond the glass. Waited . . .

And then it happened—the silhouette of a person appeared on the other side of the door, a darker cutout against a less dark background. She felt her heart seize in her chest. As she stood there watching, the figure moved. Something like an arm extended, distorted behind the textured glass. A second later, the doorknob rattled again; she could see it jiggling from halfway across the kitchen.

"Go away," she called to the intruder, her voice no stronger than a slight wind. She slid across the floor and snatched the telephone off the wall. "I'm calling the police."

The figure placed a palm on the glass. Brandy felt as though her entire body were about to crumble to powder.

"Brandy," the stranger said on the other side of the door. The intruder was male, his voice muted. "Open up. It's me."

She blinked, suddenly recognizing the voice. She hung the phone up, went to the door, unlocked it, and pulled it open.

Grinning, Jim Talbot stood there with his hands in the pockets of his varsity jacket.

"Oh my God, you scared the hell out of me," Brandy said in one nervous, shaky breath. "Jim, what are you doing here?"

"I heard you were babysitting, thought I might drop by."

"You scared the kid, too. She saw you outside her window."

"Can I come in?"

"Come on, Jim . . ."

"What do you say, Brandy?" He was glancing over her shoulder into the darkened kitchen. "Is the kid in bed?"

"She is, but you know you can't come in."

"Aw, man, you hurt my feelings," he said playfully. "You look good."

Her face went hot. "Thanks. So do you."

"What time do you get off? A bunch of us are heading into Garrett to catch a midnight movie."

"I can't. I gotta be home."

"Oh. That's too bad." He looked down at his feet, giving her enough time to admire the perfect part in his dark hair. When he looked back up at her, his trademark lopsided grin was back. "You excited about the dance?"

"Yes!" She cringed inwardly at the force of her response.

Jim laughed. "You got something to wear yet?"

"Not yet, but I know what I'm gonna get."

"I've got this pretty badass tie that lights up. You'll die when you see it."

"Sounds awesome."

Again, Jim peered over her shoulder. She thought she saw the vaguest frown in his features, but it was gone so quickly she couldn't be sure. "I really can't come in?" he asked again.

"You really can't, Jim. The Olsons would flip."

"I'll sneak out when they pull up in the driveway."

"Too risky. I'll see you soon, okay?"

He scuffed one of his Converse sneakers on the step. "Yeah, okay. Cool. Talk to you later."

She watched him hop down the stairs and vanish into the darkness. For some time she could hear his sneakers crunching over dead leaves and breaking sticks, but those sounds vanished soon enough, too.

5

It was ten-thirty when the Olsons got home and Bob Olson offered to drive Brandy home. She accepted the offer, and the drive was blessedly quick, as Bob was not the best conversationalist. As they pulled up outside the Crawly household, Brandy undid the seat belt and thanked him for the ride. Bob Olson was looking past Brandy, out the passenger window at the house.

"Looks like you got something going on tonight, hon," he said. There was an uncharacteristic tinge of compassion in his voice.

Brandy looked and saw a police car parked in the driveway.

CHAPTER FOUR

1

Ben turned and saw Wendy Crawly's daughter come through the kitchen door. She had obviously seen the cruiser out front and had a look of terror on her face. Both Ben and Wendy had been seated at the kitchen table; now, Wendy stood and went quickly over to her daughter.

"Mom?" the daughter said, her voice shaking, her face about to break apart. She hugged her mother.

"He hasn't come home yet," Wendy said. Her voice was equally as fragile. "Nothing has happened, he just hasn't come home."

Ben stood rigidly from the table. This was the second night in a row that saw him working late hours and he was exhausted. Despite his protestations, Wendy Crawly had poured him a cup of coffee when he'd arrived ten minutes ago and until now he hadn't touched it. Sighing, he picked it up and took a sip. It was very hot and very strong.

"Hi," Ben said to the daughter, setting the coffee cup back down. "You're Brandy?"

Brandy nodded, her eyes drinking him in. She seemed as though she could be knocked down by blowing on her.

"I'm Ben Journell."

"You knew my dad," Brandy said, catching him off guard.

Yes, he'd known Hugh Crawly. Though Hugh had been a few years older, Ben had gone to school with him and, for a couple of years back in the days of their unbridled youth, they'd maintained a laconic, easy sort of friendship. In a town as small and inquisitive as Stillwater, Ben was certainly aware that Hugh Crawly had picked up and left his family in the night roughly a year or so ago with a woman purportedly half his age. Ben would have never mentioned the girl's father to her, for fear of dredging up bad memories and overstepping his boundaries; now that she'd mentioned him, Ben found he didn't know how to react. His hands fumbled along the brim of his hat, which he held in front of him.

"I did, yeah," he said eventually.

Wendy smoothed a hand through her daughter's hair. "I'll make you something to eat."

"I'm not hungry," Brandy said.

Wendy went to the refrigerator anyway and began to take out some lunch meat and half a loaf of French bread. Without looking at him, Wendy said, "Ben?"

"No thanks, Wendy. I'm good."

He watched her cut frantically through the bread.

"Have a seat, Brandy," Ben said, pulling one of the kitchen chairs out for the girl. He reseated himself at the table, setting his hat on the tabletop and looping one finger in the handle of the coffee mug.

Brandy sat down, her eyes never leaving him.

She's trying to be tough, he realized. *She's trying not to cry.* He couldn't help but wonder how tough a kid suddenly had to be when their father sneaks away and never comes back. Especially if that kid had a younger sibling they felt obligated to look after. This made him think of his own father, and even as a grown adult with no siblings, he had felt completely lost and frightened when his father had died. He recalled the nights in the house after his father's death when he thought he heard the old man getting up and walking down the hall to the bathroom . . . only to remember that he was no longer among the living and it was only Ben's bittersweet memories playing games on him in the night.

"When was the last time you saw your brother, Brandy?"

"Last night. He was downstairs watching some horror movie on TV when I went up to bed."

"What time was that?"

"I'm not sure. Mom had already gone to bed. I guess around eleven."

"And what happened when you got up this morning? Your mother said you noticed he was gone."

She told him about finding the kitchen door open, mud and wet leaves on the floor. "When I went out to hang the laundry, I noticed his bike was still against the garage, too. That's when I started to get worried. Oh," she sparked to life and looked at her mother, who was still busy making sandwiches at the counter. "We found his shirt, too."

At the counter, Wendy set the knife down. Her shoulders appeared to slump.

"Yes," Ben said. "Your mom told me about the shirt."

"I went to his friend Dwight's house because I thought he might be there. He wasn't."

"Dwight?"

"Dandridge. They live a few blocks up the road."

"Did Dwight say where he might have gone?"

"He said maybe to Hogarth's Drugstore. There was something in the window he said he wanted to buy."

Wendy came over and set a hefty sandwich down in front of her daughter. Brandy stared at it with a muddled look of contempt and sadness, like someone looking at a dead animal on the side of the road. Without a word, Wendy returned to the counter and began preparing another sandwich.

"Did he have an argument with either of you?" Ben asked.

Brandy shook her head.

"He's an eleven-year-old boy," Wendy said from the counter, her voice slightly raised. "He's always arguing."

"I understand."

"Go upstairs, Brandy."

The girl looked at her mother, her face expressionless.

"You heard me," Wendy said. "I need to talk to Ben alone."

Brandy pushed away from the table, hugging herself with both arms, and crossed silently into the next room. A moment later, Ben heard the stairs creaking as the girl ascended. She'd left her sandwich behind, untouched.

Wendy sat down in her daughter's chair. Her hands shook and the worry and fear were clearly visible on her face.

"What is it, Wendy?" he said. Of course, he knew Wendy well enough, too, though she was a Stillwater transplant. Hugh had met her when he was living and working in Pittsburgh, and he'd brought her back with him like some kind of prize he'd won at a state fair. Wendy was still pretty, but she had been youthful and beautiful back then. For the first time, Ben wondered why she had remained in Stillwater after Hugh had left. This wasn't her town, wasn't her home. She owed nothing to the land or to its people. Ben doubted she felt the same obligation he'd felt in staying here to take care of his ailing father. Moreover, she did not have that obligation tethering her to Stillwater. Ben had it and it had become stronger, not weaker, after his father had died. He wondered what could be going through Wendy Crawly's head.

"Those storms we've been having," she said, her voice wavering. "The creek has been flooding and the Narrows are like rapids, Ben. And I keep thinking about that boy that was found down by the—"

Ben placed his hand atop hers, silencing her. "Matthew knows to keep away from the Narrows, Wendy. Right?"

She nodded.

"Chances are he's at some friend's house. Sometimes parents don't realize when their kids are upset and want to rebel. Maybe you guys exchanged a few words and he wants to make you worry for a night."

"I'll tan his hide," she uttered, suddenly crying and laughing at the same time.

"I'll stop by the Dandridge house when I leave here. Maybe Matthew's friend Dwight lied to your daughter and he's spending the night over there. Or maybe he's at another friend's house."

"He . . . he doesn't really have many other friends."

"Could you write down some names of the friends he does have? I'll check in with each of them."

"Okay," she said, rising from the table and going to one of the kitchen drawers. "Thank you, Ben."

She returned to the table with a pad and pen and began writing. Ben watched her write as he sipped some more coffee. He was trying not to let his uneasiness show. Brandy had said Matthew had been watching TV around eleven o'clock last night. In his head, he was doing the math, wondering if the boy would have had enough time to make it from his house out to Full Hill Road by midnight. It was a long shot, sure, but he couldn't stop thinking of Maggie Quedentock insisting that she had hit a boy with her car.

2

It had been twenty-four hours since Maggie Quedentock's incident on Full Hill Road and Evan still hadn't noticed the damage to the Pontiac.

She had arrived home last night from the scene of the accident at around two in the morning. Under the spray of a hot shower, she'd curled into a fetal position and cried, partially for the fear that still lingered in her from the accident and partially because of what she had done with Tom Schuler. After the shower, she'd dressed in a knee-length nightshirt then slipped between the cool sheets of the bed. The bedroom window was cracked open, allowing a cool autumn breeze to infiltrate the bedroom. Evan's shift wouldn't end until six—he'd be working the night shift at the plant over in Garrett for the next two weeks—and she'd struggled to find sleep before she heard the VW Beetle rumble into the driveway.

As it turned out, sleep *did* find her, but it came in fits and starts. Images from earlier that evening bled together to form a grotesque diorama of flickering motion pictures. Several times she awoke, believing she was still making love to Tom Schuler—she could actually feel his calloused hands running sloppily over her body, could actually smell the alcohol on his breath and the cologne he wore. Other times, she relived the accident on Full Hill Road, only this time with the slow motion of a frame-by-frame analysis—the darkened roadway, the swerve of headlights cutting through the night, the sudden, bright image of a small, frail figure darting out from the darkened shoulder into the bright glare of the car's headlights. She'd jerked the wheel and spun the car around in real life . . . yet in her dreams she continued to plow forward, running the child down. Sometimes she felt the car rumble over the child's body. Other times, the child was thrown up over the hood, slamming against the windshield, blackening Maggie's world.

At one point she awoke, her throat sore from possibly crying out in her sleep, and a film of sweat coated her flesh. From the partially open window she thought she heard movement out in the bushes. She got up and checked but could see nothing. There were black clouds stretched across the moon, and the fields were like pits of tar yawning all the way out to the foothills of the mountains. Terrified, she closed the window and got back into bed.

Evan got home around six-thirty in the morning, lumbering through the semidarkness of the house in his careless, noisy way. She feigned sleep when he crawled into bed beside her without showering or even brushing his teeth.

At ten in the morning, after a night of fitful sleep laden with nightmares, Maggie got up, leaving her husband snoring in bed, dreaming the dreams of the blissfully ignorant. Outside, the sky was overcast. Clouds the color of gunmetal hung low to the ground, and a soupy mist collected in the valley between the mountains. Had they owned a garage, Maggie would have salted the Pontiac away within it, and perhaps her anxiety would have been a little lower. But they did not have a garage and the Pontiac was parked around back. She'd possessed the foresight to park backward in the dirt turnabout, the rear of the vehicle facing the house. Looking at it now from the bank of living room windows, Maggie wondered how she was going to explain the accident to her husband. It was only a matter of time before he discovered it.

Evan had slept until four or so in the evening before staggering from the bedroom in search of something to eat. Maggie was pretending to read a Heather Graham novel in the kitchen when he came in. She looked up and smiled at him, overly friendly. Evan didn't seem to notice.

"How was work?"

He grunted and went immediately to the refrigerator. He was wearing pajama bottoms and a sleeveless undershirt, his muscular, tattooed arms exposed. At forty-five, Evan looked like he could have been a decade younger.

"Let me fix you something to eat."

"Up to you," he said, moving to the coffee pot on the counter. He touched the pot and frowned when he found that it was cold.

"I can make a new pot," she offered.

"I'll just heat it in the microwave." He filled a mug, put it in the microwave, and punched the buttons with the knuckle of his index finger. The appliance hummed to life as an orange light blossomed behind the tempered glass door.

She attempted to engage him several times in casual conversation. Finally, drinking his coffee while leaning against the kitchen counter, Evan Quedentock laughed.

"What? What's so funny?"

"Being so nice to me all of a sudden. Makes a guy worry."

"I'm always nice to you."

He snorted. "Yeah. Sure you are."

At some point during the rest of the evening, she fell back into her normal state of complacency. Evan busied himself in the basement while she prepared dinner and did a load of wash. The incident on Full Hill Road could have been nothing more than a waking nightmare, a bad dream. The same as what had happened with Tom Schuler—their rendezvous at Crossroads and the clumsy, wild, drunken sex at his house on the edge of town. Yes. All of it—a dream.

It wasn't until she received a text message from Tom Schuler that the reality of it all came rushing back to her. She was unemployed, had been since the bank shut down eight months ago. She relied solely on Evan to take care of her. What if he found out about Tom and kicked her out of the house? Where could she go? She tried to imagine herself moving in with Tom on the outskirts of town, but the concept was so foreign and preposterous that she couldn't do it.

She took her cell phone into the bathroom and read the text.

Had gud time last nite. More pls!

She shuddered, feeling disgusted. She quickly deleted the text then considered flushing the damn thing down the toilet.

Don't be stupid.

She thought, *More pls!*

"Maggie!"

The bathroom door shook at the booming of Evan's voice. A second later, she heard the back door slam.

"Maggie! Get out here!"

Oh, Christ . . .

"Just a minute," she called back. Bending down and opening the cabinet beneath the bathroom sink, she wedged her cell phone beneath two towels. Then she stood and caught her reflection in the mirror.

What have you done, you selfish bitch? What have you done?

"Goddamn it, Maggie! Come here!"

He was standing in the entranceway of the living room in work boots and a backward baseball cap. He had a checkered flannel shirt on over his ribbed undershirt. As he stood there he tugged off a pair of work gloves. He had just come in from outside.

"Yeah?" she said, deliberately pausing several feet away from him. He'd struck her on a number of occasions and she had developed a sense about such things. She didn't want to get close.

"What the hell happened to the goddamn car?"

Stupidly, she said, "What car?"

"The fucking Pontiac, genius."

"Oh." She blinked repeatedly. "Oh." She felt like a record player stuck in a groove.

"You hit something with the goddamn car?"

"Me?" Oh, she was digging in deep now . . .

"No, the goddamn Muffin Man. Of course you. Who else?"

At that moment, she made the decision to lie to him. "I don't know what you're talking about. I didn't do anything to the car."

Evan chewed at his lower lip as he examined his wife across the room. He had the work gloves in one fist now, the fingertips protruding like the stubby tentacles of some undersea creature.

He hooked a finger at her. "Come take a look," he said, turning and stomping out the door.

Timidly, Maggie followed. In bare feet, she descended the patio steps and crossed the overgrown lawn to the dirt turnabout. The VW and the Pontiac sat side by side. Evan marched around to the front of the Pontiac, tugging his work gloves back on. He eyed her from beneath a downturned brow. Something about his gaze reminded Maggie of the gorillas she'd seen in the Baltimore Zoo when she was just a young girl.

"Take a look at this," he growled.

She went around the car and paused in front of it, a few feet away from Evan. Experience told her his hands could be quick and close a distance of several feet in a matter of a millisecond. She would take no chances.

"There," he said, pointing to the crumpled grille. "And there," he added, his index finger gliding up to address the sizable dent in the hood of the car. "You telling me you didn't hit nothing?"

"I didn't hit anything," she said, looking at the car and not at him.

"I know what a car looks like when it hits something."

"I didn't hit anything," she repeated, glancing up at him. "I swear."

He stared at her. She found she couldn't look away. In an instant she became convinced that he could read her thoughts, every single one of them, just by looking into her eyes. Frightened, she blinked and looked back at the car.

"So you're saying you have no fucking idea what happened here," he said, not phrasing it as a question.

"That's what I'm saying."

"So . . . what? Someone came back here and smashed up my car?"

"Evan, I don't know. Maybe."

Evan Quedentock took a few steps around the car, looking for any imperfections he might have missed. He bent down and looked at one of the car's tires. When he stood, reappearing above the car's hood, he had an expression of deep contemplation on his face.

Fleetingly, Maggie considered leaving town this evening after he left for the night shift. *Stupid. Where would I go?*

(gud time last nite)

"What's the name of that kid I smacked around at Crossroads two weeks ago? The one who was staring at your tits?"

"Shit, Evan. I don't remember."

"Goddamn punk kid." He peeled his cap off his head and ran one gloved hand along the bristles of his hair. "Codger, ain't it? Ricky Codger."

Maggie knew damn well it had been Ricky Codger. But she found herself incapable of speaking now.

"If that little motherfucker did this," Evan said, his voice trailing off. All too clearly Maggie could hear the bitter aggression in her husband's tone.

Maggie tried to speak but her voice cracked.

"Spit it out," her husband barked.

"You don't know it was him."

"Who else would it be?" He scratched his chin. "You hear any noise around the house last night? In the yard?"

Her mind slipped backward to the previous night. She recalled the horrible nightmares. She recalled waking to noises in the yard—how had Evan known?—and getting up, shutting the bedroom window.

"Yes."

Evan's eyebrows arched. "Yeah?"

Maggie blinked. She caught a whiff of Tom Schuler in her nose. "I mean, yeah, I thought I heard something last night. It was loud. I looked outside but couldn't see anything. I just shut the bedroom window then went back to bed."

Evan had begun nodding midway through her little monologue. "Okay," he breathed. "Yeah, okay. Okay."

She didn't like the look in her husband's eyes.

Later that night, after Maggie had showered and dressed in a pair of sweatpants and a loose-fitting T-shirt, Evan had departed for work in the VW. His instruction to his wife upon leaving was to keep an eye on the car. If she heard any noise tonight, or caught a glimpse of something out of the ordinary, she was to call him on his cell immediately. She agreed that she would.

At eleven that night she was sitting in the living room with her Heather Graham novel open yet unread on her lap, the TV across the room on but with the volume turned down low.

He's going to do something bad, she thought. *He'll either go to the police and find out the truth or go straight to Ricky Codger and drive a fist into the kid's face. Either way, no good will come of this.*

Why hadn't she just told him she'd hit a deer out on Full Hill Road?

You know why, said a sly little voice at the back of her head. *Because he would have called the police to confirm the story and, when he found out you were out there at midnight, he'd start questioning you. He'd find out about you and Tom and what you were doing out there and then you'd be in a world of hurt.*

She could have told him the story without admitting that the police had gotten involved. She could have said she'd gone out shopping in Cumberland and that the accident had happened earlier in the day, on her way back into town. Goddamn it, why hadn't she just said that to him instead of lying?

He knows, she thought. She'd known all along. *He knows I'm lying.*

Again, she wondered where she'd go if Evan kicked her to the curb. She tried to imagine herself moving in with Tom Schuler; not only did she find the prospect implausible, but she found it wholly unappealing as well. Tom was not good looking, Tom was not polite or chivalrous, Tom did not make a lot of money and did not treat his girlfriends very well. What would it be like living with messy Tom Schuler?

This reminded her that her cell phone was wedged between two towels in the bathroom. She retrieved it to find two more messages, both from Tom.

The first: Doin ok?

The second: Cum over tonite pls.

For several long seconds she considered what to do with those texts. In the end, she deleted them without responding. If she ignored him, would he go away?

Cum over tonite pls.

Back in the living room, she turned on the floodlights that lit up the backyard. The Pontiac sat there in the middle of the turnabout like a dark secret. The windows were open, letting in a cool autumn breeze that smelled of firewood and cinders. It chilled her bones.

In her hand, her cell phone rang, startling her. She looked at the number and found that it belonged to Tom.

Don't answer it, said that same sly voice.

"Hello, Tom," she said, bringing the phone to her ear. What was the matter with her? Was she bent on a path of self-destruction?

"Hey, doll. You doin' okay?"

"No, Tom. I'm not. I messed up the car leaving your place last night and Evan's asking questions."

"Shit. What'd you do?"

I think I hit a kid, she almost said. Instead, she uttered, "I'm not sure. I might have struck a deer or something. Either way, the car's all fucked up."

"What did you tell him?"

"I told him I didn't know what happened."

"Okay, cool."

"No, Tom. It's not cool."

"He's already gone, right?"

She closed her eyes. The cold air came through the open windows and washed over her tired body.

"Maggie? Hon?"

"Yes," she said, her eyes still closed. "He just left."

"Did you get my texts?"

"What do you want, Tom?"

"I want you to come over again tonight."

"I can't."

"Don't be like that, Maggie."

"I'm not being like anything. Evan's too suspicious. I have to lay low."

"Evan's at work. What will he know?"

He's supposed to be your goddamn friend, you asshole, she wanted to shout at him. But on the heels of that, she thought, *He's also supposed to be my goddamn husband.*

Something pale and quick darted across the backyard. Maggie felt her blood freeze.

"Mags?" said Tom. "You there?"

The curtains billowed out in the wind. She leaned closer to one window and, squinting, peered out into the darkness.

"Hey, Maggie, come on. What's the problem, doll?"

A figure moved along the perimeter of the property. She could see the whiteness of its flesh—it appeared naked—and the quick, jerky, animalistic way it moved. The figure scaled the perimeter of the yard then ditched into a bay of shadows beneath a weeping willow tree. The wind blew hard, rustling the tentacular branches of the willow tree and stirring up little tornadoes of dead leaves in the yard.

"You mad at me, Mags?"

"Tom, I have to go."

"Come on, doll. Don't be—"

She hung up the phone and dropped the cell onto the sofa. Leaning forward, she tried to see into the shadows beneath the willow tree but she was too far away to make anything out. For one stupid moment, she was living in an alternate universe where all her lies were truths and the things Evan had told her to watch out for were real. She imagined the shape to be the Codger kid, slinking like a vampire in the darkness of the yard, intent on smashing the shit out of Evan's Pontiac, just like how Evan had smashed the shit out of Codger that night at Crossroads. The kid had been drunk and flirty and had been staring at Maggie's chest all night. Evan had grabbed the kid around the collar, dragged him out into the parking lot, and kicked his ass. Not that the Codger boy didn't have it coming—the kid was a complete degenerate who had served time up in Jessup for robbery and assault.

But then reality washed back to her, and she knew Ricky Codger hadn't had anything to do with the damage to Evan's car.

Maggie went out onto the patio. The town had been wracked by storms recently, and downtown had flooded and lost power; the sky still threatened its wrath, the clouds trembling with thunder, and she could almost taste electricity in the air. The wind bullied the branches of the distant willow tree. The overlong grass undulated like the surface of the sea.

"Come out!" she shouted across the yard toward the willow tree. For all she could tell, the figure had already vanished. "I see you!"

Thunder rumbled directly overhead. She thought she could make out the shape of a person behind the waving branches of the willow tree.

A cold dread overtook her.

Evan kept a shotgun in the basement, bracketed to a lacquered plaque on the wall. There were shells in a cardboard box in the bottom drawer of his workbench. She'd never fired it before and wondered now if she'd know how. Would she even be able to load it?

There's no one out there, she attempted to tell herself. *This is just my guilt and my fear messing with my head.*

The whitish figure darted out from beneath the tree and scurried across the yard. It hid behind the Pontiac, the figure itself vanishing but its shadow lengthening along the dirt turnabout in the cast of floodlights. Terrified, Maggie watched the shadow retreat along the ground until it disappeared completely behind the car.

She turned and hurried back into the house, shutting and locking the door behind her. Then she went to the bank of windows over the living room couch, shutting each one and locking it, then drawing the curtains. She was breathing heavily, her heart paining her as it slammed against the wall of her chest. For whatever reason, she thought now of the Creedence Clearwater Revival song that had been on the Pontiac's radio after leaving Tom's place last night—John Fogerty crooning about something that had fallen out of the sky and into some farmer's field.

That's what is out there now, she thought. *The thing that fell out of the sky, just like in that song. The thing I hit with the car.*

It had come back for her. She was certain of it.

No . . . please . . .

She hurried up and down the halls, closing and locking the windows and turning off all the lights. Whatever was out there, she didn't want it seeing into the house. After she had locked up all the windows, she returned to the door that led to the backyard and peered out the crescent panel of glass. The floodlights were still on. She looked frantically around the yard but couldn't see anything.

That wasn't a child you hit, said that evil voice in her head. *That was something else. That was the thing that fell out of the sky.*

She shook her head, clearing it of the voice. She'd suffered the voice when she was younger, right after high school, and for whatever reason, it had returned to her now. *No,* she thought. *Get out of my head.*

The foundation creaked and she could hear the beams in the ceiling groan in the strong wind. Maggie held her breath. Across the room, she could see the hallway and, beyond, the closed door that led down to the basement. To the shotgun.

You do horrible things, this is what happens, said the voice.

She went to the basement door, pulled it open. A mineshaft of blackness appeared before her. Feeling along the stairwell wall, she found the light switch and flipped it on. Weak, yellow light appeared at the bottom of the rickety basement stairs.

Thunder boomed, shaking the house.

Maggie hurried downstairs two steps at a time and went directly to the wall where the shotgun hung from its lacquered plaque. She yanked it down and it was heavier than she would have thought. Turning it over in her hands, she looked at the wooden stock, the sleek black barrel, the sliding bit of metal that ran the length of the barrel. She had seen enough movies to know how shotguns worked, but when she attempted to slide the movable bit which opened the chamber, it wouldn't move.

"What the hell," she muttered.

She continued to turn the shotgun over in her hands. At one side of the trigger was a circular button that protruded. There was also a lever beside the trigger. She pulled back the lever and found that the slide engaged and she was able to move it up and down the barrel. Sliding it opened a chamber in which a shotgun shell could be loaded.

The shells—they were in the bottom drawer of Evan's workbench. She set the shotgun on the floor and went quickly to the bench, pulling open the bottom drawer. There were two boxes of shotgun shells inside—one labeled *Buckshot*, the other marked as *Slugs*. Slugs sounded more dangerous, so she emptied the contents of the box onto the floor. About a dozen plastic tubes rolled out, each one capped in a helmet of brass. She had no idea what she was doing.

Maggie gathered up the shotgun slugs and dumped them back into the box. Then she took the box and, scooping up the shotgun from where she'd left it, carried both items back upstairs.

The house seemed like a different place now. She went to the crescent window in the back door and looked out upon a misty rain. The floodlights lit the grounds like a rodeo.

A blank-faced cadaverous figure crouched on the roof of the Pontiac.

Maggie shrieked and turned away from the window, throwing her back against the wall. The box of shells dropped from her hand, and a number of shells spilled out. A few rolled under the couch.

It fell out of the sky, Maggie thought frantically, bending down and snatching up a handful of shotgun shells. Crouching to the floor, she fumbled around until she found the lever on the gun again, depressed it, and managed to pull the slide back. The chamber opened on the side of the gun, just the right size and shape to accommodate one of the shells. How many of the damn things did the gun take? There were about a dozen in the box. Maybe she could load all twelve into the shotgun? Did they file down into the barrel? No, that didn't make sense . . .

Rain lashed heavily now against the windows. Her breath came in panting, rapid gasps. She took one of the shells and slipped it into the opening at the side of the shotgun. It just sat there.

"Come on!" she shouted at it.

Think, she thought. *Think about what makes sense here . . .*

With her thumb, she shoved the plastic cylinder up into the barrel until she heard and felt a click. When she withdrew her thumb, the shell was gone, having vanished up into the body of the gun.

Yes. That's it.

She tried to stick another shell into the chamber but the previous one prevented it from moving forward. She was doing something; she wasn't thinking. Her hand on the slide, she jerked it and heard a solid *clack*. Suddenly, the gun felt dangerous in her hands.

She repeated the process, shoving shells into the gun until it would take no more. *Four,* she thought. *It holds four. Remember that.*

Shaking, she stood and again peered out the crescent of glass in the door. Outside, the floodlights made the rain shimmer. The black Pontiac looked sleek as a shark.

The figure was no longer there.

Things from space can read your mind, said the head-voice. *It knows you're armed now and it's being careful. It's being sneaky.*

"Shut the fuck up," she told the voice.

The sound of her cellular phone trilling from the couch caused her to jump and sob. Still holding the gun, she rushed over to it and answered it without checking the number.

"Hello?"

"Where'd you go, darling?" It was Tom. He sounded drunk and a bit irritated.

Maggie closed her eyes. Suddenly, the shotgun seemed to weigh about two hundred pounds. Around her, heavy rain played a tattoo against the living room windows.

"There's someone outside the house, Tom," she said into the phone.

"Who?"

"I don't know," she said, simultaneously thinking, *It's the thing that fell out of the sky, just like John Fogerty said. It landed in Stillwater and I hit it with my car and now it's come back to get me.*

"You want me to come out there?" Tom said.

She considered this. Maggie Quedentock, formerly Margaret Kilpatrick, formerly a pot-smoking high school student who had lost her virginity at the age of twelve to seventeen-year-old Barry Mallick. Maggie Quedentock, who had displayed a track record of poor decisions and self-destructive behavior . . .

Into the phone, she said, "Yes. Come over."

3

After leaving the Crawly house, Ben stopped at the Dandridges' where he summoned old Delmo Dandridge to the door. Delmo looked less than pleased to find Ben Journell on his front porch at that ungodly hour. Delmo had suffered his fair share of run-ins with the police sergeant in the past, having been arrested by Ben on at least two occasions that Ben could recall off the top of his head. In an easy tone, Ben apologized for knocking on the door so late then explained the reason for his visit. Delmo grunted and told Ben to come in.

The house was a pigsty. He had to navigate a maze of upturned furniture, towers of bound newspapers, and random electrical appliances in various stages of disrepair, while following Delmo into the small, foul-smelling kitchen.

"Beer?" Delmo said, and since he didn't move from where he leaned against the kitchen counter, Ben knew he was being a smartass.

"You're familiar with the Crawly boy who lives down the road?" Ben asked.

One of Delmo's eyebrows arched. "The crawling boy?" he said, wiggling his fingers in the imitation of a scampering spider.

"Matthew Crawly," Ben clarified.

"Yeah. He's Dwight's friend. His sister was here earlier looking for him."

"When was the last time you saw him?"

"Shit if I know." Delmo was wearing sweatpants cut off at the knees and a tight undershirt that did his bulbous midsection no favors. "He gone missing?"

"Yes."

Delmo's wife, Patti, appeared in the doorway, a cigarette jutting from between two fingers, wearing a flimsy ribbed undershirt that clung to her sagging, generously nippled breasts. A large German shepherd sidled up beside her, its silvery eyes locked unwaveringly on Ben. He'd shot and killed a dog once before, as it charged him from across a barn. He had no qualms about a repeat performance if it came to that.

"What's this?" Patti rasped. She eyed Ben in the same suspicious and distrustful manner as the dog.

"He's here looking for the Crawly boy," Delmo informed her.

"Matthew?" She cocked one eyebrow.

"Do you recall the last time you saw him?" Ben asked. A second dog paced back and forth across the hallway behind her.

"Lord," she said, blowing a streamer of cigarette smoke up over her head where it seemed to collect like gossamer in the ceiling fixtures. "Maybe a week or so ago. Did something happen to him?"

"He's gone missing," growled Delmo before Ben had a chance to answer her.

"Is Dwight available to speak with me?" Ben asked instead.

Patti Dandridge's other eyebrow went up. "Now?" She made a big deal of looking at the wall clock over the stove.

"I know it's late," Ben said, "but it's important."

"I'll wake him," Patti said. She moved back out into the hall. At first, the German shepherd remained staring at Ben, quite possibly sizing him up the same way Ben had sized up Delmo Dandridge when he had answered the door just moments ago. But then the dog turned tail and padded down the hall after Patti. The second dog, no more than an indistinct black blur at the far end of the poorly lit hallway, continued to pace like a lion in a cage. The whole house stank of dog shit.

"Flood sent John Church's trash can through my basement window," Delmo said. He leaned his considerable bulk against the stove, his belly jutting from beneath the strained fabric of his undershirt. "Who do I see about that?"

"See about what?"

"About gettin' my window fixed."

"I would think your homeowner's insurance would take care of it," Ben opined, not without a hint of affectation.

Delmo grunted while he dug around in one ear with a finger roughly the diameter of an Italian sausage.

Dwight appeared in the kitchen doorway, shirtless and straining against a pair of striped boxer shorts. His hair was corkscrewed, and he winced in the harsh kitchen lighting. Ben nodded succinctly at Delmo then led the boy back down the hall and to the stairwell, where they both took a seat on the third step up from the bottom. Ben asked him about Matthew.

"We hung out after school yesterday then we went home for dinner. I haven't seen him since then." Dwight Dandridge spoke in hushed tones, either because the subject matter disturbed him or because he didn't want his parents, who lingered down the hall in the kitchen, to overhear. Or possibly it was a combination of both.

"Thanks, Dwight," Ben said, and squeezed the boy's knee before getting up off the steps.

4

The rain was coming down in sheets by the time Ben arrived back at the police station. The weather report predicted a second storm, just as bad, if not worse, than the one that had flooded the Narrows and darkened the center of town, and Ben had no doubt of its inevitable arrival. It seemed par for the course—what else could possibly go wrong?

The station was hopping this evening, at least for a department as small as Stillwater's. Ben could hear music coming from the Batter's Box. The soles of his shoes squelching on the tiles, he crossed into the Batter's Box to find Officers Eddie La Pointe and Mike Keller sitting in their respective cubicles, tossing a handball back and forth. The radio on Mike Keller's desk poured out a Tom Petty tune, all jangly guitar and harmonica.

"Hey, Ben," Mike said, tossing the handball at him. "Where you been?"

"Over at the Crawly place. Eleven-year-old kid's gone missing."

"Wendy's kid?" Eddie asked.

Mike blinked. "Missing? Like . . . gone?"

"His mother and sister haven't seen him all day. I guess he could be at a friend's house." In the breast pocket of his uniform was the sheet of paper on which Wendy Crawly had scribbled the names of her son Matthew's friends—a depressingly short list, Ben had noted. Ben didn't think that was such a bad thing; in Stillwater, the fewer friends you had, the less amount of trouble you were apt to get into. He fished the slip of paper from his breast pocket and dumped it on Mike Keller's desk. "First thing tomorrow morning, give the folks on this list a call. See if they've seen Matthew Crawly. I've just come from the Dandridge house so you can skip them."

"Roger." Mike picked up the folded sheet of paper and looked at the names on it. Mike Keller was a chunky officer in his early forties with thinning blond hair and a cherubic, pleasant face. A lifelong resident of Stillwater, he used to dress as Santa Claus every Christmas down at the Farmers' Market on Calvert Street, when there still had been a Farmers' Market.

Ben tossed his campaign hat onto one of the empty desks. He sat down in one of the chairs with a huff and began unlacing his boots. His feet ached. "Where're Haggis and Platt?"

"Out at the Shultz farm," said Eddie. "Maureen says she ain't seen old Marty all afternoon and was worried he'd gotten into a car wreck or something out on 40. My guess is he probably went out hunting with some Gentleman Jack and passed out in a tree. Prob'ly wind up falling out of it and breaking his neck."

Ben sighed. "Wonderful." At Maureen Shultz's insistence, Ben had gone out into the woods to look for her husband before, and wound up finding him in a state not dissimilar to what Eddie had just described.

"Anyway," Mike said, leaning back in his chair, "did you hear that old Eddie has finally figured out what happened with Porter Conroy's cows? Isn't that right, Ed?"

Pulling off one of his boots, Ben looked at Eddie and said, "Yeah?"

Eddie waved a hand at him. "Forget it. He's pulling your leg."

Mike Keller laughed. "Show him," he chided. "He solved the case, Ben. Big goddamn detective. Come on, Eddie!" Before Eddie could respond, Mike was out of his chair and digging through the stack of magazines on Eddie's desk. Eddie slapped his hands away, looking wholly disgusted. "Show him," Mike insisted.

"Go sit the fuck down," Eddie told him.

Snatching one of Eddie's magazines off his desk, Mike flipped through it as he carried it over to where Ben sat. Chuckling, he folded the pages back and handed the magazine to Ben. It was one of Eddie's horror magazines, Ben saw, and this particular article detailed the recent killings in a small Mexican village by a creature called the *chupacabra*.

"What the hell is this?" Ben asked, scanning the article.

"Sure," Eddie said, "you guys make fun, but that stuff is real."

"What *is* it?" Ben asked.

"A Mexican vampire. Eats livestock. The descriptions of the attacks are just like what we saw at Porter Conroy's farm last night."

Ben tossed the magazine aside. "We're not in Mexico, Eddie."

Eddie sat up straight in his chair. "That's just what they're called. Who says they can't come north? Read the article."

"I think I might head out to Full Hill Road instead," Ben said.

"You still worried about what Maggie Quedentock said last night?" Eddie asked. "Ben, you spent half the day today checking out those woods. There's no one there. She didn't hit anything. And if she did, it was just a deer, and the fucking thing already bounded off through the woods."

Ben nodded absently, frowning. He was thinking about Matthew Crawly.

Shirley Bennice, the dispatcher, appeared in the doorway. She was a squat woman in her sixties who had the pleasant, comforting face of a grandmother even though she had no children or grandchildren of her own. "You boys afraid of the rain or something?" she said, walking down the aisle of cubicles.

"Hey, Shirl," said Eddie. "Do me a favor and tell Ben here how he's gotta keep an open mind to things."

"Arguably, he kept an open mind when he had the chief hire you," Shirley responded without missing a beat. She stopped before Ben's cubicle and handed him a yellow Post-it note.

"What's this?"

"Deets over at the county morgue in Cumberland called for you earlier. He said to call him back when you got in. He said he had a possible ID on that kid that was found in Wills Creek."

Indeed, John Deets's number was scrawled in Shirley's handwriting on the Post-it. "No kidding? Great. Thanks, Shirl. Anything else going on?"

"Cumberland sent over some new equipment. Well," she added

quickly, "new for us, anyway. Some handhelds, boxes of ammunition, and a vehicle-tracking GPS."

Mike laughed. "For all the vehicular tracking we do, huh?"

"They're freebies," she said. "I ain't turning my nose up at charity from the county."

Ben leaned over and snatched the receiver off the phone, pressing it to his ear. He punched in Deets's number and listened as the line rang. He glanced at his wristwatch and saw that it was too late and Deets was probably long gone by now. Also, it was Saturday night.

"You believe in the supernatural, Shirl?" Eddie asked.

"You mean like ghosts?"

"He means vampires that eat tacos and shake maracas," Mike said, grinning.

"You just wait and see," Eddie said, tossing the handball back to Mike. "Chupacabra's responsible, all right. That's Spanish for *goatsucker*."

Again, Mike Keller laughed. *"You're* a goatsucker," he told Eddie.

On the line, Ben got Deets's voice mail. He left a cursory message, including his personal cell phone number, then hung up. Something had settled down into the back of his brain and was now nagging him. He couldn't put his finger on what it was. He picked up Eddie's stupid magazine and looked at the glossy photo of what appeared to be a hairless coyote staring at the camera with golden eyes and ears like satellite dishes. It was most obviously Photoshopped.

He could still hear Wendy Crawly's voice, as clear and sharp as a whip-crack, in his head: *The creek has been flooding and the Narrows are like rapids, Ben.* He didn't like the fact that the kid had been missing all day. Again, his mind returned to Maggie Quedentock. What had she hit last night on Full Hill Road? What had she *thought* she had hit?

Turning around in the cube, Ben powered up the computer. When the Google home page came up, he typed "livestock mutilation" into the search bar then hit Search. The first hit was a Wikipedia entry on something called "bovine excision", which was defined as the apparent killing and mutilation of cattle under unusual or inexplicable circumstances. Ben scrolled through the web page, reading the text with mounting curiosity. He read an account of a horse named Lucy who had been found by her owners dead in a field, her head and neck removed of its flesh. According to the horse's owner, there was a strong medicinal smell in the air.

"That's what it was," Ben muttered to himself.

Both Eddie and Mike turned to look at him. "Talking to yourself now, Sarge?" Mike said.

"That smell last night in Porter's field," Ben said to Eddie. "Remember it?"

"Burned my nose," said Eddie.

"How would you describe it?"

Eddied shrugged and frowned, which was his way of contemplating a question, Ben knew. Eventually, he said, "I guess it smelled like something dead and rotting."

"Did it?" Ben asked. "Are you sure? Or do you just think that because that's what you expected to smell?"

For whatever reason, Mike laughed again. The sound of it was beginning to grate on Ben's nerves.

Sucking at his lower lip, Eddie thought for a few more seconds. Then he said, "I guess it smelled like . . . well, it reminded me of maybe the locker room at the YMCA over in Garrett, you know what I mean? How sometimes the smell of the locker room stings your eyes."

"Gross," Mike Keller grumbled.

"Yes," Ben said. "Exactly."

"What are you getting at?" Eddie asked.

Ben turned back to the computer. "I'm not sure yet."

He continued to read, only to learn that Lucy's owner later brought other farmers to the field to examine the dead horse's remains. What they discovered that day were hunks of horse flesh scattered around the field. When one of the other farmers touched one of the pieces, the article attested that the hunk of flesh exuded a greenish sludge that burned the farmer's hand. The medicinal odor had lessened by this point, though the smell of it was still in the air.

Ben sat up straighter in his chair. He was thinking of the foamy, green goop that had hung from the broken half of skull, and how some of it had crusted to a hard web in the cow's large eyelashes.

"What time did the guys leave for the Shultz farm?" Ben asked.

"Just before you came in," said Mike. "You probably passed them out on Belfast when you pulled in here."

Ben stood, grabbing his campaign hat off the desk.

"Where you going?" Eddie asked.

"Home, to get some sleep. I'll be in early tomorrow. I want to call over to the sheriff's department in Cumberland, see if they'll lend us some bodies to do a search of the woods around the Crawly place."

"You really think something happened to that kid?"

Ben shrugged. "I don't know yet."

Eddie frowned. "What should we do?"

"Make some calls to Mexico. See if you can track down this Mexican vampire."

Mike Keller laughed.

5

It was twelve-thirty when Tom Schuler's 1972 Ford Maverick pulled into the Quedentocks' driveway. Leprous with rust, the car belched black clouds of exhaust, and had the words SCHULER'S AUTOMOTIVE stenciled on the doors, an irony that was lost on most everyone who utilized Tom Schuler's services.

The rain was coming down in cloudy torrents. Maggie saw the Maverick's headlights pull into the driveway and curve around the side of the house. She'd turned off the floodlights in the backyard by this point, not wanting to see the whitish figure that had been crouched on the hood of the Pontiac anymore. The Maverick's headlamps blew twin cones of yellowish light into the shadows as it circled around the dirt turnabout and came to a stop between the back patio and the Pontiac.

When Maggie opened the door, she was still holding the shotgun.

"Jesus," Tom said, rainwater pouring down his face. "Put that thing down, Mags."

"Get in here," she said, grabbing him by the lapel of his dungaree jacket and yanking him inside. She slammed the door shut and locked it behind him. Then, standing on her toes, she peered out into the darkness. "It might be gone," she muttered.

"What's that?" said Tom. He was pooling water on the floor, standing there like someone rescued from a sinking ship.

Maggie whirled around. The intense look on her face froze Tom in his tracks. He looked powerless to move.

"You didn't see anything out there?" she asked him.

"See what?"

"Anything," she said. "Something that looked like a child but wasn't."

Tom chuckled nervously. "Hon, you okay? Put the gun down, please."

Maggie thought, *More pls!* and shuddered.

Dripping water on the floor, Tom went to one of the living room windows and brushed aside the curtain. He peered out into infinite blackness. "Doll, there ain't nothin' out there."

"Don't tell me what's out there," she said.

"What'd you think you saw?"

"I hit a kid with my car leaving your place last night," she blurted, frightened by how close she was to tears. "I mean, it looked like a kid, but I don't think it was. Not really. Because he's come back and he's out there."

"Maggie . . ."

"It has skin as white as paper. I don't think he was . . . wearing any clothes . . ."

"A naked kid," Tom muttered, still peering out the window. "Don't that beat all . . ."

"I'm serious."

Tom turned away from the window. His sandy hair was plastered to his head and his light eyes, set deeply into the pockets of his skull, looked the way she imagined a blind person's eyes to look. "Seriously. Put the fucking gun down, Maggie, before you blow a hole in the floor. You're freaking me out."

She laid the gun down on the couch.

Tom sighed. "Thank you."

"I don't know why I told you to come over. I guess I was scared."

"I know why you told me to come over." He took a step toward her.

"Please, Tom. I'm not thinking right."

"Whoever is?" He laughed. It was a shrill, mechanical sound. Had she really allowed this man's mouth on her body? Had she really accommodated his erection, taking it inside her, laughing drunkenly the whole time? She suddenly loathed herself.

"I'm sorry," she said, running a hand through her hair. "I shouldn't have told you to come over."

Tom peeled his wet jean jacket off. He tossed it onto the couch, where it soaked through the fabric, though he didn't seem to notice. Maggie didn't have it in her to tell him to move it.

"If you're worried about Evan finding out," he began, but she cut him off.

"Stop. This has nothing to do with you and me. I was scared, that's all. Do you understand that?"

"Sure. But I'm here now. Things are okay."

No, Maggie thought. *No, they're not. Not by a long shot.*

Tom took another step toward her. She lifted up both hands, palms out toward him. Tom froze. "What?" he said. "What is it?"

"This should have never happened," she said. "I'm sorry."

The pleasant, helpful look on Tom Schuler's face quickly faded. It was replaced by a look of pure agitation—a look that spoke of a lifetime of betrayal and distrust. What had she done? Traded one abusive lunatic for another?

Then Tom's face softened. Holding up his own hands, he said, "Listen, Mags. You're upset. Something frightened you. That's cool, I can dig it. Just relax, keep calm. Let's sit on the couch and talk, okay?"

She didn't want to sit on the couch with him. She didn't want to talk.

Again, thunder crashed and shook the house. Lightning illuminated the yard, causing Maggie to whirl around and stare out the crescent of glass in the door. As if in the explosion of a flashbulb, she saw the silhouette of the boy back on the roof of the Pontiac, there and then gone in the brief flash of light, and she screamed.

Tom came up from behind her and wrapped his arms around her. One of his big hands covered her mouth. She felt his body against her back and winced.

"Quiet," he said. "Okay? Quiet, Mags. What is it? What's wrong?"

His hand dropped away from her mouth.

"It's back," she panted. Her whole body trembled. "It's in the yard, on the car."

Tom chuckled. He pushed her aside and peered out through the half-moon of glass. If he saw anything, he didn't say so.

Bouncing on the balls of her feet, Maggie said, "Well? Do you see it? Tom?"

"Son of a bitch," Tom muttered to himself. When he opened the door, the violent storm spilled into the house. Maggie whined and took two steps back, though she was unable to pull her eyes from the doorway. Tom hustled out into the rain, leaving the door open at his back, and marched across the wet grass. Maggie watched him until the darkness swallowed him up.

Finally, she was able to propel herself forward. She slammed into the door and threw it shut, locked it. Standing on her toes, she peered through the window at the top of the door, but the yard was too dark to make out any details. She could see Tom's form fading into the shadows, masked by a screen of silvery rain. Beyond Tom she could make out the dark, low, hulking shape of the Pontiac hiding in the darkness like a panther ready to spring.

"Fuck." She slid along the wall and flicked on the rear floodlights again. Then she returned to the half-moon window in the door. The floodlights illuminated a wide, circular patch of lawn . . . but she couldn't see Tom. His car was still there, and his muddy footprints were quickly filling up with rainwater . . . but he was nowhere . . .

You're losing your shit, Maggie, said her head-voice. *Your pot is boiling over and your beer is foaming over the top of the glass.*

"Stop it, stop it, stop it, stop it . . ."

In the darkness, beyond even the weeping willow tree, she thought she saw a flash of light. Then she heard a scream, a man's scream. Tom.

She fumbled with the lock then swung the door open. Rainwater blew into her face. "Tom!" she screamed into the night. "Tom!"

There was movement toward the back of the property. She imagined it to be a struggle. What was out there? What had happened to Tom?

A second scream cracked the night, causing the hairs on Maggie's arms to stand at attention. She retreated back into the house and slammed the door shut. As she fumbled to lock it again, the entire scene was underscored by yet another peal of thunder.

Maggie snatched the shotgun off the couch then went to the wall and turned off the living room lights. Now, only the outdoor floodlights were on, casting a dull, yellow glow over the grass, the dirt turnabout, the Pontiac, and Tom Schuler's ancient Maverick. Peering out one of the living room windows, Maggie's breath fogged up the glass. She had the barrel of the shotgun nearly pressed against her cheek. Another flash of lightning brought into brief relief an image of two figures beyond the willow tree, one smaller than the other. But she couldn't be sure. Fuck . . . she couldn't be sure . . .

Whimpering, she reached up and clicked off the floodlights. She didn't want to see anymore, didn't want to be reminded of what was going on out there.

You hit it with your car, Maggie, and it's not going to let you be.

"Shut up!" she screamed. "Just shut the fuck up!"

And you know what it is, Maggie . . . you know damn well what—

A face appeared in the living room window, a white oval with muddy, black eyes framed in darkness. Maggie screamed and jerked away. The curtains fell back into place, obscuring the hideous face. Scooting back across the floor, Maggie stopped when her shoulders struck the back of the couch. She held the shotgun in both hands and had the barrel aimed at the window, her finger on the trigger.

Hit it with your car, Maggie, said the head-voice. *Hit it with your car. But you did something much worse before that, didn't you? Oh yes, you did . . .*

Maggie wailed. Sobbing, she crawled around to the front of the couch, the shotgun dragging along the hardwood floor. She pulled the cushions off the couch and propped them up around her in some semblance of a barricade.

Yes, said the head-voice. *Pillows and couch cushions will certainly protect you from the thing that fell out of the sky.*

"Shut . . . the fuck . . . up," she rasped.

Outside, lightning lit up the world like a nuclear bomb.

6

A blast of thunder woke her. It sounded like the whole world was about to end. Somehow, she had fallen asleep amid the barricade of couch cushions and throw pillows on the floor of the living room. The second her eyes flipped open, she recalled all the events of that evening with brutal and frightening clarity. Something heavy sat across her lap. In the dark, she ran her fingers across it and discovered it was Evan's shotgun.

Tom. Tom had gone outside. Had he ever come back?

"Tom?" she called, her voice was raw from sleep.

When no one answered, she remembered locking all the doors and windows. Just how in the world did she expect Tom Schuler to get back into the house?

He won't be coming back into the house, she thought, propping herself up on her elbows as her eyes acclimated to the gloom. *Something took him. Out there in the yard, something took Tom Schuler.*

Still groggy, she managed to climb to her feet and, hefting the shotgun along with her, went to the bank of living room windows. Peeling away the curtain, she looked out upon the night. Rain still fell, churning the earth like muddy soup. The moon had cleared the strands of dark clouds, grinning down at her like the ghostly white face of a cadaver that had been cleaved in half.

Tom's car was still in the turnabout, rain pattering its windshield and roof. Beyond, the yard was a sloping black mudslide of lightlessness.

She could see nothing of substance beyond the far gate at the edge of the property.

What time was it? She went into the kitchen and checked the digital clock on the microwave. It read 1:47 a.m.

What the fuck happened to Tom?

No. She wouldn't lose her shit again. She would remain cool. Tom was out there. He *had* to be out there.

Her sweaty fingers tightened around the shotgun.

Go check. You can do this. It was the head-voice again, but this time it seemed intent on helping her through it. *Go out onto the patio and check. Call his name. Maybe he's out there and he's hurt. Maybe he needs your help.*

Trembling, she went back to the rear door. The crescent of glass at the top was foggy from her panting respiration. She had turned the floodlights off earlier—at least, she thought she had—and the world beyond was nothing but outer space. Should she turn the floods on again and see what lay beyond the door, beyond the patio? What was out there in the muddy field along with Evan's Pontiac and Tom's old Maverick?

Her hand found the light switch beside the door. The switch pressed against the sweaty palm of her hand as she pressed hard against it. In her mind's eye, she could see herself flipping on the floods . . . and seeing the horror that remained of Tom Schuler in the field, his body torn to shreds, his face mangled into a pulpy stew.

"I can't," she whined, crying again.

Do it, said the head-voice.

That thing that had been crouched low on the roof of the car earlier . . . that horrible thing that had appeared at one of the living room windows as she had looked out . . .

She pulled her hand away from the light switch and brought it to the dead bolt on the door. She turned the bolt; the sound was like opening a bank vault, and it echoed in her ears. Under her breath she counted to three . . . then, gripping and turning the knob, she yanked the door open.

Icy wind and cold pellets of rain attacked her. With a shriek she thrust the barrel of the shotgun out the door and into the night, foolishly waving it around like a sword. She could see nothing, hear nothing.

"Tom!" she shouted into the monsoon. "Are you out there? Tom! Tom!"

Only the wind howled back, frightening her even more.

When she thought she caught movement off to her right, she screamed and almost dropped the shotgun. Something quick and catlike darted out from the approximate area of the willow tree and ran toward the house along the property line. A low, animalistic groan escaped from Maggie's throat as she backed through the doorway, the barrel of the shotgun flailing about.

Back inside, terrified and soaking wet, Maggie slammed the door and bolted it again. Sobbing freely now, she carried the shotgun back to the spot on the floor where she'd erected the couch cushions and throw pillows into a makeshift pillbox and lowered herself to her knees. She pulled the shotgun back into her lap and leaned back against the couch. The roof creaked as the storm pounded against it. Outside, lightning made the windows glow like sapphires.

Maggie squeezed her eyes shut and prayed for daylight.

7

It was nearly two in the morning when Ben finally arrived back home. The house greeted him with its usual silence, and he didn't bother turning on any of the lights as he came through the front door and staggered exhaustedly down the hallway toward the master bedroom. He stripped out of his uniform, set his gun on the nightstand beside the bed, and unbuckled his duty belt, which he hung over the back of a wooden chair that faced an antique rolltop desk. From the left breast pocket of his uniform shirt, Ben took out the gold-plated Zippo lighter he always kept with him—his father's lighter. The old man's initials, W. J., were etched onto one side. Feeling more nostalgic than usual, Ben turned the lighter over in his fingers a few times before finally setting it down on the nightstand beside the bed. *Check out your only son now, Dad.* Then he peeled off his undershirt and stepped out of his underwear. Instantly he felt about seventy pounds lighter and as naked and vulnerable as a turtle without a shell.

Too exhausted to shower, he washed his face and hands in the adjoining bathroom, brushed his teeth, popped out his contact lenses, and urinated with the zeal of someone who has just come off a cross-country road trip.

Back in the bedroom, he cracked open both windows just enough to let fresh air in but keep the raging storm at bay. Then he slipped into bed and, lying on his back, laced both hands beneath his head. Moonlight filtering through the windows reflected onto the ceiling; the shadows of raindrops rolled like comets above his head.

Out in the hallway, the floorboards creaked.

Ben held his breath. Listened.

After a moment, he called out, "Dad?" Then he waited for a response, already feeling indescribably foolish.

Five minutes later, sleep claimed him.

CHAPTER FIVE

1

The sound of birds woke her. Maggie's eyes flipped open and, for a moment, disorientation caused her to question her surroundings. Stiffly, she sat up and found herself asleep on the living room floor, surrounded by cushions and pillows. Her husband's shotgun sat at an angle across her lap.

It all rushed back to her.

Grabbing the barrel of the gun, Maggie stood and wended her way around the scattered pillows and the couch to the back door. Pink dawn pooled into the room from the crescent of glass at the top of the door. The whole house was warm. She realized that all the windows were shut.

Still clutching the shotgun, Maggie staggered into the kitchen and saw that the clock on the microwave read 5:22 a.m. Evan would be home in about an hour.

Back in the hall, she undid the dead bolt on the back door and pulled the door open. Beyond, the sloping lawn glistened in the premature daylight that broke through the valley between the mountains. Tom's Maverick sat there, also glistening, and looking like a bloody fucking handprint.

Her eyes shifted toward the edge of the property and to the weeping willow tree, heavy with rain and sagging close to the earth.

Shadows pooled at its base. She could see nothing incriminating around it.

Daylight made her fear seem less palpable; she stepped down off the steps and into the yard. The wet grass tickled her bare feet. The shotgun pointed dead ahead of her, she circled around the vehicles then went straight to the edge of the property and over to the willow tree.

It was a humped, spidery thing. Its branches, which were typically notched with narrow little leaves, were currently bare. Maggie searched around the base of the tree—the exact spot she thought she'd seen Tom struggling with the pale-skinned creature last night—but there was nothing for her to find.

Was she losing her mind?

"Stop it." A nervous laugh threatened to erupt from her throat. Not wanting to take her eyes from the willow tree, she walked backward all the way across the yard to the house. When she reached the patio steps, she cautiously ascended them backward as well, the gun still aimed at the tree. In her mind's eye, she could too easily see that spidery tree uprooting itself from the wet soil and charging toward her on a system of roots like the many legs of an octopus.

Once again, she slammed and locked the door.

Inside, she set the shotgun down on the floor. Then she gathered up the couch cushions and pillows and put them back where they belonged. Tom's dungaree jacket, still damp from the previous night's rain, hung over the back of the couch. She stared hard at the tarnished copper buttons and the cigarette burns in the sleeves. A rubber key fob in the shape of a hand with its middle finger extended hung out of one pocket.

Maggie sat down on the couch and considered her situation. After several minutes, she got up and found her cell phone. There were no missed calls, no text messages. Her hands shaking, she managed to dial Tom's number. With her phone to her ear, she heard Tom's cell ring over the line. A second later, she heard a chirping sound coming from Tom's jacket.

Maggie lowered her phone. The jacket continued chirping at her until she hit End on her phone. She went over to the jacket, picked it up, and fished around the pockets. Yes, Tom's cell phone was in one of the pockets. Just holding it made everything feel too real to her, so she quickly dropped it. Her heart slammed against her ribs. Yes, in the other pocket, the middle finger key fob was attached to a set of keys which included the ignition key to the Maverick.

Tom's car couldn't be here when Evan got home. That much was clear.

Examining the keys in her hand, she felt a giddy sense of salvation rush through her like a jolt of adrenaline.

"Okay," she muttered to herself, stuffing the keys into the pocket of her sweatpants then gathering up Tom's jacket off the couch. "Okay, okay, okay . . ."

Back in the kitchen, the microwave clock turned from 5:46 to 5:47.

Barefoot, Maggie hurried out the door and went straight across the yard to Tom's car. The driver's door was unlocked, so she yanked it open and slid inside, quickly closing the door behind her. After all, whatever had been out here in the yard last night could still be around. Watching, waiting. Hiding. The thought gave her chills.

She tossed Tom's jacket into the backseat then, selecting the appropriate key, started up the engine. The car shuddered and roared, and she vibrated in the seat. The motor sounded like it belonged on a space shuttle.

Maggie spent a few minutes hunting for the gearshift before she saw that it was on the steering column. She cranked the car into Drive then, spinning the wheel, drove it around the side of the house and down the rutted driveway toward the street. It was still dark, so she patted around the dashboard until she found the knob for the headlights. It felt just like the Pontiac's cigarette lighter. She tugged the knob and the headlights blinked on, cutting through the darkness.

As she pulled onto the street, she turned left and gunned it up the hill. Had she gone right, she would have driven straight into the mountains, where an abandoned vehicle was certain to catch the eye of a vigilant police officer. Instead, she opted to head toward town, where there were always a few cars parked along the side of the road. Who knew? Maybe Tom Schuler would come stumbling out into town only to find his own car here waiting for him. Crazier things have happened, right?

You're losing your shit, honeypot, said the head-voice. This time, it was so loud Maggie glanced up at the rearview mirror for fear that someone was speaking to her from the backseat. *You're really going bughouse, aren't you, darling?*

She turned left at the first intersection. The street ahead was lined with darkened shops and lampposts that no longer worked. A few cars were parked on either side of the street. Maggie pulled alongside the curb and parked directly behind a battered old station wagon. She cranked the key and shut the car down. It chugged and chugged then finally died.

"There you go," she said then glanced up at her reflection in the rearview. She looked hideous. "Okay. Fine."

She climbed quickly from the car, pushing the door closed slowly so that it would latch but wouldn't slam. Just as the sun began to creep up over the string of darkened buildings, Maggie headed back in the direction of her home. Halfway there, she realized she still had Tom's car keys in her hands. That problem was soon solved, however, when she pitched them down the next storm drain she came to.

2

Back home, she returned the shotgun and the shells to the basement. Then she took a quick shower and got dressed. She was brushing her hair and smiling warmly when Evan came home from work a few minutes later. Greeting his wife with only a passing glance, he muttered, "You're up early," then went immediately to bed.

CHAPTER SIX

1

Ben spent Sunday morning on the phone with the Cumberland County Sheriff's Department, trying to convince one of the sheriff's deputies of the need for warm bodies to help conduct a search for the missing Crawly kid. The deputy, an obstinate bumpkin with a faint lisp, was not too keen on wrangling together a bunch of his guys on a Sunday to wander around the woods looking for a kid who'd probably run away from home and was currently holed up in some friend's tree house.

"That may very well be," Ben assured him, "but on the slim chance that something else has happened to that kid—like maybe he fell *out* of some friend's tree house and is lying with his leg or his neck broken somewhere—I think we should get out there and look for him."

The deputy grunted. "Where's Harris, anyway?"

"The chief's on vacation."

"Leaves you holding the bag, huh?"

Ben frowned at the phone. "We got a nice little diner in town," Ben went on, unperturbed. "The Belly Barn. I wouldn't mind treating your men to some good home-style dinner for giving us a hand. Bo makes a helluva meat loaf."

The deputy sighed. Ben could hear a radio or a television in the background. "Yeah, okay," he said eventually, more bored than agitated. "How many men you think you need?"

"As many as you can spare," Ben said. "This way we can get done quicker."

"What time is it now?"

It was six-thirty in the morning. Ben told him so.

"Jesus," the deputy said. "All right. We'll be out there around eight o'clock, okay?"

"Great."

"My name's Witmark, by the way. George Witmark."

"Thank you, George."

"That better be some grade-A meat loaf," Witmark said and hung up.

2

The guys from Cumberland arrived at the station at a quarter till nine—three squad cars with two uniformed officers in each car, the sheriff's logo emblazoned on each door. George Witmark got out of the first squad car. He was tall and thin, his sunken jowls crosshatched with the remnants of teenage acne. He surveyed the Stillwater police station with something akin to disdain. He had a toothpick wedged in the corner of his mouth.

Ben gave a cursory briefing to the officers in the Batter's Box then they all headed out to the Crawly house. Ben went to the front door while the other officers waited near their cars, climbing into latex gloves and forester boots. Wendy Crawly was home. She answered the door and the sight of her caused Ben's capillaries to constrict. She looked like something that had crawled recently from the grave, her face colorless and her hair a frizzy tangle. Sylvia Marsh stood behind Wendy, her plain country face a mask of worry.

"My God," Wendy said, nearly croaking.

Oh, I am an idiot, he thought, instantly realizing how this must look.

"We haven't found him," Ben said quickly, holding out two placating hands. When it looked like Wendy might collapse, Sylvia Marsh came up behind her and slid an arm around her waist. "I didn't mean to catch you like this. We just wanted to search the property. Is there someplace you could go for a while?"

"We can go to my house," Sylvia said. The Marshes lived in the next farmhouse over.

Ben thanked her then waited in his car for the two women to leave. They finally came out the front door and walked, arm in arm, up the road to the Marsh house.

The officers searched the property first, including the detached garage. From there, they spread out in four small teams to cover more ground, moving behind the Crawly property and into the Marshes' cornfield, which separated the two properties. They searched in a gridded fashion, two teams combing the field east to west while the other two teams moved north to south. The entire time, Ben conducted the search with his heart in his throat. A feeling of detachment carried him through much of the morning and well into the afternoon.

By three o'clock, with the men sweating through their uniforms, they had searched the entire cornfield and the surrounding pastures, straight up to the foothills of Haystack Mountain, with no sign of Matthew Crawly. Ben did not know how to feel about this. Of course, he was relieved that they hadn't found a body . . . but now he was faced with the increasing mystery of where the boy had gone. They hadn't even found a scrap of clothing or a goddamn footprint. No evidence whatsoever.

Exhausted, they regrouped in the Crawlys' backyard just as the sun began to creep behind the peaks of the mountain. Shirley arrived with cheese sandwiches wrapped in cellophane for all the men, a grim expression on her face. The men ate in mutual silence and most of them did not look very hungry. Peeling off his latex gloves and smoking a cigarette, Witmark approached Ben, who sat on the porch steps examining the fresh abrasions on his palms.

"You talked to the mother, right?"

"Sure," Ben said.

"My guess is they had a fight and the kid will come back once he's had time to cool off." Witmark shrugged, as if he dealt with this sort of thing on a weekly basis. For all Ben knew, maybe he did. "You know how kids are."

Ben nodded and looked back down at his hands.

"Shit," Witmark went on, a hint of compassion in his voice now. "I remember when I was a kid, I'd have some blowout with my old man and I'd jet out for Lovers' Leap with a six of Pabst and wouldn't return till the next morning."

Ben doubted eleven-year-old Matthew Crawly had cut out for Lovers' Leap with a six of Pabst under his arm, but he didn't say anything.

"I got two of my own," Witmark said. "They're always storming out of the house."

Ben felt eyes on his back. He looked over his shoulder and saw a face in one of the downstairs windows, looking out at him. It was Brandy Crawly, Matthew's sister. Ben hadn't thought to ask Wendy if her daughter was home.

"Sometimes I think they hate me," Witmark went on.

Ben glanced at his wristwatch. "You guys in a hurry to get back?"

Witmark shrugged again. He had softened over the matter in the wake of the search.

"Would you and your guys mind following me out to a road on the outskirts of town? There's some woods out that way I'd like to search, too."

"It's like we're hired help around here," Witmark commented, a bit of the old obstinacy back in his voice.

"It won't need to be as involved as this was," Ben assured him.

"What happened out on this road?"

"Local woman says she hit a boy with her car Friday night, around midnight."

"Christ, Journell. You didn't think—"

"We conducted a search of the area but couldn't find anything. She was confused and scared, and I thought maybe she hit a deer. But when I heard about this kid disappearing . . ."

Witmark nodded. "Yeah. Okay. Lead the way, hoss."

3

It was closing on five-thirty when they decided they were finished out on Full Hill Road. The sun had already set prematurely behind the western mountain and the sky was ribbed with salmon-colored bands of dwindling light. The wind spoke up, gaining courage with the oncoming night. The brown leaves in the trees shook like rattlesnakes and the occasional low moan could be heard slaloming through the valley.

Again, they found no evidence of what had happened to the Crawly boy . . . or any evidence that Maggie Quedentock had hit anyone with her car out there Friday night, for that matter. Drained and weary, Ben had every intention of keeping his promise about treating the men to a meal at the Belly Barn, but Witmark quickly waved him off. At some point throughout the day, George Witmark had warmed to him . . . or at least pitied him enough to fake it.

"Don't worry about dinner," Witmark said, sucking the life out of another cigarette. Ben guessed he'd gone through an entire pack that day. "My wife wants me home tonight, anyway. You married?"

"No."

Witmark laughed, his eyes crinkling into sparkling little gems. Ben wasn't sure what was so funny.

A light rain began to fall as the police officers from Cumberland got back in their cars and dispersed from Full Hill Road. (Before they left, Ben heard one of the officers mutter something about how creepy it was to have the sun set so early. Ben thought the guy looked pleased to be leaving Stillwater behind.) Ben sat on the hood of his car and stared up beyond the trees where stars could already be seen poking through the fabric of the sky.

Mike Keller joined him on the hood. "I just heard back from the last number on that list you gave me of the Crawly kid's friends," Mike said. "No one's seen him. He hasn't been staying at any friends' houses."

"Yeah, okay. I was beginning to think that was the case, anyway."

"What now?"

Ben rubbed his forehead. "Contact the staties, have them put out an AMBER Alert. There's also a contact number for the Baltimore field office of the FBI pinned to that corkboard in Harris's office. You know the one I'm talking about? You should notify them, too."

"The FBI?"

"Tell them there's nothing concrete, but I want them to know that it could be a possible kidnapping."

"Holy Jesus, Ben! What are you talking about?"

"It's just something I've been thinking. The boy's father split in the middle of the night a year or so ago. What if he came back just as quietly and took his son?"

"Shit. I didn't think of that."

"It's probably a long shot. But I'm sort of hoping for it, too. Know what I mean?"

"Yeah. Sure. I'll get right on it."

"Thanks, Mike."

"You interested in some dinner? Me and the guys were gonna grab something."

"Go ahead, I'll grab something myself."

"Okay, Sarge."

Three minutes later, Ben was alone on Full Hill Road, a soft rain pattering down all around him.

He decided to go into town for a quick bite, giving much consideration to stopping in at the Belly Barn for Bo's meat loaf special after all. But when Crossroads rose up on the side of the road, he pulled into the parking lot without thinking about it, as if on autopilot. Alvin Toops had run the place for the past two-and-a-half decades and, in all that time, nothing much had changed—it was a dark, dank, squalid little pit that practically oozed cigar smoke from the lathing. Country music played in rotation from the wall-mounted juke, and the usual suspects were hunched like buzzards over the bar top nursing foamy mugs of beer when Ben walked in. A few of the regulars raised their hands at him and he did the same. He sat at the end of the bar and rubbed his face with his abraded hands.

"Hey, Ben. Haven't seen you in a while," Alvin Toops said, sliding down to Ben's end of the bar. Toops was a big truck of a guy, with tattoos up and down his arms and a shaved head. A gold hoop hung from each earlobe. "Get you a beer?"

"I'm on the clock. Make it a cranberry and club soda. You still got those mini-cheeseburgers?"

"Sure do."

"I'll have some of those, too."

Alvin Toops punched Ben's order onto an LCD screen behind the bar. Then he dumped some cranberry juice into a highball glass, squirted some seltzer into it, and slid it in front of Ben. "How'd the old homestead hold up in the storm?" Toops asked.

"Got some flooding in the cellar," Ben said, "but otherwise, all is good."

"Good for you. I didn't get no flooding up at the house, or here either, for that matter. The power knocking out cost me a small fortune in supplies I had to dump, and Trish chewed my ear off about it, like it was my fault. Like I did some kind of rain dance or something."

"They're calling for another storm by the end of the week," Ben informed him, sipping his cran and soda.

"I heard. I need to get some fuel for the generator for this place. I can't afford to lose another shipment."

When the mini-cheeseburgers arrived, Ben shook copious amounts of ketchup on them then ate them slowly and methodically, like a cow chewing cud. When Ben drained his glass, Alvin Toops appeared to refill it.

"Thanks," Ben said. "Can I ask you a question? It's a police question."

Toops laughed. "Shoot. Am I in trouble?"

"Just a witness," Ben said, then added, "maybe."

"Go for it."

"Did you see Maggie Quedentock in here Friday night?"

"Sure did." Toops pointed toward the far end of the bar. "Sat right over there."

"Was she alone?"

"She came in alone," Toops said, his brows knitted in recollection, "but she talked to a few people throughout the night."

"About what time did she get here?"

"Maybe seven."

"And what time did she leave?"

"Not sure. Maybe eight or so."

"So she didn't stay very long," Ben said around a mouthful of cheeseburger.

"Nope."

"How much did she have to drink?"

"I'm really not sure, Ben. I could pull the receipts and have a look for you."

"Could you? Is that too much trouble?"

"It's either that or cater to these deadbeats all night."

"Hey," growled one of the deadbeats within earshot.

"If you don't mind," Ben said.

"No sweat." Alvin Toops swiped a dish towel across the top of the bar. "Mrs. Quedentock in some kind of trouble?"

"Just a little fender-bender Friday night," he said. "Nobody got hurt, except maybe her pride." He hoped he sounded somewhat disinterested about the whole matter.

"I'll get right on it," Toops said, slinging the dish towel over one shoulder and moving toward the bar's back room.

When he returned with a single receipt, Ben was just finishing up his meal. He downed the rest of his cranberry and soda, dabbed the corners of his mouth with a paper napkin, then took the receipt Alvin Toops handed him.

"It took me a while to find it," Toops said. "I was searching for her name but I'd forgot that Tom Schuler picked up her tab."

"Oh yeah?" The receipt showed just two beers: a Heineken and a Budweiser. She hadn't drunk much at all, assuming one of those beers was Tom's. The time on the receipt read 8:12 p.m.

"I can make you a copy of it, if you want," Toops offered.

Ben handed him the receipt back. "That's okay. Just curious, I guess. No need to make a federal case."

"Roger that," Toops said, examining the receipt himself now, as if able to divine something from it. He stuffed it into the breast pocket of his shirt just as Ben tossed his balled-up napkin onto his plate.

4

Later, Ben arrived at the station to find things quiet. Shirley was in the dispatch office, feeding her goldfish and playing her iPod through a set of small plastic speakers on her desk. Without checking the roster, he knew Platt and Haggis had the evening shift, though he was willing to cut one of them loose since they'd gotten up early that morning to assist with the search for Matthew Crawly. Let them bang it out between the two of them which one should get to go home.

"Joe and Mel around?" he asked Shirley, leaning in the doorway.

"They're out at Ted Minsky's farm on a call." She set the jar of fish food down beside the fish tank then turned around in her swivel chair. She wore a pair of bifocals halfway down her nose. "Another call about mutilated livestock."

"Oh, you've got to be kidding me."

"They just left, if you wanted to catch them."

Ben rubbed his tired eyes.

"What time did you get up this morning?"

"I don't know. Four-thirty, maybe."

"You're really worried about Wendy's kid. You think something bad happened to him."

"I do," he said. He was aware that he hadn't known how he felt until he spoke the words just then.

"Why don't you go home and get some rest? Tomorrow will bring better things."

It was a sentiment Ben's mother used to say; hearing it now caused a chill to ripple through him.

"Ben," Shirley said, like a schoolteacher attempting to gather his attention.

"I will," he said. "I'll go home, get some sleep." He coughed into one hand. "First, I think I'll stop by Ted Minsky's place."

Shirley made a barely audible sound beneath her breath and swiveled back to her fish.

5

The storm was raging by the time Ben pulled his cruiser up the long dirt drive that led to Ted Minsky's farm. The farmhouse was at the top of the hill, a stark cutout against the storm-laden sky. Ben spied Haggis and Platt's cruiser parked in front of the house beside the hull of an old artesian well, the cruiser's lights dark and the car empty. Ben pulled up the driveway, which looped around to the rear of the house. From there, he could see the sloping fields and, beyond, the rambling structure that was Ted Minsky's barn and grain silo. White fencing studded the hillside.

There wasn't a driveway that led from the house down to the barn, but Ben could make out the muddy ruts that tractor tires created in the soil, so he spun the cruiser's wheel and eased the car to a slow roll down to the barn. He flipped the high beams on but they did nothing but solidify the sheets of rain and a thin, smoky mist, so he switched them back off. The undercarriage shuddered as he coaxed it over the field. Just as he approached, he could see three figures wading toward him through the storm. One of them had a flashlight, the beam of which briefly blinded Ben as it glared across the windshield. He eased down on the brakes and brought the car to a stop.

Stepping out into the rain, he hit the floodlight on the driver's door of the car. Melvin Haggis, Joseph Platt, and old Ted Minsky each lifted a hand to block out the glare of the harsh light. The choreography was almost comical.

"That you, Sarge?" Haggis said.

"Yes. Everything all right?" Ben asked, twisting the handle of the cruiser's floodlight so that the beam shot off into space.

"Just some dead goats," Joseph Platt said. Both Platt and Haggis wore plastic shower caps over their campaign hats and they both had their hands wedged into the pockets of their chinos like two kids trying to keep warm while waiting for the morning school bus.

"Can I have a look?" Ben asked, checking his Maglite to make sure the batteries still worked. They did.

"At goats?" Platt said. His skin looked like cheesecloth beneath the wide brim of his hat. He jerked a thumb over his shoulder. "You really wanna stand out here in the rain and look at dead goats, Ben?"

Ted Minsky, wrapped in a bright orange rain slicker, made a disapproving noise.

"I do," said Ben, moving past the men. He followed their footprints in the mud until he arrived at the back of the barn. There was a corral here and some concrete slop troughs that were quickly filling with rainwater. As Ben approached, lightning briefly lit up the sky along the horizon. He could see several sodden clods of wet hair lying dead in the mud.

He paused just outside the corral and shone his Maglite into the pen. Dead goats, all right. Even from this distance, he could tell that they'd suffered the same fatal wounds as Porter Conroy's cattle the night before. A nonspecific disquiet settled over him like a shroud. Stupidly—almost ironically—he thought of the ridiculous article in Eddie La Pointe's magazine about the Mexican vampire. The goatsucker.

What the hell is going on here?

The three men came up behind Ben.

"You see this?" said Ted Minsky, his voice a low growl. When he moved, his rain slicker sounded like a plastic trash bag. "These ain't even my goats."

"What do you mean?" Ben asked.

"They're sold," Minsky said, nearly shouting. "Folks bought 'em! What am I supposed to do now? They've been paid for. Am I supposed to give the money back? And get what for my troubles? A heap of dead animals?"

"I don't know what to tell you," Ben said, moving his flashlight slowly from carcass to carcass. The beam froze on the mangled head of one of the goats. Even in the dark and from this distance, Ben could see the whitish dome of a section of its skull, the grayish hair around it looking as though it had been sheared away. And not just the hair but the flesh beneath it, too—bone gleamed in patches on the goat's head.

His heart strumming, Ben turned the flashlight on another carcass. This one's head had been opened up as well, but there was something else curious about it, too—the tapered horns at either side of its head appeared to have been broken. Glancing around, he couldn't find the sheared-off pieces near the carcass.

There was a horseshoe-shaped latch affixed to a fencepost, keeping the gate shut. Ben lifted the latch and entered the corral, his heavy boots sinking a couple of inches into the soft, wet earth. Bending down, he cast a beam of light across the ground, hoping to discern any distinctive footprints in the mud. There had certainly been a lot of commotion—the ground had been churned and kicked up—but that, coupled with the driving rain, made it impossible to identify any specific prints. Anyway, they were all filled with water now.

He went over to the goat with the sheared horns. He had expected to find them crudely broken; instead, they looked as though they had been liquefied, allowed to dribble to mere nubs, then turned solid again. Melted, almost. To Minsky, who stood on the other side of the fence, Ben called, "Did you do something to the horns?"

"Not a blessed thing," Minsky responded, his hands hanging over the railing of the corral. He exhaled a tired-sounding breath.

Ben stood. "I guess you think some bear or coyote did this," he said flatly.

"Heck, no," Minsky said. "I know who did this."

"Please don't tell me it's Porter Conroy," Ben said.

"Porter?" Minsky sounded incredulous. "Christ, no."

"Then who did it?"

"Some boy," Minsky said. "Got a face like a vampire."

"Ben!" Mel Haggis shouted from outside the pen. He had both hands cupped about his mouth. "Hey, Ben! Let's chitchat inside, okay? We're freezing our tails off out here!"

Minsky sighed with great aplomb. "I'll put some coffee on," he said, turning and kicking up clods of mud as he sauntered back toward the house.

6

"Past week or so I been hearin' noises just outside the house at night," Minsky explained while Ben sat across from him in a wingback chair in the old man's parlor. Both Haggis and Platt loitered in the hallway, half listening and dripping rainwater onto the carpet. They all held steaming cups of freshly brewed coffee. "In the mornings, I can tell someone's been in the yard. There's things moved around, some plants trampled, that sort of thing. Down at the barn one morning, it looked like someone tried to get in the night before. The doors were pulled outward but still locked, so ain't no one gettin' in or out, but someone sure as hell tried."

"When was this?" Ben asked.

"The thing with the barn was sometime last week. Don't recall the exact night." Minsky leaned forward in his chair, the mug of coffee held between his knobby knees in two hands. "Other times, I've heard this, well, sort of *scraping* noise against the windows."

Ben nodded, prompting the old man to continue.

"Then, two nights ago," Minsky went on, "I'm sitting right here watching the tube, and I hear someone outside walking around the wraparound porch. I mean, I hear the boards a-creakin' sure as I'm sitting here talkin' to you fellas. I go out and check but don't see nothing. I go down by the barn, too, because I don't need nobody messing with my livelihood. But the barn looks fine, so I come back up to the house."

Minsky set his coffee mug on a nearby end table. The old man's hand trembled as it retreated into his lap.

"But I'd left the door to the house open, and when I come back in, I'm suddenly sure whoever had been *outside* was now *inside.* Well, I get the Louisville from the hall closet and go through the house, knocking the Louisville against doorframes and peeking under beds and those sorts of things." He nodded toward the kitchen. "I was in there when I heard the door slam against the frame and footsteps racing around the porch."

"Jesus," Haggis said from the doorway.

Minsky nodded. "I hurried back in here and that's when I saw the face." He pointed to a window beside an antique mahogany cabinet which housed a prehistoric Zenith. "Right outside, pressed right against the glass, lookin' in at me."

"Who was it?" Ben asked. "Did you recognize the person?"

"Well, see, he disappeared just as quick, and I didn't get a real good look. But it was a young boy."

"A boy," Ben echoed.

"I could tell that much."

"Could you describe him?"

"Well," Minsky said, his eyes shifting uncomfortably about the room now. He was lost in recollection and, judging by the pained expression on his face, Ben didn't think the old man liked what he saw. "He was white. Like, pale." Those unsettled eyes finally settled on Ben. "He looked like a corpse, Sergeant Journell."

No one said a word for several seconds. From out in the hall, Ben could hear a grandfather clock mocking the silence.

"I thought it might've been a prank, seein' how close we are to Halloween," Minsky went on eventually. "But after I seen my goats this evening . . . well . . . I don't know nobody thinks somethin' like that's a prank. Back in my day, we strung toilet paper in people's trees and lit bags of dog shit on fire on their front porches. You hear what I'm saying?"

"I do," Ben said after sharing a look with his two officers in the doorway.

Minsky leaned closer to Ben in his chair. This close, Ben could see the large pores in the man's thick nose, the network of red threads in his eyes, and the peppery tufts of hair that sprouted from the man's ear canals like kudzu. "You tell me, Sergeant Journell," said Minsky. "What kind of kid does somethin' like that to goats?"

Ben could only shake his head. He had no answer for the man.

CHAPTER SEVEN

1

Monday was Ben Journell's day off. He spent the morning jogging along Full Hill Road, crossing from shoulder to shoulder in the spot where Maggie Quedentock claimed to have struck a pedestrian with her car last Friday night. All evidence, or lack thereof, led to the fact that Maggie had most likely hit a deer which then bounded far off into the woods. It was even probable that she had hit nothing at all, that she had enjoyed a few too many drinks at Crossroads on someone else's tab and nothing more. The dent in the car's hood and the broken grille, which he had observed when he showed up on scene, could have been there all along, as far as Ben knew. And to top it all off, the guys over in Cumberland probably thought he was an overreacting moron.

It was on his third pass around the bend where the supposed accident had taken place that something occurred to him. He paused beside a stand of leafless trees and checked his pulse while his breathing regulated. Overhead, predatory birds circled like tireless acrobats. Full Hill Road ran from midtown straight up into the undulating foothills, which was where Ben stood now. After looping around a few remote farmhouses up here, the road continued toward the mountains where it eventually denigrated to a muddy service road dead-ended into the trees. Though he wasn't sure on exactly which street the Quedentocks lived, he knew they were somewhere around midtown. Crossroads—the tavern Maggie had claimed to be coming from—was only a few blocks outside midtown. What in the world had she been doing way up here?

A squirrel loped out into the middle of the roadway. It stood abruptly on its hind legs, its hands held together before it in a mockery of prayer, and surveyed its surroundings. When it spied Ben, it froze, though its tail continued to twitch spasmodically.

Was he reading too much into Maggie Quedentock's statement? Should he swing by her place later, ask her a few more questions? He supposed he could, although that wouldn't help alleviate the thing that was bugging him, even more than the rash of mutilated livestock. Eleven-year-old Matthew Crawly was still missing and, with each passing day, the outcome became bleaker and bleaker.

When he returned to the old farmhouse on Sideling Road, he took a long shower, dressed casually in a pair of jeans and a T-shirt, and made himself a hearty breakfast of four scrambled eggs, sausage links, toasted Italian bread, and strong Brazilian coffee. Outside, the temperature simmered at around the seventy-degree mark, so he carried his breakfast to the back porch that overlooked the southern field. The air smelled swampy from the previous night's storm and large black crows drank out of puddles in the marshy topsoil. When he was a boy, this field had brought forth countless crops, lush and Edenic in all its greenness. Now, it was a desolate, barren landscape, the only foliage being the spiraling helixes of vines that grew around the fenceposts. Somewhere over time, the soil had adopted a grayish hue and looked no more fertile than a sand dune. The previous spring, overcome by grief at the loss of his father, Ben had planted some seeds: cucumber, tomato, squash, parsley. Nothing unmanageable. Yet the land had yielded nothing. Some nights, he would dream of the seeds hatching just beneath the soil, the tendrils of their fragile roots seeking out one another like hands uniting, until they formed a firm network under the earth. In these dreams, vines like the tentacles of a giant squid would burst from the ground in a shower of dirt and stones and engulf the farmhouse, wrapping it up like a gift. Then, gradually, the farmhouse would be pulled down beneath the ground, Ben still inside it, screaming, until only the stone chimney protruded from the dirt. And after time, even that, too, would be sucked down until nothing remained except a flat, empty, desolate plot of land.

After breakfast, he read a book for a bit, but he became too antsy as his mind began to wander and he found himself rereading the same paragraphs over and over again without retaining any of it. Finally he closed the book and went to the bedroom down the hall that, in his youth, had belonged to him. Since then, he had fashioned it into a comfortable little home office, completed with a handsome desk, two leather chairs studded with brass tacks, and a bookcase containing various law books and awards. Some of his father's medals from Vietnam hung on the wall in shadow boxes.

There was a Rolodex on the desk. Ben flipped through it until he found the card he was looking for. He punched the numbers into his cell phone and waited.

"Lieutenant Davenport," said the man on the other end of the line after a series of rings.

"Hey, Paul, it's Ben Journell over in Stillwater."

"Hey, buddy. How've you been?"

They engaged in idle chitchat for a few minutes before Ben asked about the mountain lion.

"Damnedest thing," Davenport told him over the line. "I mean, it didn't really look that big when you just saw it out walking, but when you see it up close, well, it's something else, man. Teeth like carpentry nails."

"So the rumors are true. Eddie La Pointe told me about it but I didn't really believe him."

"Oh, it was true, all right. Damn thing had everybody talkin', and half the town scared to go out after dusk."

"It still doesn't?"

"Not no more," Davenport said.

"You mean the thing's dead?" Ben asked. "You guys killed it?"

"Three days ago," said Davenport. That would have been on Friday. "Wasn't us, though. We just responded to the call after it had been shot. Turned out the damn thing had gotten into someone's garage through an open window, but it got stuck and couldn't get out. Some locals went out and fired a few rounds at it with a goddamn Glock, of all things."

"Oh."

"Yeah, well, I'm guessing they didn't want to mess it up too badly, figuring they'd take it to a taxidermist and have it stuffed or whatever. Either way, by the time we got there, the sucker's days of digging through people's garbage cans was over."

"Had it been attacking any livestock?"

"Livestock? No, man—just knocking over dumpsters and shit. Pulled some dead rabbits out of a trap, too, I think. They're actually pretty timid and don't like to get too close to humans." Davenport cleared his throat. "Why? You got livestock being killed out that way, Ben?"

Ben's laugh held no humor. "Right now, I've got two farmers in town looking to hang me up by my suspenders if I don't figure out what's going on out here."

"It's that bad?"

"It's just . . . I've never seen anything like it. You know of any animal that goes after another animal's brain?"

"Shit. You're talking parasites."

"No, Paul. I mean cracking the fucking skulls apart and eating what's inside."

"Jesus in a sidecar." Davenport whistled. "You're putting me on, right? What does something like that?"

"You tell me."

"Wish I could, Ben."

"And it's the way they're killed. It's like the flesh around the wound is . . . I don't know . . ."

"Yeah?"

"Dissolved."

Davenport made a breathy acknowledgment that wasn't actually a word.

"I don't know what to do about it, or even where to start, really," Ben said. "I figured I'd just give you guys a call, see if you were experiencing the same thing."

"Sorry I can't help you, Ben."

Ben sucked on his lower lip for a second. "You think that mountain lion would attack a kid?"

"Wow. I guess it's possible. If it was provoked or really hungry, I guess. But it seemed more frightened of people than anything else. Why do you ask?"

"I'm probably overthinking things," Ben said. "We got a missing boy out here. I'm just turning over every stone."

"Oh boy. When'd he go missing?"

"Between Friday evening and Saturday morning."

The silence on Davenport's end of the line was telling.

"About what time did those guys shoot the thing on Friday night?"

"It was late," Davenport said, knowing it wasn't the information Ben wanted to hear. "The bar had let out. Two in the morning, or thereabout."

"Do you still have the carcass?"

"Couple guys from Fish and Wildlife picked it up this morning. Were you thinking about opening up its stomach and seeing what's inside?"

"If it had eaten anything . . . suspicious . . . I would think . . ."

"Christ, Ben. I'm thinking of that scene in *Jaws* where they slice that shark open on the pier and that license plate comes out."

"You have the number to those Fish and Wildlife guys?"

"Sure do, but it's back at the office. I'm on my cell now."

"Could you call me back with it when you get the chance?"

"Of course. And I'm sure you're right, that you're just overreacting. This kid will probably pop up anytime now."

"Thanks. You're probably right."

"And hey, Ben?"

"Yeah?"

"I was sorry to hear about your old man. I'd been meaning to call out there after I heard but, well, you know how it is . . ."

"Thanks, Paul. I appreciate it."

"You take care, all right?"

"You, too."

He hung up the phone, feeling no better and no worse.

Later that afternoon, he went into town to pick up some Halloween candy to leave on the front porch for the trick-or-treaters at the end of the week. He would be working Halloween night and knew from experience that a dark house with no candy on the porch suffered the wrath of neighborhood children scorned. Down at Lomax's, he picked up a few bags of the pocket-sized Snickers and Butterfinger bars, some M&M's, and an assorted pack of hard, sugary candies. He'd leave them all out in a big Tupperware bowl on the porch with the porch lights on, bright as day. He had made the mistake of taping a sign to the bowl last year recommending each trick-or-treater take just one candy bar each, but for all the good that did he could have left a sign that said PLEASE TAKE ALL MY CANDY THEN THROW THE BOWL INTO A TREE. He'd learned his lesson on that one.

In his youth, when Stillwater was still a flourishing blue-collar town, the streets would teem with children of all ages on Halloween night. Ben himself had raced up and down those streets, a plastic dime-store mask cinched to his face, an old pillowcase bursting with goodies banging against his shins as he ran. Christ, how things had changed. Nowadays, he was surprised if he came across a dozen kids schlepping their meager satchels of goodies up and down the sun-faded streets. They were sad and derelict in their costumed campaign along the otherwise empty sidewalks. Families had picked up and moved, and the ones who stayed mostly didn't have children of their own. Stillwater had become a barren womb.

In another ten years, Ben thought, counting out his change at the checkout counter of Lomax's, *this town will be nothing but dilapidated shotgun shacks, paranoid hermits, career alcoholics, and weekend hunters. This is what happens when a town folds in on itself.*

If nothing else, the Stillwater Police Department was just a microcosm of the town it served and protected. Just a handful of years ago they had had nine officers, two sergeants, a lieutenant, and a chief. Now, they were left with four officers, a working sergeant (which was Ben), a lieutenant who had recently transferred out east and whose position had yet to be filled, and Chief Lom Harris, who was now—and always seemed to be—out of town on vacation with his wife. True, there was very little in the way of crime in Stillwater to warrant a well-staffed department. Much of the action came in the form of drunken brawls, traffic violations, and the occasional domestic dispute.

He left Lomax's and walked up Hamilton, enjoying the cool autumn air on his face, the crunch of dead leaves beneath his sneakers, and the smell of fireplaces coming from the residential streets just a couple of blocks over. Many of the shop windows were dark and soaped over. The businesses that remained, like random teeth in a diseased mouth, tried their best to appear upbeat and festive, their windows decorated in seasonal attire and jack-o'-lanterns glowing on the front stoops. In the front window of a liquor store, a cardboard decoration depicted a cadre of skeletons in top hats wielding slender black canes, their fleshless arms intertwined in some semblance of camaraderie.

That's us, Ben thought morosely. *That's all that's left of the proud Stillwater PD—a bunch of skeletons marshaling through the streets of a ghost town.*

At the corner of Hamilton and Susquehanna, Ben jaywalked in the direction of Hogarth's Drugstore. The drugstore's windows issued a soft, yellow glow and Ben could see a variety of Halloween costumes—masks and hats and capes—on pedestals behind the glass. He hopped up the curb and entered Hogarth's.

It was a cramped little store that had an old-fashioned soda fountain toward the back. Godfrey Hogarth was back there now, toiling away with something underneath the counter. At eighty-eight, Godfrey Hogarth was one of Stillwater's eldest residents. Despite his age, the man's memory was as sharp as a tack, and he was known to tell stories about Stillwater's heyday—or what passed as Stillwater's heyday—with much fanfare and animation when he was down at Crossroads, enjoying some dandelion wine or Wild Turkey. He'd run the drugstore since Ben had been a kid, though back then it had taken up the whole block and had employed roughly a dozen people.

"Hey, Mr. Hogarth."

"Hello, Ben!" The old man's eyes lit up as he peered at him from over the counter. "Haven't seen you in ages."

"I'm either working or holed up at the farm. You know how it is."

"You want a float?"

The notion struck him as almost comically appealing. "You know what? What the heck, let's do it."

"Fantastic!" The old man opened a freezer chest and took out a small container of vanilla ice cream. He opened it and scooped some into a fountain glass then poured cola over it. The drink fizzed and the ice cream bobbed like a tiny iceberg.

"I came in to ask you about a boy named Matthew Crawly," Ben said as Hogarth slid the ice cream float in front of him. "Do you know him?"

"Sure. He's been coming around some days after school with another boy, looking at the costumes in the window."

"His mother reported him missing Saturday night."

"Oh, no. What happened?"

"We don't know yet. Do you remember the last time you saw him?"

"I certainly do. It was Friday afternoon." He pointed toward the front of the store with one hooked, arthritic finger that reminded Ben of a knotted tree branch. "He stood right outside on the sidewalk with his friend and looked at the costumes and masks in the window."

"Did he come inside?"

"No."

"Did you go out there and talk to him?"

"I would have, but I was on the cash register."

Ben sipped the float through an accordion straw. It was delicious and reminded him of childhood.

"Do you think something bad has come down on the poor kid's head?" Hogarth asked. There was genuine concern in his ancient turtle eyes.

"I don't know much yet," Ben said truthfully.

"That's a shame. He seems like a nice boy." With speed Ben would have thought impossible for the old man, Godfrey Hogarth jerked one finger up beside his face. He had the tired, drooping face of a scarecrow, capped with a wild nest of thick, iron-colored hair. "You know, I may be a crazy old man, but I haven't felt right since that other boy was found down in the Narrows, Ben."

"I know what you mean."

"I've seen a lot of things. I've felt a lot of things, too." Hogarth shook his head, his eyes wise yet distant, like the eyes of an old reptile. "I know when to listen when my heart tells me something."

This sparked something else inside Ben. "In all the time you've lived here, have you ever heard of any animal eating—God, this sounds so stupid—any animal eating the brains out of other animals?"

Hogarth brought his hand back down. His muddy-brown eyes narrowed. "Eating brains, did you say?"

"I know how it sounds." *Like something out of one of Eddie La Pointe's horror magazines,* he thought. "We've had two cases of farmers whose livestock have been killed."

"Since you've mentioned the brains, I'm assuming you mean *only* the brains, correct? Nothing else was eaten?"

"Not that I can tell."

"Well," the old man huffed, "that *is* strange."

"That's not something a mountain lion would do, is it?"

Slowly, Godfrey Hogarth shook his shaggy head. "I couldn't say, Ben. I suppose anything is possible. A mountain lion?"

"Some folks in Garrett shot and killed one Friday night."

"Would get cougars come down from the mountains on occasion," Hogarth said. "You know that as well as anyone, having grown up here in Stillwater, Ben."

Ben nodded. But that didn't help him. He was trying to narrow things down, not broaden them.

"I've heard tell of strange things come down from those mountains in my lifetime, and stranger things pulled from the Narrows," Hogarth went on. "I've seen a few, myself. Mutated toads and tadpoles bristling with more legs than a goddamned centipede, if you pardon an old man his language. Stuff like that. These things happened with more frequency back when the factory was in operation, of course."

"The plastics factory."

"Pollutants in the water, runoff, things like that. Used to be a guy up on Yew Drive claims to have caught a rockfish with a fully working eyeball growing right outta its side. Can you imagine?"

"Do you believe that story?"

"Sure. Why the hell not?"

"I've never seen anything strange down there."

"That's because the factory's been closed long before you were ever born. And mutations like that don't breed and they don't live long, neither. It's God's way of making sure nature corrects whatever man done screwed up." He shrugged, as if the whole conversation was suddenly inconsequential. "Heck, I suppose there's still some freakish things down in the Narrows—and in the mountains beyond—but they's mostly just legend now."

"When I was a kid I actually used to swim in there."

"As did I," Hogarth said. "Maybe that's why I've lived so long." The chuckle that followed was a low, rumbling growl clotted with phlegm. "Of course, back then, the Narrows used to flood much worse than it does now, so maybe all the bad that collected in there got flushed out more regularly. Year I was born, most of what was then downtown Cumberland was destroyed when Wills Creek flooded, and all the runoff came right through Stillwater, tearing down bridges, knocking the walls out of homes, and uprooting trees. A baby went missing in that flood, too. The sorry little thing was just pried from its mamma's arms, was how I heard it told. I remember, when the floodwaters finally receded, there were dead horses and livestock all over the streets. The smell was unbearable. After that, many of the residents moved their farms higher into the mountains.

"It wasn't until the fifties that the Army Corps of Engineers finally came in and assisted the city in putting in a pump system and retaining walls around the creek down by Route 40 to help alleviate the flooding problems. That was what created the Narrows as we know them now. At the time, it was one of the most costly public works projects in American history. The price tag was something like eighteen million dollars, if I remember correctly."

Ben whistled.

"Took ten years to finish the project, too," Hogarth went on. "And while I don't believe Cumberland has ever had a bad flood since, us folks here in the river valley of Stillwater still get dunked occasionally."

"I remember one summer when my dad's entire harvest was washed away," Ben said. "There were three feet of standing water in the south field. And when the water went away, I remember seeing someone's front door lying in the mud. Just some random front door to a house, washed up in our yard. It had a decorative oval of glass in its center, completely whole and unbroken. I remember being amazed at how a flood could cause such destruction—destruction enough to tear a door off a house—yet leave the oval of glass completely intact."

"Crazier things have washed up." Like that poem about Santa Claus, Hogarth pressed one finger to the side of his nose. "Craziest thing I ever found was a Viking helmet—bullet-shaped thing with the horned tusks coming out of the sides."

"No kidding."

"Saw it wedged up in the fork of a tree," Hogarth said. "I must have been about seven or eight at the time, and a hell of a tree climber. I scaled that tree, pulled the helmet down, and took it home to show my old man. I remember him examining it by the firelight in the hearth that evening—we were living in a tar-paper shack out along what is Tillman Road now—and how he turned it over and over in his big hands. He was afraid of it, thought it meant there were soldiers hiding somewhere in the mountains plotting some attack. My father was a descendant of English pig farmers. He hadn't the slightest clue what the hell a Viking was, let alone what sort of headgear they wore."

"What about animals?" Ben asked. "Did any nonindigenous animals ever wash up?"

While the look on the old man's face conveyed a lack of familiarity with the word *nonindigenous*, he understood the context and did not miss a beat in answering Ben's question. "There was a snake once. A big one. And I'm not talking your garden variety mountain snake, Ben. This thing looked like it had come straight out of the Amazon."

"A python?"

"Lord knows what it was. It was pale yellow with these whitish, wavy markings down its back. It had drowned in the flood and washed up at a dirt intersection that eventually became Calvert Street, right where the Farmers' Market used to be. Damn thing was as long as a school bus and, at its widest, thicker than a grown man's upper thigh. Midway along its body was a massive bulge, an indication that it had eaten something before it died."

Ben finished his ice cream float and slid the glass across the counter. Lost completely in the past, Hogarth did not appear to notice.

"Some men came out of the cannery—there used to be a cannery at the far end of Susquehanna, where all those homes are now—and one of them had this long buck knife. We all gathered around in the street and watched as he cut into the belly of the snake and all this greenish-black ooze spilled out. I remember it taking him some time and effort to cut that belly open, and when he finally got it, the gash separated like a purse."

"What was inside?" Ben asked. His voice was close to a whisper.

Hogarth said, "A little girl."

Ben blinked.

"She had been maybe six years old, judging by her size, though it was hard to tell because she had been partially digested. Her features had been melted and worn away by the snake's stomach acids, giving her this faceless, inhuman appearance. I was in my thirties back then, but I still suffered about two weeks' worth of nightmares after seeing that girl's featureless body slide out of the opening in the snake's belly, splayed out there on the muddy road in a pool of bile, blood, and digestive juices."

"Jesus," Ben breathed.

"Yeah. So maybe the Viking helmet wasn't the craziest thing ever washed up around here after all."

"My father never told me stories like that."

"Your dad had stories to beat the band, Ben. I once saw him save the little Winterbarger girl when she was chokin' on a bit of stewed lamb at the county fair."

"I've heard that story," Ben said. "I meant stories about the land, the town itself. I was told never to go up into the mountains by myself and, when I got older and could go out beyond the highway, I was told never to swim in the Narrows alone. But I was never told about . . . well, the way you speak of it, there was a sort of . . . power, I guess, that the land held. I hear you talk about this town, and it's like listening to stories from another planet."

"Every small town has power," Hogarth said. "The people are aware of it in the way we're aware of electricity humming through the walls of our homes or that our water is delivered through a network of pipes underground. We sense it like animals sense a tornado coming. You feel it just as much as I do, Ben. I've just been around long enough to recognize what it is."

He thought about the cold, empty nights in the farmhouse now that his parents were dead and buried. He could not deny the sense of indefinable power that seemed to radiate up through the old, warped floorboards on certain winter nights . . . the power that funneled down the old stone chimney and moaned like a bear from the cave of the hearth . . .

"Lately," Hogarth said, snapping Ben from his reverie, "I've been having trouble sleeping. It started before the last storm and it's just gotten worse. Not insomnia, per se . . . but a certain wakefulness that I feel is partially thrust upon me and partially my inbred responsibility. I feel like a warrior keeping watch in the tower of some medieval castle."

"If that's supposed to make me feel better, it doesn't."

The old man's smile looked pained. "Me either, Ben. Me either."

2

The moment he stepped back out onto the sidewalk, Ben's cell phone trilled. He anticipated that the call was from Paul Davenport over in Garrett County with the number for the Fish and Wildlife folks who had come and collected the carcass of the dead mountain lion, but he was wrong.

"Ben Journell," said a man's voice, vaguely familiar. "It's John Deets over in Cumberland."

"Oh. Hello, John." Deets was the county medical examiner whom Ben had brought in to deal with the drowned boy who'd washed up along Wills Creek almost two weeks ago. He'd forgotten that Deets had been trying to reach him.

"Listen," Deets motored on, talking in his clipped and rushed way, "I'm sorry to bother you on your day off, Ben, but I've been trying to get in touch with you and, well, it's your name I've got listed down here as the case sergeant."

"I heard the boy has been identified," Ben said. "Is that correct?"

"Well, we did happen to hear from a couple whose son went missing a few days before the body was found. They were on a road trip and had stopped at a motel off Route 40. The kid went outside to walk the family dog and never came back. The father went out looking for him and found the dog sniffing around some dumpsters out behind the motel. No trace of the kid."

"Have they identified the body?" Ben asked.

"They were going to." Deets's voice sounded unsteady. Apprehensive.

"John," he said. "What is it? What's wrong?"

"Ben," said Deets. "The boy's body is gone."

3

"What the heck are you doing here?" Eddie said, peering at Ben from around the side of his cubicle. He had one of his horror magazines open in his lap. "It's your day off."

"I'm just grabbing some stuff to take home," Ben said, going immediately to his desk. A stack of slim blue case folders sat at the corner of his desk. He picked them up and hastily thumbed through them.

"What's the emergency?" Eddie asked as he flipped casually through his magazine.

"I just heard from John Deets at the morgue."

"They get an ID on that kid?"

"The kid's gone." Ben set the folders back down on his desk. He met Eddie's eyes from across the Batter's Box.

"What the heck are you talkin' about, gone?"

"They're not sure if the body's just been misplaced or if this is some kind of theft—"

"Who'd steal a body?"

"All I know is *they* don't know where the hell the boy's body is."

"Maybe it's a Halloween prank?"

Ben frowned at the ridiculousness of the statement. It reminded him of what old Ted Minsky had said last night, after they'd come in from examining his slaughtered goats—*I thought it might've been a prank, seein' how close we are to Halloween. But after I seen my goats this evening . . . well . . . I don't know nobody thinks somethin' like that's a prank.*

"Where's the kid's case file?"

Making a face as if he smelled something foul, Eddie sat forward in his chair and scrounged around the top of his own desk. When he found the slender blue folder, he handed it to Ben. "What're you gonna do about it?"

"I'm not sure yet. Just seems awfully coincidental that it's been one thing after another around here for the past two weeks or so, don't you agree?"

Lethargically, Eddie La Pointe nodded. "It's the storms."

"How's that?"

"Storms like we been havin' are bad juju."

"I don't believe in that stuff."

Eddie shrugged, obviously disinterested in Ben's opinion on the matter. "Your whatchamacallit has been chirping its head off in the sally port. I think it's hungry."

He'd forgotten about the bat. "So now it's *my* whatchamacallit? You guys were the ones who wanted to keep it, remember?"

"Hell," Eddie drawled, "not me. Bats, they freak me the hell out."

4

Before leaving for home, Ben stopped off in the sally port with some fresh slices of apple. The bat was upright, clinging to the bars of the birdcage with the fang-like little hooks at the apex of its wings. It sniffed blindly at the air, its tiny pink mouth open.

"You hungry?"

Yet as he approached, he saw a few half-eaten bits of apple still at the bottom of the bat's cage.

"What's the matter?" He spoke in a low, soothing baritone. "Are you getting picky all of a sudden? You want some caviar or something instead?"

He squeezed a fresh wedge of apple through the bars of the birdcage.

"What the hell's going on around here, huh?"

The bat tittered.

CHAPTER EIGHT

1

Just as Ben Journell stood outside Hogarth's Drugstore speaking to the county medical examiner, Brandy Crawly awoke from a fitful sleep. For a moment she remained lying on her back, wondering if her waking hours had somehow become her dreams, while her dreams had somehow become reality. It was Monday, a school day, but she had no intention of going to school; in fact, she had slept through much of the morning.

There was a dull ache at the center of her head. *Matthew is gone.*

She got out of bed and passed by her beveled mirror without pausing, going straight to the bedroom windows. The windows looked out onto the road that ran along the front of the Crawly house, twisting and curling like a ribbon of asphalt until it disappeared over the nearest hill toward town. On the other side of the road, the sloping green fields yawned all the way out to the tree-studded foothills. Within the shadows of the mountains, heavy darkness still pressed low to the ground out beyond the fields, and the hillsides looked mottled with alternating blackness and spangles of red and white sunlight. What leaves were still in the trees blazed with all the colors of an inferno.

Downstairs, her mother dozed on the couch, still propped up in the approximation of a sitting position. The living room windows were partway open and a cool autumnal wind had dropped the temperature. Brandy unfolded an afghan that hung over the back of one of the wingback chairs and spread it over her mother's sleeping body. Wendy Crawly did not even stir. Then Brandy clicked off the television, which was tuned to some ancient black-and-white movie, the volume turned down so low it could have been a silent film.

In the kitchen, she dumped five scoops of Maxwell House into the coffee machine then clicked on the red Power button. The machine hissed and burped. There was still some food left out on the counter from the sandwich her mother had made her the previous night—sliced turkey, crusts of bread, an empty jar of mayonnaise, a wilting head of lettuce. There were some open Tupperware containers and ceramic dishes out along the countertop as well, and she assumed her mother had taken these items out of the refrigerator late the previous night after Brandy had gone to bed.

Brandy opened the window over the sink, hoping some fresh air might combat the aggressive odors of the stale food. There were plastic trash bags in the cupboard beneath the sink; she took one out and flapped it like a matador's cape until it opened. Systematically, she moved down the length of the counter, dumping the Tupperware containers into the trash, whether they were disposable or not. She scraped hunks of pot roast, foul-smelling chicken legs, and congealed, quivering cubes of stew out of the ceramic dishes and into the trash bag. The bag sufficiently weighted down, she hauled it out onto the back porch and, hefting it over the railing, dumped it into one of the Rubbermaid trash bins that were lashed to the porch by bungees. A swarm of flies spiraled up out of the trash bin and dissipated like smoke into the atmosphere.

Matthew's bike still slouched against the garage. It troubled her to look at it, so she decided to stow it away in the garage until Matthew returned. Kicking on her mother's sandals that still sat by the door, she went down into the yard and was making a beeline for the bike when she paused in mid stride. Bats, like little black pods covered in bristly hair and pointy devilish ears, hung from the eaves of the garage. As she stared at them they seemed to vibrate as if alive with electrical current. Some of them opened and closed their wings with mechanical rigidity. There was even one hanging upside down from the clothesline that stretched from the garage to the back porch.

Like most everyone in this part of the country, she was no stranger to the creatures. Customarily, they came out around dusk and zipped through the sky in erratic, confused patterns that could not be confused with those of birds. Once, she had spied a tiny one nesting in the latticework around the raised back porch. It had looked like a leaf until it cranked open its fragile little wings in a manner that reminded Brandy of the hydraulic doors on the school bus.

She had never seen this many before, all in one place. And they were usually gone before the first shimmer of daylight painted the eastern sky.

After standing there in a mixture of fear and deliberation, she decided to forego moving the bike into the garage and went back into the house.

2

Her mother awoke around three in the afternoon, shambling out of the living room and into the kitchen to fill up a mug of coffee that had already gone lukewarm. Brandy was at the kitchen table, one of her school textbooks before her, a partially eaten apple browning beside an untouched glass of milk.

"I don't suppose anyone called?" her mother asked, drinking her coffee while looking out the window over the kitchen sink.

"No."

"What time is it?"

"About three."

"Why'd you let me sleep so late?"

"You looked tired. I didn't want to bother you."

Her mother said nothing.

"Do you . . ." Brandy faltered. "Mom?"

"Hmmm?"

"Do you think we should call Dad?"

Just by staring at the matted hair at the back of her mother's head, Brandy could tell that a wave of emotions coursed through her. The hand holding the coffee cup shook.

"He might want to know, is all," she added quietly, turning back to her textbook. True, her father might want to know that the son he'd left behind had now similarly disappeared . . . but that wasn't the only reason for Brandy's suggestion. Her reasons were deeper than that, but they were so pitiful that she did not want to even acknowledge them herself. Before he'd left, Hugh Crawly had been the family protector, the strength and the decision-maker. To the extent of Brandy's knowledge, he had never been broken or weakened or brought to his knees a single day in his life. To have him back home now would be—

Stop it, she chastised herself, feeling a hot flush spread across her face. *He walked out on all of us two years ago. Remember what it did to everyone? Remember how it felt?* Brandy Crawly remembered. She hated feeling a childish need for him now.

Her mother dumped the rest of her coffee into the sink then went out onto the back porch. A minute later, Brandy heard her sobbing. She contemplated going to her and attempting to comfort her, but the simple prospect of doing so seemed to weaken her spirit. Instead, she went up to her bedroom and switched on the stereo. From one window she could see Dwight Dandridge seated on the curb across the street. He had something tucked under one arm and was looking at something else on the pavement between his sneakers.

Unable to help it, she thought about the boy who had washed up along the shores of Wills Creek two weeks ago. When news of the boy's discovery had hit the town, Brandy had simply assumed that the boy, who had not been identified as a resident of Stillwater or any neighboring towns, had been careless, fallen into the swollen waters of the Narrows, and drowned. Now, she was not so sure. What if his death were the work of something more sinister? What if something had attacked and killed that boy? She found she could not recall if the newspapers had spoken of a cause of death. Rumors were that he had been hairless and pale and naked, but had there also been . . . injuries?

Feeling sweaty and unclean, she showered quickly, changed her clothes, and went out the front door without saying a word to her mother. Across the street, Dwight was still perched on the curb looking at whatever it was on the ground between his feet.

He looked up at Brandy just as her shadow fell across him. "Hey," he said. The thing between his feet was a tiny turtle.

"What are you doing?"

Dwight shrugged and looked back down at the turtle. "Just hanging around, I guess."

She sat down beside him on the curb.

"Is that your turtle?"

"Nah," said the boy. "It was just here. I ain't messin' with him. Just watching where he goes."

She glanced at the thing tucked beneath Dwight's arm. It was a plastic bag, though she could not make out its contents. "What's in there?"

Dwight pulled the bag between his knees and opened it. He took out a rubber vampire mask from which the price tag still hung and seemed to appraise it longingly. Something about the boy's sullenness resonated with Brandy.

"Picked it up for him this morning, before school," Dwight said. "You know, before anyone else could grab it. Figure I'll hold on to it until he comes home."

The back of Brandy's throat tightened.

Dwight looked at her. His eyes were moist. "A cop came to our house the other night and asked me questions."

"Yeah?"

"I didn't know what to tell him."

She could tell he was frightened. "They just want to find Matthew. You're not in any trouble."

"I know that. I just didn't know anything that could help them find him."

"It's okay," she told him.

"And I don't want to get Matthew in trouble."

"In trouble for what?" She leaned closer to him.

Dwight stuffed the mask back into the bag then set the bag down on the curb. Between his feet, the turtle trudged lethargically across the pavement. There were incongruous yellow racing strips along the sides of its neck.

"In trouble for what, Dwight?" she repeated.

"I know he's not supposed to go out to Route 40 and down to the Narrows," Dwight began before tapering off.

"Do you know something you didn't tell the police? It's okay if you do. You can tell me. Matthew won't get in trouble. And I won't tell anyone you told me."

Dwight sawed an index finger back and forth beneath his nose. "Well, I was thinking . . . I mean, I don't know for sure, but maybe he . . . maybe he went out to that old factory. You know the place I'm talking about?"

For a second, no, she didn't know what Dwight was talking about. But then an image surfaced in her mind—the squat, stone building on the other side of the Narrows, abandoned and condemned since the fifties, or so she understood. She knew that many residents of Stillwater had once made their living working at the plastics factory before it closed down all those decades ago. According to her father, the closing of that plant had been the precursor to the death of Stillwater. After the plastics factory closed down, many people left town to find new jobs, leaving houses vacant and dark. Soon after, the shops along the main thoroughfares dried up. Ironically, having once been the lifeblood of the rural Maryland hamlet, the plastics factory had also facilitated its ultimate demise.

But why would Matthew go out to the old plastics factory? She asked Dwight as much.

"Promise you won't tell and get him in trouble," Dwight said flatly.

"I promise."

"No," Dwight said. "You have to swear."

"I swear."

"Now spit on the ground."

"What?"

"You have to do it or else it doesn't count." The boy was dead serious.

"Okay, okay." She spat on the pavement. "See? I swear."

Dwight stared at the speckle of spit and nodded. This seemed to suffice. "The last time I saw him—the last day we hung out—we went down to the Narrows across from that old factory," he said. "I wanted to see the dead deer Billy Leary said was down there—and it was, Brandy, we saw it—and I swear I made Matthew go. He didn't want to go."

Vaguely, Brandy recalled her mother chastising Matthew about going down there Friday evening while at the dinner table. If she recalled correctly, someone had seen Matthew and Dwight down there while driving along Route 40. She couldn't remember all the details now, however.

"When we were there, Matthew thought he saw someone up by the factory." He paused, contemplating his choice of words. Eventually, he said, "He thought he saw your dad, Brandy. He thought . . . he said he saw him hiding in the trees up by the old factory."

Brandy simply stared at Dwight, not quite sure what to make of this new information. In fact, she wasn't immediately sure she had heard him correctly.

"You said . . . my dad?"

Dwight nodded. "We went up to the factory and looked around but there wasn't nobody there. We looked in the windows, too, but they were really old and dirty and you couldn't see anything inside." Again, his face twisted in contemplation. Quite possibly the memory troubled him, seeing how it was the last time he had been with his best friend. "At least, *I* couldn't see anything. But I hoisted Matthew up and I think Matthew saw something. He didn't say it, not exactly, but I think he did. He wanted to go inside."

"Inside the factory?"

"Yeah. Like, he wanted to go inside really bad."

"Did he go inside?"

"No. But he would have." Dwight hitched his meaty shoulders. "I guess I got scared. It's a creepy place and, anyway, it was getting late. And it just . . . well . . . I mean, I don't know how to say it . . ."

"Just say it," she told him.

"Well," he said, "it's just that Matthew . . . see, he's never really up for doing anything where we might get in trouble or where things might get . . . I don't know . . . dangerous or scary or anything." He grunted the approximation of a laugh, which summoned a timid smile to Brandy's face. "He's a bit of a sissy, is what I mean."

Brandy nodded, still smiling. "Yeah. He really is."

"So I thought it was strange that he wanted to go inside so badly. It wasn't like him. It scared me a little."

"So what happened?"

"He said he would go in without me if I didn't come along. But somehow, I managed to talk him into going home, so we left."

"And you didn't tell this to the police?"

Dwight hung his head and seemed intent on examining the turtle's slow progress. He didn't answer her.

She put a hand on the boy's sweaty back. His entire body seemed to radiate a tremendous amount of heat.

"I get it," she said quietly. "You didn't want to get him in trouble. It's cool. You're a good friend."

"You won't tell on him, will you?"

"No." Sweat dampened her own brow. "You think he went back out to the factory alone?"

"Maybe."

"Wouldn't he take his bike?"

"Maybe, maybe not. You can't ride your bike across the field and down to the Narrows. It's too tough and rocky and, anyway, there's all this garbage lying around that the flood left behind. It's easier to just walk."

"Wouldn't he have asked you to go with him?"

When Dwight looked at her again, she could see that his eyes were threatening tears and that he was doing his damnedest to fight them off. He was a boy who refused to cry in front of some girl.

"I don't know," he said, his voice cracking. "I wouldn't have gone, anyway. Maybe he knew it. I would have talked him out of it."

She shook her head. "Why would he want to go back there so badly?"

"I don't know. He saw something. He saw his dad, Brandy." After a time, he could only repeat himself. "He saw his dad."

3

Under the influence of Valium, her mother fell asleep on the couch again by five o'clock that evening. Careful not to wake her, Brandy took the truck keys from the pegboard by the back door and went out into the yard. Darkness had fallen prematurely, the sun eclipsed by the mountains, and the yard was alive with the sound of restless crickets. As she went to the truck, she gave the garage a wide berth; the bats still hung from the eaves, swaying gently in the wind like fruit dangling from tree branches.

Since she had turned sixteen and gotten her license, Brandy had driven the truck less than a half-dozen times, her mother barking instructions at her from the passenger seat. Only once had she driven by herself, and that had just been down to Lomax's for groceries. Now, she winced as she cranked the key in the ignition. The pickup's engine roared loudly. She realized she was already standing on the accelerator. Switching her foot to the brake, she dropped the truck into Drive. The truck jerked back and forth, alerting Brandy to put on her seat belt. She expected her mother to come storming out onto the back porch at any second, but that never happened. The poor woman was inside, dead to the world.

The steering wheel turned stubbornly. It was an old truck and didn't have power steering, so unless she was already in motion, turning the steering wheel was like cranking open the hatch on a submarine. Nevertheless, she managed to turn the wheel and simultaneously ease off the brake. The truck bounded forward, crunching over stones and fallen branches. She drove around to the front of the house and made a sharp right when she hit the road. Gunning the accelerator, she headed in the opposite direction of town.

When she hit Route 40, the damage caused by the recent rash of storms was readily apparent. There were downed trees and muddy corrugations in the earth. As the highway curved around the mountain, she could see the silvery slip of the Narrows below. The water was high and ran with the potency of white-water rapids.

Spinning the wheel with more ease now, she took a gravel access road off Route 40 that eventually became Highland Street. In the truck's rearview mirror the mountains appeared to surreptitiously rearrange themselves. Brandy suddenly felt very cold.

The land grew darker as she left the highway behind. She fumbled one hand along the dashboard until she located the knob for the headlights. Dull light cleaved through the gloom ahead of her. Skeletal trees shuttled by. When the road graduated toward an incline she pressed down harder on the accelerator. She crested a hill then sped quickly down the other side, loose change vibrating in the cup holder between the seats, and she leaned forward over the steering wheel to see ahead of the headlights into the darkness. Though she wasn't too familiar with this stretch of road, she knew the Highland Street Bridge was likely to appear directly before her at any moment—

Yet only blackness rushed toward the dashboard.

Then the blackness *moved* and she realized she was heading straight toward the swirling water of Wills Creek.

Shrieking, she spun the wheel and slammed on the brakes. The pickup fishtailed and the reek of burning motor oil stung her nose. Loose change peppered the dashboard like buckshot. A second later, the truck jerked to a stop, the chassis rocking on its undercarriage. Clouds of road dust and bluish exhaust engulfed the vehicle as bits of gravel rained down against the windshield.

For several seconds, she sat straight as a ramrod, unable to move. Both her hands clenched the steering wheel. As the dust cleared outside, she could see the truck's headlights carving through the gloom to the other side of the creek. Just a few scant yards from the front of the truck, the Narrows roared below.

The bridge was gone. She recalled hearing on the news that the previous flood had weakened the shoreline and sent the pylons crumbling into the water below. The bridge itself was either on the floor of the Narrows or had been carried out to the Potomac.

Her heart still overexerting, she climbed out of the truck and crept to the muddy ridge of the Narrows and peered down. The water looked like liquid mercury and about as cold and inhospitable as the moons of Jupiter. A sickening feeling overtook her as she imagined her little brother losing his footing and sliding down into the rapids below.

Matthew would have taken the footbridge to get to the old factory on the other side of the Narrows, she rationalized with herself. *The bridge was only for automobiles.*

But could she be so sure?

Still trembling, she climbed back inside the truck, turned around, and went home.

CHAPTER NINE

1

Up until about a week ago, Maggie Quedentock would have had a difficult time identifying the worst thing she had ever done. She had been promiscuous and slept with married men prior to her own marriage to Evan. She had shoplifted small items from Lomax's as well as some of the big department stores in Cumberland on occasion when she thought she could get away with it. She had even walked out on her tab at Crossroads a few times when the bartender and owner, Alvin Toops, had been too drunk or preoccupied to notice. And now, of course, there was the issue of infidelity with Tom Schuler. *What is the worst thing you have ever done, Maggie?* It wouldn't have occurred to her to acknowledge the abortion she'd had when she was seventeen.

In fairness, she hadn't thought about it in many years. Also in fairness, a different type of person might not have termed it a horrible act. However, having been brought up in a strict Catholic household, such things as abortions (or even premarital sex, for that matter) were unacceptable.

Her father, Aaron Kilpatrick, had been a brutish factory worker who had believed that anything shy of corporal punishment—for both his daughter *and* his wife—was tantamount to shirking his domestic responsibilities. By the time Maggie was in high school,

Aaron Kilpatrick had already fractured her jaw, broken the pinky finger of her left hand, and tattooed a pattern of black-and-blue bruises along her buttocks and upper thighs on so many occasions she had lost count. The man had done similar things to his wife, Katrina, a timid and soulless woman who always seemed to suffer the abuse with the acceptance of the biblically damned. Maggie grew to hate her father because of his behavior, but she grew to categorically *loathe* her mother because of her helplessness, her weakness. When compulsion struck—and when her father wasn't home to mitigate such things—she felt perfectly justified raising a hand to Katrina herself, cracking the woman across the face for piddling bullshit reasons . . . or sometimes for no reason at all.

When she was twelve years old, she found herself in a car with Barry Mallick, a seventeen-year-old high school dropout who smoked dope and carried a switchblade everywhere he went. At twelve, she was too young to be attracted to Barry's delinquency—arguably, she was too young to comprehend the intricacies of genuine attraction at all—but she *did* achieve a certain sense of acceptance from him that made her feel good. In the backseat of his car, she had willingly taken her pants off for him. And while she did not believe it had been Barry's intention to cause her physical pain, he did not seem all that bothered by the fact that he did.

She pretty much lost part of herself after Barry. In high school, sex was the only sword she wielded. It was a sliver of power to the otherwise powerless. Often, she would allow these boys—these clumsy, smelly, greasy, bad-tasting boys—to do what they wanted with her, and she would willingly oblige their requests, too. Most times, they did not even have to ask—she found it thrilling to be the aggressor. Sometimes, in the middle of doing these things, she imagined that whatever smelly, greasy, bad-tasting boy was having her was in fact her father. It had nothing to do with physical attraction or even with sex. It had simply to do with something *she* had that *he* did not. Something he would want, as all boys and men wanted it. Her power over the man who otherwise held her powerless . . .

At seventeen, when she learned she was pregnant, she went to a boy named Lyle Pafferny and told him the baby was his. (What she didn't tell him was that, at the time, he had a one-in-three chance of being the baby's father.) Lyle cried. He was about to graduate high school and he wanted to move to Miami to work on boats with his older brother. A baby would crush that dream, he told her, and yes, she agreed that it would. But he was off the hook, she said, because she didn't want to keep the baby. She was willing to go to a clinic in Garrett County and have an abortion. She just needed the money for the procedure and someone to take her there to get it done.

So Lyle Pafferny came up with the money and borrowed his old man's Toyota pickup to drive her to the clinic in Garrett. She'd spent the next three days at home in bed. Her father was easily convinced that she had a terrible fever and was gravely ill. Her mother never said a word, though a part of Maggie Kilpatrick thought the woman knew something suspicious was going on.

And that had been that. She'd never thought about the abortion again.

Until now.

"What are you doing?" Evan said. He leaned in the doorway of the living room, eating macaroni and cheese out of a microwavable container.

Maggie turned away from the window. She was sitting on the couch, an unread book beside her. Outside, the floodlights illuminated the backyard. "I was reading," she lied.

"Yeah?"

"I mean, I *was*. I thought I heard something outside." This part wasn't a lie.

"Yeah?" It was as if he knew no other words. Cocking one eyebrow, Evan sauntered into the living room and peered casually out one of the windows. "I don't see nothing." His mouth was full of food.

Maggie pulled the book into her lap. "Was probably just a coyote."

"Nothin' there now."

He backed away from the window, chewing loudly. Maggie knew that something was wrong with him. He had been more subdued than usual, even friendly with her. When she had forgotten to make dinner he had said nothing; he'd nuked some food and had even offered her some, which she had politely declined. Not to mention that today was his day off, which he usually spent down at Crossroads, but for whatever reason he had opted to stick around the house with her. He was like a dark and lingering shadow haunting the periphery of her vision at every turn.

She turned a page and hoped he didn't notice the way her hand trembled. At her back, she could feel the encroaching darkness pressing against the windows, against her shoulders and the nape of her neck. Even with the yard's floodlights on, the darkness could creep into the house and get her, like living smoke.

That's because you can't escape from the things you've done, said the head-voice. She winced as it echoed through her skull. *The things you've done will always come back home to you.*

At different times in her life, she'd heard the head-voice. It usually came to her in moments of stress or self-doubt, and it *always* came to her in moments of self-loathing. It had been there chattering away in her head—albeit less pronounced than it was now—as she prepared to meet Tom Schuler at Crossroads. It had been even louder after she had made love to him. And then later that night, out on Full Hill Road . . .

She had always assumed that the head-voice had belonged, in some way, to her father. Aaron Kilpatrick had found a way to haunt her from the grave, to always be with her and tell her what a pathetic loser she was, and how she would never have a good life because she was not a good person. *You are not a good person, Margaret.* The sound was like a ringing in her ears.

But she had been wrong; the head-voice was not some clinging filament of her dead father.

It was the baby. The baby she had so recklessly dismissed in her jaded youth.

And now, somehow, the head-voice had finally manifested itself in tangible form—in *life.* The child she had hit with her car out on Full Hill Road was *her* child. After all these years, after all the horrible things she had done, it had finally come back for her . . .

It had come back.

Evan grabbed the remote off the coffee table and turned the TV on. Grunting, he dropped into the armchair and flipped absently through the channels, his half-eaten bowl of macaroni and cheese balanced on one knee. Maggie hardly registered him; she was still worried about the encroaching darkness and the child that was out there waiting for her, probably standing out there just beyond the reach of the floodlights. It had gotten Tom Schuler—she had seen Tom standing beside the smallish figure that night by the willow tree, though not clearly and without definition. And then . . . when it had come up to one of the windows, its pale and hairless head gleaming like a skull in the moonlight . . .

I'm home, Mom.

Her moan must have been audible because Evan glanced over and met her eyes. The look on his face was not one of confusion or concern. Maggie thought her husband looked like he knew something was going on with her. Almost as if he knew *specifically* what was going on.

Without saying a word to her, he turned back to the TV. Some old John Wayne movie was on AMC.

Maggie closed the book. "I'm going to take a shower."

Evan said nothing.

"I can make you something else to eat when I get out," she added.

"This is fine," he said, picking up the bowl of macaroni and cheese. "This is dandy."

He's making fun of me. He doesn't talk that way. He knows something is up.

Still trembling, she made her way down the hallway and into the bathroom off the master bedroom before hot and silent tears spilled down her face. She did not turn on any lights. Instead, she went to the small bathroom window and peered through the slatted blinds into the yard. In the dirt turnabout, the VW and Pontiac sat side by side. Shapes capered in the darkness beyond the reach of the floodlights. The longer she stared at the darkness, the more shapes seemed to taunt and tease her.

I'm out here, Mom, but I'll be home soon. I'll be inside soon. I've come back. Just wait till you see where I've been all these years when you thought I was dead, when you thought I was nonexistent. Just wait till you see what I look like . . .

While she stared out the window, the floodlights went off. At the far end of the house, she could hear Evan moving around, mumbling to himself.

She turned on the shower and waited for the water to turn warm while she undressed. She kept the lights off, for she did not want to allow anything outside to see in through the blinds or even know what room of the house she was in. Her body felt alien, her skin pimpled with goose bumps that felt like braille. Her nipples pained her, engorged and hard for some reason. Her feet felt numb.

In the dark, it was like showering in a coffin. She smelled the mildew between the tiles and felt the needling of the water. When the water turned cool, she wondered how long she had been standing beneath it. She hadn't even washed—just stood there, weeping silently to herself, terrified.

It was after ten when she got out, toweled off, and dressed in sweatpants and a Crossroads tank top. The house was eerily silent. She went into the living room to find it empty. The kitchen was also empty, as was Evan's work area in the basement. Back upstairs, she flipped on the floodlights and found the VW Beetle gone. Evan had left.

He knows. Somehow, he knows.

She turned the floodlights back off then went into the kitchen. From the cabinet over the refrigerator, she pulled down a bottle of red table wine. With trembling hands, she uncorked it and filled a wineglass. Dead leaves, curled like clamshells, blew against the window over the sink.

Maggie felt her heart seize at the sight of eyes watching her from the darkness on the other side of the window. Taking two steps back, she reached out one shaky hand and flipped off the kitchen lights. Darkness swallowed her like an abyss. The square pane of glass over the sink radiated with a deep blue moonlight and, in the distance, she could make out the pinpoints of streetlamps lining the road.

No longer able to reflect the light coming through the kitchen window, the eyes vanished. Maggie rushed to the sink and nearly pressed her nose to the glass. At first she could see nothing in the blackness . . . but then she could see a small, fluid form moving across the top of the wooden fence. Maggie held her breath as the thing glanced back up at her, apparently able to see her just as clearly in the dark.

It was the Morelands' cat.

Maggie released a shuddery breath. She was aware of wetness on her hands and arms and the front of her tank top felt damp. She turned the kitchen lights back on to find that, in her momentary panic, she had spilled her wine. The wineglass lay on its side on the kitchen counter and there was a blood-colored puddle on the floor. Tearing a length of paper towel from the dispenser on the wall, she hastily mopped up the mess then stuffed the wine-soaked wad of towel into the kitchen trash. She forced herself to laugh at least once to prove that she once again had things under control, but it came out as a sharp, disharmonious cackle.

She filled the wineglass again then carried it into the living room while pulling her hair back with one hand. She could put a CD in the CD player, something melodious and soothing, and try to wade through her book while drinking her wine, not worrying about what Evan might or might not know, not worrying about what might or might not be out—

A slight, pale figure stood in one of the living room windows. As Maggie's eyes fell upon it, the thing receded into the darkness, the way something will gradually vanish as it descends into a murky pond.

A prickling heat caused the skin to rise on her arms. Again, she felt her nipples tighten painfully into knots. For what seemed like an eternity, she remained motionless. It wasn't until she saw—or thought she saw—the milky, ghostlike form cross behind the crescent of glass in the back door that she regained control of her body. She dropped the wineglass and ran to the door, double-checking that it was bolted. It was. Peering out, she could see nothing.

A cry that sounded pathetically like steam whistling from a tea kettle issued from her throat. She went to the wall, slammed her palm against the switch that activated the floodlights, and shoved it up with the heel of her left hand.

The face of a cadaver stared at her from the nearest window. It was human, though just barely—its scalp was a hairless dome of flesh, its brow disarmingly smooth above colorless eyes as swollen as jellyfish. The thing's mouth hung open, and Maggie caught a glimpse of rigid black gums and square, blunt teeth.

I'm home.

Maggie screamed and flipped the floodlights back off.

A colorless hand slammed against the windowpane, hard enough to vibrate the glass.

Her first instinct was to curl into a ball and weep. Instead, she followed her second instinct, which was to run down into the basement and grab the shotgun off the wall. She tripped at the bottom of the stairs and crashed into the basement wall, a sharp, hot pain bursting to life in her right ankle. Using the wall for support, she managed to stand and swing one arm blindly before her in the dark, searching for the chain that turned on the basement light.

You took care of me all those years ago, said the head-voice, *but now I'm back, Mom, to take care of you.*

"No," she breathed, shuddering. Her fingers grazed the chain and she closed a fist around it, tugging the light on.

The shotgun no longer hung from the wall. Frantically, she looked around. It was nowhere. She'd put it back here, hadn't she? Where the hell could it have gone?

She thought she heard floorboards creak above her head.

"No!" she screamed back. "No! Go away! *Please!*" But the "please" came out as a shrill whine, not even a word.

In the face of self-preservation, she reverted to her initial instinct and backed into a corner, crouching down and pulling her knees up to her chest. If it came down here, she'd be trapped. There was nowhere to go, no way to get out.

Suddenly, in her mind's eye, she was seventeen again and trundling along in a Toyota pickup that belonged to Lyle Pafferny's father. Steve Miller was on the radio and there was a look of seasickness on Lyle's face. They hadn't said more than a handful of words to each other on the drive into Garrett and they'd said absolutely nothing on the drive back.

Maggie blinked tears down her cheeks and shuddered at the memory.

2

A sharp pain raced up her neck as she jerked awake. Somehow, amazingly, she had fallen asleep.

Something had woken her up . . .

"Evan?" Her voice sounded like the lone wail of a loon reverberating off the basement's cinder block walls. She waited. No response came.

After several more minutes passed with the lethargy of a steamship on the horizon, Maggie was able to coax herself to her feet. Her entire body was stiff. There were little red welts on her forearms and the tops of her feet that she immediately identified as bug bites.

It seemed to take an eternity to climb the basement steps. Upstairs, the house was as silent as a crypt. Listening, she could hear the hum of the refrigerator and the ticking of the hallway clock. Nothing more. When she crossed through the kitchen and into the living room she spied her broken wineglass on the floor. Shards of glass sparkled like jewels and wine spread from the epicenter like a bloodstain. Beyond the windows the night was still dark, though there was a predawn shimmer of pink light in the fork between the two mountains.

Somewhere inside the house, Maggie's cell phone rang. She cried out at the sound and felt her heart threaten to push up into her throat. When it rang a second time, she became aware that this had been the sound that had woken her up in the basement just moments earlier.

Having forgotten where she'd put her phone, she wandered quickly through the house, following the digital chirping until she located it on the nightstand on her side of the bed. She snatched it up mid-ring, her blood running cold as she read the name displayed on the screen: *Schuler, Tom*.

She let the phone clatter to the floor. Though it could have been a coincidence, the ringing stopped. She had the desire to kick it under the bed and forget about it. Or take the battery out first.

She didn't realize she had backed up against the bedroom wall until the phone rang again, startling her into striking her head on a picture frame. From where she stood, she could see the phone's display with horrific clarity: *Schuler, Tom*.

Shimmering in digital light like an accusation.

Too easily she could imagine the phone ringing and ringing forever until it drove her insane.

Grab it, pop the battery out, she thought. *And if that doesn't silence it, flush the fucker down the toilet.*

The phone was already in her hands before she'd even finished the thought. Yet instead of prying out the little rectangular battery, she hit the button and accepted the call. It was like someone else was controlling her now.

With an arm that felt like it was made of rubber, she brought the phone to her ear.

"Come out back," Tom said. It was his voice . . . but, at the same time, it had changed. Something had turned Tom into something else. *My child,* she thought frantically. *My child did that to him.*

The sound she made into the phone approximated a bullfrog's croak.

"Maggie," Tom said firmly. It was then that she knew it wasn't Tom at all. Somehow, it was Evan, her husband. "Did you hear me? Come out back. Now."

Trembling, she hit the End button. Just moments ago she hadn't wanted to touch the phone at all; now, walking back down the hall to the living room, she found she could not let go of it, as though it had been fused to her flesh. On the living room wall, she toggled the switch for the floodlights but they did not come on. Either the power had been cut or the bulbs had been removed.

When she reached the back door, her hand paused in midair on the way to unlock the dead bolt. Things were happening too fast; she didn't have time to think things through clearly enough. How did Evan get Tom Schuler's cell phone? None of it made sense.

Dreaming, she thought, undoing the dead bolt. *I'm dreaming.*

She opened the door.

3

In the wine-colored light of dawn, Evan sat on the sloping hood of the Volkswagen. The shotgun lay across his lap and he had one boot on the front bumper. His eyes locked on Maggie, who remained standing in the doorway. Seeing him there, coupled with the sheer impossibility of Evan having called her from Tom Schuler's cell phone number in the first place, Maggie's hold on reality slipped yet another notch. Absently, she wondered when exactly reality had ended and the nightmare had begun. Had she actually had the affair? Was she still a little girl under the oppressive rule of an abusive father?

"Come 'ere," Evan called to her. His voice boomed.

Maggie didn't move.

Evan held up something small in one hand. He kept his other hand around the maple stock of the shotgun. "Recognize this?" he asked her. "Your boyfriend's cell phone." He looked at it himself now. "Saw the call log. Read the texts." Then he fell uncomfortably silent.

Maggie tried to speak but found her voice absent and her throat impossibly dry.

"Just answer me one thing," Evan spoke up eventually. There was a pathetic crack in his voice this time that jabbed a barb into Maggie's heart. Mostly masked in shadows, she couldn't make out the expression on his face. "How long has it been going on?"

She thought she spoke. Her face burned.

"Answer me!" he shouted. "How long?"

"It was just once," she said.

"What?"

She realized she'd just muttered the words, and that they'd come out in a jumble of nonsense. "Just one time, Evan," she repeated, more loudly and clearly this time. "I swear it."

Evan stood the shotgun up, the butt planted firmly on one of his thighs. He looked like the photograph of a prideful hunter slouching over a kill. Looking at him turned Maggie's blood to ice.

"Went by his house earlier," Evan said. "Son of a bitch wasn't home. I waited for a while but he never came. Lucky motherfucker."

"Evan, please—"

"Shut *up!*" It came out as a partial sob, as if something vital had just broken deep down in his throat. "You just shut the fuck *up,* you *whore!*"

She took an instinctive step back into the house.

Her husband leveled the shotgun at her. "Don't you move."

She froze.

"I bust my ass at that fuckin' factory while you sit home, and what do I get for all my trouble? A cheatin' goddamn whore of a wife and a friend who sticks a knife in my back. A so-called *friend* who sticks it wherever he wants."

She wanted to tell him he'd misunderstood the situation. She wanted to tell him that it wasn't how he thought it was and that there was nothing—no feelings at all—between her and Tom Schuler.

Tom Schuler is dead, said the head-voice. *Tom Schuler is—*

A slight shape materialized out of the darkness behind Evan. Maggie's heart seized. The shape shuffled its small feet through the dirt, its body pale and exposed and seeming to glow in the moonlight that still spilled over the peaks of the mountain that bordered Stillwater to the west. Maggie shook and found herself powerless to move. Evan caught her gaze and spun quickly around, the barrel of the shotgun swiveling away from her and over to the frail shape shambling out of the shadows. Even from such a distance, Maggie could hear the shotgun begin to quake in her husband's unsteady hands. Then he lowered the shotgun and muttered, "What the hell is this?"

It was the boy. His pale skin bluish in the cool predawn, his knobby little knees practically buckling beneath him, he managed yet another step closer to Evan. He wore no clothes, and his abdomen and hips appeared to be dappled with something that could have been—

(blood)

—dried mud. His eyes wandered, like great roving searchlights, beneath a perfectly smooth, white brow. The boy's scalp was not completely hairless—strands of tawny gossamer sprang out in sparse patches. He was a boy, but not wholly . . . more like the skin left behind after a reptile molts.

"Who're you?" Evan barked at the boy. "What are you doing here?" And then he actually laughed, possibly at the child's nudity and overall awkwardness.

The boy took another awkward step closer to Evan. Maggie watched, unable to move, unable to scream.

"You hurt?" Evan asked.

The boy staggered right up to the side of the Volkswagen and gazed up at Evan. When he turned his thin little body just the slightest bit, Maggie could make out a quartet of what looked to be tiny puncture wounds moving vertically down the center of the boy's back.

Evan extended one leg and thumped the boy's chest with his boot heel. The boy rocked unsteadily but his large, black eyes never left Evan.

"Hey," Evan said to the boy. "I'm talking to you."

Maggie saw it begin in the boy's pale and narrow chest—a gathering of essence, followed by a fullness, a welling, in the breast. Something akin to a bubble of air seemed to rise up through the boy's chest where it fattened the stovepipe of his thin, white neck, bulging it out like the throat of a bullfrog. The boy's lips formed a perfect *O* just as his large eyes rolled back into his head like those of a great white shark preparing to strike. The boy's cheeks quivered as—

(oh god something is going to come out something is about to burst right out of that)

—Evan scooted backward on the hood of the Volkswagen.

"Hey," Evan said. His voice quavered then broke like glass in the night.

A gout of greenish fluid burst from the boy's mouth. It arced through the air like a party streamer toward Evan's face. Evan bucked his hips and jerked his head back but he wasn't quick enough—the liquid pattered across the upper portion of his face.

Evan cursed and backed up till his spine struck the Volkswagen's windshield. His boots scrambled blindly for purchase on the sloping hood of the car while he pawed frantically at his eyes with one hand. The shotgun's muzzle waved like a white flag back and forth, back and forth. The boy leaned against the hood of the car just as his small and inadequate chest swelled once more. His neck fattened, engorged with the greenish, snot-like substance, and his head tipped back slightly on its thin stalk of a neck.

A second ribbon squirted from the boy's mouth, splashing against the side of Evan's face while droplets pattered down into Evan's lap and along the hood of the car. Again, Evan cried out . . . and now Maggie thought she could see steam or smoke rising from the snot-like sludge stuck to her husband's face. Evan screamed and rolled off the hood of the car and, a second later, Maggie also screamed as the shotgun exploded and fire belched from the muzzle. In the sudden flare of firelight, the boy's profile flashed into quick relief—his pale, almost hairless body and indistinct features reminiscent of the blind creatures that live deep underground or on the floor of the deepest oceans.

Again, Maggie saw the barrel of the shotgun wave back and forth in the air. One of Evan's boots kicked out from behind the car.

"Evan!" she screamed, suddenly finding her voice.

Evan sprang up from behind the other side of the car, his face a mask of steaming, disintegrating tissue. Somehow he managed a strangled noise that sounded as if he were trying to mimic birdcalls; the sound still hung in the air as a section of his skull slid away in a bloody mudslide, taking the gelatinous white orb of one eyeball with it.

Evan threw himself over the hood of the car. Scrambling like a cat looking for purchase, he bucked and kicked and groped blindly at the windshield wipers. His fingernails sounded like creaking hinges as they scraped down the hull of the Volkswagen's hood. Bits of Evan's face puddled in the windshield-wiper well.

That was when Maggie ran back into the house.

She slammed the door then spun the dead bolt. Peering through the crescent of glass in the door, she was horrified to find her husband's body on the ground now, having been dragged off the car by the pale-skinned boy. Evan had stopped struggling and now lay like a sack of wet grain in the dirt beside the car.

As she watched, the boy walked around the side of the car and crouched down beside the mutilated bulb of Evan's skull. Just before Maggie Quedentock passed out, she saw the boy dig around inside her husband's skull and bring a wet and bloodied tendril of gray matter to his mouth.

PART TWO

SUNDOWN

“How sweet it was to see the clouds race by,
and the brief gleams of the moonlight
between the scudding clouds . . .”

—Bram Stoker, *Dracula*

CHAPTER TEN

1

For the first time in years, Ben Journell showed up late for his shift at the station. He'd spent much of the previous night combing through the case file for the unidentified boy. There were the photos he and Eddie had taken at the scene; there were Deets's photos as well, taken after the ME had arrived on the scene to officially pronounce the death; there was their official report; the coroner's report, notification letters, and other official documentation. He had hoped that by going through it again he might be able to uncover some previously elusive bit of information that might open some secret door for him. And was there a connection between what had happened to this boy and Matthew Crawly's disappearance? He was becoming increasingly worried about the Crawly boy. It was now Tuesday and there was no further news.

"Hey," Mel Haggis said as they nearly bumped each other's shoulders in the doorway of the Batter's Box. "You feeling okay?"

"Yeah, why?"

"Looks like you didn't get no sleep last night."

"I didn't." Ben went over to his desk where he dumped the case file on the unidentified boy. "Anything exciting going on?" He could hear the dullness in his own voice. It made him tired.

"Dorr Kirkland just had Tom Schuler's car towed from a no-parking zone outside his store," Haggis said with about the same amount of enthusiasm as Ben. "And Poorhouse Pete's in lockup again. Poor fool seems really out of it today." Haggis shrugged, looking bored. "That's about it."

"You guys ever get in touch with the FBI about the Crawly kid's disappearance?"

"Oh, yeah," Haggis said, his small, blue eyes brightening. "They located the kid's father."

Ben sat wearily in his chair. "Hugh? Where is he?"

"Salt Lake City. A couple of feds showed up at his place and interviewed him. He said he hadn't seen the boy since he left Stillwater about a year or so ago and hadn't been back to Stillwater since. Feds said his story checks out."

"Damn." Ben had been hoping the father was involved. It boded better for Matthew that way.

"Guy picks up and leaves his family like that," Haggis went on. "You think he even cares that his boy's gone missing?"

"I don't know, Mel."

"I mean, how does a guy do something like that?"

Again, Ben said, "I don't know."

Haggis looked at his wristwatch. "I'm gonna grab some lunch. You want anything?"

Ben waved a hand at him. "I'm good. Thanks."

"Suit yourself." Haggis turned to leave then paused and turned back around. "Oh, I almost forgot. There's a kid waiting for you in Shirley's office."

"A kid?"

"Some girl."

"Yeah? She's waiting for me?"

"Says she wanted to talk to Ben Journell. That's you, last I checked."

"Okay. Thanks."

"You got it," Haggis said and sauntered out of the Batter's Box.

Ben thumbed through the stack of Post-it notes Shirley had left on his desk—she didn't believe in leaving voicemails—and saw, with much relief, that nothing more serious than the dissemination of a few parking tickets had happened in his absence.

When he pushed open the door to the dispatcher's room, he saw Shirley talking to Brandy Crawly, who sat in one of the molded-plastic chairs against the wall. She looked small and lost and had her hands clenched between her knees. As he entered, the girl looked up at him. A fierce helplessness flashed behind her large, dark eyes.

"Hey, Brandy," he said. "I heard you were looking for me."

Brandy stood, looking as unstable as a foal. "Mr. Journell? Um, I mean . . . Officer Journell?"

"Call me Ben," he said. "Is something wrong?"

"Can I talk to you?"

"Sure." He held the door open and waved her through. Then he shared a quizzical look with Shirley before leading the girl back to his desk in the Batter's Box.

Brandy walked slowly down the aisle of desks, peering all around.

"You look disappointed or something," Ben said, pulling an extra chair over to his desk. They both sat down.

"I thought you'd have guns and stuff all over the place."

"We've got guns but we keep them locked up in the back." He tapped a thumb against the firearm at his hip. "I've got this, too." He folded his hands on his desk and tried to sound casual. "So what can I do for you?"

"I have some . . . information," she said.

"About your brother?"

She nodded. "His friend Dwight Dandridge said Matthew might have gone out to the old plastics factory on the other side of the Narrows. Do you know the place?"

"Yes."

"He said he didn't tell you because Matthew's not supposed to go out there and he didn't want to get him in trouble."

"Why does Dwight think he went there?"

"Because that's where they went Friday after school. Dwight said Matthew thought he saw someone inside the factory and he wanted to go in after him."

"Someone who?"

"Oh," she said, "Dwight said he thought maybe . . . well, he thought he saw our dad."

Ben blinked. "Dwight said he saw your dad go into the factory?"

"Well, outside the factory, not in it. I don't think so, anyway." She paused and thought about it. "And no, Dwight didn't see him, but he said Matthew did. I think."

"And Matthew said it was your dad?"

"That's what Dwight said."

"Did they go into the factory? Dwight and your brother?"

"Dwight said they didn't. He said he got too scared. But Matthew really wanted to go in there."

Ben nodded and chewed on his lower lip.

"I drove out there last night," Brandy said, "and I would have gone up to the factory but the bridge was out."

"I guess I can drive out there and take a look," Ben said.

"I want to come with you."

"Shouldn't you be in school today, hon?"

"I skipped out." She seemed nervous admitting this to him, as if she were facing jail time for truancy.

"Why don't you go home and keep your mom company and I'll drive up to the—"

"I really want to go with you, Ben. Please."

"Yeah." He rubbed his chin, feeling the bristles of his beard that he'd forgotten to shave that morning. He supposed it couldn't hurt anything having her come along. The poor kid looked terrified. "Okay. You can come. But then I'm driving you straight home, okay?"

She nodded fervently. "Okay."

Together they walked down to the sally port where Ben switched on the large ceiling light and punched the mechanical button that raised the garage doors. He went to an equipment locker, opened it, and rooted around for the industrial bolt cutters he knew were in there. Finally he located them toward the back of the locker, hidden behind someone's rain slicker. Ben examined them, noting that they looked like the wishbone of some large prehistoric animal, and put them in the trunk of the cruiser.

Brandy stood in front of the bell-shaped birdcage, staring at the bat.

"Pretty neat, huh?" he said, coming up beside her.

"How come it's here?" She sounded uncomfortable.

"It got caught in the garage. The guys wanted to keep it as a sort of mascot."

"Will you keep it forever?"

"No. We'll let it go soon enough."

"Does it drink blood?"

Ben laughed. "It eats fruit. Bugs, probably, too." He put a hand on her shoulder. "Let's get in the car, take a ride."

They drove out to Route 40, mostly in silence. Ben's attempts at small talk failed—he had no idea how to make idle chatter with a sixteen-year-old—and it wasn't until Brandy initiated conversation that things took a more dramatic turn.

"My dad called the house today."

Ben nodded firmly but said nothing.

"It was early when he called. I heard my mom on the phone with him. She cried."

"We had the FBI locate him and tell him about Matthew. I guess he wanted to speak with your mom about it."

"He hurt Matthew the most when he left," she said. "I mean, my mom cried a lot and I was upset, too, but I was also mostly angry. But Matthew, he was really devastated. He didn't really understand what was going on, either. He would spend hours sitting in the garage, which is where my dad kept his workbench and did little projects and stuff, like he was waiting for him to come back. It made my mom sad to see him sitting in there and it made me angrier."

"I can understand that."

"You said you knew my dad, huh?"

"We grew up in Stillwater together, yeah." He braced himself for more questions about Hugh Crawly, but she did not ask any more. So he asked one of his own. "Have you seen your father since he left Stillwater?"

"No." She looked at him and he felt her eyes weighing heavily on him. "You said the FBI found him? My dad, I mean."

"Yes."

"Is he . . . close by?"

"No, hon. He's living in Salt Lake City."

"Oh."

"That's in Utah."

"I know where it is." She turned and faced forward again. "So then Matthew was wrong. He couldn't have seen our dad, could he?"

"Doesn't look like it."

When they came around the bend of Route 40 that overlooked the Narrows and, beyond that, the incline of the mountain where the old factory sat halfway up, Ben slowed the car and turned off the highway. The tires crunched over gravel and the ride was bumpy.

"There's a turnabout down here where we can park," he told her, craning his neck to peer through the dirt-speckled windshield. "Since the Highland Street Bridge is out, we'll have to walk across on the footbridge."

In the passenger seat, Brandy nodded numbly and looked out the window.

The turnabout was halfway down the embankment that led toward the Narrows. Ben parked and stepped on the emergency brake. "Fall out," he said, attempting to sound jovial, and pushed out the driver's door. The air was humid this afternoon, the sun a blazing eyelet in the sky directly overhead. He went to the trunk and took out the bolt cutters while Brandy meandered down to the edge of the Narrows and peered down.

Ben came up beside her. "Be careful."

The tips of her sneakers were overextending the concrete barrier. Inches below the lip of the barrier, the grayish waters of Wills Creek shuttled by. Typically the water was no more than four or five feet deep, but after the series of storms and all the flooding, the water was high enough for someone to lean over the barrier and touch it with their fingertips or graze the surface with a boot heel.

"It's deep," she said. "I've never come this close to it before."

Ben knew what the girl was thinking, mainly because he was thinking the same thing. Had her brother come down here on his own and fallen into the Narrows? Christ, he hoped not . . .

"Listen," he said then. "You can come along with me but you do whatever I tell you to do. You do it without question, okay? I don't need to argue with no kid out here, okay?"

"I'm not a kid."

"Well, you get what I mean, right?"

She averted her eyes from his. "Yeah."

"Good. Now come on," he said, turning away from the water and heading across the sloping field toward the stone arch of the footbridge. Brandy followed, her shadow mingling with his in the brownish grass.

"This is where you found that other kid, right?" she asked.

I knew it was only a matter of time before she brought that up, he thought, feeling uncomfortable and unprepared nonetheless.

"A bit farther down," he said. "Where Wills Creek empties into the river."

"Do you know who he was?"

"No."

"But he wasn't from town, right?"

"He wasn't."

They crossed the footbridge. At the apex, Ben peered over one side and examined his smeary reflection in the running, black water.

"What killed him?" Brandy asked. She appeared beside him now, also gazing down at her reflection.

"I assume he drowned."

"How can you be sure?"

"I'm not sure," Ben said. He was growing increasingly perturbed talking to this girl about the strange boy's death. "The autopsy hasn't been done yet."

"When will the autopsy be done?"

When they find the goddamn body, he thought eerily. *If it just got up and walked away, maybe it will come walking right back.* Which made him even more uncomfortable thinking about it . . .

"Was that all?" she asked.

"What do you mean?"

"Did he have any other injuries or anything?"

"No." They stepped off the footbridge and began climbing the grassy slope toward the factory. Sweat already ran down Ben's forehead.

"Are you sure?"

He paused and glanced at her. He felt himself offer her a crooked smile though it was more out of discomfort than humor. Wincing in the bright light of day, she looked up at him, her face otherwise expressionless.

"Of course I'm sure," he said evenly. "Was there something else you wanted to ask me?"

"You said my mom already told you about the T-shirt we found in the yard? Matthew's T-shirt?"

"Yes."

"Okay." She nodded. "I guess that's it, then."

They continued up the incline until the trees parted and the massive stone facade of the ancient plastics factory rose out of the earth. As recently as a few years ago, the factory grounds had been part of the department's patrol area, in an effort to keep an eye out for potential drug users or neighborhood delinquents who found it exhilarating to throw bricks through windows and spray graffiti on walls. But it seemed no one ever trespassed on the property. When the land eventually reverted back to the county, officers stopped coming up here. There was no landowner to complain if anything ever happened, and it seemed that nothing *did* ever happen. Quite often, Ben forgot the place even existed.

It seemed to greet him now, however. *If buildings could smile,* he thought, and shivered.

He moved around the side of the building and Brandy followed, her footing as delicate as a fawn's. The shrubbery was overgrown back here, obscuring most of the windows and doorways. Back when he had still patrolled up here, there used to be a dirt access road that toured the circumference of the building. That road was gone now, and Ben could not even see remnants of it beneath the overgrown grass.

"Where are we going?" Brandy finally asked after the two of them had spent a substantial amount of time stumbling through the underbrush.

"There's a set of doors back here somewhere," he told her.

"There," she said, pointing through a part in the trees.

Ben bent down and peered through a curtain of crispy red leaves behind which stood a set of double doors made of oxidized copper. A thick chain wound itself around the rectangular door handles.

"Nice lookout," Ben said, stepping through the trees while brandishing the bolt cutters. He held branches out of the way so that Brandy could follow him, unimpeded.

"What's that smell?" she said, wrinkling her nose.

Ben whiffed the air but didn't smell anything. "What does it smell like?" he asked.

"Like the cleaner my mom uses to scrub the bathroom."

Ben gathered a link of chain between the teeth of the bolt cutters and squeezed. A second later, there came an audible pop and the link widened into a *C*. Ben cut the same link again and the chain came apart and dangled from the door handles like a mechanical snake. With one hand, Ben unwound the chain from the handles until it coiled to the ground. His fingers came away orange with rust.

"Matthew would have found another way in," Brandy said at his back.

"Yeah," he responded, though he was already quite certain her brother had not found a way into the old building. He was more curious about who else might have found a way in—whoever it had been that Matthew Crawly had thought he had seen in here . . .

Ben took a step back, already breathing heavily though he hadn't done anything except walk here. "You know what," he said. "Take a few steps back. I don't know what might come jumping out when I open these doors."

"Jumping out?"

"A raccoon or possum, I mean," he said, though he was thinking *mountain lion.*

"Oh. I thought you meant . . ." But her voice trailed off, her thought unfinished. Brandy took a few steps back, the boughs of the trees sweeping down over her like curtains after a stage exit. Ben dropped the bolt cutters onto the ground and grabbed the door handles in both hands. The doors were enormous, pitted monstrosities, like the doors on an old battleship.

"Here goes," he said, and heaved them open.

The stubborn hinges squealed and flakes of rust snowed down on him. They came only partway open, either impeded by the encroaching trees or simply refusing to budge any farther on their uncooperative hinges. A panel of darkness—of varying shades of darkness—appeared before Ben. Stale air breathed onto his face. There was another smell, too. Suddenly, he could smell what Brandy had smelled just a moment ago—the acrid, chemical stink of industrial cleaner. Though more potent, it was similar to the smell at Porter Conroy's and Ted Minsky's farms.

"Yuck," Brandy commented from behind the tree branches.

Ben stepped inside, cautioning Brandy to be careful as she followed him. He entered into a room as spacious as an airplane hangar. The upper portions of the walls were lined with tiny square windows that reminded Ben of tic-tac-toe grids, the windowpanes so thick and grimy that only the barest hint of sunlight permeated. The floor was a level plain of concrete covered in an ancient blanket of dust. Large machines stood at intervals about the room, looking like a cross between an oil rig and dinosaur bones. The ceiling, with its exposed iron girders and sheets of hammered tin, reminded Ben of the high school gymnasium. Some sections of the ceiling were missing, allowing shafts of sunlight to slide like rapiers into the factory.

"This place," Brandy said. Her voice was almost reverent and hushed as she walked slowly across the floor. "This place doesn't seem like it belongs here in Stillwater."

Ben thought it was a pretty astute comment, particularly coming from a sixteen-year-old. "Don't wander off too far," he warned her.

"Matthew!" she shouted, startling Ben. Her voice echoed off the walls and the corrugated-tin ceiling. Flocks of birds lifted off rafters and funneled through the rents in the roof.

"Quiet," he told her.

"He could be anywhere."

"Yeah, well, we don't need to start an avalanche."

He unhooked his flashlight from his belt and went over to one of the large industrial machines. It was enormous, and looked like something that had been conceived and engineered on some distant planet.

"What do these do?" Brandy asked. She was examining one of the machines, too.

"I have no clue. It looks like an old printing press, only bigger. Much bigger."

Brandy opened a small hatch on the side of the machine and peered in. "Dusty," she commented.

"Stay here," he told her. "I'm going to take a look around."

"I want to come with you."

"Just stay here. It's too dangerous."

"He's my brother," she challenged.

He pointed his flashlight at her face. "I thought we went over this outside? You do as I say."

She continued to stare at him until he softened.

"Okay," he relented. "But stick close to me."

She followed him into an adjoining room where the ceiling wasn't as high. Enormous lights were recessed into the hammered tin and caged with a metal meshwork, similar to the light in the sally port back at the station. The floor was empty, though there were piles of sawdust everywhere. What looked like jewels glittered on the floor as Ben panned his flashlight across the room. He bent down to examine some only to find that they were little metal shavings in the shape of fingernail clippings.

"Tetanus city," he muttered to himself.

Brandy said, "Huh?"

"Never mind."

At the end of the corridor they arrived at a wall of iron grates, blackened and fire-scarred. Ben assumed medieval prisons probably looked no worse. He went to one of the grates, shone the flashlight into it. The throat of a narrow pipe carried the light to an elbow that bent up into the stonework.

"What is this?" Brandy asked.

"Some sort of kiln."

"What's a kiln?"

"Like an oven. Don't you take pottery classes or something in school?"

Brandy shrugged and peered through the slatted iron bars.

"I think these pipes all go up into one of those smokestacks," he said.

She pulled away from the bars. "I don't like this place."

"I don't think your brother came in here, Brandy."

By the expression on her face, he could tell she didn't think so, either.

She's trying to hold out hope, he thought. *In all likeliness, the kid probably did come out here and fell into the Narrows. I should alert the state police and they should keep an eye on the mouth of the Potomac. Jesus fucking Christ.*

Ben felt sick.

"What's that stuff?" Brandy asked. She pointed to a series of wooden rafters along one wall. The rafters themselves looked like some sort of scaffolding, yet there was something dripping from them that reminded Ben of spelunking as a child in Shenandoah. Specifically, he was reminded of the stalactites, those calcified horns of stone that hung from the ceilings of caves. Similarly, this stuff had hardened into corkscrews and hung from the scaffolding, a mottled white and black and gray in hue. On the floor beneath the scaffolding, mounds of the stuff rose up. As Ben shone the flashlight on the mass, large black flies spiraled dizzyingly into the air.

"That's guano," Ben said.

"What's *that?*"

"Bat shit." He shot her an apologetic glance. "It's, uh, bat feces. Like, uh . . . bowel movements or . . ."

"You can say *shit.* I know what shit is." She stared up at the hanging columns of dried dung, nearly mesmerized. "There's so much of it."

"We've been having a bat problem lately. I guess this is where they've been roosting."

"But where are they now?" Brandy took a few steps back, her eyes still trained on the rafters. "It's daylight out there. They should be in here sleeping, right?"

"I don't really know too much about bats," Ben said, though he thought, *She's right. Bats are nocturnal. Where are they?*

"He's not in here, is he?"

Ben clicked off his flashlight. "No, hon. I really don't think so." He caught another whiff of that antiseptic stink—that burning, medicinal smell that reminded him of doctors' offices. It made his eyes water. "Let's get you home, okay?"

Back in the car, with the ribbon of asphalt that was Route 40 curving around the mountain ahead of them, Brandy said, "Thanks for taking me out here and for taking a look around."

"It's okay, Brandy. I wish I could be more help." He glanced at her profile against the passenger window. "We're doing all we can."

"I know." She played with the door lock while she watched the countryside shuttle by. "I still have the shirt, in case you want to take it for evidence or whatever. I didn't wash it and kept it just like we found it."

"The shirt?"

"Matthew's T-shirt," she said. She looked at him. "You said my mom told you about it, right?"

"Your mom said she found one of his shirts out in the yard. She said it probably blew off the clothesline."

"Maybe," Brandy said. "It's the holes that bother me."

"What holes?"

"The holes in the back of the shirt." With an index finger, she dotted the air in a vertical line. "There were these little holes going down the back of his shirt. I do his laundry all the time and never noticed them before."

Ben's skin went clammy. "Yeah?" he said, realizing his mouth was suddenly dry. "Holes?"

"Yeah." Brandy turned back to the window.

"Tell you what," he said. "Why don't you give me that shirt, huh?"

"For evidence?" she said.

"Yeah." His mind was reeling now. "For evidence."

2

Ben pulled up outside the Crawly house and Brandy got out of the car. The door still open, she peeked in and said, "I'll be right back." Then she took off toward the house, leaving the door ajar.

Unsettled, Ben turned on the goodtime radio, located a classic rock station, and tried to grow comfortable with one of his favorite Bruce Springsteen songs. Yet his mind was on other things.

The unidentified boy's body had been found by some watermen late in the day. Both Ben and Mike Keller had responded to the scene. What they found was the doughy outline of a young boy, naked and bloated, strewn in the reeds at the mouth of Wills Creek where the creek joined the Potomac River. They had rolled the boy over and found his face a sodden, swollen mess. The boy's eyes were like jelly in their sockets. There had been a stiffening rigor to half the face, giving the corpse the frozen grimace of a stroke victim. Lord knew how long the boy's body had been in the water, but it had been long enough to pull body hair out by the roots and turn the skin into glue. Ben had called Deets in from Cumberland, and the fastidious little medical examiner addressed the scene perfunctorily, taking pictures of his own and scribbling in a notebook. Deets called the death, and he assisted a pair of medics in loading the corpse into the back of an ambulance.

That evening, Mike Keller had gone with Ben down to Crossroads where they tilted back a number of beers. "Don't think less of me for saying this, Ben," Mike had told him while perched on a bar stool beside him, "but that was just about the worst thing I've ever seen. I feel like crying about it a little, too, but it feels like my insides are all dried up."

That's how Ben felt now—as if his insides had all dried up.

Brandy returned with her brother's T-shirt wadded into a ball. She tossed it onto the passenger seat. "Maybe there's fingerprints on it or something," she said, and he felt miserable hearing the hope in her voice. "Like they find in those cop shows."

She's just a goddamn kid. Life is so unfair.

"Maybe," he said.

"Thanks again."

"You got it."

Brandy shut the door and Ben turned back out onto the road. When he got out of eyeshot of the Crawly residence, he pulled onto the shoulder and put the cruiser in Park. Reaching over, he grabbed the T-shirt off the seat and flapped it open so that it draped itself down the front of the steering wheel.

The front of the shirt looked fine. There was nothing wrong with it.

Chewing again on his lower lip, he turned the shirt over. The small holes in the fabric running down the back of the shirt caused a slight tremor to course through him. Distantly, he felt his left eyelid spasm.

"Goddamn it," he muttered. His words seemed to shatter like glass as they came out of his mouth and his whole face felt like it was on fire. On the radio, Springsteen sang about going down to the river, as if it were some sort of baptism, a holy rite. "What's going on around here?" Ben muttered, his breath fogging up the windshield.

CHAPTER ELEVEN

1

Ben's discomfort only intensified by the time he returned to the station. He carried with him the balled-up T-shirt Brandy Crawly had given him—the T-shirt with the peculiar but all-too-familiar series of puncture marks down its back—and a sense of nonspecific apprehension.

Blessedly, the Batter's Box was empty. He went straight to his desk, flipped open the case file on the unidentified boy, and set the T-shirt down on his desk. As he looked over the photographs in the file, he flattened out the shirt and spread it out along his desktop. The line of tiny, frayed holes along the back of the shirt stared up at him. A tasteless lump formed at the back of Ben's throat.

There it was—one of the photos of the unidentified boy. Mike Keller had taken these pictures, crouching down over the bloated and pallid corpse and snapping shots like a consummate professional. (It wasn't until later, knocking back those beers at Crossroads, that Mike told him just how much he had been affected by the boy's body, and how he was sure to lose much sleep over what he'd seen.) He'd taken photos of the body just as they'd found it—facedown, one bony arm crooked in a nest of reeds, one leg partially submerged in the brown, brackish water. Looking at the photo now, Ben could see the twin shoulder blades at the child's back . . .

the S-shaped curve of the boy's spine . . . the bloated hubs of the boy's buttocks . . .

There were four small puncture marks trailing down the boy's back, the first one starting from just between the shoulder blades while the final one ended just above the boy's buttocks. Peculiar little holes drilled right into the fishy flesh . . .

Ben examined Matthew Crawly's T-shirt again. Smoothing it out along his desk, he counted one, two, three, four holes running vertically down the back.

There was a connection here . . .

He just didn't know what it was.

Fifteen minutes later, he was listening to the telephone ring a number of times before John Deets of the county coroner's office picked up.

"John, it's Ben Journell over in Stillwater."

"You sound panicked."

"Christ. Is it that obvious?"

"What is it?"

Ben closed his eyes, attempted to catch his breath. When he spoke again, his voice was calmer and more decisive. "First off, is there any news on the whereabouts of the boy's body?"

"No. No one saw a thing. No one had even come in here in the two days before the body went missing. It's an anomaly, Ben. I'm really embarrassed about all this, you have no idea." John Deets laughed nervously on the other end of the line. "It's like the fucking thing got up and walked out on its own."

Again, Ben closed his eyes, then said, "Those marks on the boy's back. Do you remember?"

"Yes. Circular puncture marks."

"Did you get a chance to identify them before the body went missing?"

"Officially?" Deets sighed like a locomotive. "No."

"Unofficially?" Ben prompted.

"Unofficially, they looked like the kind of wound a scorpion makes with the stinger on the end of its tail."

"A scorpion?"

"Yeah," Deets said, "if the fucking scorpion was the size of a grizzly bear."

Ben made a clicking sound way back in his throat.

"I never got a chance to do an autopsy, Ben. Nothing I can tell you has any scientific backing. You understand that, right?"

"How deep did those puncture wounds look? Like, could those have been the cause of death?"

"I can't really say for sure. I examined one of the wounds and it looked like it went straight through the tissue down to the vertebrae. Maybe the kid fell on a two-by-four that had some nails poking up from it."

"Why'd you say it looked like a scorpion's wounds?"

"Hell, Ben," Deets said, and Ben could tell the coroner was already regretting having made the comment to him. "It's just the first thing that came to my mind."

"Why?" he pressed.

"Because when I used to live in Albuquerque, a neighbor's kid got stung by a scorpion on the back of his hand. The wound looked identical to the wounds on the back of the kid you shipped over to me—the entry small and hooked, not straight in, and the surrounding area of flesh irritated, red, puffy . . . Christ, Ben, I don't know . . ."

He was staring at Mike Keller's photos of the dead boy in the case file. "Okay. You'll call me if you hear anything else?"

"You know I will."

"Thanks, John."

"What's going on out there, Ben?"

He drummed his fingers on the photographs of the dead boy. "I don't know," he told the coroner. "I don't know."

2

What had been seated at the back of John Deets's mind during his discussion with Sergeant Ben Journell was the comment Dougie Overland, one of the morgue attendees, had made after being questioned on the whereabouts of the unidentified boy's body. Dougie, who was in his twenties and had blue-dyed hair and gold hoop earrings, had assured Deets that no one had come into the facility the night he was on duty, which happened to be the night the boy's body disappeared. What bothered Deets—and what he found himself unable to relay to Ben, lest he feel like a complete fool—was what Dougie Overland had admitted to later that evening: that he swore, on a few occasions, he could hear muted thumping sounds coming from the room where they kept the bodies in their steel drawers. "It was like someone was trying to get out," Dougie had said.

3

After he hung up with Deets, Ben went into the dispatcher's office where Shirley monitored the phones. On the console, a small television set showed one of Shirley's soap operas.

"Hey, Ben."

"Hey, Shirl. You got the chief's personal cell number handy?"

Both of Shirley's eyebrows arched. "His *personal* cell?"

"I want to bring him up to speed. I'm not... I'm a little overwhelmed here, hon. Know what I mean?"

She leaned forward and lowered the volume on her portable TV. Sliding her bifocals down her stubby nose, she stared hard at Ben. "People are saying we got some wild animal killing off livestock around town," she said. It was not a question. "People are saying it could be a bear or a cougar or something. Other people, they're saying it might even be something else."

"Something else?" Ben said.

She gave him a look that suggested she knew more than she was willing to let on. "Did something eat all of Porter Conroy's cows this past weekend? Be honest with me."

"Something got at them," he acknowledged. "Ted Minksy's goats, too."

"People are starting to worry, Ben."

So am I, he felt like adding.

Shirley scribbled Chief Harris's personal cell phone number down on a Post-it and handed it over to Ben. He looked at it then folded it up and stuck it in his pocket. He knew Harris would be annoyed at the interruption in his vacation with his wife, but things were getting out of hand.

One of the phones lit up and started ringing. Shirley's sharp eyes lingered on him for a moment longer before she turned to address the telephone, picking it up and pressing it to her ear. Into the receiver, she said, "Stillwater Police Department," then went silent as she listened to the caller on the other end of the line.

Ben went out into the hall and stared for a time at the shafts of daylight that angled in through the wire-meshed windows. He thought he heard someone moving around at the far end of the hall. He went down there and peered into the chief's empty office, one of the supply closets, and eventually into lockup. Three jail cells lined the far wall, and the first two were unoccupied. A slovenly dressed figure sat hunched over on the bench in the third cell, a mane of iron-colored hair draped down over the man's face.

Ben walked up to the cell, taking in the familiar, unwashed scent of the lockup's most frequent visitor. "Hello, Pete."

Pete Poole, more infamously known as Poorhouse Pete to the guys at the station, looked up at Ben. The man's face was blotchy and haggard, his eyes red-rimmed and moist. Whitish beard stubble looked like it had been hastily applied with a paintbrush.

Pete shook like a tuning fork. "Hi, Ben."

"How come you're still here? You haven't sobered up yet, bud?"

"Ain't come in drunk," Pete advised him. "Not this time."

"Then what are you doing in here?"

"Knocking over trash cans on Hamilton."

"Why would you do that, Pete?"

"Wanted to get arrested."

Ben dragged over a wooden chair from behind one of the desks and sat before the cell. "And why would you want to do *that?* It's not that cold out yet." Once the weather grew cold and winter came, Ben could always count on Pete Poole to act up and cause a scene with hopes of getting locked up and thus be given a warm place to sleep and some hot meals. Everyone knew the routine and, last year, Shirley had even bought Pete a Christmas present—a knitted cap and some gloves—which she'd placed in the cell while awaiting the man's inevitable Yuletide arrival.

"Don't wanna be out there on them streets tonight," Pete said. His long hands shook fiercely in his lap. "Things are fallin' apart out there, Ben, and I'm gettin' a little scared."

Ben leaned closer to the bars of the cell. "What's falling apart, Pete? Tell me what's going on out there."

"It's not something I can see," Pete said, also leaning toward Ben.

"I can feel it, though. I feel it the way some animals feel it when a storm's coming. It's in my bones."

"What is?"

"Uneasiness." Pete placed one hand against his abdomen. "Makes me sick to my stomach."

I know the feeling, old friend, Ben thought.

"Can I tell you something . . . without you thinking I'm crazy?" Pete asked.

"Sure. Go ahead."

Pete shuffled his feet beneath the bench. He was wearing scuffed boots with high laces, the cuffs of his pants tucked into them. "First off," the man began, "I wasn't always this guy sittin' here. You know what I mean? I came from someplace else and had things in my life, Ben. You've known me as old Poorhouse Pete—"

"Now, Pete—" Ben began.

"—and that's just fine, but that ain't who I always been." Pete cleared his throat and Ben could see his eyes welling up. When he opened his mouth again to speak, his lower lip quivered. "I once was married, did you know it? Way out in a different part of the country. I was much younger and damn if some ladies didn't think I was a fine-looking fellow."

Ben smiled sadly at the man.

"We had a daughter and she lived to be five years old," Pete said. "She was a beautiful child and the light of my life."

Ben felt his body go numb. "Oh, Pete. I didn't know. I'm sorry."

"Was struck and killed by a drunk driver right out in the street where she was playing," Pete said. "Right in front of our house." Pete looked at him, his colorless eyes like chunks of granite, his complexion as ruined and asymmetrical as a topographical map of the Sahara Desert. "Well, as you can see, a tragedy like that breaks a man down. People say men are stronger than women, and maybe in some regards that's even true, but not when it comes to the people we love being taken away. My Holly. My little girl, Holly." He made a quavering, paper-thin sound. "Maybe I'm weak because I wound up here, all the way at the opposite end of the country, covered in filthy clothing and drinking too much whenever I have enough money to do so. Maybe that makes me weak, Ben. I don't know." He held up one crooked finger. The fingernail was black. "But what I *do* know . . ."

"What?" It came out in a reverent whisper.

"What I know is my Holly came back last night. She was down by the Narrows, standing right there on the water, Ben, looking up at me. It was going on dusk so it was hard to tell for certain, but I didn't need to be able to see with perfect clarity to know it was her and that, after all these years of being dead, my little girl Holly had come back."

Ben felt instantly cold. He opened his mouth to speak but could find no words. *He's drunk, that's all,* he thought, though wondering if he actually believed it. *Old Poorhouse Pete's off the wagon again. Nothing unusual about that.*

"But I ain't crazy," Pete continued, "and I know nothing good is gonna come from seeing my poor sweet girl down by the Narrows. That's why I'm here. That's why I don't wanna go back out there, Ben."

Ben stood up. He dragged the chair back behind the desk. "You can't stay in here forever, Pete. It's not a motel."

"I know it ain't. Just for tonight though, Ben, okay? Please?"

Rubbing the back of his head, Ben said, "Yeah, okay. Sure. Have you eaten?"

"Shirley brought me a sandwich earlier."

Slowly, as if in a dream, Ben nodded. He went to the door and paused in the doorway. "You want me to turn out the lights so you can get some sleep?"

"No." Across the room, Pete's eyes were like twin headlights. "Leave the lights on, for God's sake, Ben."

"All right."

Ben walked back down the hall, suddenly feeling the weariness of the past two weeks pressing firmly down on his shoulders. The goddamn storm, the unidentified boy washed up at the mouth of the river, the slaughtered cattle, and now the missing Crawly boy . . .

In truth, it was almost comical. But Ben didn't feel like laughing.

He returned to the Batter's Box to find Eddie La Pointe settling in his cubicle with some cartons of Chinese takeout. "Hey, Ben. Hungry?"

"Not really."

Eddie switched on the small black-and-white TV that sat at the corner of his desk and turned it to one of his beloved horror-movie channels. He cracked open the lid of one of the cartons of Chinese food and the smell was instantly overwhelming.

Ben sat at his own cubicle and looked forlornly at the massive amount of paperwork stacked on his desk. His head hurt and his eyes burned from lack of sleep. Absently, he rummaged around the top of his desk for the bottle of Advil he knew was there, somewhere, among the madness.

"Second storm front moving in later this week," Eddie said around a mouthful of noodles. "Cumberland Public Works already put out their flood warning."

"Fantastic," Ben bemoaned. He located the plastic bottle of Advil behind his Rolodex, popped the cap off the bottle, and shook two into the palm of one hand. After brief consideration, he shook out a third tablet. He dry swallowed them, one at a time.

"I just dried out my goddamn cellar from the last flood," Eddie went on. "Lousy sump pump is fine as long as the power stays on. Well, we both know the score on that."

Ben leaned forward in his chair. "What are you watching?"

"Huh?" Eddie glanced up from his container of Chinese noodles at the black-and-white TV. On the screen, a disfigured humanoid creature was vomiting acid onto another actor's arm. "Oh! Man, this is a classic! Well, a remake of a classic, anyway, but it's a classic remake, too. *The Fly,* with Jeff Goldblum. Ever see it?"

"Once," Ben said, his eyes locked on the television. On the screen, the actor's arm sizzled and withered beneath the gout of acid. "That's what happened to the animals."

"What's that?" Eddie said, stuffing more noodles into his mouth.

Ben jabbed a finger at the screen. "That. That's what it looked like happened to them. Porter Conroy's cows and Ted Minsky's goats."

Eddie turned around and leered at Ben from over one shoulder. Around a mouthful of food, he said, "Are you serious or just screwing with me?"

"The way the flesh was eaten away . . . the melted look of the bones and the goats' horns at Minsky's place . . ." Ben leaned back in his chair, one set of fingers rubbing circles into his left temple. His head continued to bang like a drum.

"Come on, Ben. Who would do something like that?" Eddie coughed into one fist and swallowed the rest of his food. "*How* would someone do that?" he added.

Ben just shook his head. "I don't know. Maybe I'm wrong, but . . ."

They both turned back to the television. Goldblum was in full insect mode now, his face having split down the middle to reveal the bulbous, hammerhead eyes of a giant fly.

The telephone at Eddie's desk rang. Eddie set his carton of Chinese food down and scooped up the receiver. "La Pointe," he said into the phone.

Still watching the TV, Ben reached over and snatched one of the cartons off Eddie's desk, along with a pair of chopsticks. He had just gotten the chopsticks out of the cellophane when Eddie hung up the phone and looked at him. The blood had drained from Eddie's face.

"What?" Ben said. "What is it?"

"That was Platt," Eddie said, switching off the television set. "He and Haggis are over at Bob Leary's place. Bob's kid, Billy, is missing."

4

Bob Leary and his son, Billy, lived out on Town Road 5, a perilous twist of unpaved roadway that wound with the discipline of a jumbled garden hose up into the foothills of the mountains. Their home was a run-down ranch house with a stone facade and chimney that looked about one good storm away from falling down. When Ben and Eddie approached, they found Haggis and Platt's cruiser already parked in front of the house, its bar lights casting intermittent red and blue light into the neighboring trees.

Inside, Bob Leary sat forward in a tattered La-Z-Boy recliner, a can of Coors Light on one knee. There was a look of hollowed desperation on his face. Across the room, Officers Haggis and Platt sat like matching bookends in their uniforms at either side of a cramped little sofa. Melvin Haggis had a notepad flipped open on one thigh and a look of consternation on his face.

"Where's the chief?" Bob Leary said the second Ben and Eddie came into the house. "Where's Harris?"

"Out of town." Ben took his hat off. Beside him, Eddie swayed from foot to foot like a player waiting his turn to take the football field. "Your son's gone missing, Mr. Leary?"

"I was just telling the guys here." He jerked a pointy chin at Haggis and Platt, who looked like they were being punished and had been told not to move. "The boy's been gone two days now and I'm fixing to worry."

Ben said, "Two days?"

"It ain't unusual for him to stay out late or sometimes at some friend's house. But even then he usually comes home the next day. And see, I been out of work, so's I been home more. I catch his comings and goings. He ain't been around and I don't like it."

"He says the last time he saw him was Saturday afternoon, Ben," Haggis said, consulting his notepad.

"He was out in the front yard patching up a tire on his bike," Leary said. "I went out to Crossroads and when I come back, he was gone."

"His bike was gone, too?" Ben asked.

"Yeah," Leary said.

Melvin Haggis scribbled something in his notepad.

"Have you tried contacting any of his friends?"

"Made a few calls." Leary sounded irritated having to answer the questions. "Nobody's seen him."

"Okay. You want to give a list of these friends to one of my guys, Mr. Leary?"

"So you can double-check on me?"

Ben ignored the comment. To Platt and Haggis, he said, "Why don't you guys check around the area, see if you can find anything." He knew the foothills could be dangerous, and that danger had little to do with blood-starved carnivores; the sudden drops and unsteady footing were the real dangers. Though nothing of the sort had ever happened in Stillwater, Ben had assisted on a few occasions over in Garrett County when some careless hikers had gotten lost or hurt—and sometimes killed—in the mountains.

"You got it, Ben," Platt said, rising quickly from the sofa. Haggis struggled to get up and join him.

"I'd like to take a look at your son's room, Mr. Leary," Ben said.

Leary set his can of beer on the carpet then peeled himself out of his La-Z-Boy. "Follow me," he said.

Leary led Ben and Eddie down the hall to the last door on the right. It opened up to a tiny room with one window facing a stand of elm trees. There was an unmade bed wedged in one corner and there were toys and clothes all over the place. Posters of horror-movie monsters hung on the walls and some classic Aurora monster models had been carefully arranged on a desktop, bookshelves, and the solitary windowsill.

"Don't know what you expect to find," Leary said. "Room's a goddamn pigsty."

Ben went to the closet, opened it. He dug through a heap of unwashed clothing, board games, and random toys until he found an empty backpack. He held it up so the missing boy's father could see it. "Is this the one he uses for school?"

Leary lifted one pointed shoulder. "Beats me."

"School one's over here, Ben," Eddie said. He was peering over the small desk that was pushed beneath the single window at another backpack that was unzipped and loaded with textbooks.

"What's it matter?" Leary asked.

"When kids run away they sometimes pack some stuff in a backpack. It seems Billy's are accounted for."

Leary grunted.

"Is something wrong, Mr. Leary?" Ben asked him.

"Why would Billy run away?"

"I'm not saying he did. I'm just looking around."

"I got a good relationship with my boy, Journell."

"I don't doubt it," Ben said, tossing the backpack back into the closet. "You mind if I check the papers in your son's schoolbag?"

Leary made a face that suggested he didn't care one way or another.

Ben emptied the contents of Billy Leary's schoolbag onto the desk as Eddie came up beside him. Pencils, erasers, a broken ruler, notebooks, and balled-up wads of lined notebook paper spilled out along with a collection of textbooks. There was also a half-eaten sandwich in a Ziploc bag, so old and festooned with mold that the identity of the lunch meat remained suspect.

"How have your son's grades been?" Ben asked.

"He does okay," Leary intoned from the doorway.

Eddie sighed audibly.

Ben knew that sometimes kids ran away instead of having to confront their parents with a bad report card or a failed test paper that needed to be signed and turned back in to the teacher. And while there were plenty of poor test scores among the contents of Billy Leary's schoolwork, Ben did not think the boy would have worried too much about showing them to his father. Abruptly, he felt like he was wasting time.

"Okay," he said, dumping the boy's items back into the schoolbag. "I think we're done here."

"You figure anything out?" Leary wanted to know.

Ben offered him a wan smile and said, "Not just yet."

Back outside, Eddie lit a Marlboro while Ben stood surveying the property with his hands on his hips. Bob Leary remained inside, though he occasionally appeared in one of the windows to stare out at them.

"Explain to me how we got two missing kids in one week," Eddie said, exhaling a column of smoke.

"I have no idea."

"And then the livestock mutilations? I mean, how fucking bizarre is all this?"

"Pretty bizarre."

"It's all got to be related, right, Ben? It can't just be a bunch of coincidences, can it? All at once like this?"

Ben had no answer for him. He couldn't see how they could possibly be connected . . . though he found the timing of all these seemingly unrelated events more than just troubling.

"And let's not forget that kid who washed up in Wills Creek," Eddie added.

"Don't remind me."

"Seems to me this whole town is being overrun."

"Overrun by what?"

"You name it," Eddie said. "Take your pick. Fuck if I know. But it's almost like that dead kid who washed up in Wills Creek was the trigger to all this madness."

This struck Ben as oddly poignant. He looked at Eddie, but Eddie was peering casually around at the yard and the rusted vehicles up on blocks around the side of the house, looking infernally bored and exhausted. To Eddie La Pointe, it was nothing more than a passing comment.

CHAPTER TWELVE

1

Amid a dream of plowing through rich autumn leaves, Brandy Crawly awoke to find it was the middle of the night, the darkness penetrating her bedroom like a sonic shock wave. Her fleeting thoughts still resonated with her peaceful dream—scampering through crunchy, brown leaves in the forest and overturning stones at the edge of Wills Creek to find their undersides fuzzy with moss, horned owls noiselessly circling overhead. The juxtaposition was jarring.

Flipping the sheets off her sweating body, she climbed quickly out of bed and hurried over to one of her bedroom windows. Outside, the road looked like a glowing blue ribbon coursing its way through the valley and up into the foothills of the mountains. She could see the large, black trees crowding the road and the moonlight that dripped from their branches. For whatever reason, she recalled summers spent in her youth when she'd walk up and down that road, searching for toads in muddy puddles after rainstorms. Tonight, the world seemed to close in around her like some constriction, nearly suffocating in all its claustrophobia. In nothing more than her nightshirt and panties, she hurried out of her room, into the upstairs hall, and down the steps that led to the first floor of the creaky old house.

It was the garage that bothered her. Even when she could not remember it, she knew she had dreamt of it in the night. It was a subliminal text hidden between the pages of her pleasant and youthful dreams of summers among the tree-lined roads while kicking up balls of dead leaves as she bulldozed through the forest. Tree frogs croaked and the summer crickets sounded like mechanical sprinklers going off. Yet this notion of darkness—a closet of darkness opening up into more darkness, like those Russian fertility dolls—right here on the property, right here in the yard, never fully left her.

She passed now through the kitchen, the moonlight coming through the curtained windows and the glass in the back door the color of the moon. No different would it be if the Crawly house—right here, right now—existed on the moon. She thought of the great horned owls and tried to remember if they were from real life or her dreams.

Brandy opened the back door. Frigid air rushed into the kitchen, rattling papers on the corkboard in the laundry room and twirling dead leaves around the slouching porch. In the distance, she could hear wind chimes.

Maybe I'm still asleep, she thought . . . but didn't think it was true. *Maybe I'm not standing here at all.*

Across the yard, she could see the dark frame of the detached garage. Wind rattled the bushes and moaned through the eaves of the house. It chilled Brandy's bones and her skin prickled beneath the thin fabric of her nightclothes.

Without giving it a conscious thought, she stepped out onto the porch. The floorboards creaked beneath her bare feet and the screen door slammed against the frame as she let it go. There was a rusty, scraping sound, and it took her several seconds to realize it was the wind bullying the clothesline that hung from the porch to the garage; the line jounced fiercely in the metal wheel that was hooked to the side of the garage.

The chrome on Matthew's bike glowed in the moonlight. It still lay slouched against the side of the garage, causing a weakening tremor to vibrate up through the center of Brandy's body. Before she realized what she was doing, she descended the porch steps and stood in the cool dirt of the yard, facing the garage.

And the garage was *alive.* Seeing this, she stopped moving and stood in absolute fear and immobility at the foot of the porch steps. The garage *moved.* Or, rather, *parts* of it moved: she could see them clearly enough even in the dark. Swarthy, undulating husks of deeper darkness hidden among the black. It—

Bats, she knew.

They still hung from the eaves of the garage. There were several of them dangling upside down from the clothesline, too. The nearby hedges were alive with them. Their fluttery wings and scrabbling claws and high-pitched chirps were suddenly all she could hear. It made the hairs on the back of her neck stand at attention.

Just then, a cold wind whipped down from the mountains and coursed through the gutted valley of the dying town. The sound of the wind in the trees was like the clash of the ocean's surf on a rocky shore. The wind emanating from the hollowed trunks of trees moaned like the mournful cries of the ghosts of anguished mothers.

As she stood there, she heard something move inside the garage. It was a subtle sound, like the repositioning of feet on a gritty floor, but she heard it nonetheless. This was followed by a much louder sound, the sound of something crashing from within the garage . . . items being knocked to the floor and kicked about.

Brandy took several steps closer to the garage. In the eaves, the black bats' claws scrabbled for more secure footholds along the perimeter of the garage. Off to her left, the bats in the hedges twittered and hummed like electronic equipment. This close to Matthew's bike, a dizzying wave of sadness threatened to collapse her to the ground. She fought it off with all the strength she could muster.

Someone is in the garage . . .

"Matthew?" Her voice was shaky and unsure. Above, the bats squealed like pigs and Brandy blinked, suddenly realizing there were at least twice as many as she had originally thought—the darkness was playing tricks on her eyes.

Then, for reasons hidden too deeply within her subconscious to be examined and fully understood, she thought of a summer where she'd bounced about in the passenger seat of her father's pickup truck, some Americana rock song straining the speakers of the truck's radio, a set of fishing poles and a five-gallon bucket stowed in the bed of the truck. Just Brandy and her dad, driving out in the early predawn hours to his favorite fishing hole at the crook where Wills Creek emptied into the cold and gray Potomac River, hot air pumping from the dashboard vents and the smell of her father's cologne filling the cab. In her mind's eye, she could see her father clear as day, the unshaven scruff at his cheeks, his chin, his neck; the somber blue eyes hidden beneath the shadowed bill of the Orioles baseball cap he wore; his big-knuckled hands gripping the steering wheel while he occasionally spit gobs of tobacco juice into an old plastic Gatorade bottle. Tattered paperbacks slid back and forth across the top of the dashboard—old Aldo Leopold essays and a book called *Four Seasons North* that was about arctic and subarctic exploration.

Land is important, Hugh Crawly would tell his daughter. *Land is most important, Brandy. This town used to be alive. Now it's dead. People do that to the land. We build things up and make machines that fly and crush and swim and kill, but people do it. It's our fault Stillwater is dying.*

She could *smell* him, even now—a smell like gun oil and cheap cologne. Those were the same scents he would leave on the couch cushions after he'd sat there watching an old black-and-white movie on the weekends or football on Monday nights.

Somehow, she had arrived at the side door of the garage, one hand extended to grip the doorknob. Directly above her, the bats were so close she could hear their commingled respiration, a sound like air wheezing out of an old accordion. A vague medicinal odor pricked the hairs in her nose, but the smell itself was too fleeting to be properly identified.

She gripped the doorknob.

Turned it.

There arose a shriek no different than the wail of a passing ambulance, though this sound came from *inside* the garage, followed by a scrabbling of sounds. Her hand frozen to the doorknob, Brandy couldn't move. The sound that followed was of breaking glass, as whatever had been inside the garage had broken out of the window at the opposite side. She heard it—whatever *it* was—strike the ground outside. It emitted a piggish grunt that seemed to coincide with all the bats' wings opening around the perimeter of the garage.

Brandy shoved the door open to an empty garage. Items from her father's work shelf were strewn about and the floor was covered in countless screws, nuts, bolts, washers, carpentry nails. Opposite her, the small window high on the garage wall had been shattered and triangular bits of glass glittered on the floor beneath it. As she stared at the busted window, she heard the thing directly on the other side of it breathing its labored respiration. Then there came a shock wave rattle as the thing leapt the chain-link fence at the back of property and, on the heels of that, the rustling of the tall grass as it ran.

Brandy ran back out into the yard just as the bats lifted off the eaves and darted up into the night. Moving quickly around the other side of the garage, she found the chain-link fence still shaking and the field of tall grass parting as something unseen carved its way through it toward the wooded foothills.

Bats spiraled up into the sky, briefly blotting out the scythe-shaped moon. They seemed to vanish as the darkness claimed them.

And a moment later, all was silent in the Crawlys' backyard, save for the wind that still troubled the hollow trees and whistled flutelike through the nearby reeds.

There were bits of broken glass out here, too, scattered in the dirt in an almost decipherable pattern.

Among them were the undeniable footprints of a boy roughly Matthew's age.

2

No stranger to trouble, nineteen-year-old Ricky Codger pushed out the back door of Crossroads and stumbled across the darkened parking lot. There were lampposts here but the lights had been busted out some time ago. Ricky knew it was the perfect place to hide and wait for the son of a bitch. He got in his Camaro and drove it around to the side of the parking lot, never turning the headlights on, so that the front door was framed perfectly in the windshield.

See? This is smart. This is using the old melon. The last thing I need is to rip the fucker's face open in front of a bunch of witnesses and wind my ass up in Jessup again.

No. He most certainly did not need that.

The fucker in question was Donald Larrabee, a sponge-faced lush in his mid-twenties who lived out on Susquehanna and worked days over in Cumberland at Allegheny Power. Had Ricky not been pacing himself all evening and thinking rationally, the fucker in question would have already been picking his teeth up off the sticky floor of the tavern. But as it was, Ricky was skating on thin ice. Some folks might argue he was a lunatic, but Ricky would be damned if they would think he was a *careless* lunatic.

Ricky Codger lived with his grandmother on a sterile plot of land off Full Hill Road. It had once been the Codger family farm, back when Ricky's grandfather had been strong enough (and alive enough) to keep it up. But that was several years ago now. Currently, the Codger family consisted of just Ricky and his grandmother (and given her rapid deterioration into the muddy swamp of dementia, Ricky questioned how much longer she'd stick around). They survived off his grandmother's Social Security checks, bought food with her food stamps, and collected a monthly pittance from the state as a farm subsidy, despite the fact that the Codger farm hadn't produced a single crop in just under a decade. On occasion, Ricky would pick up some hourly work at Tom Schuler's garage, but, other than that, it was slim pickings in Stillwater as far as the job market went. And the places that *could* hire him didn't, due to his stint up in Jessup for armed robbery back when he was sixteen. (Armed robbery? Okay, sure, he'd gone into a feed store in Garrett with a handgun and asked for the money out of the register, but, son of a bitch, he knew the asshole behind the register and was only joking. Well, half-joking. What did him in was that he took the money and that the sorry son of a bitch had called the cops.) He supposed he could leave town, head out for the East Coast, and start fresh in a place where people were strangers and didn't already know your business before you shook their hands and introduced yourself. Stillwater was a secret cracked down the middle, bleeding its guts all over the sidewalk. Every asshole stepped in the puddle and tracked your business down the fucking street.

No matter. As long as his grandmother was still hanging on, those checks rolled in like clockwork. He would deal with the repercussions of her death when the time came and no sooner.

There was a part of Ricky Codger that often wondered how anyone would actually *know* when his grandmother died. The woman had no friends and no other family. She never left the house. With the exception of her biannual doctor visit in Westlake, no one else on the planet ever saw the woman. So he wondered . . . with the part of his mind that was darker than even he liked to acknowledge . . . just how plausible it would be to keep the old woman alive even after her death. That same dark part of his brain had, on more than one occasion, imagined himself digging a deep grave at the far end of the farm's southern field. And maybe, just maybe, that would work.

He realized he was fading in and out of consciousness behind the Camaro's steering wheel. Maybe he'd had a bit too much to drink after all. He rubbed his eyes then flipped on the Camaro's radio and located a hard-rock station out of West Virginia. A few people stood huddled together beneath the awning of the tavern, smoking cigarettes. Donald Larrabee wasn't among them, and he feared he might have missed him come out already.

An hour earlier, Ricky had been shooting pool, minding his own business, and in a rare state of complacency bordering on a good mood when Larrabee ambled over and complained that he'd been hogging the pool table all night. "As long as I'm paying, I'm playing," Ricky had responded coolly. But then Alvin Toops came over and told him that the tables were on a rotating basis unless it was league night. Alvin Toops was a big son of a bitch, with a shaved head and tattoos on his neck. He kept a shotgun beneath the bar and had threatened Ricky with it on more than one occasion. "See?" Alvin said, waving an arm at the other two tables. "Look how nice everyone else is sharing."

Ricky didn't like the condescending tone of Alvin's voice. He might have even told him so if Alvin's brother, Jimmy Toops, hadn't risen from his stool at the bar. Jimmy owned a towing company and junkyard. Ricky knew better than to mess with some bastard who could hook up your ride when you weren't looking.

"Come on, Codger," Alvin went on, making a face as if he were tasting something sour. "Cut me some slack here, will ya?"

So Ricky cut Alvin Toops some slack. He cut Donald Larrabee, that whiny little bitch, some slack, too . . . by not shoving his boot heel up his ass. He'd dropped his pool cue and paid his bar tab while hastily chugging down the last of his Yuengling, then shoved out into the night while the eyes of the men at the bar hung on him like fishhooks. All the regulars had been there, watching the scene unfold and no doubt hoping for a little entertainment in the form of a bar fight—Elmer Watts, Delmo Dandridge, the Kowalski brothers, Flip the Drip, Lombardo, Davey Kingfield, the lot of them—and Ricky knew what they were thinking. Oh yes, he did. They were thinking, *That pussy Codger can't do shit 'less he wants to wind up back behind bars. The poor bastard's easy meat now.*

Yeah? Well, that was bullshit. He wasn't easy meat for no one.

Nonetheless, following his release from Jessup, he hadn't come straight back to Stillwater for just that reason—to avoid confrontations with the local hillbillies and rednecks who thought they could give the Codger kid a few shoves without getting shoved back. They were wrong, of course—Ricky had never let anyone take advantage of him like that and he didn't plan on starting now—but he had had no real desire to jump back into that mess right away. Instead, he spent a few months living on his own in Cumberland, renting a small room in a boardinghouse and paying his rent with money he withdrew from his grandmother's bank account.

But like all good dogs, he eventually came back home. In the time he'd been gone, which had been about a year and a half, Stillwater had dried up considerably. Even if he'd wanted to snare a job, even a part-time gig, his choices were woefully limited. He wondered what the hell brought him back to this shitty little town after all, aside from a free roof over his head and the luxury of leeching off his grandmother. He couldn't come up with any answer except for the most obvious—a dog like him knew nothing other than the master who whipped him.

Everyone goes back to what they know, no matter how horrible and pointless and static it all is. There was a strange sort of mundane comfort in predictability.

Ricky blinked and rubbed his eyes just as he saw Donald Larrabee pushing his way past the clot of smokers beneath the tavern's awning and hobbling down onto the uneven pavement of the parking lot. He looked drunk, and Ricky wondered just how long he'd been sitting in his car, waiting for the fool. As Ricky watched, Larrabee meandered over to one section of the parking lot where, presumably, he looked for his car. When he couldn't find it, he unbuckled his pants and released a potent arc of urine onto the tire of a green Chevy van. After shaking off, he buttoned up his jeans and staggered back across the lot to where his sad little two-door Civic sat beneath a darkened lamppost. Ricky watched the headlights come on. A long while passed before the Civic pulled out of the space. Larrabee pulled a wide arc around the lot, nearly clipping the front fender of an old Buick Skylark in the process, before emptying out onto the road. Ricky watched the Civic's taillights flare briefly before the vehicle chugged forward into the dark.

Ricky followed.

One-on-one, he'd teach the motherfucker to embarrass him in public. He'd teach him, all right.

When both cars crossed the intersection at Highland and Gracie, Ricky shook out a Camel from the pack he kept wedged in the visor and lit it. He was feeling pretty upbeat now. The Civic continued up Gracie, and Ricky followed. They were the only two cars on the road at this hour and in this part of town—where the barns were all unoccupied and dilapidated monstrosities, and the radio signals fuzzed in and out—but if Donald Larrabee realized he was being followed he did not show it in the casual, sloppy way in which he drove.

The right side of Gracie Street sloped down toward the Narrows.

Ricky peered out the passenger window and down at the silvery concourse of water that snaked through the valley, and he marveled silently at how high the water had risen. With another storm on the horizon, he wondered just how much Stillwater could take.

It's like fucking Armageddon, he thought, chuckling.

Ahead of him, the Civic's taillights swerved right, the tires leaving smeary black skids on the pavement in the wake of their sudden movement. For one second, Ricky thought Donald Larrabee was about to drive his goddamn car down the embankment and into the Narrows. But then Larrabee overcorrected and swerved left.

At this point, it was clear that Larrabee was no longer in control of the vehicle. Ricky eased down on the Camaro's brakes, leaving a nice distance between the two of them, and he eventually came to a full stop just as Larrabee plowed the Civic off the road and straight into a tree.

Ricky stared at the scene, dumbstruck. On the radio, a Metallica song came on. Ricky quickly switched it off, popped open the driver's door, and climbed out of the Camaro.

The air smelled of gasoline and scorched rubber. Steam billowed out from beneath the Civic's hood, which, from where Ricky stood, appeared to be wedged against the trunk of a thick spruce. The taillights looked like beacons on a sinking ship.

Ricky flicked his cigarette into the woods and slowly approached the wreck. By no means did this let Larrabee off the hook—not in Ricky's book—but the suddenness of the whole thing had shuffled the world into a sort of replay mode in which Ricky kept seeing the car swerve and strike the tree over and over again. Trying to catch up to reality was like trying to run through a pool of syrup.

When he reached the rear of the car, Ricky knocked one fist against the Civic's trunk. He knocked again as he approached the driver's side of the vehicle, this time on the driver's side window. The windows were fogged up with condensation and it was difficult to see inside. From what Ricky could make out, it looked like the airbag had been deployed.

A shape moved from within. Ricky hopped back a few steps, suddenly aware of the slimy sheen of sweat that coated his forehead and the palms of his hands. The driver's door cracked open and Donald Larrabee fell out. Larrabee's skin was the color of ancient parchment and there was a lightning-bolt gash vertically bisecting his forehead. He crawled, trembling, on his hands and knees away from the car. Through the open door, Ricky could see that the airbag had indeed been activated and that fine, white powder—or possibly smoke—clouded up the whole interior.

Larrabee crawled to Ricky and looked up. There was dislocation and confusion in his eyes. There was something else in there, as well.

Fear, Ricky thought, recognizing it instantly. *Absolute fear.*

"What . . . the fuck . . . was *that?*" Donald Larrabee gasped as blood drooled out of his mouth.

"A car accident, you shit heel," Ricky said . . . but then he froze as he looked past Larrabee and out onto the road. Something pale and vaguely humanoid stood there, watching him. When it began to creep forward and Ricky registered the unnatural way with which it walked, a cold dread closed around his heart. When moonlight struck the side of the figure's face and he saw that it was, in fact, a young boy, the realization only heightened his fear. He turned and ran for all he was worth back to the Camaro.

He never paused to look back over his shoulder, even when Donald Larrabee began screaming.

Ricky dove into the Camaro, slammed the door, and cranked the ignition until the engine roared. He jerked the gearshift into reverse and spun the wheel while slamming the accelerator. The car lurched dizzyingly backward until Ricky jammed on the brakes with both feet.

Only then did he pause to glance up at the rearview mirror.

What little he saw would haunt him till his dying day: the pale-skinned child atop Donald Larrabee's writhing form, pinning him down, down, with brute and unnatural strength, a gout of steaming liquid belching forth from the child's face and splattering against the back of Larrabee's head—

Ricky Codger had seen enough. He slammed the car back into Drive, jumped on the accelerator, and got the hell out of Dodge.

3

As a strong wind blew hard against the house, old Godfrey Hogarth awoke from some disremembered nightmare that had left him covered in perspiration. He crept slowly out of bed, his heart racing and his skin seeming to tingle. Around him, the house creaked and moaned in the wind, and it was like walking through the belly of an old whaling ship. Hogarth went directly to the bathroom and, without turning on the light, pulled on the faucet. Beneath a cool stream, he washed first his hands then his face and, lastly, the nape of his neck. He remained standing there at the sink in the dark, the water still running, for some time; time enough for his heartbeat to regain its regular syncopation and for his nerves to calm.

Before going back to bed, he paused before the tiny octagonal window in the hall that looked out upon the cold blue curl of asphalt that was Trestle Road. In the moonlight, the asphalt looked like polished steel.

Something's fixing to happen, sure as I'm standing here breathing, he thought then, feeling the creeps overtake him all over again. He was an old man and possessed an intuition about certain things, much as infants know when they're hungry and mothers know how to provide the milk. *Something bad.*

Like an electrical current, it radiated through the marrow of his bones.

4

His mother's pointy foot poked him awake. Dwight stirred and blinked open his eyes. He'd fallen asleep again in front of the television in the living room—some black-and-white horror movie playing on the public-access channel out of Pittsburgh—and was temporarily disoriented. His mother's tired face hung above him like the disapproving face of God.

"Trash needs to go out to the curb," Patti said around the cigarette jutting from between her lips. "Your father's probably gonna forget when he gets home. I'm going to bed."

If he even makes it home tonight at all, Dwight thought, already scrambling to his feet while pawing the sleep from his eyes. There had been more than enough instances—where Delmo Dandridge, after a night of getting shit-faced down at Crossroads, had either fallen asleep in his car in the tavern's parking lot (or on the side of the road) or been hauled into jail—for there to be more than an ounce of truth to Dwight's musing. He shut the TV off and headed down the hall where his sneakers sat in a heap beside the front door while his mother climbed the creaking stairs to go to bed. Gideon, the German shepherd, lifted his head up off his paws. The dog had been snoozing in the foyer and he looked now at Dwight with the sleepy disorientation Dwight himself had felt just a minute earlier when his mother's toes had jabbed at his ribs.

"Good boy," Dwight told the dog. Gideon rested his head back down on his front paws and narrowed his eyes to slits.

The house was cold and he assumed it was even colder outside, so he snagged a sweatshirt with a John Deere logo on it from the hall closet and tugged it on over his head before he stepped out onto the front porch.

Outside, the night was absolute. Insects and frogs exchanged heated dialogue in the long grass and the three-quarters moon looked sharp enough to cleave a wound in the sky. The trash cans were at the side of the house, and Dwight hurried down the porch steps now, not pausing to look around and survey the rest of the property. It was the same way he went down into the basement to retrieve tools for his old man when Delmo got what he called the "fixin' bug"—a quick dash down the stairs, grab the item, and a quick dash back up. Slam the door, too, for good measure. (It was always on these dashes back up the stairs that he swore he heard a second pair of feet hurrying up right behind him, moving at the same speed as he was but just a half-second off.) Taking out the trash was no different . . . particularly since he'd been hearing someone moving around outside the house at night.

Those noises outside his window began roughly around the time the hairless boy's body was found along the banks of Wills Creek. It might have been a week earlier, though he couldn't remember exactly . . . though after the boy's body was discovered, he recalled thinking about those noises he'd been hearing and wondering if whatever had gotten the hairless boy had also spent the previous week lurking outside the Dandridge house. Or . . . worse yet . . . he had wondered if those noises had been the boy himself. Had he been lost? Searching for help? He quickly realized it couldn't have been the boy since the noises continued after the boy's body was found. The boy was dead; the noises were made by someone or something else.

At the side of the house, Dwight found the two metal trash cans overflowing with bags of refuse. He tried to drag them both along at the same time but they were too heavy. Instead, he grabbed the handle of one in both hands and, sliding backward through the muddy lawn, pulled the first can around the side of the house and out to the curb. It was on his return trip back for the second can that he heard the noise.

Dwight's feet skidded to a halt in the dirt. He jerked his head to the right, where overgrown foliage and bamboo stalks rose up over a rusted and bent chain-link fence like aboriginal spears. Suddenly, he was aware that his mouth had gone dry.

"Is someone there?" he croaked. The words practically stuck to the roof of his mouth like peanut butter. "Dad? You back there?" It wasn't unusual for someone to drive Delmo home when he'd had too much to drink, and he often passed out in the yard until morning came to sober him up . . .

The foliage rustled but no answer came.

Dwight thought of Miss Sleet's classroom, now with those two empty desks—Matthew's and Billy Leary's—as incontrovertible as craters made from bombs dropped from a great height. It was the loudest silence Dwight Dandridge had ever heard in his life.

He thought he saw some of the bamboo shoots separate.

His compulsion was to run back into the house and forget the other trash can. But then he thought of his father's wrath when he sobered up the following afternoon and found the second trash can still overflowing against the side of the house, and, for whatever ill-defined reason, Dwight found himself even *more* terrified of that scenario. So he dashed quickly back around the side of the house, grabbed the second trash can by the handle with both hands, and hurriedly hauled it across the lawn to the curb, too. When he'd finished, breathing heavily and prickling with perspiration under the John Deere sweatshirt, he staggered a few steps backward toward the front of the house, his eyes still trained on the bamboo shoots and the rustling, heavy foliage. There was definitely something back there.

He reached down and pried one of the walkway flagstones up out of the dirt. The thing was heavier than it looked and as cold as a thick sheet of ice. Like a discus thrower, Dwight heaved the large flagstone over the fence and into the bushes. The bushes rattled and some of the bamboo shoots bent out at awkward angles. There came a resounding *thong!* as the stone struck one of the galvanized fenceposts.

Frozen with fear, Dwight waited for whatever was back there to spring out and charge him.

But nothing happened. And when he regained mobility a moment later, he ran back into the house, certain that he heard footsteps chasing after him as he sprinted up the porch steps.

5

Some noise woke Bob Leary from a fitful sleep on the living room couch. He roused with a series of meek little grunts, already muttering nonsense to himself, as he swung one leg over the couch and knocked it against the coffee table. Empty cans of Coors Light and a carton of partially eaten Chinese food slid off the table and onto the floor. All around him, the house stank and the smell of it infiltrated his dreams.

Sitting up, he blinked wearily as his eyes became acclimated to the lightlessness of the house. Outside, the wind blew hard and unforgiving through the old trees, a sound like creaking floorboards. Was that the sound that had awakened him?

He staggered to his feet and wended across the darkened living room to the front door. He opened the door and peered out. The wind whooped down and gathered up the dead leaves in the yard into miniature tornadoes. Whistling sounds emanated from the cavernous hollows of the rusted automobiles up on blocks at the side of the house. In a hoarse voice, Bob Leary shouted his son's name out into the freezing darkness. Then, shivering, he went back inside, bolting the door behind him.

Billy was a good kid, though maybe a little slow. Bob had known that since Billy's birth—that writhing, pink, hairless, squealing little contraption that had been wrenched from Lorraine Leary's womb via caesarean. Their only child, the kid had blinked his gummy eyes up at Bob and had worked his toothless mouth as if desperate to speak but unable to form words. Sounds came from the infant child, but they weren't the sounds of a living creature. Rather, they were the sounds of Bob Leary's life being changed for good and permanent, because the eyes that looked up at him had been trusting and needful, and what are you supposed to do with that? And when Lorraine died a few years back from the Big C, it was just the two of them—Bob and his squinty-eyed, puffy-faced son. The Leary men. It was—

A low groan emanated throughout the house, causing Bob Leary to pause in his tracks. This time it wasn't the wind; this had been the noise of an animal, surely. *It was in the house.*

He kept a revolver in the kitchen cabinet. He retrieved it, clicking on all the lights in the house as he went. Then he went down the hall, systematically checking the bedrooms, the revolver shaking in his unsteady hands. "Is that you, Billy-boy?" he called as he stood in the doorway of his son's bedroom. The room was silent and undisturbed. Bob Leary's voice echoed off the walls, and, if he had closed his eyes, he would have easily imagined himself shouting into an empty bank vault or some underground cavern. "You come home, son?"

No answer.

Back in the living room, he went to the sliding-glass doors that looked out onto the back deck and, beyond that, the dense forest. He finagled the light switch beside the door but the bulb outside did not come on, and he couldn't remember the last time he'd changed the bulb. Beyond the property, tall black trees swayed in the wind.

They're calling for another storm, he thought, *and that means another flood. That damn kid better get his ass on home before the waters rise up again, so help him . . .*

Again, that low, guttural moaning sound. This time, it came from directly behind him. Bob jumped and spun around, clutching the revolver in both hands while surveying the living room. The sound was not unlike a raccoon. He'd spent his entire life in the hills of western Maryland and knew the sounds animals made when they were frightened, trapped, or angry.

He heard a scraping noise and flung his eyes toward the stone hearth in time to see a cloud of soot drop down into the fireplace. When he rubbed the back of one hand along his forehead, he realized he was sweating. He laughed nervously, though he did not lower the gun. Goddamn animals were always getting caught in the chimney. Just last winter, he had a goddamn squirrel drop down into the fireplace and tear pell-mell around the living room before Billy got the front door open and Bob was able to chase the little fucker out of the house with a couch cushion.

There was a flashlight on the mantel. He crept over to the hearth, his footfalls silent on the carpeted floor, and snatched it up. He clicked it on and saw that it held a strong and steady beam. He eased himself down on his knees in front of the fireplace, the gun in one hand now, the flashlight in the other. There would be no chasing any oversized rodents around his living room this evening; if he got a bead on the fucker, he'd pull the revolver's trigger and blow it to pieces.

He swiped aside the chain-link curtain just as a second plume of soot rained down from the chimney. Bob could taste the soot at the back of his throat. It made his eyes water. Crouching forward, he propped one shoulder on the ledge of the fireplace then scooted himself up so that his head was inside the hearth. He brought the revolver and the flashlight up beside his head as he peered up the pitch-black channel. The revolver shook. The flashlight beam swung along the brick wall of the fireplace's interior then angled straight up through the open flue.

Bob blinked.

What in the—

A jumble of wiry, black fur vibrated within the beam of the flashlight, no more than four or five feet above Bob's head. It took him a second or two to realize what it was he was looking at—*bats that's bats Jesus fuck that's bats up there*—but when he did, he felt his heart stutter in his chest. *Rabies!* screamed his next immediate thought.

Just as he began to inch his retreat back out of the fireplace, the bats began to flap their wings, causing great roiling clouds of soot to rain down on Bob Leary's face. He sputtered and coughed, swiping absently at his eyes with the back of the hand that held the flashlight. When he blinked his eyes back open and repositioned the beam back up into the flue, he found his son's slack face staring back down at him. The skin fish-belly white, the eyelids purple and swollen shut, Billy Leary hung upside down in the flue, his body wreathed in bats.

Bob felt his bowels loosen.

And just as he opened his mouth to scream, young Billy's eyes flipped open.

CHAPTER THIRTEEN

1

It had been Brandy's intention to stand watch throughout the night, yet, despite her terror, the long and lumbering hours had ultimately conquered her and put her down. She awoke hours later, in the stillness of a Wednesday morning that already promised rain, from sleep in the wicker loveseat on the back porch.

The first thing she realized was that she was freezing—her teeth chattered, the sound not unlike someone tap-dancing across her skull, and the exposed flesh of her arms and legs was broken out into hard little knobs of gooseflesh. Stupidly, she'd fallen asleep out here in nothing more than her nightshirt and panties. It was a wonder she hadn't frozen to death in the night.

Or worse, she thought, her eyes already on the garage that faced the back porch. In the daytime it certainly looked less ominous. The bats were no longer dangling like Christmas decorations from the eaves. Matthew's bike had fallen over on its side—had she done that last night in her panic?—and looking at it again sent a wave of sorrow through her.

Then a piece of last night's dream returned to her—her eyes opening to a darkened world, where bitter winds whistled through the valley and the mountains groaned like restless giants in slumber. Matthew stood down in the yard, staring up at her. He was nude except for his underwear and his scalp was patchy where clumps of his hair had fallen out in places. His eyes took on the predatory black stare of a shark. He dug his toes into the black soil and spoke to her telepathically without actually opening his mouth. Yet his words—if they could even be deemed as such—were like a thousand bleating trumpets at the center of Brandy's brain. In her dream, she shrieked into the night. Her brother—or the thing that had once been her brother—fled back through the cornfield.

Sitting here now, in the bright light of day, she wondered if it had been a dream after all . . .

Also, she had to piss so badly she could taste it.

She crept back into the house, conscious of the fact that her mother was probably still asleep (which she was), and went directly to the upstairs bathroom. She urinated then washed her face and hands before heading to her bedroom. There, she dressed in a pair of running sweats and tied her hair back with an elastic band. She laced on her good running sneakers, too—the Adidas with the cleats. They were a bit dirty, and the cleats had been worn to ineffectual little nubs, but it felt good to climb back into them again.

Back outside, she stood for some time, staring at the shards of broken glass in the dirt then up at the small window in the side of the garage, jagged glass spearheads still protruding from the frame. She went around to the other side of the garage, took a deep breath, and put her hand on the doorknob. Then she shoved the door open, expecting the unexpected.

2

It occurred to her at that moment that prior to last night she hadn't actually stepped foot in the garage since before her father had left.

The small, musty work area was filled with his personal belongings: his tools, his workbench, his lawnmower and Rototiller and gardening supplies, his various automotive supplies, paint cans stacked into pyramids, ancient stereo equipment, including several old turntables blanketed in dust as thick as fur, a Baltimore Ravens cheerleaders calendar pinned to one wall, countless other sundry items. Yet it wasn't just the items but the place itself that channeled Hugh Crawly. The smell of the wood mingled with turpentine mixed with the overly sweet scent of antifreeze and motor oil . . .

All of it.

She found herself fighting off tears. And she hated herself for it. She hated her father, too. *This has nothing to do with you,* her mind quipped, addressing the father who had abandoned the rest of them. *This is about Matthew right now. You have no right intruding on me right now, damn you.*

She took a deep, shuddery breath and was able to bring herself back under control. Looking around, she realized that she had no idea what she had expected to find coming in here. She considered going to the police, maybe talking with Ben Journell again, but she really had no idea what to tell them. That someone had been hiding in her garage, probably for several days now? That she had the horrific impression that the *someone* had, for some inexplicable reason, been her brother? No, she couldn't do that.

Instead, she went back out into the yard and over to where the rickety chain-link fence separated their property from the Marshes' cornfield. Brandy leaned over the fence and saw a perfectly outlined footprint in the hard soil on the other side of the fence. She looked up and could make out a subtle parting of the cornstalks, which suggested the direction the person might have traveled the previous night as they cut through the field.

Without giving it a second thought, Brandy hopped the fence and proceeded through the corn.

3

Bryant and Sylvia Marsh owned about a hundred acres of farmland, much of it utilized for the growing of maize. The fields abutted the Crawly property, close enough that Brandy and Matthew, when they were younger, could reach over the fence and pluck the ripe ears right out of their silky husks without leaving their backyard. The Marshes, who were kind people, encouraged this and would often bring barrels of the crop over to the Crawly household after a plentiful harvest. The cornfields yawned clear across the southern crook of Stillwater, right out to the bristling green-and-brown foothills of Wills Mountain. To the west, the fields overran the wooded hillsides straight out to Gracie Street, where abandoned farmhouses and barnyards stood eerily like props from some long-forgotten movie set.

Brandy followed the trail of broken cornstalks for close to forty-five minutes before the trail grew cold. Something immense and mechanical loomed just ahead so she continued in that direction. It was a large combine harvester, yellow as a school bus, its reciprocating head filled with rows of metal teeth. She walked a complete circle around the machine, still not sure what she was looking for. Satisfied that she hadn't found anything out of the ordinary, she pressed on through the maize, leaving the combine harvester to diminish in her wake.

By the time she emptied out onto Gracie Street, the sky had already been grumbling for some time. A light patter of rain fell but it only lasted a brief time. It felt good against her face. She had worked up quite a sweat hoofing it across town. On the shoulder of the road, she scraped the dirt out from between the cleats on the soles of her sneakers then picked aphids, spiders, and stalk borers from her clothes and hair. Across the road stood the first wave of abandoned farmhouses, their roofs sagging or completely sheared off, their windows like holes punched in drywall. Rising above the rooftops and farther in the distance, the crumbling grain silo rose up like a missile. NO TRESPASSING signs were posted everywhere, but Brandy also saw scads of empty beer cans, fast-food wrappers, and tire tracks in the mud. This was where many residents had lived and farmed until years of flooding had prompted their inevitable evacuation. Even now, the damage done to these structures was still clearly evident in the way they slouched and sloped and sank down into their foundations. The earth itself was still a muddy quagmire from the last flood.

Brandy crossed Gracie Street and trod across the muddy field, surveying the closest farmhouses with something akin to reverential silence. For the first time, she could understand why her father would have wanted to get out of a town as desolate and ruinous as Stillwater. These people had left, hadn't they?

He could have taken us with him.

Again, she chased the thought away. This had nothing to do with her father.

As she crept closer to one of the farmhouses, she was overwhelmed by the smell of the Narrows coming off it in potent, suffocating waves. It was the smell that, following the flood, had permeated the whole town, including the Crawly household. It was stronger out here, however, and Brandy had to hold her breath when she peered into a doorway that no longer had a door hanging from the hinges.

Inside—crumbling darkness and warped, waterlogged floorboards. Animals had made nests and dens, and the vaguely sweet perfume of feces mingled with the reek of the flood. Great streamers of moss, as lush as carpeting, crept up and down the walls. Large rents in the roof showed the iron-colored sky and allowed rain to spill in. With one hand she reached out and touched the doorframe. It was spongy and forgiving. She thought she might be able to push the entire structure over on its side with one sturdy shove.

She crossed between two dilapidated barns where weathered beams and struts poked out from the walls and through the roof like ribs through a rotting carcass. Between the two crumbling barns, a structure slightly larger than an outhouse gathered her attention. There was something rusted and metallic inside—some piece of farming machinery she didn't recognize—and there was what looked like a bloody handprint on the outhouse's open steel door. Brandy veered clear of it, cutting through the marshy ground to a small, square little house made of white brick. The roof was furry with moss that dripped over the front windows. There was a little porch off to the right where a door was set into the front of the house, off-center. The door itself looked like something scavenged from a junkyard. Determined weeds sprang up between the porch's floorboards.

Something moved in one of the house's windows. Brandy jerked her head and peered at the window, trying to see past the film of muck on the glass, but it was impossible. When the thing moved again, she was startled to find that the movement hadn't been coming from *inside* the house, but from right above the window itself. Two bats, their wings intertwined about each other, dangled upside down from the drooping eaves of the house.

A second later, it seemed she was suddenly allowed to see the rest of them. They were clinging with clawed wings to the walls, scrabbling along the rooftop, hanging precariously from a slouching brick chimney, huddling together in damp, hairy pods beneath the porch . . .

Even as she moved toward the house, she couldn't comprehend exactly what she was doing. Had she been watching herself on some instant reply, perhaps projected onto a movie screen, she would have denied that the figure moving slowly toward the house was her—surely *she* would have no intention of going up to that run-down, bat-infested shack. Yet here she was, and she moved with the silent and unwavering determination of a wildcat stalking prey through the underbrush.

The bats nearest the porch did not move as she mounted the waterlogged stairs and arrived before the closed front door of the abandoned house. She was suddenly alive, more alive than she had ever been, and she could feel the blood whooshing through her veins and the sweat bursting through the pores on her face and the agitation tickling the back of her throat. Her heart pumped like a piston.

She pushed against the door, and it opened.

CHAPTER FOURTEEN

1

When Maggie Quedentock finally opened her eyes, she could see the soft glow of daylight behind the drawn shade of the bedroom window. Stiffly, she sat up. She was on the floor of the master bedroom, curled in a fetal position like a child who'd fallen asleep on their parent's lap. What time was it? *When* was it?

The next thing she noticed was the blood on her left forearm, tiny crimson pinpricks that wiped off when she pawed at them.

Her throat felt sore and abraded. Moreover, it felt like someone had run a metal rod straight down into her head, through her neck, and down through her spine. Moving *hurt.* She looked around the room, strands of hair wafting like cobwebs in front of her eyes. The bedroom looked untouched and perfect—yet almost alien to her. She struggled to assemble the events of the past seventy-two hours (or had it been longer?) in her head but found it as fruitless as tossing pieces of a jigsaw puzzle into the air in hopes that they would assemble themselves before striking the floor.

A part of her recalled with perfect clarity what had happened to Evan out in the backyard. However, a wholly separate part of her brain countered that event with falsities and sparkly, curtained gauze, forcing her to question the authenticity of such an incident, which in turn allowed her to function without completely breaking down.

That brick wall was rooted firmly at the center of her brain, and she was torn about whether she should knock it down and bulldoze straight through it or just pretend it wasn't there, content to walk around in circles like a blind cat.

She stood on legs that felt as unsteady as broomsticks. Her mouth tasted stale, and her tongue was a swollen lump of cloth. At the window, she peeled away the shade and looked out on the backyard. It did not make her feel any better that there was no evidence out there of what had occurred two nights ago. Either that *thing* had been real . . . or she was quickly losing her mind. Either way, there was no positive outcome.

The Pontiac and the Volkswagen both glistened in the silvery light that managed to peek out from behind dark clouds. Now, with the darkness of night behind her, it seemed possible and even plausible to believe that everything had been a dream, a nightmare. It hadn't been real.

The shotgun was out there. She could see it in the dirt, its inky-black barrel sticking out past the VW's front tires. She stared at it for a full three minutes, until her eyes burned from not blinking.

Trembling, she went into the bathroom. The visage in the mirror grimaced at her. There was blood on her lower lip where she had apparently bitten down too hard in her sleep, which accounted for the patter of blood on her left forearm. The wine stain was still front and center on her tank top with the Crossroads logo emblazoned across the top. Vaguely, she recalled spilling her wine last night . . . or two nights ago . . .

What the fuck day is this?

Beneath a spray of lukewarm water, she washed her face and hands then pulled her hair back and manipulated it into a hasty ponytail with a fabric hair tie.

She'd wanted to call for help the past two nights but couldn't. This realization rushed back to her now like a tidal wave. They didn't have a land line and she'd dropped her cell phone out in the yard two nights earlier, before running back into the house. Trapped. Helpless. She could risk going back out there to find her phone, sure . . . but that *thing* might still be out there . . .

She stripped off her clothes, needing to get rid of that accusatory wine stain, and dressed in a pair of jeans and a halter top. Back at the bathroom sink, she brushed her teeth, nearly sobbing the whole time. It was such a pragmatic and domesticated thing to do, brushing one's teeth in front of the bathroom mirror, and she thought it would help calm her down, but all it did was make her more anxious and upset. She spat into the sink and threw her toothbrush into the basin then rushed out into the hallway as if someone were chasing her.

The hallway clock ticked ominously. She listened but the rest of the house was incriminatingly silent. At the far end of the hall, where shadows shifted and twisted and looked nothing like the objects which they belonged to, a shape ambled into view, large and hulking. Maggie felt her throat tighten.

It was her father, as big in death as he had been in life, standing there in the suit she and her mother had buried him in. His face was a peeling mask of flesh through which the ridges of his cheekbones protruded. His eye sockets were hollow pits at the bottom of which issued a faint red illumination. His nose was gone, revealing in its absence a spade-shaped cavity that reminded Maggie of hands pressed together in prayer.

—You hated me but all I ever did was try to prepare you for the hardships of this world, he said. His voice was clogged with dirt from the grave.

"I didn't hate you." Tears stung her eyes.

—Things you do come back to haunt you, he said. Things you forget about never forget about you.

She cried out then, grabbing the sides of her head while her tears burned hot rivulets down her cheeks. A moment later, when she opened her eyes, her father was gone.

Losing my mind, losing my mind, losing my mind . . .

In the living room, the broken wine glass still sat in a puddle of spilled wine. She went quickly to the back door and peered through the crescent of glass. It provided a slightly different perspective of the yard than the bedroom window had, but she could still see no more than the tip of the shotgun poking out from behind the Volkswagen. Her cell phone was out there somewhere but she couldn't see that, either.

Daylight is my best chance. If I keep myself holed up in this house, that thing will come back when it's dark—it always seems to come back when it's dark—and then I'm a goner. Daylight is my best bet.

A part of her brain was still trying to convince her that none of this was real and it was all a nightmare and Evan was out working at the plant and he would arrive home tonight in time for dinner and maybe she should shoot out to Lomax's for groceries . . .

It was the same mantra she had convinced herself of last night. Now, she tried to recall specific details of yesterday but found that, aside from brief and flashy snapshots of jumbled, nonsensical images, she could remember very little. She had slept most of yesterday away, hadn't she? She'd been practically unconscious with fear for a full twenty-four hours.

Or possibly longer, she thought now, trembling all over again. *I could have been asleep for days. Or even a week . . . or a month. What if everyone else in Stillwater is gone? What if I'm the only one left and that thing is still out there, waiting?*

Ceiling beams creaked. She froze, petrified. Could something be on the roof? Christ—in the fucking *attic*?

Can someone die from fright?

From the kitchen window, she could see a scrabble of footprints in the dirt. They were erratic, like those of some frantic animal. Sunlight angled off the dent in the Pontiac's hood and winked at her. That damn shotgun barrel seemed to be pointing straight at her.

She forced herself under control. Closing her eyes, she grew conscious of her breathing and forced it to regain some semblance of composure. From the roll of paper towels on the wall, she ripped off a streamer of paper and went into the living room, where she cleaned up the spilled wine and collected the pieces of broken glass like someone hunting for treasure on a tropical beach.

Through the window over the sink, she could see the fenceposts and, beyond that, the backyard. The wet grass rippled in the wind.

You can't stay in this house forever. It was the head-voice again, although this time she couldn't tell if it was her unborn, undead child or some other ethereal voice booming down on her from the heavens. She couldn't be sure. Nothing was real and nothing made sense. If she stayed in this house, she was certain she'd crisp up like something excavated from a fire . . . that she'd blacken and turn to a heap of muddy soot. Her soul was shrinking.

"Daddy?" Her voice carried down the hallway and echoed through the empty house like someone shouting down into the belly of a mineshaft.

Momentarily, she was confused again . . . uncertain about who she was and where she belonged . . .

Again, she thought she heard the beams above her head creak. *Someone is up there . . .*

No. She couldn't stay here.

Couldn't.

In the living room, she found her hand on the dead bolt. Holding her breath, she turned the bolt until she heard and felt it slide home. When she opened the door, daylight slivered into the living room like a laser beam. She could feel the cold wind against her skin and hear insects buzzing in the grass. Beyond the patio steps, she could see the footprints her bare feet had made in the soft earth two nights ago. Retracing those footprints should bring her to where her cell phone—

Not bothering to complete this thought, she rushed out into the yard and ran pell-mell across the lawn, the dew-covered grass cold and slick against the soles of her feet, the cold autumn wind in her hair. Her breath rasped in her throat. She stopped halfway across the yard, the chrome on the Volkswagen Beetle glinting in the sunlight that managed to poke out from behind angry-looking thunderheads. Looking down, she saw her toes and her feet were grungy with mud. There was no cell phone but there were striations in the dirt and dime-sized holes in the hood of the Beetle where the creature's acidic sludge had burned through the tempered steel.

Full-fledged panic didn't strike her until she turned around and saw just how far she was from the house and the door. A trembling began at the base of her spine and quivered, like a knife stuck in a piece of plywood, up to the base of her skull. Her blood suddenly felt like ice water.

Her cell phone was nowhere to be found.

When she turned back around, she found that her feet had unconsciously brought her closer to the Volkswagen. With horrific vividness, she could see the barrel of the shotgun jutting up out of the dirt from behind the VW. There were tufts of fabric on the ground, too—shreds of Evan's flannel shirt.

Unable to help herself, Maggie drew closer and closer to the vehicle until she was able to peer over the VW's hood.

Evan's body was gone. The shotgun was still there, as were a few tattered ribbons of fabric that Maggie was certain had come from Evan's shirt, and there were clawed trenches in the dirt and blood on the ground and splattered against the hood of the car . . . but the body of her husband was not there.

Losing my mind, losing—

Bits of bloody flesh speckled the Volkswagen's windshield.

She felt herself begin to hyperventilate. In the periphery of her vision, she saw figures shifting, taunting her like blurry jesters. When she looked directly at them, they disappeared. The pounding of her heart actually *hurt.*

Losing—

A high-pitched keening rose up from her throat. It broke through to the air like an alarm. Clumsily, she pivoted in the dirt and began running back toward the house. Mere feet from the house, she believed she saw the image of her dead father standing behind one of the living room windows, a cadaverous grin spread across his colorless, skeletal face.

Screaming, Maggie cut to the left and tore across the western field. The gate in the fence was wide open and she ran straight through it, knocking over a couple of trash cans. While she ran, she imagined someone's hand falling on her shoulder. This only caused her to run faster. And finally, when hands *did* grab her, she passed out.

2

Fifteen minutes later, Ben's squad car pulled up the Morelands' long driveway toward a whitewashed, two-story farmhouse. As he approached, a figure rose up from a bench on the front porch. It was Jed Moreland, nervously rubbing his bristling chin and neck with one large hand. Jed nodded and said Ben's name as Ben mounted the porch steps and took off his campaign hat.

"Hey there, Jed. I've got Eddie La Pointe on his way out here, too." The porch creaked beneath Ben's boots. "What the hell happened?"

"I caught her about a half-hour ago running through the field," Jed said, opening the screen door. He was nearing sixty but looked younger; working in the fields year-round kept him healthy and in good shape. "She was screaming her head off and nearly socked me in the face when I grabbed her. When she finally got herself under control, she said someone did something to Evan. I didn't quite know what to make of it so I figured I'd best call you guys. She's inside with Bev now. She's calmed down some but she still ain't makin' a whole lot of sense. Talkin' gibberish, if y'ask me."

Ben followed Jed Moreland into the house. It was a traditional country home, the ancient wallpaper bearing a corncob pattern and adorned with framed needlepoints. Miniature tractors and hand-carved angel figurines stood on shelves in the hallway that led into the kitchen. The kitchen itself was spacious, with a bay window overlooking the Morelands' property and, beyond, the immense panorama of the Allegheny Mountains.

Maggie Quedentock sat at the kitchen table with Jed's wife, Beverly. Beverly was a stout, stone-faced woman in her fifties who looked both concerned and unnerved sitting at the table with Maggie. There were two cups of coffee on the table between the women, but it didn't appear as if they'd been touched.

Maggie looked up at Ben, and he was immediately taken aback by the swimmy, unfocused quality in her eyes. It was like looking at an asylum inmate.

"There's some stuff out in the yard that needs tending," Jed said to his wife, who rose quickly from the table and appeared more than happy to be ushered out of the room.

Once they left, Ben pulled out one of the kitchen chairs and sat down. On the tabletop, Maggie's hands gyrated like seismographic instruments. Having spent his whole life in Stillwater—among the *people* of Stillwater—he often tried to put his own opinions about certain people out of his head when he was acting in an official capacity. As someone with little interest in gossip and innuendoes, he was usually able to do this without difficulty. Therefore, it bothered him when he suddenly found himself sitting here with Maggie and hearing his father's voice rise up into his head from the grave, warning him to steer clear of the Kilpatricks. *That Aaron Kilpatrick,* his father had once told Ben when he was just a boy, *he ain't too right in the head, boy, and I don't trust what he'd do if he ever caught you over there doing something he didn't like.*

Ben shook the thought from his head. "Seems like you've been having one busy week," he said, putting a hand atop one of Maggie's. "Did something happen to Evan?"

"There's something going on," she rasped in a partial whisper. Her voice sounded hoarse, and her hand vibrated like a tuning fork beneath his.

"What's that?" he asked gently.

"I don't know what it is." Then her eyes went distant and seemed to stare right through Ben and at the kitchen wall behind him. "Or maybe I do. I don't . . . I don't know . . ."

Ben squeezed her hand but then slid his off hers. He felt uncomfortable touching her and feeling the bones trembling beneath her flesh. He glanced over his shoulder, following Maggie's gaze to the wall. A large silver crucifix hung there. A chill in his bones, he turned back to Maggie. "You told Jed someone hurt your husband," he said, deliberately phrasing it as a statement. "Do you remember?"

"Not a *someone.*" She began to slowly shake her head. Her eyes refocused and clung to him now, burning holes in his flesh. He almost preferred her staring at the wall. "I don't know exactly . . ." Her voice trailed off.

"Maggie, what happened to Evan? Tell me what you know."

"What I *saw.*"

"Okay. What did you see?"

"Evan was out in the yard yesterday. Or maybe it was two days ago. I can't really remember what day it was. Time's all screwed up." On the table, her hand trembled audibly. "We'd had a . . . a fight. It was dark so I couldn't see. Something . . ." She squared her shoulders, her body going rigid. "Something came out of the dark and got him."

"Could you see who it was?"

"It wasn't *anyone!*" she screamed, startling him. Her own chair skidded against the tiles. "It was a *thing!* It looked like a person but it *wasn't!*" She jerked forward and clutched at Ben's shirt. "It was the thing I hit with my car. Remember? Remember what happened?"

"I remember," he said in a small voice, trying to pry her claws from his uniform. "You said it was a boy."

"It looks like a boy," she said, "but it's not."

"Do you—"

"It's haunting me and breaking me down. It's making me pay."

"Pay for what, Maggie?" He managed to get one of her hands off him, though it still retained the hooked shape of a bird's talon. When she didn't answer, he said, "Why do you think it's the same person from the accident?"

"It's not a person," she reiterated, more calmly this time.

"Okay. But the night of the accident you said it looked like a child had come—"

"It may be a child and it may *look* like a person, but it isn't. Don't let it fool you."

"No one's going to fool me," he told her.

She froze and gaped at him, as if she suddenly forgot who he was. Almost too casually, she withdrew her hands from him and brought them close to her body, crossing them at the wrists over her chest. Ben watched as her nostrils flared and sweat began trickling down her temples.

Ben stood. *Something's seriously wrong with her,* he thought. "Do you want to go to the hospital?" he asked her.

"No."

"Are you sure? I can have someone take you."

"I don't need a hospital. I don't need doctors."

She's afraid they'll lock her up in the loony bin, Ben thought.

"I'm going to go over to your place and check things out," he said. "Is the house unlocked?"

"Yes."

"Where did you say this happened to Evan? Out in the yard?"

"Yes. In the back. By the cars."

"Okay. Now I want you to try and relax. We'll talk about this again when I get back. Meantime, you stay here with Jed and Bev."

"Be careful over there," she said in a near whisper.

Nodding, Ben stepped backward out of the kitchen. He found Jed and Beverly Moreland on the front porch, Beverly sitting ramrod straight on the bench while Jed leaned over the porch railing, smoking a Capone cigarillo.

Jed turned and looked at Ben as he came out of the house. "Well?"

"I'd appreciate it if you guys could keep an eye on her until I get back from checking out her house."

"Something's funny with her," Beverly Moreland intoned. She had the strict, no-nonsense voice of an aged schoolmarm.

"She and Evan have always been a little off," Jed opined, waving a hand at his wife.

"This," said Beverly Moreland, "is more than just off, Jed. Something scared that girl."

Another squad car pulled up the Morelands' driveway, its heavy tires splashing through puddles. It parked beside Ben's car and Eddie La Pointe got out, blotting his sun-reddened forehead with a handkerchief. He held his campaign hat in his other hand.

"Don't worry, Ben," Jed told him. "We'll keep an eye on her till you get back."

Ben intercepted Eddie at the bottom of the porch steps.

"Shirley said to hump it out here ASAP," Eddie said, looking puzzled. "Something about Evan Quedentock . . ."

Still within relative earshot of the Morelands, Ben dropped his voice as they both walked back to their squad cars. He filled Eddie in on what Maggie had told him then added, "She sounds completely out of it. Whatever happened over at her place, it scared her half to death."

"Goddamn," Eddie muttered.

Ben said, "Let's take my car."

Since the Quedentock house was just on the other side of the Morelands' farm, the drive took less than two minutes. Ben swung the squad car around to the rear of the house where the Quedentocks' two vehicles sat at the center of a muddy turnabout. The house did not appear to be disturbed and Ben could make out no overtly obvious signs of a struggle—broken windows or items strewn about on the lawn—that would have caused him any further concern. Yet the quietness of it all was what bothered him most.

Maggie's right about one thing, he thought, shutting down the car's engine. *Something's going on, all right.*

Ben and Eddie got out of the car just as a cool autumn breeze swept down from the mountains, shaking the orange leaves in the trees like maracas. The fronds of a weeping willow tree at the edge of the property waved at them, unfurled like the tentacles of some undersea beastie.

Ben pointed at the two vehicles. "She said it happened over here."

They walked toward the cars, their pace seeming to slow down simultaneously as the items on the ground came into view—a shotgun and what appeared to be torn ribbons of clothing. What first looked like mud patterns along the side of the Volkswagen revealed itself to be a spray of blood as the two men drew closer.

"Jesus," Eddie intoned. "That's blood."

There were bits of matter stuck to the windshield. Ben leaned forward and examined the gore.

"What?" Eddie asked, his voice high and panicky. "What is it?"

Ben dropped down beside the shotgun and felt the barrel to see if it was hot. It wasn't. Looking around, he could see the dirt had been disturbed, and there were two distinct trenches leading away from the vehicles and into the grass. Ben stood uncomfortably.

"This ain't good," Eddie said.

"What's that?" Ben asked, pointing to something on the ground beside one of Eddie's boots.

Eddie bent and picked it up. "Looks like pieces of a shirt," he said, examining the frayed ribbon of fabric. "She said this happened when?"

"She wasn't clear. Maybe two nights ago. The blood is dry."

"That's really all blood, isn't it?"

"Looks that way."

"What's she been doing since then?" Eddie asked. "For two days? Hiding in the house?"

"I don't know."

"Doesn't make sense."

Ben uttered, "Christ." He bent down and picked up a spent shotgun shell from behind the tire of the Volkswagen Beetle.

"Lord," Eddie said, his face going slack as he stared at the hollow cylindrical tube Ben held. "Do you think . . . ?" He didn't need to complete the thought.

"Seems likely." Ben glanced around. "Looks like there's only one."

"One's enough," Eddie commented. "What do you think that means?"

"Can't mean anything good, I don't think," Ben said. "Not with all that blood." He leaned over the Volkswagen's hood. Aside from the blood and flecks of spongy matter, as well as a number of rust holes that had burned straight through the hood to reveal sections of the engine block underneath, the car was in otherwise fine condition. Curiously, there was a dried greenish crust around the perimeter of the holes that looked suspiciously like the slimy webbing he'd seen around the wounds of Porter Conroy's Holsteins. "Come take a look at this," Ben said.

Eddie peered at the hood of the car then looked up at Ben and shrugged. "What about it?"

"That stuff doesn't remind you of that gunk that was stuck to Porter's dead cows?"

"I guess." Eddie seemed unimpressed. "That stuff on the cows was like jelly, though."

"Well, maybe this stuff had time to dry out." Ben scraped at some with his fingernail, and the grayish flakes were scooped up by the breeze like dandelion seeds.

Overhead, the sky darkened. Eddie looked up warily. The smell of rain was in the air. "Perfect," Eddie muttered.

Ben stuffed the shotgun shell in his pocket. He moved down the length of the car, searching for more of the strange greenish substance or any other evidence. There was none. He crossed over to the Pontiac and checked that car out as well. Still nothing.

"Christ, Ben. You don't really think Maggie shot him, do you?"

"I don't have an opinion on anything just yet."

Eddie shook his head, his eyes like searchlights. He looked like he wanted to throw up.

"Grab some rubber gloves from the car, would you?" he told Eddie.

"Rubber gloves?"

"They're in a box in the trunk."

Confused, Eddie mumbled, "Okay . . ."

Ben followed the twin trenches in the dirt until they disappeared in the grass. Damned if those trenches didn't look like the impression someone's heels might make if they were to be dragged somewhere . . .

Ben walked through the grass, his eyes scrutinizing the ground. The trail was lost here. He looked up, his eyes following the slope of the property to the billowing willow tree and, beyond the tree, the chicken-wire fence that surrounded the property. Directly overhead, thunder growled.

Ben stopped. There was something small and black on the ground next to his shoe. Ben picked it up. It was a cell phone.

Okay . . . so what was this about? A domestic situation gone awry? Evan's out here yelling about the dent Maggie put in the Pontiac, the fighting escalates . . . a shotgun makes itself known? It was a leap, though stranger things had happened. *Would Maggie have gone back into the house to get the gun? If she'd shot him right here, where's the blood? Where's the body? And it's not like she did anything to cover up her tracks, so why not admit to it back at the Morelands' place?*

He slid the cell phone into the breast pocket of his uniform as he approached the willow tree. Its tendril branches seemed to finger the air, summoning him with a come-hither gesture. There'd once been a similar tree at the corner of the Journell property when he was a young boy. It had been the perfect tree for climbing. Once you were nestled securely in the upper branches, no one could see you. You were hidden from the world. Sometimes, as a kid, Ben would sit up there for hours.

Like separating a curtain, Ben brushed the spindly branches aside and stepped under the umbrella of the tree. It was incrementally cooler and darker in its shade. He bent and examined the earth around the base of the tree and then he examined the tree itself, searching for anything—though he knew not what—that he might perceive as out of the ordinary. He hadn't liked the way Maggie had been talking back at the Morelands' house and he didn't much care for the shotgun and spent shotgun shell he'd found out here in the yard. He didn't much care for the blood sprayed along the side of the car and smeared on the windshield, either.

If she shot him . . . where the hell is he?

Back by the cars, Eddie handed Ben a pair of latex gloves. "What are these for?"

"So we don't leave fingerprints and corrupt the scene."

Eddie frowned, his eyebrows knitting together. "Fingerprints on what?"

"Let's go check the house," Ben said.

3

Yet, with the exception of a broken wine glass in the kitchen trash, the house was otherwise undisturbed. In the basement, Ben located a box of slugs that matched the brand of the shotgun shell he'd found out in the yard. After twenty minutes of fruitless searching, Ben and Eddie returned to the yard just as a light rain began to fall.

"Let's bag up the shotgun as evidence before the rain washes away any prints," Ben advised, and the two men began wrapping the shotgun in a sheet of plastic tarp Ben kept in the trunk of his squad car.

4

The rain was coming down in sheets by the time Ben returned to the Moreland house. Eddie had already left in his own car to bring the shotgun back to the station and to write up the chain-of-custody form he would have to send to the county police, along with the shotgun, in order to have it dusted for prints. It was the most action Eddie had seen in a long time and, to Ben, he seemed both nervous and excited.

Beverly Moreland was in the kitchen preparing dinner when Jed let Ben into the house. Jed looked utterly exhausted. He worked a toothpick around one corner of his mouth as he shook Ben's hand. "She's on the back porch," he told Ben. "Didn't want to come inside. Said she wanted to keep watch on whatever's out there."

"Thanks for keeping an eye on her, Jed."

"Bev gave her a Valium. It seemed to calm her down. I hope that was okay."

"That's fine."

Jed led him out onto the back porch but didn't follow him out. Maggie was perched like a bird on the porch steps, her hands folded in her lap, her eyes trained on the downpour that was already filling up craters in the earth. Cornstalks heaved and swelled in the wind like ocean waves.

Ben folded his arms and leaned against the porch railing. He was quiet for quite some time, watching the rainwater sluice down the eaves of the porch's roof. Eventually, he cleared his throat. "What were you and Evan fighting about, Maggie?"

She looked up at him, her stare as lifeless as a wax dummy's.

"Maggie?" he said when she didn't respond.

She turned back and looked out over the cornfield. "He accused me of sleeping around on him."

"Had you been?"

She didn't answer.

"Where'd the shotgun come from?"

"It's Evan's. He keeps it in the basement."

"I meant, why was it out in the yard?"

"Evan had it."

"Did he threaten you with it?"

Silence.

"Maggie? Did Evan threaten you with the gun?"

"I. . . can't remember . . ."

"Think harder."

"He was yelling at me. He was sitting on the car with the gun in his lap, yelling at me."

"Did someone fire a shot?"

Again, she said, "I can't remember."

"There's blood on the car, too." When she didn't respond to this, he added, "Do you know whose blood it is?"

"I guess it's Evan's."

"Did you shoot Evan?"

"No."

"Are you sure you don't—"

"I didn't shoot him. I didn't kill my husband."

"At least one shot was fired from that shotgun, far as I can tell right now. Who did it?"

"It must have gone off when . . . when he was being attacked . . ."

"Evan, you mean? Attacked by who?"

She trained her dark, vacuous eyes back on him. "I don't know," she said in a barely audible voice.

"Didn't you see the person?"

"No." She looked back at the rain.

Ben sighed and leaned on the railing. "Let's talk some more, but not here, okay?"

Maggie stood up sharply from the stairs. "I don't want to go back to my house." There was genuine fear in her eyes.

"We'll talk down at the station," Ben said.

5

She was silent for much of the ride from the Morelands' house to the barracks. The only visible sign of life came when she turned her head to look out the passenger window at the carved roadway that was Full Hill Road trailing up into the wooded hillside. To assuage his discomfort, Ben turned on the radio. R.E.M. came on, singing about the end of the world. He snapped the radio back off.

"Am I under arrest?"

Though there was enough probable cause to lock her up right then, he said, "No, ma'am."

They got soaked going from the car to the station. Ben pointed to a restroom and told Maggie she could go clean up in there and he'd see if he could locate some towels. In the dispatch office, Shirley Bennice sat at her desk reading an issue of *People* magazine. She looked up at him as he came into the office and made a *tsk tsk* sound. "Lord, Ben, you're soaked."

"It's coming down in buckets now. We got any towels?"

"There should be some clean ones in the storage closet. I'll run and grab some if you want."

"Sit tight, I'll get them. Did Eddie come back yet?"

"He's at his desk."

In the Batter's Box, Eddie sat curled over his desk filling out the chain-of-custody paperwork for the shotgun in large block letters. He wrote with the intensity and concentration of a schoolboy, his tongue cocked into one corner of his mouth.

"I brought Maggie Quedentock back, gonna ask her a few more questions," Ben said, opening the storage closet. There was a stack of clean white towels on the bottom shelf. He bent to pull two out when the cell phone he'd found in the Quedentocks' backyard fell out of his pocket and clattered to the floor. He had forgotten about it.

"This whole thing gives me the creeps," Eddie said from his desk.

Ben flipped the phone open. The phone was on but the battery icon in the corner of the screen was red, indicating that it needed to be charged. Was there enough juice left to make a call?

"I'm gonna dial your desk phone," he told Eddie. "Tell me whose name appears on the caller ID."

Eddie swiveled around in his chair and watched Ben dial. A moment after he hit Send, Eddie's desk phone rang. Eddie leaned over and examined the narrow digital screen on the top of the phone. "That's weird," Eddie marveled. "It says *Tom Schuler*."

Ben ended the call and flipped the phone closed.

"He's my goddamn mechanic," Eddie said, turning back around in his chair to face Ben. "How come you got Schuler's cell phone?"

And then it hit him: Tom lived off Full Hill Road, up the hill on the outskirts of town—the same road where Maggie's accident had taken place last week. On the night of the accident, Maggie had claimed to have been heading home from Crossroads in town. Full Hill Road was not only out of her way, it was at the other end of town.

What had she told him back at the Morelands' place? *He accused me of sleeping around on him.* And when he'd asked her if this was true, she hadn't responded.

Things in his head began to turn and snap together with a series of nearly audible clicks.

"Ben?" Eddie stood. "You okay?"

"Wasn't that Tom Schuler's car that Dorr Kirkland had towed recently?" Ben asked, though he already knew the answer.

"Yeah, Ben. What's wrong? What's that mean?"

Maggie appeared in the doorway. Her face blotchy and her hair stringy and wet, she looked like a corpse that had just washed up on a beach somewhere.

"What happened to Tom Schuler?" Ben asked her from across the Batter's Box. Eddie's eyes jumped in her direction.

"Maggie?" Ben said.

Maggie said nothing.

Ben turned to Eddie. "Go out to Tom's place, see if he's home."

Eddie picked his campaign hat up off the corner of his desk. "Sure thing."

"You won't find him," Maggie said from the doorway.

"Where is he?" Ben asked.

"He's gone, too. Just like Evan."

6

After Eddie left, Ben sat opposite Maggie at a table in the small kitchenette that also functioned, when needed, as an interrogation room. He asked Maggie various questions—about her relationship with Tom Schuler, about the argument with Evan, about whether or not she believed Evan had done something to Tom or if Tom had done something to Evan—but she provided no responses. Her eyes grew increasingly distant. Ben began to think that she could no longer hear him speaking, that his words were barrages of nonsense that whistled uninterrupted and undigested through the hollow space at the center of her mind. After ten minutes of this foolishness, Ben told Maggie to stand up. He had to repeat this command two more times before she actually complied. It wasn't that she was being deliberately insubordinate; to Ben, it seemed that some vital fluid was slowly leaking out of her, leaving nothing but a glaze-eyed zombie wearing Maggie Quedentock's clothes.

He led her into lockup. Poorhouse Pete still occupied the third cell, and as Ben and Maggie entered, Pete perked up and watched them intently, like an owl in a tree. Maggie said nothing when Ben led her into the first cell. She went and sat down on the bench and stared out at him with dead eyes as he closed and locked the cell door.

I think I'm currently witnessing someone on the verge of losing their mind.

"My baby did it," she said, startling him. "That's the big secret, Ben. That's what got Evan and what got Tom, too. My baby."

"Who's your baby, Maggie?"

"He died before he was ever born, back when I was just a girl. But now he's back and he's making me pay. He got Tom and he got Evan and now he's coming for me next."

From memory, Ben recited Maggie her Miranda rights. Then he went to Poorhouse Pete's cell and unlocked it.

"Hey," Pete said, his old face suddenly slack and innocent. "What'd I do?"

"Time to go. This isn't a boardinghouse."

"You said I could—"

"I'm not in the mood tonight, Pete. Please."

Pete rose and shuffled out of the cell. Ben gave him a few dollars and one of the rain slickers they kept in the supply closet then ushered him out the front doors of the station. The rain was coming down harder now, the sky deepening toward dusk. Before passing through the front door and out into the rain, Poorhouse Pete gave Ben one last doleful look from over his shoulder. Under his breath the homeless man muttered, "You really gonna make me go back out there, ain't you?"

Ben sighed. "Have a good night, Pete."

Pete shuffled out into the night, his body trembling beneath the rain slicker. His longish hair hung in wet ropes around his face as he peered up at the darkening sky. That was how Ben left him.

He went back to the dispatch office and leaned exhaustedly in the doorway. The look on his face must have been one of pure misery, judging by the empathetic look Shirley gave him from over her magazine.

"Maggie Quedentock is in lockup," Ben said.

"Maggie?"

"I think she did something to her husband. And maybe Tom Schuler, too."

"What do you mean 'did something'?"

"She may have killed them."

Outside the windows, lightning lashed across the sky. A peal of thunder followed.

Ben's cell phone rang at his hip. He snatched it up and saw Joseph Platt's name and number scrolling by on the digital screen. Ben answered. "This is Ben."

"Can you . . . Ben? Hello?"

"Your phone's breaking up, Joseph."

". . . problem here . . ."

"Come again?" Ben said. The worry on Shirley's face increased.

". . . need to get out here . . ."

"Where? Where are you? What's going on?"

Through quips of static, Ben heard Platt say, "Gracie Street . . . old farmhouses . . . we found . . . think we . . . the Crawly boy . . ."

Ben's left eyelid twitched.

On the other end of the line, he thought he heard Platt say, ". . . dead."

CHAPTER FIFTEEN

1

Joseph Platt was in the middle of Gracie Street waving his arms when Ben approached in his squad car. Ben pulled onto the shoulder of the road and got out. He tugged a rain slicker over his uniform as he hustled across the swampy field, his boots driving craters into the soft mud. Platt met him halfway, talking fast.

"He's up here in one of the houses," Platt said, rainwater streaming down his face. His hair was plastered to his head.

"He's dead?" Ben asked, following Platt between the skeletons of two run-down barns. Platt's cruiser was parked in the mud before a square little house the same color as the storm-filled clouds above. Mel Haggis was wending around in the mud with an extendable baton in his hand.

"God, yes." It came out in a sickening wheeze. "Me and Mel were up here checking out a car that had hit a tree and this girl, she comes running up the goddamn street—"

"What girl?"

"The sister," Platt said. "She found the body."

No no no no no, Ben thought. *None of this is happening.*

"Brandy Crawly?"

"Yes."

"Where is she now?"

“In my car,” said Platt.

Indeed, as Ben hurried past Platt’s cruiser, he could see Brandy Crawly’s face staring out at him from the backseat. She was a ghost.

“Hey, Sarge,” Haggis grumbled when Ben arrived at the foot of the little house. Rickety steps led up to a door that was partway open.

“What’s with the baton?”

“Bats,” Haggis said. “Had to shoo ’em away from the house.”

“Terrific. Where is he?”

“Inside,” Platt said, moving up the porch steps and unclipping a penlight from his gear belt. “I’ll show you.”

Ben followed. Passing through the doorway was like being inhaled by the house. Inside, the air was stifling and musty, redolent with the stink of mildew, bat shit, and decay. Curtains of gauze crisscrossed the entranceway, strung up to the rotting beams in the ceiling and billowing gentle in the breeze. It took Ben a second or two to realize these were cobwebs.

“Be careful,” Platt warned. “Floor’s spongy. Don’t break an ankle.”

It was like walking on a mattress.

“There,” Platt said, shining his light at one corner of the room.

Ben thought, *Holy Christ.*

Momentarily, Ben was back on the banks of Wills Creek, staring down at the unidentified corpse of a hairless child. This creature looked no different—a pale white form frozen in a fetal position on the floor of the abandoned house, the gleaming dome of its skull like a giant hard-boiled egg, patchy with strands of blondish hair. The corpse’s face was Matthew Crawly’s face, though just barely. His eyelids were swollen shut and his skin looked taut and nearly transparent.

“What the hell happened to him?” Platt asked him. “I mean, Jesus fuck, Ben, *look* at him. That’s not . . . I mean, that’s . . . what *happened* to him?”

"I don't know." Ben's voice shook. Slowly, he advanced toward the boy. When Platt told him again to be careful, he wasn't so sure he was talking about the floor anymore.

Ben knelt down beside the body. The boy's skin was colorless and practically translucent. Ben could make out the assemblage of veins and arteries, like fine blue cables, networked just beneath the paper-thin flesh. The joints—the kneecaps and elbows—were bony protrusions that reminded Ben of knots in a tree's trunk. The fingernails and toenails were ragged and blackened; there was mud and some other grit beneath the nails. And, of course, the face . . . the face was a taut membrane of skin stretched across the protuberances of the skull. Those horrific eyes bulged beneath purpled lids that had been seemingly fused shut. Within the slash of the boy's mouth, Ben could see the protrusion of a tongue, swollen and black. When he reached out and touched the corpse—the skin was as cold and unyielding as the skin of a dead toad—Platt sucked in a breath and moaned, "Ben . . ."

Ben ignored him. The boy's body rocked forward and Ben peered down at the boy's back. Shoulder blades like dorsal fins. Four circular wounds ran vertically down the boy's back. A suppurated, yellowish discharge had dried in crusty ribbons along the interlocking knots of the boy's spinal column.

Boy, Ben thought. *This is no boy.*

"What do we do, Ben?"

Ben thought for a minute then stood up. The corpse rocked back on its side with sickening rigidity. "We take the body back to the station. I'll call the medical examiner's office and see if Deets will come out tonight, but I don't want to leave the body in here." The abandoned house seemed to groan all around him. Ben shivered. "I'm gonna call the sheriff's department over in Cumberland and have them send some guys out, too. This is beyond anything we're prepared to handle."

Joseph Platt just stood there, unmoving. He still had his penlight trained on the corpse.

"Is there a problem?" Ben said.

"You want us to . . ."

"Take the body back to the station for right now."

Platt still didn't move.

"Would you rather tell Wendy Crawly her son's dead?" Ben asked.

Platt gave no response.

"I've got some tarpaulin and fire-retardant blankets in the trunk of my car," Ben said, tossing Platt his car keys. Catching them shook Platt from his stupor. Some color returned to his face.

"We better get Haggis back in here with his stick first," Platt said. He was looking up at the ceiling where his penlight fell upon the wet, matted black fur of several bats. They dripped like ink from the ceiling.

2

Opening up the rear door of Platt's cruiser, Ben climbed in and sat next to Brandy. "Hey. You okay?"

She looked hardly there, hardly real . . . as if the slightest breeze might reduce her to a pile of white sand.

"We're gonna take care of this here," he went on, "and we're gonna do a good job. I can take you home if you want to go there, or—"

"Where are you taking him?"

"To the police station."

"And then what?" There was a pragmatic decisiveness to her tone that seemed out of place. Ben assumed she was still in shock.

"Well," he said slowly, thinking things through as he went along, "we'll call the county sheriff's department and they'll come take care of your brother. But for right now, you and I need to go by your house and speak to your mom. We need to tell her what happened to your brother."

"He isn't dead," she said flatly.

Ben nodded. "Okay. I know this is hard, honey. I'm going to help you and—"

"He isn't dead. He's just . . . changed."

"Changed?"

"He's some kind of . . . vampire now."

"Okay," Ben said. He reached out and put a gentle hand on her shoulder.

"He's been in our garage all along, sleeping during the day. He's been in there all along." She looked at him. Her eyes were dead sober. "Didn't you see what he looked like?"

He looked just like that kid we found washed up in the creek two weeks ago, Ben thought. This notion made him uncomfortable.

She looked away from him, facing forward. Ben felt the seconds tick by like millennia. After he'd aged considerably, Ben's hand slipped off the girl's shoulder. "Let's get you home," he said.

Brandy said nothing.

3

Eddie La Pointe eased the squad car to a slow crawl as he advanced along the gradual incline of Full Hill Road toward Tom Schuler's place. It was dark now, without even the occasional streetlamp to brighten the way out here.

This part of town was about as rural as it got in Stillwater—a place where the small dirt roads were named after the families who lived off them and where, over generations, the houses had become sagging, weather-ruined monstrosities that looked more like the wooded landscape than anything constructed by the hands of man. Back before the Army Corps of Engineers came and put in the pumping system and retaining walls in the 1950s, the more cautious of Stillwater's residents, tired of constant flooding and losing their livestock and crops, had taken to this place up higher in the mountains. For the most part, the bloodline of these cautious families had remained in town and up here in the high hills, and many of the dilapidated houses up here on Wills Mountain still provided sanctuary for the descendants of those very families. Although Eddie La Pointe had been born and raised over the line in West Virginia, he had lived and worked in Stillwater long enough to become attuned to the town's history and to the families with whom it was populated.

Now, pulling along the narrow twist of muddy roadway that led through the trees up to Tom Schuler's place, the rain laying a tattoo against the car's windshield, Eddie could already see that all the lights in the house were off and Tom Schuler's old Ford Maverick was nowhere to be seen. It was possible that the car was around back. It was likely Tom had already gone to bed, too. Once he left here, he could make a call out to Jimmy Toops's lot and see if the vehicle had ever been picked up after Kirkland had it towed.

Eddie did not feel too comfortable. He pulled alongside the slouching porch, shut off the squad car's headlights, and switched off the ignition. The house looked silent and empty, radiating that hollowness that all abandoned houses seemed capable of emitting, like some kind of sonar.

He could readily recall the abandoned building that had stood at the end of Maple Lane in his own hometown of Truax, West Virginia. It had once been an old soda shop and burger joint but, when Eddie was just a boy, it had already become nothing but a graffiti-laden concrete shell, its row of empty windows as foreboding as black ice, the paved parking lot gritty with sand and overgrown with blond weeds. Kids from the neighborhood had said it was haunted, and indeed young Eddie La Pointe swore on more than one occasion that he had seen a *figure* drifting behind those black windows like a corpse moving through the ether of space. Eddie and all his friends would have to walk past the place whenever they went down to the sandlot to play baseball, which they did most days in the summer. It hadn't been so bad in the daytime, but come dusk, when Eddie and his friends had to return home for supper, and with the sun already beginning to set while painting great sweeping shadows across the land, the run-down burger joint seemed to come alive. If Eddie happened to walk by it alone, he would break out into a run halfway across the weedy parking lot, certain that the building had come alive and was somehow capable of reaching out and snatching him up off the ground . . .

Looking at Tom Schuler's house brought back those memories of the old burger joint in Truax, and Eddie shivered behind the squad car's steering wheel. He hadn't thought of that old place in years (it couldn't still be standing on that corner at the edge of town, could it?) and having it resurface in his mind now felt like a bad omen. Still shivering, he popped the door and stepped out into the cool, rainy night.

Trees applauded in the wind. A mist of clouds sailed slowly across the sky, blotting out the early stars. In the woods that surrounded him, he could hear all sorts of noises that let him know that he wasn't the only living creature out here after all. The thought gave him little comfort. After a moment, he convinced himself it was only the rain and nothing more.

He mounted the creaking porch steps of Tom Schuler's house and rapped on the front door. Though he couldn't be certain, he swore he heard his knock echo through the entire house. It was like shouting down into a well or out over the Grand Canyon.

That's just my nerves.

He knocked again.

"Hey, Tom, you in there? Wake up, bud. It's Eddie La Pointe."

Things hidden in the darkness of the woods made whispery noises at him.

Just my stupid imagination, he told himself again. *Reading too many horror magazines and watching too many bad movies on late-night television. This is what you get, you chickenshit.* He couldn't argue with that logic. It even caused him to chuckle a little, though there was hardly any humor in it.

Eddie pulled his flashlight from his belt and turned it on as he slid away from the door and peered into the nearest window. He pressed both the flashlight and his nose against the windowpane, shielding some of the glare with one cupped hand around his eyes. The beam illuminated only a small bit of Tom's front parlor—an armchair and the grate over a stone fireplace—but nothing more. He repeated this at several of the other windows, too, but from what he could see, nothing appeared to be in any state of disarray.

Out back, he knocked on the door then took a few steps away from the house so he could shout more audibly to the second-floor windows. His heavy boots sank an inch or two into the mud.

"Hey, Tom! Wake up, will ya?"

His voice shook the night but no lights came on in the upstairs windows. The only response he got was from a clash of thunder.

He could be at Crossroads, he thought, glancing at his wristwatch. He could drive by the place, see if Tom's car was in the parking lot. . .

Eddie keyed up his handheld radio and called into Shirley Bennice in the dispatch office.

"Hey, Eddie," she said, her usual cheerfulness gone. "You okay out there?"

"Yeah. I didn't want to bother Ben. I know he's got his hands full tonight."

"Eddie, what's going on around here?" There was a desperate, pleading quality to old Shirl's voice that Eddie didn't much like to hear. "Ben said Maggie Quedentock killed her husband. Tommy Schuler, too. And now Platt and Haggis are on their way back here with a dead body."

"Jesus," Eddie said, not meaning to say it aloud. Thankfully, he hadn't keyed the radio yet. "Whose body?" he asked into the radio.

"The missing Crawly kid. Can you believe it?"

No. He most certainly could not believe it.

"Swell time for the chief to go on vacation, huh, Shirley-cue?" he said finally into the radio, an attempt at humor. When Shirley didn't respond, he quickly added, "Let Ben know I checked out Tom Schuler's place. He ain't home and his car's gone, but nothing seems out of the ordinary." He glanced around the yard to make sure everything was still copacetic.

"You heading on home now?"

"Well, my shift was over an hour ago, but I'll keep the radio on in case anything else comes up." His mind was still whirling. He thought, *How can the Crawly boy be dead?*

"Have a good one, Eddie. Stay safe."

"Goodnight, Shirley-cue."

He clipped the portable radio back onto his belt and was about to do the same with his flashlight when a noise rose up from somewhere in the yard. He turned the flashlight in the approximate direction but saw nothing but an overturned birdbath and the handle of an axe protruding from a tree stump.

Reading those stupid monster magazines, scaring myself half to death so that I'm jumping at every noise, every shadow—

Something moved just beyond the trees at the periphery of his vision. It was a blur beyond the curtain of rain.

Eddie jerked his head in its direction in time to see something recede quickly into the shadows. Over the patter of rain, he heard the crunching of footfalls over dead leaves and fallen branches and tried to convince himself it was just rain or possibly a deer, only a deer. *Fuckin' whitetail are all over the place this time of year. Open season, halle-fucking-lujah!*

But it wasn't a deer.

Somehow, he knew that.

He swung his flashlight around and let the light play along the stand of trees that rushed up to meet Tom Schuler's backyard. The light illuminated very little.

His breath clouding the air, Eddie took a step toward the line of trees . . . then another step, slowly passing the flashlight beam back and forth along the tree trunks like a searchlight in a prison yard. Rainwater spilled over the brim of his hat, down his shoulders and his back. Water drained from an old birdhouse that hung from a nearby tree branch.

A pair of silvery eyes flared up out of the darkness. Eddie's bowels clenched. Even as he tried to convince himself once again that this was a deer, a fucking whitetail—*all the fuck over the place this time of year, swear to God they are, all the fuck over*—he knew that this was no goddamn deer. To begin with, the eyes were situated right next to each other and faced forward, faced *him.* They were the eyes of a predator, not the eyes of prey.

"If . . ." he began, attempting to address the owner of those eyes, but he wound up choking on his words.

Just as quickly as they had appeared, those silvery eyes vanished . . . then reappeared a few yards to the right, shining like dimes through the space between two trees. Eddie tried to swing the flashlight over to it but was too slow. The thing repositioned itself yet again, toying with him it seemed, and the sounds of its footfalls seemed to come from various locations all at once, audible all too clearly over the storm.

"Fuck this," he muttered, sidestepping around the side of the house yet unable to take his eyes away from the stand of trees.

Something stretched forward out of the tree line, the barest hint of moonlight illuminating what looked like the small, pale arm of a child. The tattered sleeve of a dark-colored flannel shirt hung from the thin white arm in ribbons.

"Who's that?" he called, his voice a reedy whine. "Who's there?"

The arm withdrew back into the shadows. He could make out the silhouette of someone back there—slight, narrow, frail, childlike.

"Come out."

The shape ambled out of the trees. A tattered flannel shirt hung drenched from small shoulders. Eyes like silver discs.

"Jesus," Eddie breathed.

It was Bob Leary's kid. Yet it *wasn't*. . .

The kid took a shuddery, uncertain step toward Eddie, and Eddie felt himself flinch. In an unsteady voice, he called out, "That you, Billy? You okay, son?"

The boy did not respond. There was a feral look in the kid's eyes, which looked unnaturally large. When the Leary kid cocked his head quizzically to one side, the way a curious dog might, Eddie could make out striations along the kid's scalp where tufts of his dark hair had fallen out.

Billy Leary's eyes shimmered with an unearthly light.

"Christ. . ."

Eddie lowered the flashlight, the world spinning out of view. Coldness ran through his veins like arctic wind. To say he made it halfway to his squad car would be an exaggeration; Eddie La Pointe staggered backward a few steps, never taking his eyes off the pale-skinned boy who was not actually a boy at all. When the boy lowered his head and charged at him from the thicket, Eddie turned and started to run. Yet he made it only a few feet before one foot snagged on the exposed root of an oak tree arching out of the earth. He came down hard as stars exploded before his eyes, all his weight driving him down into a puddle of freezing water. His campaign hat flipped backward off his head and disappeared into a whirlwind of sightlessness. He sensed rather than saw the thing as it closed the distance between them, Eddie's heartbeat rising and his head screaming before any actual sound could manage to escape his throat. When he rolled over on his back, the thing was suddenly upon him, pinning him down to the earth with impossible strength. The face that looked down upon him was not of some snarling beast nor some vaporous phantom, but the soft, white face of a child, only with eyes like glass balls and flesh the color of candlewax. Water traced down the contours of the child's face, glittering like diamonds and pouring into Eddie's open mouth and spilling into his eyes. The child's mouth unhinged, snakelike, revealing a corrugated tubular void of ribbed, quivering flesh. The child's blackened tongue lashed out.

In a fit of fury, Eddie swung his head to one side just as a belching sound emanated from the boy. A second later, a molten hot gout of fluid spilled onto Eddie's upper shoulder and bicep.

Eddie screamed and bucked his hips. The Leary boy hung on, his small, bony fingers planted firmly in the flesh of Eddie's arms. His vision blurry, Eddie turned his head again and managed to make out the hideous white face with its mouth agape and inching closer to his face. Pale foam dripped and sizzled from the open mouth. Eddie screamed and bucked his hips some more, managing to pry his arms up off the ground and roll onto his side. Distantly, he heard a second belching sound and was faintly aware of a thick, warm fluid splattering down the shaft of his right arm.

He rolled onto his stomach, splashing again in the icy water, and shoved himself to his feet. Through his bleary eyes, he could see the squad car only a few yards away, parked at a slant at the front of the house, rain tap-dancing across its hood. He staggered toward it but quickly lost his footing, driving his face down into the cold, hard, compacted mud. He felt his jaw crack. Somewhere behind him, a wicked shriek echoed through the night.

Then came the pain. It came in a hot molten swelling, all along his right fist and arm, straight up to the shoulder and the right pectoral muscle. He made the mistake of glancing at his pained appendage and found that a greenish sludge was oozing down the length of his arm. Where the fingers of his right hand should have protruded up through the muck, there was only the fast-melting sludge of muscle and tissue, along with the startlingly bright nubs of bone. Acid burning through his flesh, Eddie La Pointe howled in pain.

Static buzzed over his radio. He hardly heard it. With his good hand—his left hand—he managed to drag himself a foot or two closer to the squad car before his attacker leaped onto his back, driving him down. He made a pathetic *uff!* sound as the wind was knocked out of him. Uselessly, he tried to claw through the dirt with his right hand, only to realize that he no longer *had* a right hand. The pain caused fireworks to explode before his eyes.

The thing on his back emitted another belch. The sound was like a creaking door or an old tractor turning over in cold weather. Again, Eddie screamed. He felt hot sludge spill out across his shoulder blades and down his back, and for the first time he could actually smell the stink of his own burning flesh.

With his left arm—his good arm—he managed to swing an elbow and knock the creature off his back. Ahead of him, the squad car doubled and trembled and looked like something out of a bad 3-D movie. For whatever ridiculous and inexplicable reason, he pictured himself sitting on the edge of his bed earlier that morning, pulling on a pair of gym socks. Fucking gym socks. That was what went through his mind at that moment.

With his one good hand, he managed to hoist himself to his feet and propel himself toward the squad car before the thing took him back down to the ground. He struck the earth hard, teeth gnashing together in his busted jaw, and rolled over halfway onto his good shoulder. Above him, a whitish blur lashed out and tore into the flesh of his right cheek with fingernails that felt more like claws. His feet kicking, he tried to buck the creature away from him yet again, but he was unable to succeed this time. Through bleary eyes, he saw the channel of its wide mouth zeroing in on him. There was a smell like cleaning products—the fucking Lysol they used on the pews at St. Bernadette's was the first thing that came to his mind—followed once more by that guttural belching sound. A moment later, Eddie felt hot magma spill out across his face. He screamed and felt it run down his throat, scorching his esophagus and loosening the teeth in his gums.

A moment later, he was dead.

4

On the ride back to her house, Brandy Crawly sat quietly in the passenger seat of Ben's police car. Ben kept waiting for her to break down and cry but she never did. In studious contemplation, she looked out the passenger window at the flooding streets and the trees that bent in the strong gusts of wind. By the time they arrived in front of her house, the sky was fully dark. Rain fell steadily and the streets were already beginning to flood.

When he put the car in Park and shut the engine down, Brandy offered him a small thank you.

"I'll need to go in and tell your mom," he told her.

She nodded then looked through the rain-speckled windshield

of the police car and up toward her house. Only a single light was on in one of the downstairs windows.

"Can I ask you one thing?" Ben asked.

She looked at him again. In the rain-shadowed moonlight, her face was a glowing patchwork of pale light and deep, lightless grooves. "Yeah," she said.

"How did you . . . you know where to look for him?"

"The bats," she said. "The bats go wherever he goes. I mean, I think so, anyway."

Brandy Crawly's eyes seemed to briefly lose focus. Then she blinked and looked back up at the house again. "He's been staying in the garage the whole time. He'll probably come back tonight. I'll be waiting." Almost as an afterthought, she said, "He can still be saved. You just have to kill the head vampire."

It was surreal, all of it. Was he dreaming? Surely none of this was actually happening.

As she looked back at him, she suddenly looked much older than her sixteen years. "You have to kill the head vampire, Ben."

Before he knew what he was doing, he nodded. "Yeah," he whispered to her. "Okay."

Wendy Crawly began yelling the second Ben and Brandy walked through the front door, exclaiming how worried she'd been and where the hell had she been all day, anyway? But when Wendy turned the corner and saw Ben standing in the foyer, she went immediately quiet. Before Ben could say a word, Brandy ran to her mother and, as if by maternal instinct alone, her mother's arms sprang open to receive her. They embraced for what seemed like an eternity, and Ben thought he could actually *see* some heavy load transfer back and forth between mother and daughter via some indescribable parent-child osmosis.

"We found your boy, Wendy," Ben said, taking a step toward them. He didn't have to say the dreaded word and Wendy did not need him to say it. She had known, it seemed, the second she turned down the hallway and saw Ben standing there, dripping rain on the oriental runner.

Wendy closed her eyes and just nodded, over and over, like someone being prodded with a jolt of electricity. Then she buckled and folded to the floor, crying out. Brandy held her mother's head against her stomach and let her tears fall in her hair. But her eyes, dark and pleading yet viciously intense, remained on Ben. It was as though she was swearing him to some blood oath.

CHAPTER SIXTEEN

1

Back in the car, Ben drove a block or so down the street from the Crawly house before he pulled over onto the shoulder, put the car into Park, and paused to catch his breath. His eyes burned and his face radiated heat. When he looked down, he saw that his hands were trembling. He was not a religious man or a superstitious man, but at that very moment, Ben Journell believed the world to be on the verge of ending. Or maybe it was just Stillwater that was ending. Maybe this was how small towns died. It starts slowly enough, with factories closing up and people relocating to different parts of the country in search of jobs. Houses go dark and street corners go empty. Before long, whole stretches of highway have been evacuated as if some great plague had come and swept through the countryside. Faces vanished. People dematerialized into nothingness, into vapor. The great American dreamer has awakened. Wasn't that what was going on now? Was this no different than the spoils of some great plague?

Or maybe it's just the reverse, he thought, watching the street ahead of him fill up with water. *Maybe the plague seeks out a town that is already on the verge of collapse—that is already very much near death—and it grabs hold and takes root and plants its virulent claws into the soil. Maybe when a town dies, it becomes this rotting, festering corpse that attracts the sorts of things that feed off corpses.*

He thought of his father at that moment—and not just the man, but the things that had made him the man he was. The farm out on Sideling Road where his father had sweated and bled and ached and worked hard, and where both his parents had created a home for their only child, their only son. Ben had stayed and watched his mother die and then he had remained and watched the farm die all around him. His father's death now seemed like more of a resignation than anything else, a futile surrender as the rest of the world was similarly reduced to dust. *I was a fool to have stayed.*

But he had, and he carried a burdensome responsibility. The Crawly boy was dead. Something horrific had gotten to him, just as it had gotten to the unidentified boy a few weeks earlier. Quite possibly the same thing had happened to Bob Leary's son, too. And then there was Maggie Quedentock . . . and whatever had happened to her husband and Tom Schuler . . . and Ben couldn't wrap his mind around how all these random things could possibly be connected. Could they be? Could they?

He punched the car back into Drive and continued along the road until he came to the turnoff for Route 40. The rain still pounded, and the driving was treacherous. Across the gulley, he could make out the ominous bulk of the old plastics factory with its twin parapets rising like lighthouses against the stormy sky. He felt like someone's father, patrolling the house at night as his children slept soundly, checking the locks on the windows and the bolts on the doors. When he turned a bend, he jumped on the brakes, sending the car fishtailing back and forth across the asphalt. A moment later, the car came to a shuddering stop across both lanes.

A mudslide had avalanched down from the hill, tossing mounds of black sludge and twisted, skeletal trees across the highway. To his left, the water of the Narrows had already risen above its concrete basin and was slowly climbing the embankment toward the road.

Wills Creek was flooded, which meant the water was shuttling quickly toward downtown.

Ben took out his cell phone, scrolled through the phonebook, and hit the number to the Allegheny County Sheriff's Department in Cumberland. The phone never rang. When he looked at the screen, there was no signal. The storm must have knocked out some towers.

He shifted into Reverse but the tires spun without traction. The engine roared but the car did not move.

"Of course. Fantastic."

Switching between Drive and Reverse, he jockeyed the car back and forth until the tires gripped solid roadway and he was able to execute a functional if not very pretty three-point turn that faced him back toward town. But he only had to drive another few yards to realize one of his tires was flat.

"Goddamn it!"

He slammed both palms against the steering wheel. Lightning filled the sky, a dazzling artery of electrical fire. He got out of the car and, sure enough, the passenger tire sagged dramatically off the rim. Cursing, he leaned back into the car and keyed the CB radio but got nothing but static.

"Shirley? Hon, you there?"

Static . . . and then a dull silence.

Ben switched frequencies and tried it again. "Shirley? It's Ben. Come in, Shirley. Come in, HQ."

The only response was the electronic crinkle of static.

At that moment, he was overcome by the sensation that he was being purposely segregated from the rest of the community by some unseen and preternatural force. *The shepherd has lost his flock.* It was such a potent feeling that it nearly caused his legs to weaken and surrender beneath his weight.

Keep it together, keep it together . . .

He dropped the CB and went around the car to readdress the ruined tire. He had a spare and a jack in the trunk. Question was, would he be able to change it out here on the sloping tarmac of Route 40 in the middle of a torrential downpour?

"I guess we'll find out," he said, already shivering as he popped open the trunk and dragged the full spare out. The water in the road was already rising over his shoes. He didn't have much time, if he had any time left at all . . .

When he looked back up and back out toward town, the storm and the protruding mountainside blocked the lights of Stillwater completely from view. He could see nothing. Only darkness.

Why do I have the unsettling feeling that I'm suddenly the only human being left alive in Stillwater?

And just like that, Ben Journell was standing on the moon.

2

"Oh Lord," Shirley said, standing from behind her desk. She brought her hands to her mouth and watched as Joseph Platt and Melvin Haggis carried between them some small figure wrapped in blue tarpaulin and a heavy gray blanket. She had been working dispatch for over a decade and this was by far the most horrific sight she had ever seen. She knew the Crawly family in passing and could summon an image of the young boy from memory—blond, bowl-cut hair, frail, with a light smattering of reddish-brown freckles across his nose—but she found it impossible to equate that lively and lovely child with something packaged in blankets and plastic and carried by two grim-looking police officers.

Shirley squeezed out from behind her desk and followed them down the hall. The officers did an awkward two-step, as if deciding what room they were taking the body to and who should go in first. Haggis suggested the lockup and Platt nodded his assent.

In the room, they carried the bundle to the nearest desk. Haggis swiped a hand across its surface, throwing the ink blotter and a few pens to the floor. They set the bundle down and Shirley saw, with mounting sadness, that the figure beneath the blanket still retained the shape of a small boy.

"Where's Ben?" she asked.

"He went to see the kid's mother," Platt said, hiking up his gun belt. His eyes remained on the boy beneath the blanket. He looked defeated.

"What are we supposed to do?" she asked.

"Ben was going to call the sheriff's department over in Cumberland and have them come out and take over," Mel Haggis interceded. He looked about as pasty and out of sorts as his partner. "This is beyond us, Shirl."

"This is *horrific,"* Shirley told them.

"Christ," Platt barked, his voice cracking. He was looking across the room at Maggie Quedentock, who still occupied the first cell. "Who's that?"

Shirley walked around the desk and addressed the woman in what she hoped sounded like a semi-cheerful voice. "You okay in there, Maggie? You need anything?"

Maggie lifted her head up the slightest bit and addressed Shirley with dark eyes. She gave no reply.

"Why's she locked up?" Haggis asked, dropping his voice to a whisper.

Shirley shot him a glance that said *I'll fill you in on everything the moment we're in the next room.* Melvin Haggis seemed to comprehend.

Shirley looked back at Maggie. "You want some water or something, dear?"

Again, Maggie said nothing.

"Let's step out in the hall," Platt said.

3

Maggie watched them go out into the hallway. Part of her—the part that was still in the police station holding cell—could hear the rain pounding the roof, could feel the cold steel bench beneath her thighs, could hear the muted whispers out in the hallway. Another part of Maggie—arguably the more conscious of the two halves—sat down on the bench seat of her father's truck. Her father, Aaron Kilpatrick, sat beside her behind the wheel. Daylight glittered against the windshield and the distant sky looked like an impressionistic painting.

They were driving along one of the old logging roads far up in the hills. It was summer—she could tell by the fullness of the trees and the heat against her flesh, magnified as it radiated through the truck's cracked windshield—and she was eleven years old. Dressed in a pair of pink denim shorts and a loose-fitting white blouse with short, scalloped sleeves, her long brown legs slid into the passenger footwell while her hands fumbled with each other in her lap. She smelled her father's pungent and medicinal aftershave coupled with the ghostly aroma of pipe tobacco that always seemed to linger in the cab of the truck and on Aaron Kilpatrick's clothes.

"You know why we're out here, Margaret?" he asked her, shattering the peaceful silence.

"No, sir."

"It's your momma's idea. You've made her very angry. She wanted me to have a talk with you."

A cold dread gripped her by the hand. Her mouth went dry.

A million possible violations shuttled through her head. Had someone seen her smoking? Had one of her friends ratted her out about shoplifting candy and sunglasses from Lomax's? Sometimes she skipped school with Susan Winterbarger—had her folks found out about that?

"You just gonna sit there, being quiet?"

"No, sir."

"You have any idea what your momma's so off the rails about, girl?"

She had to fight off the urge to respond that her mother was *always* going off the rails about *something*. She knew damn well that her father knew this, too.

Instead, she said, "I don't know what it is. I didn't do anything."

The truck crested a hill that overlooked Stillwater and, beyond, the serpentine ribbon of glittering diamonds that was the Narrows. Her father whipped the truck around so that the town below was framed perfectly in the windshield. At this hour, she could see the shadow of the mountain sliding in slow increments across the town as the sun sank behind it. Even at such a young age, Maggie Kilpatrick had always felt an imprecise sadness at this time of day, knowing that while the rest of the countryside would enjoy a few more hours of daylight, Stillwater was doomed to a lifetime of premature night. Even now, young Maggie was overcome by despondency.

Her father shifted the truck into Park but kept the engine idling. With his window rolled down, he poked an elbow out as he surveyed the darkening landscape below. Cars twinkled like sapphires along Rapunzel and the lampposts along Hamilton blinked on. Her father dug a pack of Marlboros out of the front pocket of his overalls. He shook a cigarette into his mouth then seemed to reflect on something for a second or two before offering Maggie the pack.

She looked at him with stark confusion.

"I know you smoke," he said, the Marlboro bouncing between his lips.

She felt like she was being set up. "I don't want one."

He shook the pack so that the tip of one cigarette poked out from the cellophane. "Go on." There was an uncomfortable insistence in his voice that made Maggie's heart beat faster.

Reluctantly, she plucked the cigarette from the pack then stared at it numbly as if she'd never seen one before. Sure, she had smoked plenty of them behind the schoolhouse or down by the Narrows with her friends, but this was something different. This was like being shoved out onto a stage and told to dance because her life depended on it. Just the thought of smoking the cigarette in front of her father made her ill.

Aaron Kilpatrick lit his cigarette with a flashy gold Zippo then extended the flame toward Maggie.

In a tiny voice, she said, "I really don't want—"

"Smoke it," he barked, uncompromising.

She poked the cigarette between her lips and inhaled as her father held the flame to the tip of the cigarette. Afraid to inhale in front of him, she just let the thing dangle lifelessly from her mouth.

Her father capped the lighter then tossed it onto the dashboard where it joined a container of Skoal and a scattering of bottle caps. In silence, he smoked and admired the view through the windshield.

After a little while, he said, "Your mother is concerned that you've been hanging out with some boys." The word *boys* caused her to cringe inwardly. "Is that true?" And before she could answer—not that she was quick to answer—he followed up with, "Don't lie to me, now, Margaret."

She swallowed foul-tasting spit. "Sometimes me and Susan Winterbarger and Caroline Hunt hang out in the park with some boys from school."

"Mmm-hmm," her father hummed, nodded. He was still looking over the hill and down at the town. "What you girls been doin' with them boys?"

What had she been doing? Images flashed like a filmstrip before her eyes—all the inappropriate things she had done with the boys, Bobby Douglass in particular. She had kissed him on the mouth several times and she had let him touch her chest (even though there wasn't much there to touch, unlike Suzie Winterbarger, who actually had *boobs*). Once, Bobby had even showed her his *thing*. They had been in the woods behind the elementary school and completely unprovoked Bobby had taken down his pants, revealing a horrific little mushroom that Maggie found at once both ridiculous and terrifying. He'd asked her if she wanted to touch it and she had said no . . . but there had been a part of her that *had* wanted to touch it. What did it feel like?

But Christ, she couldn't say these things to her father. She just stared at him, her face slack, the Marlboro pinched between two fingers.

"You been doing things with boys you shouldn't be?" he rasped through a cloud of cigarette smoke.

"No, sir."

"You been kissin' up on some boys?"

"No," she said. Her lower lip trembled and her vision abruptly blurred.

"You been showin' boys what you got?"

"No . . ."

One of her father's big, meaty, workman's hands shot out and gripped her hard around the forearm, eliciting a weak cry as he dragged her closer to himself across the bench seat.

"What you got to show anyone, huh? What you got?"

"Daddy!" She screamed and closed her eyes and felt his big paws suddenly all over, suddenly everywhere. She bucked and kicked her legs and one of her shins cracked against the underside of the dashboard. She howled and her father cracked her firmly across the face. The smell of his aftershave mingling with the stink of his cigarette smoke caused her throat to burn and her eyes to spill tears.

"What you *got,* Margaret? What you *got*?"

She screamed again . . . and this time the scream traveled straight through space and time until it finally resonated now in the center of Maggie Quedentock's head as she sat motionless in the jail cell. The power of that scream caused her eyes to water and her hands to tremble in her lap. She thought she could feel her blood pumping throughout every single vein and artery in her body. In her shoes, her toes felt like cold little marbles.

Across the room, the bundle on the desk moved.

It was *almost* imperceptible, and Maggie would have missed it had she not been staring straight at it. She blinked and cleared her vision just in time to see the gray blanket—or whatever was wrapped in the gray blanket—move again. Something was shifting within.

Her eyes shifted to the doorway. Shadows moved back and forth out there and she could still hear people talking in hushed voices. When she looked back at the thing on the desk, she found the shape beneath the blanket sitting upright. A cool sweat prickled Maggie's scalp. She saw a pale hand slide out from beneath the blanket and felt her heart seize in her chest. The suggestion of a foot pressed against the dark fabric of the blanket.

No—

A section of the blanket fell away. In the half-light, a face was revealed to her. Eyes like simmering white-hot coals and a wide mouth dotted with tiny teeth, the fucking thing actually *grinned* at her.

Maggie tried to scream but could not find her voice.

The thing slipped off the table amid a flutter of blanket and crinkling tarpaulin. She heard its bare feet strike the floor on the other side of the desk. As it scurried across the room in the dark, she could see its childlike form briefly silhouetted as it passed in front of the doorway that led out into the hall.

Then Maggie *did* scream—a throat-cracking, strangled bleat.

The voices out in the hall rose. Both officers filed into the room. One of them—the skinnier of the two—came over to the cell and peered through the bars at her, his sallow face twisted into grim incomprehension.

"What's—" he began, just as the officer behind him screamed shrilly. He spun around and Maggie rushed against the bars in time to see the larger officer stagger blindly until his back struck one wall. He was covering his face . . . and there was something *over* his face—a greenish slime in which his fingers sank up to the knuckles. What looked like steam radiated from the ooze, and Maggie thought she could hear a faint sizzling sound. A second later, the stink of burning flesh filled her nose.

"Mel?" the skinny officer croaked weakly. Under any other circumstances, it would have been a comical sound.

Maggie heard a woman scream out in the hallway.

The larger officer's hands then sank *straight through* the mask of slime, impossibly far, and Maggie had time to think, *There is no longer a face behind that stuff; there is no longer a head back there.*

The sludge splattered against the wall, bubbling like acid, and the officer's body—*sans* head—fell forward and slammed lifelessly against the floor. The white nub of the man's spine protruded from the ragged hole of his neck where the skin still sizzled and melted away.

A small figure darted from behind one desk to another. The skinny officer must have remembered he had a gun at his hip; he dove for it now with one hand and tugged at it, tugged at it, tugged, seemingly unable to recall how to pull it out. Then Maggie heard the snap on the holster give and the officer was just preparing to yank the handgun free when the creature sprang out from the shadows at him. The officer staggered backward and slammed against the bars of Maggie's cell. The gun clattered to the floor and spun away into the darkness.

Maggie backed up until she struck the far wall of her cell. On the other side of the bars, the officer bucked and cried out and struggled with the creature that was now situated on his chest. An arc of green slime belched out of the creature's mouth and spattered across the officer's face. Some stray drops passed through the bars and struck the concrete floor of the cell, where they sizzled like plutonium and left steaming craters in the cement.

The officer's head narrowed and melted to a mushy pulp beneath the flesh-eating slime. It did not take long for the officer's body to fold into a heap on the floor, dead.

Maggie shuddered. A piece of her mind seemed to break away at that moment, floating like a raft out across a moonlit sea.

On the other side of the bars, the creature rose. It wasn't a creature at all. It was a boy; hairless, pale-skinned, bug-eyed . . . but a boy nonetheless. A *child*.

Mine. You're mine. You came back for me after all, didn't you? I knew that you would. Somehow, I knew someday that you would. You've come back home to your mother.

The boy's eyes hung on her. She could smell him standing there, a smell like industrial cleaners and detergents.

"I'm sorry," she said, just barely above a whisper. "Don't hurt me."

The child's eyes hung on her a moment longer. Then he shifted his gaze back down to the cop who lay dead at his feet. The skin on the cop's face had dissolved into a puddle of bubbling soup that seemed to be eating through the floor. The skull itself melted like wax. Maggie thought she could make out a pair of eye sockets slowly receding into the sizzling liquid. The boy positioned his slender body so that his face hung directly above the mess that had just moments ago been the officer's head. The boy's mouth worked itself into an *O* as the skin stretched and elongated to form some sort of tubular appendage. Once the appendage had grown to a length of several impossible inches, like the proboscis of an insect, the boy dipped it into the sludge and proceeded to noisily slurp the mess up.

"Don't hurt me," Maggie continued to murmur. It was like a mantra now, a prayer. "Don't hurt me. Don't hurt me. Don't hurt me."

When the child-thing had finished, it stood up off its haunches and regarded Maggie once again through the bars of her cell. As she stared back at him, the tubular appendage retreated toward the child's face until it changed back into a mouth. It was a boy once again, wide-eyed and innocent, his tight little lips smeared with blood.

"Don't hurt me. Don't hurt me. Don't hurt me."

The child-thing's hands closed around two of the cell's bars. It slid one pale, splay-toed foot between the bars and into her cell.

"Don't hurt me. Don't hurt me."

It was thin enough to squeeze through the bars, its body sliding toward her unimpeded. The boy was as insubstantial as smoke.

"Don't hurt me." Her voice was a shrill tremolo now as she cowered in one corner of the cell. "Don't hurt me. Don't hurt me. Don't hurt me."

It hurt her.

CHAPTER SEVENTEEN

1

The streetlights along Belfast Avenue blinked on and off, as if signaling to some spacecraft high above the clouds. Rain slammed the earth, and the windshield wipers of Ben's squad car could hardly keep up with such ferocity. As he turned into the parking lot of the police station, his concern quickly mounted . . . though he could not necessarily identify why. Cold, wet, and covered in mud, it had taken him a good half-hour to change the tire back on Route 40. On the first attempt, he had the car jacked up and was about to spin the last lug nut off when the jack bent to one side and the car crashed back down to the pavement, the entire undercarriage shuddering. By the time he'd managed to jack the car up again, replace the ruined tire with the spare, and lower it back to the ground, Ben's clothes were soaked through and his nose was running like a sieve. Then, on the drive back to the station, he'd attempted to use both his cell phone and the police radio again, but each proved useless. The storm wreaked havoc.

He parked right out in front of the station and ran into the building to find the sodium lights in the ceiling fizzing. Likewise, the lights in the dispatch room threatened to blink off and stay that way.

"Shirley?" He poked his head into the dispatch room to find it empty. One of Shirley's *People* magazines lay flat on the counter.

Back out in the hall, he shouted a "hello." Aside from the echo, there came no response.

When he entered lockup, the world threatened to break apart all around him. He saw Melvin Haggis's corpse first. Haggis's large body was on the floor, straining the blood-drenched fabric of his khaki police uniform. Where his head should have been lay a pulpy, scarlet stew through which Haggis's lower jawbone protruded like a tree root arching out of a swamp. His hands were melted down to the wrists, where knobby bones jutted from the shredded wounds.

Ben's gun was out before he moved over to the second corpse, that of Joseph Platt, although he was only able to identify the man because he knew he'd been with Haggis earlier. Platt's head was gone as well; where it should have been was a sizzling crater in the floor, clogged with blood and hair. Platt's gun was gone. There were bloody slashes across his pant legs and sleeves. He had one white, rigid hand wrapped around one of the bars of the first cell.

And *in* the first cell was what remained of Maggie Quedentock. She lay slumped in one corner, her legs splayed out before her, one shoe off. Her head lay at an unnatural angle against the wall, the top portion of which had been sheared away to reveal a hollow cavern in the center of her nest of wet, stringy hair. The skull was an empty bowl that dribbled a pinkish fluid down her forehead. Her eye sockets dripped blood.

Ben leaned over one of the desks and vomited on the floor. Heat whooshed out of his shirt collar, causing sweat to spring out across his face. It took him several seconds to regain some semblance of composure. Through bleary eyes, he could see small bloody footprints on the floor tiles. They led in various erratic directions, like some animal trying to evade capture . . . or like some predator darting after prey.

The boy, Matthew Crawly . . . his body was gone. The fire-retardant blanket and the sheet of blue tarp lay on the floor, kicked away and discarded like bedsheets in the middle of the night.

Trembling, Ben struggled to his feet. He planted one hand against the nearest wall for support while his pistol shook in his other hand. He scanned the rest of the room but saw nothing but hidden shadows and empty spaces. Rain slammed against the roof. His eyes kept returning to the three bodies scattered throughout the room. He was in no frame of mind to even begin to question what had happened here, to even try to formulate some kind of hypothesis.

Moving strictly off instinct, Ben made his way back across the room and out into the hall. His gun jumped and shook as he clenched it in both hands.

"Anybody here?"

No one answered him. From Shirley's office, he could hear the ticking of the wall-mounted clock above her desk—a ghostly electronic toll. In the ceiling, the lights continued to blink. The air was charged with a faint medicinal odor, one that Ben readily recognized . . .

A soft, muffled whimper came from nearby. Ben looked around, his eyes finally landing on the closed door of the supply closet directly in front of him. Listening, he could hear something shuffling around on the other side of that door. He extended a shaky hand and gripped the doorknob with one sweaty palm . . .

The door swung outward before he could even grasp the knob. Ben uttered a small cry and, staggering backward, repositioned his handgun at the figure that burst out into the hallway.

It was Shirley. Her eyes, large as saucers, found him instantly. Her skin was bloodless and she held her hands out timidly before her in some mockery of Frankenstein's monster. As she stared at Ben, a gasp of pent-up breath escaped her lungs. She looked about ready to collapse. Then she shrieked.

Ben holstered his gun and slung an arm around the woman, just as she went limp against him.

"Are you okay? What happened?"

She sobbed against him for a time, and he didn't bother asking her any further questions until she was able to get herself under control.

"The b-boy," she stammered after a while. She was a tough old bird, and Ben could tell she was struggling to keep it together. "He wasn't dead. He w-wasn't d-d-dead, Ben."

"Where's the boy now?"

"I don't know."

"Did you see what happened? *How* did it happen? What did you see?" He knew he was talking too fast for poor Shirley's addled mind to keep up. He squeezed her shoulder. "Are you hurt?"

"No." Shirley righted herself against him, swiping tracks of runny mascara off her cheeks. "I don't think—"

Something banged at the far end of the hall, the reverberation of its echo like a gunshot. Both Ben and Shirley froze and whipped their heads in unison in the direction of the sound—the sally port. Shirley began making a shuddery, whimpering noise.

"Stay here," Ben said as he began to creep down the hall toward the sally port, his gun leading the way.

"Don't," Shirley intoned. "Don't leave me alone." She clutched at the back of Ben's shirt and followed him as he proceeded down the hallway. Just before they reached the door to the sally port, the lights blinked out and the phones ringing at the opposite end of the hallway went dead. Again, Shirley moaned.

"Shit," Ben whispered. The station fell as silent as a crypt.

Then the lights winked back on, the electricity humming through the circuits in the walls, and Ben's heart began beating again. On the other side of the sally-port door, something metallic clanged around, grinding against the cement floor.

Ben kicked open the door, shoving his gun straight into the darkness with one hand while his other hand went quickly for the light switch beside the door. The lights jumped on, stinging Ben's eyes. He swatted blindly at the air then gripped the gun again in both hands. Shirley's fingernails dug deeper into his back.

The noise came from the bell-shaped birdcage. It had fallen to the floor and scraped along the concrete as the small bat inside beat frantically against the bars of the cage. It unleashed a series of aggravated screeches that cleaved through the center of Ben's skull.

"Oh," Shirley sighed at his back, her breath warm along the pockets of sweat that had broken out across the back of Ben's shirt. The relief was evident in her voice. She managed it a second time. "Oh . . ."

Despite the insanity all around them, Ben felt a burst of laughter borne on the waters of his own stark relief threaten his throat. "I forgot that thing was in here," he said.

"It's going berserk," said Shirley.

The bat raged against the bars of the cage with enough force to drag it several inches across the floor. It screeched and tittered, its clawed wings and scrabbling feet clanging against the cage. At one point, it hooked a pair of fangs around one of the bars and hung suspended by its snout.

"Looks like it wants to get out," Shirley said. She took a step closer to the cage, still clinging to the back of Ben's shirt with one hand.

A nonspecific disquiet settled around Ben like a shroud. Piping up in his head was Brandy Crawly's voice, whispering, *The bats go wherever he goes. I mean, I think so, anyway.* And on the heels of that, *He isn't dead. He's just . . . changed. He's some kind of . . . vampire now.*

Again, the lights blinked off then back on. Very soon, the storm would knock the power out for good.

"It wants to get out, all right," Ben said, crouching down beside the bat's cage. Its beady little eyes stared at him. Its fangs, still clinging to one of the bars, looked like the fangs of a rattlesnake. "It knows something. It wants to get somewhere." Ben stood. "I want to know where it wants to go."

"What are you talking about, Ben?"

"This thing's a homing device." *I mean, I think so, anyway,* Brandy added in his head. "If I let it out, I bet it takes me straight to . . ."

"To where?" Shirley asked.

You have to kill the head vampire, Ben.

Yet he couldn't bring himself to speak the words aloud. Despite all that had transpired in Stillwater in the past two weeks, it was still too ridiculous to think about . . . still too insane . . .

"To whatever has been going on in this town," he said at last. It was the best he could do to speak the truth of it. He holstered his handgun and found that his hands shook terribly. "How do you follow a goddamn bat, Shirley?" He wondered if Eddie would know—Eddie, with all his ridiculous horror magazines, Stephen King novels, and beloved gory vampire films. When was the last time he'd heard from Eddie? Ben's mind raced. He couldn't think straight.

"Ha!" Shirley cried, startling him. When he faced her, he found a surprising grin stretched across her otherwise bleary face. Her eyes were alight. "You don't *follow* a bat, Ben. You *track* it."

"Yeah? And how do you do that?"

Shirley released her grip on the back of Ben's shirt then went immediately to one of the two-by-four shelves that were hammered straight into the drywall. She rummaged through stacks of boxes until she found what she was looking for—a plastic case roughly the size of a laptop. Shirley set the case on an overturned five-gallon bucket and opened it. Pressed into the foam padding was a GPS screen, a jumble of wires, and four nondescript black boxes, each one approximately the size of a silver dollar.

"What is that?" Ben asked.

Shirley picked up one of the black boxes and examined it more closely in the palm of her hand. "A tracking device. Don't you remember? Cumberland sent them over to us, in case we ever needed to track a vehicle. Mike laughed."

"You don't mean . . . I mean, you think . . ."

"Why not?"

Ben peered down at the tiny black box in the center of Shirley's hand. "Holy crap, Shirl. You're a goddamn genius."

"I want a raise when this is all over," Shirley said.

2

Her mother took a Valium, poured a glass of red wine, and fell asleep on the living room sofa. Once Brandy was confident her mother was out, she went up into her mother's bedroom and opened the bottom drawer of the dresser. There was a pink shoebox in there and it was filled with her grandmother's belongings—various trinkets and bits of costume jewelry that the woman had left to Wendy, her only daughter, just before she died many years earlier. Brandy had very few memories of her grandmother, but she knew about the shoebox. On occasion, whenever her mother felt nostalgic, they went through the ancient and tarnished relics together. There were large, spangled rings and great looping necklaces, and earrings that looked as though they'd been made from the shells of tortoises. But those were not the items Brandy concerned herself with on this night.

Brandy's grandmother had been a devout Catholic. Inside the box, Brandy located a silver crucifix, nearly seven inches long. It was heavy and cold and felt strangely powerful in Brandy's hand. There was also a rosary in the box. Brandy didn't know if rosary beads harbored the same power against vampires that crucifixes did, but she didn't think there was any harm in taking that, too.

She hung the rosary beads from the doorknocker on the front door. Beside the back door, she slipped the silver crucifix into the rusted eyelet beside the doorframe where Hugh Crawly used to plant an American flag when he was feeling patriotic. She knew vampires couldn't enter someone's home unless they were specifically invited, but she wasn't so sure if that rule applied if the home had previously belonged to the vampire. Better safe than sorry.

There were garlic cloves in the refrigerator. She broke them apart, getting stink on her fingers, and scattered the remnants around all the windowsills throughout the two-story house. Once she'd finished, she deliberated on one final precaution. While arguably the most vital, she did not know if she could actually bring herself to do it.

Stakes. Wooden stakes. You were supposed to drive them through the vampire's heart.

There were brooms and mops and all sorts of things with wooden handles in the laundry room. It wouldn't take much effort to whittle the handles into points with a kitchen knife. The hard part, she knew, would be summoning enough courage to actually *use* the stakes if and when the time came. Could she do it?

She didn't realize she had fallen asleep until a clash of thunder jarred her awake. She was sprawled out on the kitchen floor, a broom handle angled across her lap. The tip of the handle was sharpened to a point and there were curled bits of shaving scattered around the tiles. In her right hand, Brandy still clutched the kitchen knife.

Something was wrong. She felt it in the center of her animal brain.

She got up and checked on her mother, who was still asleep on the sofa in the living room. Rain slammed against the windows and lightning briefly lit up the sky. The lamp beside the sofa dimmed but stayed on.

She went through the house a second time, methodically checking the locks on the doors and windows. In the kitchen, she picked up the telephone to make sure there was still a dial tone in the event she needed to call the police. There was.

With the kitchen lights off so that nothing could see inside, she cleaned up the wood shavings off the floor then shook them into the kitchen trash. Then she systematically lined up the brooms and mop beside the laundry room door like rifles in an armory. Her hands reeked of garlic.

Hungry, she took out a dish of cold chicken from the refrigerator and poured herself a cold glass of milk. In the dark, she sat at the kitchen table and ate. Around her, the house creaked and moaned. The storm was unforgiving.

The epicenter of her animal brain remained on high alert. Her skin tingled. After only a few bites of chicken and a few sips of milk, she broke down, crying silently into her hands. *Wake up,* she told herself. *Wake up, wake up! You're dreaming. This is all one bad dream.* But it wasn't a dream. The tingling intensified as thunder shook her bones.

She waited, a blood-sense promising her that something would soon happen. The way parents know when something bad has happened to their children . . . the way twins sense each other's pain and grief and happiness . . . the way dogs know when their master is about to arrive home . . .

All those things.

She waited for her brother.

3

Wearing a pair of rubber gloves, Ben carefully extracted the small bat from the birdcage. The thing struggled futilely in his grasp, its one free wing batting uselessly in the air. High-pitched squawks funneled up from its throat as its blind head bobbed like some windup toy. Even through the gloves, Ben felt the heat radiating off the tiny creature, and the power of its struggle to break free. He held it delicately but firmly.

"Don't let it bite you," Shirley said. She seemed calmer now, more like her old self. "Rabies City."

"Thanks," Ben grunted.

With Shirley's assistance, he secured the tracking device to the bat's back by Velcro bands, tight enough so that it wouldn't fall off but not too tight as to restrict the bat's mobility. Shirley switched on the battery-powered GPS and waited for the signal to load.

"Are you sure this is gonna work?" Ben asked.

Shirley smiled her grandmotherly smile at him. There was terror in her eyes. "I have no idea, Ben. I really don't."

The GPS beeped and a red dot appeared on the screen. A map of Belfast Avenue and the surrounding streets blinked on. The red dot appeared just off Belfast on the map—right where the police station should be.

"Well, look at that," Ben marveled. "It's pretty damn accurate."

Shirley's hands trembled as she held the GPS. "What now?"

"We let the little fella go," Ben said, looking around. Rain lashed a small porthole window inlaid in the wall. He went to it, carefully holding the bat in two gloved hands now. Shirley followed him, footfalls nearly silent. Ben shoved the window open several inches, allowing the cold wind to spear through the crack and chill his bones. Rainwater wasted no time spilling over the sill and pooling on the concrete floor.

"Wait a minute," Shirley said. "Can bats fly in weather like this?"

"I have a feeling this one can," he said, holding the bat up to the opening in the window. The creature's tiny head bobbed and its triangular nose sniffed the air. Its little black eyes were like two dollops of oil. "Godspeed, little buddy."

He released the bat and it took off like a shot into the night.

Shirley held the GPS closer to her face.

"I hope the rain doesn't wreck the electronics," Ben muttered, more to himself than to Shirley.

"Seems to be working." She handed the GPS over to him. "Look."

On the screen, the red dot moved in jerky increments across the digital map, heading northeast from Belfast toward the copse of trees that separated Belfast and Susquehanna. Just before the red dot hit Susquehanna it darted left and arced across the digital screen. Ben watched it run parallel to Susquehanna, moving farther north.

Then suddenly Ben knew where it was going. Again, Brandy Crawly's voice surfaced in his head, this time sending shivers down his back: *He's been staying in the garage the whole time. He'll probably come back tonight. I'll be waiting.*

Susquehanna ran directly in front of the Crawly house.

"I think I know where the boy is," Ben said.

Shirley said, "He's no boy. Not anymore."

4

She cried out, startling herself in the process. Her eyes blinked open and the first thought that shuttled like a locomotive through her brain was, *I fell asleep!*

She was on the kitchen floor, half-propped against the wall beside the table. There was a crick in her neck. She rubbed her eyes and immediately felt them burn as the garlic from her hands bit into her. Then the reality of it all rushed back to her in one destructive tidal wave.

There was someone out on the back porch. Rather than seeing or hearing anything, she felt things, the way wild animals sense the approach of a predator. Across the kitchen, the rank of broom handles filed into points caught her attention and caused her hands to tremble and her feet to grow cold.

Footsteps moved from one end of the back porch to the other—this time she *could* hear them. A shape passed briefly behind one sheer-curtained window. *Matthew.* He was moving toward the door.

Her heart thudded loudly in her ears. Brandy rose quickly and went to the sharpened broom handles, picking two of them up and holding them both together in her unsteady hands. Right then, she knew there would be no way for her to drive these through her brother's chest . . . and wasn't that just the stupid stuff of horror movies, anyway?

The shape behind the window vanished. She heard more footsteps treading the creaky floorboards of the porch just on the other side of the wall. Rain sluiced down the windows and thunder boomed in the distance, threatening to send her screaming. Somehow, she kept it together.

The doorknob jiggled.

"Brandy . . ."

Then she *did* scream, dropping both broom handles. They clattered at her feet and one of them rolled underneath the kitchen table.

It was her mother, the vague impression of confusion on her groggy, sleepy face. She had wandered in from where she'd been sleeping in the living room, her hair a frizzy hive, her expression one of bleary incomprehension.

Brandy clung to her.

"What is it?"

Again, the doorknob jiggled.

"Someone's at the door," said Wendy.

"Don't open it," Brandy said, looking back at the door from over her shoulder as one arm clung to her mother's waist. "Don't let him in."

"Let who in?" She spoke with an eerie calmness that troubled Brandy. "Who is it?"

The doorknob stopped moving. Except for the storm raging outside and their own ragged breathing, everything went silent.

Then the glass window in the door exploded, sending glittering shards in a dazzling burst into the air and raining down onto the floor. Both Brandy and her mother screamed . . . but they were too paralyzed by fear to move.

A small, white arm snaked in through the broken window. A child's grimy hand, tiny fingers splayed, searched for the dead bolt. Found it. The fingers turned the dial, and across the kitchen Brandy heard the tumblers turn and the bolt click open. With mounting horror, she watched as the hand then found the slide lock. Those small white fingers delicately—almost lovingly—slid the bolt back into its housing.

You have to invite vampires in! her mind screamed at her. Wasn't that part of the folklore? *But what if they return to the place they previously lived?*

What if—

As if on a gust of strong wind, the kitchen door blew open.

Matthew's silhouette stood framed in the open doorway. Rainwater dripped from his pale, unclothed body, the left side of which was silvered with moonlight. The boy's mostly bald head cocked slightly on the thin stalk of his neck, his eyes glittering like jewels in the darkness. As Wendy uttered the boy's name, the silhouette executed a single footstep through the open doorway. The sound of the bare and wet foot striking the kitchen tile was sickening.

"Matthew?" Wendy repeated, taking a step toward her son.

"That's not Matthew," Brandy warned.

The silhouette took another step into the house . . . then another . . . then another . . .

"Mom!" Brandy cried, attempting to grab the back of her mother's shirt as Wendy rushed across the kitchen toward her son. Wendy dropped to her knees before the boy and wasted no time wrapping up his small, wet frame in her arms. As if nature disagreed, this act was underscored by a flash of lightning then a boom of thunder.

"Where the hell have you been?" Wendy cried at her son, holding him out now at arm's length. If she noticed the horrid state of the child—if she could see him clearly enough in the poor lighting—she did not seem to register it. "What happened to you, Mattie? Where did you go? Where did you go?"

Brandy backed up against the wall, one hand groping blindly for another one of the sharpened broom handles propped against the laundry room door.

"Oh, Mattie," Wendy sobbed, and hugged the boy against her again.

Matthew's pale, ghostlike face watched Brandy from over their mother's shoulder. His eyes probed into her like drill bits, a faint greenish light radiating far back in his pupils. He reached one of his hands out toward her, his arm a colorless, formless shaft, the tine-like fingers of his tiny hand splayed like a starfish. The stink of ammonia filled the kitchen.

Brandy's hand closed around a sharpened broomstick.

Matthew's body shuddered. His eyes rolled up like window shades.

"Mattie," Wendy said flatly, separating herself from the boy just as his small body started to buck. His frail chest appeared to slowly expand, as if he were taking in a deep, deep breath, and his mouth slowly unhinged and dropped open like a glove compartment in an old car. The stink of ammonia grew stronger, stinging Brandy's eyes and tickling her nose.

The bulge in Matthew's chest ascended up into the boy's neck, stretching it impossibly wide. The mouth gaped, drool spilling out in copious torrents.

"Mom!" Brandy cried out. "Get away!"

Wendy skidded backward on the floor, still on her knees. Her arms were still frozen in a mock embrace.

A sound not dissimilar to the croak of a bullfrog ratcheted up Matthew's throat. A second later, a web of snot-like liquid burst from the boy's mouth and spattered across Wendy's right forearm. Brandy could smell the stuff—an insulting, medicinal smell that reminded her of cleaning products—and her eyes watered.

Brandy took a step forward, instinctively holding the broomstick like a baseball bat instead of a stake. As Matthew's chest began to expand a second time, Brandy rushed beside her mother and knocked her over and out of the way. Matthew's pallid face turned in Brandy's direction. His eyes blazed with an inhuman, predatory light. Foam dripped from his agape mouth.

Brandy swung the broom handle and cracked her brother against the side of his head. She felt it connect—a sickening *whump!* that resonated up her arms—and immediately dropped the broomstick. The thing that had once been her brother toppled over on his side against the kitchen floor. His limbs scrambled for purchase on the tiles, to no avail. As she stood over him, his face turned and scrutinized her with those soulless eyes that were as black as coals.

Her mother began screaming. Brandy looked and saw steam rising off her mother's arm, right where a slab of dark slime clung to her shirtsleeve. The stuff was eating through her mother's flesh like acid.

On the kitchen floor, the thing that had once been her brother began climbing to its feet. He wore nothing but a filthy pair of underwear, covered in mud or blood (or both). The boy settled into a crouch. His head pivoted in Brandy's direction. The boy hissed like a wildcat.

Brandy groped for her mother, who was rising unsteadily to her feet. Wendy sobbed her son's name again but Brandy was already dragging her backward through the kitchen and into the adjoining living room.

"He's—"

"Mom! Come on!"

Matthew appeared in the doorway that connected the kitchen to the living room. He looked strikingly like himself again, except for the bloodless skin and the patches of scalp that gleamed through missing swatches of hair. Ropes of saliva dangled like entrails from his lips. Her mother paused, and Brandy had to yank her backward to set her feet in motion again.

Matthew crossed into the living room, the moonlight coming in through the windows making his face look like that of a corpse. *He is,* Brandy thought wildly. *He is a corpse. He is undead.*

In the hallway, Brandy feigned for the front door. Matthew took the bait and charged the door, his small frame slamming hollowly up against it. Brandy turned and shoved her mother up the stairs, shouting, "Go! Go!" Wendy used her hands and feet to scramble up the steps like a child. Brandy urged her along, two hands against her buttocks. When they reached the landing, Wendy rose, trembling on legs that threatened to send her toppling back down the stairs. Brandy looked down the stairwell and saw Matthew at the bottom, looking up. He was awash in shadow; only his eyes, like two searchlights, radiated through the darkness.

"Matthew!" Wendy Crawly shrieked down at her son. It caused Brandy's heart to lurch.

Matthew set one naked foot on the first step. One white hand gripped the handrail.

Brandy grabbed her mother's hand and tore down the hallway toward the nearest room, Matthew's bedroom. Inside, she slammed the door and flipped on the light. Wincing at the brightness, she glanced around as her mother stood motionless against one wall. Her forearm bled through her shirt and blood dripped onto the floor.

"Help me move the desk in front of the door," Brandy said, out of breath.

"What's going on?" Her mother's voice possessed the detachment of someone recently roused from a coma. "Let your brother in."

"He's in," Brandy assured her, "and he's not my brother, Mom. He's not Matthew. Not anymore." Grunting, she slid Matthew's desk away from the wall. A Superman lunchbox clattered to the floor. "Please help me with this, Mom."

Her mother didn't move.

5

Siren blaring, Ben raced through the empty streets of Stillwater toward the Crawly house. The streets were already beginning to flood, torrents of water and debris rushing down toward the center of town. The storm raged.

In the passenger seat, Shirley stared nervously out the windshield. She held the GPS in her hands but did not look at it. "Where is everyone?"

"The storm's keeping them at home," Ben said . . . though he worried that the storm wasn't the only thing. He was thinking of Matthew Crawly and of the hairless, unidentified boy who had washed up along Wills Creek . . . and subsequently disappeared from the morgue in Cumberland. How many others were out there, stalking through the night?

"Ben," Shirley said, her voice just a hair above a whisper. "What's going on here, Ben?"

Something evil came in on the storm, he thought. *Just like Godfrey*

Hogarth said—strange things wash up in the Narrows. Crazy things. Unnatural things.

"I don't know," Ben told her . . . yet he wasn't so sure that wasn't a lie.

6

The banging started on the other side of the bedroom door. Both Brandy and her mother cried out. They had scooted to the far end of the room and huddled now in one corner between the wall and Matthew's bookcase. With each bang, the bedroom door shook and slammed against the back of the desk Brandy had shoved in front of it. As she watched, the desk jerked forward an inch . . . then another inch . . .

It would only be a matter of time before—

A set of fingers curled around the door, which had opened a crack.

Beside her, Wendy struggled to stand up. Brandy pulled her back down. "No, Mom. Please."

"Mattie!" Wendy shouted at the bedroom door. Tears streamed down her face. "Oh, Mattie!"

"No, Mom." Brandy's hands were slick and red with her mother's blood. "Mom . . ."

"Mattie!"

The door bucked again. An arm appeared.

It was then that a part of Brandy Crawly's mind threatened to break apart and sail up out of her body, dissolve right through the ceiling and up through the roof, and float unanchored out over the house. From there, it could disappear into the storm, leaving the husk of Brandy's body to whatever fate awaited it. At the last moment, Brandy clamped down and held strong to her sanity, astounded by the sheer *practicality* of such a feat, as if it were no different than wrapping a fist firmly around a door handle.

The desk screeched across the floor as the bedroom door shoved open a few more inches. Matthew's pale face flashed within the opening, eyes blazing. That single arm shoved blindly against the back of the desk, kicking it forward a few inches more. A moment later, Matthew was in the room. He climbed up on top of the desk, his back arched like a bow, his small face now only vaguely human.

"Stop!" she shouted to the thing that had once been her brother. She was crying freely and uncontrollably now, her body shaken by sobs. "Matthew, *please!* Stop! Stop!"

Matthew did not stop. He climbed down from the desk and was in the room with them. His white legs were marbled with bruises and streaked with filth. Dried blood clung to his bare stomach and chest. As she stared at him, a tuft of blondish hair liberated itself from his scalp and wafted like a cobweb to the floor.

Brandy screamed and wedged herself into the corner. Her mother wrapped her up in her arms, blood oozing over both of them now from her wound. Panicking, Brandy shoved the bookcase down to the floor in an effort to provide one last obstacle for her brother to tackle before he tore into them. The bookcase cracked when it hit the floor and items blew everywhere. Three plastic cups filled with soil on top of the bookcase flew across the room and one of them landed on Matthew's bed. An ultraviolet lamp that had been on top of the bookcase struck the floor as well, the light blinking on and casting an arc of radiant white light across the bedroom.

Matthew hissed and backed away from the light.

It took Brandy a moment or two to realize what had happened. Mopping the tears away from her eyes, she reached down and snatched the UV lamp off the floor, then held it out, her arms fully extended, the light shining directly on Matthew. In the garish, overly bright light, Matthew's body was a hideous mockery of a human being.

He cried out then backed away, crawling behind the desk. Brandy saw the dome of his head retreat back into the hallway where silver eyes stared back out at her from the darkness. Those eyes hung there in the black like stars piercing the night.

"Please, Matthew," she sobbed. "Please . . ."

"Brandy," her mother whispered into her sweaty hair. She repeated her daughter's name over and over again, as if in prayer against the undead. "Brandy, Brandy, Brandy . . ."

7

Out along U.S. Route 40, the water of the Narrows rose up to overtake the highway, sending a cascade of cold, black water down into the heart of Stillwater, Maryland.

8

The UV lamp, along with the bedroom light, blinked and fizzed then finally died. Out in the hallway, Brandy heard the smoke alarm beep once then fall silent. The power had gone out.

"Shit," she said beneath her breath.

Wendy gripped the lamp in Brandy's hands and shook it, as if such an act would restore its power.

How much time had passed? How long had they been sitting here? Brandy did not know. Her whole body ached and she was rank with sweat. The wound at her mother's arm still leaked black blood onto the carpet. There were crimson smears along the wall, too.

There were noises out in the hallway. Brandy sobbed and held the useless UV lamp against her chest like a shield. Her mother said, "Shhh . . ."

"He's coming back," Brandy said breathlessly.

"Okay, baby," Wendy said, smoothing back her daughter's sweaty hair. Some semblance of her old self had returned, though Brandy was only vaguely aware of this. "Okay. Shhh. Okay."

The bedroom door swung open and slammed against the desk. The figure out in the hallway grunted. Another arm appeared and found the desk, gave it a good shove away from the door. A second later, a man appeared in the doorway, the badge at his chest glimmering like salvation in the moonlight coming in through the window.

"Someone in here?" he said.

"Help us," Wendy called.

The man stepped into the room and looked around. He held his shotgun at the ready. "Where are you?" It was dark.

"Here!" Brandy shouted, struggling out of her mother's embrace. "We're right here!"

The man clicked on a flashlight and located them in its beam. Brandy winced. She wondered how much of this was actually happening and how much of it was a horrible nightmare.

The man settled down before them on one knee.

"Okay," he said. The weariness in his voice was all too evident. "Okay, now."

It was Ben Journell.

9

"Are you hurt anywhere else?" Ben asked. They were still in Matthew's bedroom and Ben had just finished wrapping Wendy's wound with a gauze bandage he'd located in the medicine cabinet in the hallway bathroom. A woman was with him, too—Brandy recognized her as the older woman who worked in the police station answering phones.

Brandy had seen her the day she had gone to the station to talk with Ben. The day they had driven out to the old plastics factory on the other side of the Narrows . . .

"I don't think so," Wendy said. She turned her big eyes up to Ben. "Did you see him? He's out there."

"No," he said flatly. "I didn't see him. But I know he's out there. Somewhere."

"What . . ." Wendy began . . . but the crux of it all was too much for her to formulate into coherence and her question died before it ever truly began. Her face collapsed into tears while her chest hitched with sobs. The older woman from the police station settled down on the floor beside Wendy and slipped an arm around her shoulders and told her that everything would be okay.

Brandy didn't know if she believed that.

"Okay." Ben Journell addressed his flashlight onto her mother's bandaged wound and nodded, apparently satisfied with his work. "That should be okay for now." Then he turned to Brandy. "How about you? Are you okay?"

Brandy just stared at him. She was trying to think of the most appropriate response, but just considering it rendered her into stagnation. Like a television set when the cable is out, her mind filled with static.

"Hon?" he said, and placed a gentle hand on her leg.

She said, "The light."

"What's that?"

"I scared him off with the light." She pointed to the lamp that now lay dark and unused on the carpet beside the toppled bookcase.

Ben looked at the lamp then looked back at her. There was a firm expression on his face that afforded Brandy some indescribable comfort. Then he stood and looked out one of the bedroom windows. His shotgun was propped against the wall and Brandy's eyes fell on it. She felt a contradictory mixture of respite and unease.

"The whole town's dark," he said, still looking out the window. The sight of him standing there with his hands on his hips reminded Brandy of—

(her father)

—a marble statue in some museum somewhere. "It's the storm," Ben continued. The badge on the front of his uniform glimmered in the moonlight coming in through the window. He turned away from the window and said, "What's the GPS say now?"

The woman who had come in with Ben—Brandy believed her name was Shirley—paused while comforting Brandy's mother and began digging around in her purse. She withdrew a small device that cast sickly white light onto her face from an electronic screen. The woman scrutinized it then looked up at Ben. "It's still moving," she told him.

He went to her and she handed him the device. Ben's face glowed blue as he held the device up to view it. The screen was doubly reflected in his eyes. "It's moving toward the center of town," he said.

"What is?" Brandy asked.

"The bat," he said. "We put a tracking device on a bat."

"The one in the cage at the police station?" Brandy asked.

Ben looked at her. Then he said, "Yes. I think you're right. I think those bats are . . . I guess—"

"Harbingers," said Shirley. "They're harbingers, Ben."

Although she did not know what a harbinger was, Brandy said nothing.

Ben took the shotgun up off the wall. "I'm going to follow it," he said to them.

"No," Brandy said. They all looked at her. "We should wait, is what I mean. Go in the daytime. I think they sleep in the daytime."

Ben said, "They?"

"There's something else out there," Brandy said. "Something had to do that to my brother."

"She's right, Ben," Shirley said.

"Don't hurt my boy," Wendy Crawly said, her voice just a hair above a croak. It hurt Brandy's heart to look at her, to hear her plead like that. "Don't hurt my boy, Ben Journell."

Brandy said, "He's not—"

"I ain't hurting no one's boy," Ben said, cutting Brandy off while shooting her a sideways glance.

"The fake sunlight scared him off," Brandy reminded him, pointing to the UV lamp again. "And I think he's been sleeping in the daytime." With a sinking feeling in her stomach, she added, "In the garage."

Slowly, Ben nodded. He glanced back down at the GPS device . . . then set it down on the desk that sat slantwise across the bedroom floor. He lowered himself to the floor and set the shotgun back against the wall. When he drew his knees up and rested the back of his head against the wall, Brandy heard him release an audible sigh. She could see his hands shaking in the moonlight.

10

"That boy we found down at Wills Creek," Ben said after the silence became too great. "He had a series of puncture wounds going down his back."

"Like Matthew's shirt," Brandy Crawly said, not missing a beat.

"And the hair had fallen out with both boys," Ben volleyed. He was disgusted. Tired. He couldn't stop thinking about how similar both boys had appeared . . .

"What happened to my little boy?" Wendy Crawly whispered. Shirley was back at her side, her arm around her shoulders again, their heads nearly propped against one another.

"I'm not sure," Ben admitted. He exhaled loudly. "Something got to him. The same thing that got that other boy." After a pause, he added, "I think the same thing happened to Bob Leary's kid, too."

Brandy said, "Billy?"

"Yeah. He went missing, too."

"When?"

Ben shook his head. The days all blended together. It could have been yesterday or six months ago for all he knew.

Then young Brandy said something that caused a chill to radiate through the center of his bones: "How many more are out there, do you think?"

Ben did not answer. He took the GPS off the desk and set it in his lap. The battery still registered as full. He asked Shirley how much time they had before the batteries in the GPS and the tracking device went dead.

"Seventy-two hours," she responded, sounding sleepy and very far away.

"Isn't that something," he muttered to himself. "That's a smart idea," he told Brandy, "waiting for daylight."

"It is," she said. "And I'm coming with you."

He was too tired to argue.

At some point, he slept.

CHAPTER EIGHTEEN

1

Official sunrise for Allegheny County on Thursday morning registered at 6:29 a.m., but the sun did not begin to peek over the eastern mountain and cast its predawn light onto the town of Stillwater until ten after seven. Ben had woken up around five and had sat in the silence of the bedroom, listening to the others sleep, thinking the same catalog of thoughts over and over while keeping one eye trained on the bedroom windows. The rain had let up to a light drizzle, but he knew it was too late. The Narrows had already flooded and the power would be out for some time yet.

What does it matter? he wondered. *What will be left after today? What happened to Stillwater while I sat in this house, waiting out the night?*

Waiting for daylight had seemed like the smart move last night, but now he felt as though he'd allowed some virulent strain to work its poison, sickening the veins, ruining the body, corrupting the heart. Had his hometown died quietly in the night while he slept and waited?

Someone stirred across the room just as the eastern sky began to change. It was Brandy. She stretched and made half-sleep sounds before crawling over to Ben. She leaned against the wall beside him.

"I should go now," he said.

She looked warily out the window and due east. "It's still dark."

"It'll be daylight soon enough. Besides, I can't sit here and wait any longer."

"What does your thing say?"

"Huh?" he grunted.

"Your whatsit," she said. "That little screen."

"Oh." In the night, he must have kicked it under the nearby desk. He slid it out and looked at it. The red dot was no longer moving. It appeared to have roosted at the far end of town, in the abandoned section of town beyond Gracie Street.

"Where is it?"

"Off Gracie Street," he told her.

"What do you think we'll find out there?" she said, her whispery voice dropping even lower.

Ben grinned with half his mouth and said, "We, huh?"

"Yes. I'm not going to let you shoot my brother."

He nodded, but thought, *It would be doing him a favor, I think, darling.* Yet even thinking that made him feel horrible.

Brandy pointed to something on the carpet between them. "What's that?"

He picked it up and turned it over in his fingers. "A lighter. It was my dad's. It must've fallen out of my pocket while I slept."

"Your dad's dead, isn't he?"

He nodded. "How'd you know?"

"It was the way you said it."

He handed her the lighter. "Flip it open. Here. Like this."

He showed her. It took her a few times to get it down, but she eventually did. She handed it back to him and he dropped it in the breast pocket of his uniform shirt. Then he stood up, grunting as his back creaked. Across the room, Shirley said his name in a small voice that was just barely audible over Wendy's light snores.

"It's time for me to go," he told her. "You stay here with Brandy's mother."

"And the girl?" Shirley asked.

"I'm going with him," Brandy said.

Ben put a hand on the girl's shoulder. "She's coming with me," he said.

2

Outside, freezing rain drummed against the roof of the front porch. Across the road and in the direction of town there was nothing but black space where streetlights and house lights should have been. Looking into that emptiness caused Ben's resolve to weaken. It was as if Stillwater had been erased from the face of the planet in the middle of the night. Pervaded by a series of queasy tremors, Ben wondered just how prophetic that thought was.

Brandy appeared beside him, zipping up a nylon jacket with her name embroidered at the breast.

"Is that a school jacket?" he asked her.

"Yes. I used to be on the track team."

"Good. Because if anything happens, I want you to run."

They made a dash for Ben's squad car, which was parked at an angle in front of the house, their footfalls splashing through icy puddles while the rain pelted them. Ben secured the shotgun in the trunk while Brandy climbed into the passenger seat. In the car, Ben set the GPS on the dashboard, keyed the ignition, then spun out into the street and headed in the direction of the town square.

"Seat belt," Brandy said, pulling hers over her chest and clicking it home.

Ben nodded and buckled up. Ahead, the squad car's headlights chased away a chasm of darkness. The faintest ripple of pinkish light stood off to the right now, just beginning to crest the mountain range. The streets were flooded and driving was treacherous. When they reached the intersection of Hamilton and Cemetery Road, Ben had to detour around the main drag and opted for one of the higher, unnamed service roads that ran behind the cemetery.

"There's no one on the roads," Brandy said, her voice small.

"It's the storm," Ben assured her . . . although he did not think his voice sounded all that confident.

"Do you know the Talbots?" Brandy asked out of nowhere. "They live out on Drury."

"I think so."

"I was supposed to go to the school Halloween dance this Friday with Jim Talbot."

Ben said nothing, not sure why she was bringing this up now.

"He's got a younger sister," she went on, "and we were making fun of her a couple of weeks ago, teasing her because she said there was a troll living under the Highland Street Bridge. You know, like in that story about the three goats?"

"I know the one."

"She said she saw a troll living under the bridge when she drove past the Narrows with Mr. Talbot. She's only seven, so she could have seen anything down there, I guess." But the tone of her voice informed Ben that she suddenly believed Jim Talbot's seven-year-old sister, and that there *had* been a troll hiding beneath the Highland Street Bridge after all.

He cut the wheel and detoured along Schoolhouse Road even though the service road had not yet flooded. Brandy asked him where they were going.

"I think it would be smart to round up some backup," he told her. "Do you agree?"

Brandy said nothing but continued to look out the passenger window at the encroaching darkness. Here, the trees blotted out the mountains and any hint of daylight that was working its way up over them. It could have been the middle of the night.

Ben slowed the car as they passed a series of small brick houses that flanked the right side of the road. All the lights in the houses were off, making it appear as though the entire block had been evacuated.

Or worse, Ben thought.

He pulled up in front of Mike Keller's house, which was the last house at the end of the road before the road dead-ended into dense woods. The place was as dark as an underground mine. Mike's police car was still in the driveway. Moonlight limned the shape of what appeared to be a pair of boots pointing up out of the overgrown grass of the front lawn.

Christ . . .

He popped open his door and Brandy did the same. "No," he told her. "Wait here for a sec." Then he snatched his cell phone out of the console and tossed it into her lap. "See if you can get a signal. If you do, call 911."

The girl glanced at the cell phone. "There's no bars."

Ben climbed out of the car and hustled across the front lawn in the rain. At the side of the house, Mike's live-in girlfriend, Judy Janus, had parked her Chevy Blazer. One of the Blazer's doors stood open but no interior light was on in the cab.

The figure on the lawn was Mike Keller, still in uniform. He lay with his face down on the lawn. Someone had unzipped the back of his head, leaving behind a ragged split in his skull which was already overflowing with rainwater.

Ben unholstered his gun and approached the Blazer next. The driver's door stood ajar and the keys still dangled from the ignition, though the engine was off. There was a tremendous amount of blood on the vinyl seats and dark, soupy matter congealing in the footwells.

When he got back in the car, he was breathing heavily. He sat for a few moments behind the wheel, not speaking.

"What happened to your backup?" Brandy asked. She sounded nervous, her voice as taut as a rubber band stretched to its limit.

"I changed my mind."

She set his cell phone back on the console. "No signal. I guess the storm knocked the towers out or something."

"Yeah," he said. Then he pulled back out onto the road.

3

The sky had just begun to lighten when Ben swung the car onto Gracie Street. To the left, the cornfield that flanked the road had been pulverized by the power of last night's storm. To the right, the muddy swamp and stoic, empty houses that made up the abandoned part of town looked now like a prophecy. When they motored by the old house where Brandy had discovered her brother yesterday evening, the girl hung her head low, brownish tangles of hair covering her face.

According to the GPS, the tracking device—the bat—was located on the other side of the field, past the husks of the empty houses. Brandy looked up and out the window and Ben followed her gaze. The razorback silhouette of the eastern mountains stood in sharp relief against a sky that was brightening to a bland yellow at the horizon.

And then he saw it and he knew.

"There," he said.

"I see it," Brandy answered breathlessly.

The turret that climbed almost three stories into the air was that of the old grain silo off Gracie Street. Weather-rotted and the color of bone, it was like the beacon of some lost dystopian civilization. This monster was comprised of wood staves that were gapped and split and bleached from decades in the sun. The cupola resembled a domed hat, capped with an ancient weather vane that did not appear capable of turning in even the strongest wind. Bats hovered around the top of the silo like giant flies, and more of them clung from the railing that encircled the structure just beneath the cupola. A few more darted in and out of rents in the staves.

"Jesus Christ, look at them all," Ben mused.

Brandy said nothing. The expression on her face was one of unmitigated terror.

"Are you gonna be okay?" he asked her.

After a couple of seconds, she nodded . . . but said nothing. She looked about as fragile as fine china.

Ben cut the wheel and bounded over the muddy field. Twice, the car got stuck and he had to switch back and forth from Drive to Reverse to jockey it loose. Finally, he turned onto a paved yet potholed slab of roadway that curled up an incline toward the silo. When they got to within a hundred yards of the structure, Ben geared the car into Park.

"What do we do now?" Brandy asked. Their commingling respiration was fogging up the windshield.

"I guess I go in there." He was peering through the windshield and up at the silo. Sunlight had just begun to strike the eastern side of the structure.

"I'm coming with you."

"I think it's probably best if you—"

"No. I'm not sitting here alone. I can't. I'm coming with you."

He said nothing more.

Surprisingly, Brandy got out of the car first. Ben followed. He went around back and opened the trunk. He took the shotgun out of its rack then filled the pockets of his uniform with extra shells. He handed some to Brandy and told her to fill her pockets, too.

"You know how to use this thing?" he asked, hefting the shotgun. "Just in case something happens . . ."

"Yes. My dad taught me."

He nodded sharply. "Okay. Good." He took the bolt cutters out of the trunk then slammed the trunk closed. Wincing, he looked across the field at the looming cylindrical structure. The rain had lessened to a hazy drizzle but the air had turned bitterly cold. Storm clouds hung low to the ground. "If I tell you to run, to get the hell out of here, I want you to do it. Understood? No arguments. We won't have time for it."

"Understood." She looked as insubstantial as a mirage standing there in the lightlessness of a predawn drizzle. Ben thought that if he closed his eyes, counted to ten, then opened them again, the girl would have disappeared. "What do you think we'll find in there, anyway?"

"I have no idea, but I guess we'll find out soon enough," he said honestly. "All right. Let's go."

Together they crested the gradual incline toward the ancient, weather-ruined grain silo. It had stood there for all of Ben's life, the familiarity of it tantamount to the streets of the town he had navigated since childhood or the various rooms and hallways of the old farmhouse on Sideling Road. But there was a sinister darkness cloaking it now, like how maturity brings with it a certain clarity of distinction between good and evil, and with each step that carried him closer to the thing, he felt his heartbeat amplify and quicken in his chest, and his flesh, despite the cold, begin to perspire.

"Do you smell that?" Brandy asked. "It smells like chemicals."

Indeed, that ammoniacal stink was growing stronger the closer they came to the silo.

It seemed to radiate from it like waves of heat off a desert highway.

There was a single wooden door at the base of the silo that slid open on an old, rusted track. The door was bound shut by a length of chain and a padlock, much like the door on the old plastics factory. Looking at it, Ben guessed that door hadn't been open for the better part of a decade. When they approached it, Ben handed the shotgun over to Brandy—"Be careful," he warned—then clipped the chain with the bolt cutters. The rusty chain fell away from the door handle and coiled at Ben's feet like a cobra. He set the bolt cutters against the side of the structure then took the shotgun from Brandy.

"I've got this, too," she said, showing him the string of black rosary beads she wore around her neck. "They were my grandmother's. I don't know if they work or not but I guess it couldn't hurt."

He wanted to tell her that he did not believe in vampires—even now, he did not believe in them, or in any other type of monster—but he could not find his voice at that moment. Instead, he just nodded succinctly and readied the shotgun with one arm. With his free hand, he gripped the bracket-shaped door handle. He clung to it for seemingly an eternity without breathing.

"You ready?" he whispered eventually.

"I guess so."

"Okay."

He shoved the door open.

4

Absolute darkness greeted them. The chemical smell was unbearable, striking Brandy like rancid breath. Warmth surrounded her and, when she looked up, she could make out slivers of sunlight burning through the gaps in the staves at the eastern-facing wall of the silo, all the way up the channel to the top. Both she and Ben took a few steps in. A faint rectangle of light spilled in through the open door and projected onto the opposite wall, framing their distorted shadows. One of her sneakers sank into something.

The sense that they weren't alone was pervasive and all-encompassing, as if the walls of the structure themselves were alive and dangerous.

"I'm stepping in something," she whispered very close to Ben's face.

"So am I."

Ben clicked on a flashlight and directed the beam at the ground. The entire floor was covered in heaping, reeking mounds of bat shit. She had her right foot in it up to the ankle. A sickly heat puffed up through the collar of her shirt and she held her breath and tried not to think about it. Ben turned the flashlight up toward the ceiling and Brandy snapped her head back to look up . . .

At first, it seemed there was nothing but shadows up there, darkness swimming across darkness through inky, liquid space. But then she realized it wasn't darkness at all, but the dark, fur-cloaked, squirming pods of thousands and thousands of tiny bats. It was an entire colony of them, so many that the whole ceiling was completely covered with them, bulging and rippling like a great beating heart. They crawled over each other, clung to each other, writhed like maggots covered in bristling, brown hair. The susurration of their bodies swarming over each other created a sound like the shushing through dead autumn leaves. The sight of them nearly made her gag.

Like the parting of the Red Sea, the bats at the center of the flashlight's beam began to spread outward, expanding away from the light as if disturbed by it.

What they revealed as they cleared away would haunt Brandy Crawly until her dying day.

5

"Jesus," Ben breathed.

What had been hidden behind the wall of bats was revealed to him not all at once—for the human brain could not comprehend such madness in one unified punch—but piecemeal, like glimpsing individual pieces of a jigsaw puzzle, which helped prevent his sanity from shattering like a pane of glass.

The hairless boy from Wills Creek hung suspended in the air, his nude body a pallid fetal question mark. He was suspended in what appeared to be an enormous web that stretched across the ceiling of the silo. The web itself looked organic, comprised of living tissue, the spokes of the web made of thick veins and arteries that, even as Ben stared, seemed to pulse with some preternatural blood flow. Something was at the center of the web—or perhaps it was part of the web itself, the way the body of an insect is attached to its wings or a turtle is affixed to its shell—that seemed to alter its physical appearance the longer Ben stared at it. It was vaguely humanoid . . . but then it resembled a mollusk . . . and then some tyrannical insect. Something akin to a segmented tail unfurled from the—

(scorpion)

—thing. It was twice as long as a grown man's arm and concluded in a rough bulb that bristled with spiny, black hairs like porcupine quills. Four distinct hooks protruded from the flattened side of the bulb. As Ben watched, the tail came around and encircled the fetal boy in a mockery of a lover's embrace. Clear fluid dripped from the four prong-like hooks as they came up to meet the boy's arched back.

Like the teeth of a zipper fitting neatly together, the four hooks inserted themselves into the four puncture marks that ran down the hairless boy's spine. A moment later, a gush of fluid could be seen pumping through the semitransparent flesh of the thing's tail.

The hairless boy's eyes opened. They appeared blind and did not seem to register the flashlight's beam. As Ben watched, the boy cocked his head at an unnatural angle. The lipless mouth came together to form a crude circle . . . and then the flesh of his lips stretched to an impossible length until it was less a mouth and more like the tubular proboscis of some bloodsucking insect. The proboscis needled itself into a divot-like opening in the flesh of the mother-creature where it proceeded to pump stark-black fluid into its transparent body.

It was a symbiotic exchange, where the child fed the mother and the mother fed the—

"Run," Ben said.

6

She burst from the silo and streamed across the muddy field to find daylight cracking the sky. She tried to scream—and perhaps even thought she had—but no sound came out.

Yet in her head, she was screaming.

7

Ben aimed the shotgun toward the abomination at the center of the ceiling and pulled the trigger. The explosion was deafening. Bats swarmed over the two creatures, which remained locked in their otherworldly symbiosis, filling up the space like darkness in the absence of light. The flashlight dropped and the beam cut off, leaving only the rectangle of pallid predawn light that issued in through the doorway at Ben's back. Ben fired two, three more shots at the ceiling, the tornado of bats whirring in the muzzle flashes and spiraling like a hurricane down the throat of the silo toward him. Dead ones rained down on him, while others struck his face and shoulders, still partially alive, screeching like tortured cats. He went to fire a fifth round but found the shotgun empty. Stupidly, his mind whirled. Above him, something large was moving through the darkness—had become the darkness—and was descending upon him.

Ben remembered the extra shells in his pockets. He pulled out a handful, losing most of them in his panic, and tried to reload the weapon with hands that shook like seismographs. Bats whipped his face and he threw himself backward, hoping the wall of the silo would catch him. But he was too far away from the wall and he fell backward into a mound of reeking, partially hardened feces.

Something large continued to move down the throat of the silo, its formless bulk temporarily cutting in front of the slivers of daylight that cut through the slats in the wood.

Ben groped blindly at the darkness with both hands, desperate to reload the weapon and continue firing.

It seemed to take him an eternity to realize he had dropped the shotgun.

8

She stopped running by the time she hit Gracie Street. Her lungs burned, as did her eyes, and she collapsed to her knees in the mud by the side of the road where she unleashed a woeful, terrified sob. Her terror was great, but she forced herself to close her eyes and count to ten in an effort to reclaim some semblance of control. It took her to twenty before she began to feel steady again . . . and to fifty before she was able to open her eyes and stand.

It was her brother she was thinking of, but it was her father who forced her to stay and stand her ground. Unlike him, she would not run away.

She turned and ran back up the hill toward unimaginable horror.

9

Oddly enough, it was the fact that he was thinking of his own father at the same moment that probably saved Ben Journell's life. He recalled the Zippo he carried in his breast pocket, felt for it . . . and gripped its solid, heavy, cold frame between two fingers. It ignited on the first spin of the knurled wheel. Dim yellow light illuminated the erratic fluttering of the bats' membranous wings all around him. He swatted at them and cried out as they battered against him, shrieking in their unnatural, high-octave voices. When he dared glance up, he could make out something pale and formless creeping down the throat of the silo toward him—the extended dual limbs of impossibly long arms and eyes that gleamed briefly like mirrors facing the sun . . .

The shotgun lay several feet away. The shotgun shells had vanished into the shadows. The hand holding the lighter trembled and the flame threatened to blow out from the air stirred by the wings of the bats.

He thought of his father at that moment, in the weeks before his death when the old man had stood out in the back field of the farmhouse off Sideling Road and had held a conversation with a wife who was no longer there.

His hand still shaking, Ben brought the lighter down to the ground. The flame touched a heap of guano and the guano, rich with nitrogen, ignited instantly. The flames wasted no time spreading across the terrain of feces, the firelight a dazzling yellow-white and reeking. Ben rolled over just as the fire rushed toward him, slamming down onto the ground with a shoulder that immediately thronged with pain. One hand shot blindly out, his numb fingers closing around the butt of the shotgun. He slid it toward himself as flames raced up the dry wood of the silo's walls, the bat shit providing fuel that bested the sodden state of the wood.

He stood and raced out the open door, the entire floor ablaze while flames crawled up the walls of the silo. Cold, wet air struck him like a wall as he burst through the door and into oncoming dawn. He spun around and grabbed the bracket-shaped handle of the silo's door. He gave it a tremendous yank and it slid along its rusty runners until it closed. When he let go of the door handle, he left a bloody handprint behind.

10

He caught Brandy as she came rushing toward him. Her eyes were fearful but there was a set determination to her jaw. She screamed and struggled to break from his grasp, her eyes locked on the silo. Ben hugged her to his chest, cradling the back of her head with one hand.

"Calm," he told her. "Calm down. I need your help more than ever right now."

She broke out in tears and began crying audibly against him. He held her while he watched the flames shoot out from the staves at the base of the silo. Columns of thick, black smoke poured out of rents in the wood, and the bats, whipped into frenzy, spiraled out of the open cracks, filling the sky in a black blizzard.

When she pulled her face away from his chest, she looked over toward the burning silo. The rain was reduced to a fine mist now and the fire burned the entire base of the silo so that it looked like a rocket about to blast off into space.

"I didn't see him in there," she said in a small voice.

"He wasn't," Ben said, knowing she was talking about her brother.

"Do you—" she began, and that was when a low moan escaped the confines of the burning structure. Brandy whimpered softly and clung to Ben, fearful that he might run and leave her there by herself.

"I'm not going anywhere," he assured her. "I need your help."

She nodded numbly but she wasn't looking at him and he didn't think she truly heard him.

"Brandy! I need you!"

She jerked her head back in his direction. Her eyes were wide, lucid. "Yes. Whatever it is . . ."

"Unless it dies from smoke inhalation or the fire itself, it's going to try to get out," he told her, already digging in his pants pockets for more slugs. "I'm going to keep an eye on the door. I'll shoot it if it tries to come out. I need you to go to the other side of the silo and make sure it doesn't get out another way."

She nodded but he wasn't sure she was getting it all. He gripped her forearm in one tight fist. "Honey, do you hear what I'm saying?"

She blinked. Rainwater cascaded in torrents down her face. "Yes," she said. "You want me to go around to the other side in case it tries to escape from there."

"Very good. Now go!"

She ran, steadier than he would have thought possible at the moment.

Ben turned and crouched in the cold mud, facing the closed door of the silo. The flames had blackened the wood around the base but the storm was keeping it from burning out of control. He proceeded to reload the shotgun, filing the shells systematically into the body of the gun while keeping his eyes trained on the silo's door. He supposed he had struck it with at least one blast from the shotgun as it descended the throat of the silo, but if it had done any damage, he couldn't tell.

This is where we die, he thought with bitter finality. *We die now.*

Something slammed against the other side of the silo's door. Ben could hear it like a cannon blast and he could see the door itself rattle in its frame. Fiery bits of sheathing rained down as a second strike shook the entire structure.

This is where—

And then the silo collapsed.

11

The bottom of the structure gave out first, the old wood—coupled with the guano as an accelerant—consumed by the fire despite the soft patter of rain. The silo appeared to telescope straight down at first, releasing a noxious black cloud from its base that rose up like a death shroud to cover the entire structure. Rows of staves blew outward in a shower of splintered wood, iron rivets, and steel bands. As it did so, great scores of bats burst forth and whirled up into the atmosphere in a dizzying black flurry, their numbers so great they temporarily darkened the sky. Their shrill cries, unified in an orchestra of hackle-raising discord, resonated in Ben's molars like fingers down a chalkboard.

Then the silo canted to one side, the remaining staves coming apart as the flames licked up from the foundation. The cupola collapsed in on itself and a mushroom cloud of black smoke billowed out of the hole at the top like the smokestack of a steamship. The silo then appeared to sway like a house of cards before the whole thing came crashing down. It struck the earth in a belch of black smoke and fire.

12

It seemed to take forever for the fall to end. Debris rained down. Dead bats missiled earthward from the sky and exploded in shallow, muddy puddles. Circular bands of iron struck the ground and rolled like hula-hoops until their momentum ceased. Filaments glided and wafted and slowly fell.

Trembling, Ben stood on quaking knees, his entire body shaking so horribly that he did not trust his finger resting on the trigger of the shotgun. Only vaguely was he aware of Brandy running back toward him through the commotion, his eyes locked on the fallen structure, as bits of wood still showered the ground. The air itself was acrid with the stench of smoke.

Brandy arrived at his side, breathing heavily. "Is it dead?"

Ben tightened his grip on the shotgun. "I'm going to find out."

He tramped across the sodden earth until he arrived at the wreckage. Brandy was a step or two behind him. She said, "Look," and pointed at the wreckage—at the steaming, buckled boards and the whitish smoke that corkscrewed up from them. Dead bats littered the ground and some flapped their mangled wings futilely while drowning in puddles of mud.

"What?" Ben asked... but then he saw what had attracted Brandy's attention—a section of boards bucked and heaved. There was something underneath struggling to liberate itself. "Stay here," he instructed.

The smoke-scarred boards were unstable beneath his feet. He trod upon them with the discipline and heed of a tightrope walker, avoiding the sections of wood that still burned or looked weak enough to surrender beneath him and cause him to break an ankle. The stench that engulfed him was one of burning wood, shit, and hair . . . with an underlying medicinal odor. Ben stepped atop the charred boards and walked to the place where the boards bucked. The wood here was shattered and splintered and blackened, like the remains of a house fire, and the thing that moved beneath this sharp and indelicate shrapnel did so with the lassitude and fast-fading resolve of a deer fatally wounded after being struck by a car on the highway.

With his boot, Ben kicked away planks of wood and bits of ancient, twisted metal. A hollow opened up beneath the boards. Something was writhing within. Ben crouched and stared down at it, the gun shaking in his right hand. His breath whistled in and out of his throat and sweat stung his eyes.

A segmented tail retreated beneath the heap of smoldering wood through a crack in one of the boards. It left a trail of snotty fluid on the boards that glistened like semen.

A few feet away, one of the boards rose up and separated itself from the rest of the wreckage. A pale and impossibly long arm extended out from beneath it, stretched halfway to the muddy earth that was just out of its reach. Whatever the creature was, it was seeking solace on solid ground. A second arm appeared . . . and then the creature itself extended out from beneath the smoldering planks of wood.

The thing possessed only the most rudimentary humanlike appearance, in that it appeared to have a central trunk from which limbs diverged. Its head suggested some strange mutation between plant and insect, though there were really no specific details to identify it as such. The longer Ben looked at it, the more formless and indecipherable it became. At one point, he believed he was looking at a gigantic insect crawling out of a hole in the ground. At another point, he swore the thing was amphibian in nature, almost toad-like. Yet again, it also appeared to resemble a hybrid between a human being and some alien species of vegetation. It dragged its organic web behind it like a paratrooper dragging a deployed chute through unwieldy terrain. The tendrils that connected the web to the creature pulsed with lifeblood—or some otherworldly variation thereof—and the web itself, like a glistening sphere of bonelike spokes, appeared to deflate until it more closely resembled a wind sock on an eerily calm day.

Ben approached it, the shotgun up and the butt pressed against his right shoulder. The thing dragged itself out from beneath the wreckage and was in the mud now, the soft rain pelting its formless, colorless hide. The segmented tail carved a muddy swath in the ground as it pulled it up underneath its body. Ben saw the four hooks suppurating like infected sores, bleeding milky fluid onto the ground.

Ben stepped down off the ruined planking, his boots sinking in the mud. He took a few steps toward the creature as it clawed its way along the earth. It had a destination in mind—Ben could tell by its determination and from the direction it was heading, which was clear across the field toward the dip beyond the trees that was a tributary of Wills Creek. The creek itself was flooded now, and water simmered at the cusp of the wooded embankment, black as night itself.

I can't let it reach the water. That's how it got here and that's how it wants to leave. I won't let it leave. I'm going to kill the son of a bitch.

Ben leveled the shotgun at it. The creature must have sensed its impending doom, for it paused in its campaign and leaned to one side. For a brief moment, Ben saw it how it really was—bulbous, inhuman eyes, a nasal cavity like that of a human corpse whose nose has been eaten away, semitransparent skin through which its network of internal organs could be glimpsed pumping and throbbing and dilating and expanding and retracting. Where its mouth should have been there was a small and reddened anus-like cleft.

You're a vampire after all, Ben thought. *Only you can't drink our blood or eat our flesh. You use that tail to poison us and turn us into monsters that do your killing and eating for you. Then we return to your lair and regurgitate all of it back into you. And in return, you pump your poison back into us so that we can continue doing your bidding.* It was a hideous, gruesome, synergistic dance.

And then it was his father.

Ben exhaled a shuddery breath. His lower lip quivered. Sweat peeled down the sides of his face and stung his eyes.

"Dad . . ."

The old man smiled wearily up at him, his moist eyes socketed in a seamed and unshaven face. Bill Journell's mouth moved, and although no words came out, Ben was certain he heard the man speak in his head, a chorus of whispering voices that said a million things at once.

So that's how you do it, Ben thought, fighting back tears. *You reflect our own thoughts back at us . . . show us the people we most want to see. That's why you go after the children first—they believe what they're seeing to be real.*

"You're not my father," Ben told it.

He pulled the shotgun's trigger.

What sprayed out was not so much blood as it was a pale-green sludge. It oozed like molasses from the gaping wound that most closely approximated the creature's neck. It writhed and squealed, though Ben could see no orifice through which such a sound could emanate. Its segmented tail whipped furiously along the ground, cleaving through the mud in a horrid mockery of a snow angel. Once again, as it died, Ben could only see it in pieces instead of one complete whole: the papery, transparent skin; the network of veins just beneath the flesh, congealing with green mucus; the snakelike appendages of its limbs; the crimped and segmented tail with its quadruple hooks and black hairs sprouting like poison-tipped porcupine quills . . .

It was still shuddering when Brandy came up beside him. She looked down at it and a soft moan escaped her. Ben thought he heard her say, "Daddy." Then she picked up one of the loose boards that was shaped serendipitously like a wooden stake and held it reverently against her chest before handing it over to Ben. "Please," she said.

He said, "What?"

"Stake it through the heart. I . . . I just can't . . ."

He set the shotgun down then gripped the makeshift stake in both hands.

If I do this, I risk losing my sanity. I am on the cusp, on the verge. The world as I know it is crumbling down all around me.

But it didn't matter. Not anymore.

He lifted the stake above his head and drove it down through the center of the creature's body. He felt the flesh yield with surprising pliability as he sank the stake all the way through it to the ground. Something popped and air hissed from the carcass. More green ooze frothed out from the fresh wound. As Ben stared down at it, the creature continued to change its appearance before his eyes. *Like flipping through pages of a book.*

"Just in case," Brandy said.

Then she dropped to her knees and cried.

13

Surrounded by a misting rain, they retreated back across the field toward the squad car. They did not speak to each other, opting for silence, as if they had just completed some religious ceremony. And perhaps they had.

Halfway back to the car, they paused to stare at the body of the hairless boy, dead in the mud. He was partially covered by debris from the collapsing of the silo. He was dead and projected all the morbidity and hideousness of a dead body . . . but he was also a boy once again, as if the stopping of his heart had instantly released him from whatever unimaginable horrors had kept him prisoner.

"Who was he?" Brandy asked.

"I'm not sure."

"Do you think . . ." she trailed off on her own. She didn't need to ask the question. Ben knew what she was thinking, anyway.

She took off her rosary and laid it on the body. When she rejoined Ben, she was crying silently.

CHAPTER NINETEEN

1

Ben awoke to a world that was already half a memory. The farmhouse was still dark, the mustiness of the place greeting him in its customary way. A soft rain fell against the roof. He listened to it for a time, and found the world otherwise silent. No power hummed through the walls of the farmhouse. No one drove cars up and down Sideling on their way to work. For a change, there wasn't even the sound of generators off in the distance. Ben glanced at the clock on his nightstand and saw that it was just after seven in the morning, though there was still night pressed against the windows.

It was Friday, Halloween Day. The power was still out on the outskirts of town, including the Journell farm, but that didn't bother Ben all that much. He stripped the bedsheets from his body and climbed out of bed. In the kitchen, he lit a few candles then drank two tall glasses of water from the tap. Rain sluiced against the windowpanes.

He turned on the gas stove and lit the burner with a match. He filled an old percolator with coffee and stood there in the semidarkness waiting for it to brew.

Ten minutes later he went out onto the covered back porch and sat in the coolness of the early morning listening to the storm and watching the craters in the untilled soil overflow with water. Due east, warm pastel light bled up the horizon, forming a sharp and jagged silhouette of the mountains.

He sipped his coffee and contemplated taking up smoking.

2

And he thought, *Every small town has power. The people are aware of it in the way we're aware of electricity humming through the walls of our homes or that our water is delivered through a network of pipes underground. We sense it like animals sense a tornado coming.*

3

And he thought, *Maybe the plague seeks out a town that is already on the verge of collapse—that is already very much near death—and it grabs hold and takes root and plants its virulent claws into the soil. Maybe when a town dies, it becomes this rotting, festering corpse that attracts the sorts of things that feed off corpses.*

4

There were no reports filed and there were very few phone calls made. The death toll was never officially stated, though the number of lives lost came to just over two dozen. In a small, rural town the size of Stillwater, that was quite a lot of people.

At daybreak, Ben made the rounds in his squad car. Some of the water had retreated from the town square but there was still a lot of damage. Out on U.S. Route 40, the receding water left articles of clothing, discarded couch cushions, and pieces of antique furniture in the roadway like roadkill. Similarly, a number of cars at Jimmy Toops's tow yard—including Tom Schuler's beat-up old Maverick, which had been there for the better part of the week—were casualties of a mudslide that sent them tumbling down to the banks of the Potomac River. The stockpile of automobiles created a makeshift dam that caused the cold, black water of the Potomac to rise at an unusual rate, overtaking Beauchamp Avenue and flooding the root cellars of all the homes along Town Road 5. An avalanche uprooted trees and spilled their remains across Schoolhouse Road while the basement of the elementary school gradually filled with septic, black runoff. The school janitor, Odom Pulaski, would return to the building over a week later to a rancorous stench that would remind him of Vietnamese killing fields.

The water left bodies behind, too . . . although it was apparent these people did not suffer a death from drowning. Among the human detritus were the fetid and bloated corpses of Evan Quedentock and Tom Schuler, their faces sheared off and their skulls cracked right down the middle. (A black river snake might have been discovered curling up in the empty cranium of Mr. Quedentock.) Their mutilated corpses would be discovered by some thrill-seeking teenagers looking for valuables left behind in the wake of the flood. Bob Leary's body would eventually be found, too, his skull having been split open like an overripe melon, his legs still protruding from his fireplace. Floodwaters scooped Mike Keller's body right off his front lawn and sailed him like a parade float down Schoolhouse Road. He would be found nearly a week later, snared in the *Y* of an oak tree, but by that time his face, fingers, and neck had been eaten away by wild animals. Judy Janus, his live-in girlfriend who drove the Chevy Blazer, would never be found. No one would ever know that it had actually been Officer Mike Keller who had shot and killed her that night following her tearful confession of infidelity. When Mike was attacked and killed on his front lawn by the Leary boy, he had been on his way into Garrett County to plant a bullet between the eyes of Judy's lover.

In fact, there were a great many things that had happened in Stillwater that no one would ever know, although some folks would come close to knowing them. Ben himself had come close to learning that the unidentified hairless boy who had washed up along Wills Creek had spent the weeknights prior sleeping in a semi-catatonic state up in the trestles of the Highland Street Bridge. He was the troll that Jim Talbot's seven-year-old sister thought she had glimpsed while traveling along Route 40 with her father. He would have also never been found had the Highland Street Bridge not been washed away in the previous flood, casting his hibernating body into the muddy reeds where it was discovered the following day by a group of drunken watermen.

On this day, the Narrows itself continued to gurgle and roil and spill over its concrete barrier. It took some things with it and deposited others as it saw fit, just as it always had throughout the years. Ben pulled over onto the shoulder of Route 40 and climbed halfway down the embankment toward the rushing gray waters. It was a difficult climb and he nearly lost his footing twice. He decided not to descend any farther and merely remained halfway down the embankment, clinging to the old Witch Tree as he watched the risen waters moving at a quick clip. On the other side of the Narrows and up the hillside, the plastics factory held court over the town, the mummified corpse of a king presiding over an abandoned kingdom. Ben turned away with a feeling of dread crawling around inside his belly.

He stopped by Hogarth's Drugstore on Hamilton but the place was dark and locked up tight. The storefront hadn't been properly sandbagged, and, peering into the darkened front windows, Ben could see rubber masks, Halloween decorations, and various other sundries floating about in what looked to be fifteen or so inches of murky brown water. A three-eyed toad was perched on a box of tampons that floated by the window while Ben peered in. He left and drove out to Hogarth's place on Trestle Road. The front door was unlocked and there was rubbish, sodden and mildewing, strewn about the front porch. He entered the house, calling out the old man's name, but no response greeted him. Eventually, he found the old man's body in the back bedroom. He lay in repose on his back, his hands balled together on the swell of his stomach. A St. Christopher medal was clenched in both his hands. By Ben's estimation, the old fellow appeared to have died of a heart attack sometime in the night.

He stopped by Shirley Bennice's house out on Truckhouse Road to say good-bye. Yet he found the place dark and locked up, Shirley's Grand Prix gone from the driveway. He nodded, as if confirming her decision to run away from Stillwater, and turned back to his car.

When he arrived at the police station, he didn't bother to go inside. Instead, he locked the front doors then put a note in the mail slot that read:

This station has been abandoned.
Contact the Cumberland Sheriff's Department
or 911 for assistance.

He thought about adding something about the three dead bodies inside, but in the end, he decided against it.

5

It was closing on dusk when he finally made it around to the Crawly house. He knocked several times on the front door but no one answered. Wind chimes tinkled in the cool breeze. After a while, he climbed back down the steps and headed toward his police car before pausing then cutting around to the rear of the house.

Brandy sat on the top step of the back porch in a sweatshirt and jeans. Her hair was pulled back in a ponytail and her face looked stoic and clean. When one of his boots snapped a twig, she looked up at him without an expression on her face at first . . . but then she smiled softly at him. *She's going to be a beautiful woman someday,* Ben thought, surprised and a bit frightened by the fatherly nature of such a thought.

"Hi," she said. "You look different in regular clothes."

He was dressed in jeans, an old Towson University T-shirt, and a lightweight windbreaker. Her comment caused him to smile, too. "How are you feeling?"

She shrugged. "Okay, I guess."

"How's your mom?"

"She's getting better. She spends most of the time asleep, but I guess that's best."

"Her arm?"

"It's healing."

"That's good." He followed her earlier gaze out across the yard and beyond the Marshes' cornfield. "You out here waiting for someone?"

"Not really," she said . . . and he knew instantly that she was lying to him.

He didn't press the issue. "Well, I just wanted to say good-bye."

"So you're really leaving?"

"I am," he said. "I've been meaning to do it for a long time. Got no reason to stay now."

"I guess not," she said. "Mom says we're leaving, too."

"Everyone's leaving. They're blaming the floods and maybe they even believe that, but these families put up with the flooding for generations without batting an eye. Whether they know it or not, they've sensed what happened here. And now it's time to go."

"People are gonna want to know what happened," she said with genuine worry in her voice.

He sighed. "Probably. But there won't be anyone around to tell them." And he winked. "You dig me?"

Again, that smile. "I do," she said. There were other thoughts flitting around just behind her eyes that Ben could see clear as day. "What do you think happened to the other boys?" she asked. "To my brother and Billy Leary?"

He had given this much thought, too. "I don't know, hon."

She nodded. "Yeah."

He walked over to her, fishing around in the pocket of his jeans. "Here," he said, handing her his father's Zippo lighter. "I want you to have it."

She looked at the lighter then looked up at him. Tears were already welling in her eyes. "Are you sure?"

"Yes. You just take care of it, okay?"

"I will."

"Thanks." He slipped his hands in the pockets of his windbreaker. "You stay safe, okay?"

"I will. Are you leaving tonight?"

"I am. But you hear me about staying safe, right?"

"Yes."

"Promise me."

She spat on the ground and said, "I promise."

Ben smirked. "That's some habit."

"You stay safe, too," she said. "Don't do foolish things."

"I won't," he promised her . . . though he was already thinking foolish things.

"Go on, now," she told him. "Get lost."

He got lost.

6

At the farmhouse, he exchanged the squad car for the dusty old Packard that had sat idle in the barn for several months. It took a few cranks of the ignition to get the Packard started, but when it awoke, it did so like a lion rousing from a deep and restful slumber. He drove it around to the front of the house and popped the trunk. For the next hour, he loaded some items into the Packard's trunk—some clothes, toiletries, his father's war medals, some other items. Midway through packing up the car, Ben was startled by his cell phone ringing in his pocket. He answered the call and found it was Paul Davenport calling with the number to the Fish and Wildlife folks he'd promised Ben earlier in the week. Ben just laughed, wished Paul Davenport well, and hung up the phone. Then he powered the phone off so as not to be disturbed.

Before leaving the old farmhouse, he paused in the front hall and surveyed the place. The halls were musty with deepening shadows, the windows gilded with fading daylight. For a brief moment, he could see himself as a small boy playing with Tonka trucks on the living room floor while his father, old Bill Journell, sat in his recliner reading a newspaper with a pipe propped in his mouth. The image was so clear it was as if it were a stage play going on right before his eyes. Watching it, Ben felt something solid and heavy clench quickly at his heart and squeeze. His breath came in labored gasps. He had stayed to take care of his father and that had been noble. But there was no need to hold stewardship over old ghosts.

Ben left.

7

Fifteen minutes later, at the intersection of Cemetery Road and one of the unnamed service roads that wound up into the hills, Ben stopped his car and rolled down his window to get a better look at the rubber vampire mask—surely some kid's Halloween costume—that had gotten snared by a low-hanging tree limb. Ironic laughter threatened to burst from his throat. He drove quickly away, leaving the town of Stillwater behind him to die its silent death.

EPILOGUE

1

But she had lied to him. She *wasn't* careful. Quite the opposite, in fact. The nights that followed saw her on the back porch while her mother slept soundly in the master bedroom, her grandmother's silver cross in her lap, her brother's UV lamp beside her, trailing an extension cord back into the house. The most recent storm had brought with it the frigidity of winter. Trees shook loose the rest of their leaves and the sky appeared gray and brooding no matter the time of day. Bundled in heavy sweaters and two pairs of socks, she spent every night on the porch, keeping watch.

One by one, the people of Stillwater picked up and left. Ben had been right. They blamed the storms and the flooding . . . but Brandy recognized a deeper, darker truth in their eyes. Even the folks who hadn't been affected by the terror still smelled it on the wind, like dead things hidden and rotting. Deep coils of stink perfumed out of the ground. You couldn't go anywhere in town and escape it. Anyway, there were no places left to go. The shops along Hamilton were all dark now and filled with water.

Once, Dwight Dandridge stopped by while she was sitting on the back porch. They talked for a while about nothing in particular and then Brandy went inside only to return with two steaming mugs of hot chocolate. Before Dwight headed home, Brandy hugged him.

He shied away at first but then let her do it. Matthew's name never came up.

Matthew . . .

He came back in the middle of one night, though he did not approach the house. He lingered just beyond the shrubbery that bordered the property, his pallid ghost-face seeming to hover like the moon. Brandy stood and walked halfway down the porch steps. She even called out his name, her voice dull and flat in the cold night. The sound of her voice appeared to have startled him, for he turned and rushed off through the Marshes' cornfield. Expressionlessly, Brandy turned back around and reclaimed her seat on the porch.

He returned twice more. The next time, some brazenness urged him onto the property where he wavered like a ribbon of steam in the space between the detached garage and the hedgerow. This time she did not call his name, not wanting to frighten him away. This time she just waited for him, sitting motionless in the darkness of the porch. He moved now with a humanity that recalled the child he truly was—the *brother* he was—and it hurt her heart to see it. Yet she was silent. She said nothing.

He fled back out into the night.

The final time, he appeared with another figure who Brandy guessed was Billy Leary. Both boys trod through the corn and crept into the yard, just as Matthew had done the previous time by himself. By this time, however, the power had been restored to Stillwater, and the boys' movements caused the motion sensor light above the garage to wink on. Bright-white light spilled out across the yard, spotlighting the two frail little figures who quickly retreated into the darkness where they disappeared almost as silently as they had come.

The following morning, just as daylight seeped up into the sky over the eastern mountains, Brandy took the pickup truck out to Route 40 and then down to the turnabout where the stone footbridge crossed over the Narrows. She parked the car and zippered up her jacket then got out. The air was stingingly cold. With her grandmother's crucifix in her jacket pocket and a flashlight leading the way, she crossed the footbridge and ascended the hillside on the opposite side of the Narrows. Toward the plastics factory.

The shrubbery was denuded, making it easier for her to locate the double doors at the rear of the old building. In fact, one of the doors had been left open a few inches, revealing a vertical sliver of darkness. She shone the flashlight into the sliver while she eased the door open with one sneaker. Its hinges squealed.

Inside, only the vaguest shafts of early morning light permeated the milky windows at the far end of the building. Industrial machinery loomed like prehistoric creatures frozen in time. The air smelled unused and musty, coating the back of her throat like dust. The flashlight's beam washed back and forth. Muddy footprints stamped trails about the concrete floor.

She found them in a back room, asleep on a mound of sawdust and dead leaves. Matthew lay curled on his side, his thumb propped in his mouth just as he used to do when he was a toddler. Even in the limited light of the flashlight, Brandy could see his hair had started to grow back. His flesh had taken on some color, and his face even looked rosy. Beyond Matthew, Billy Leary lay on his back, asleep. There was sawdust and dead leaves in his hair.

"Matthew," she whispered.

He sat up, blinking into the light. Dirt streaked his face. His eyes focused on her and warmed instantly.

"Brandy," he said, already beginning to tremble . . . already beginning to cry. Behind him, Billy Leary stirred and woke, too. "Brandy."

She turned off the light. "Time to go home," she said.

2

But he had lied to her. He *wasn't* careful. Quite the opposite, in fact.

Shirley had been right—the battery on the GPS lasted for nearly seventy-two hours. When the signal finally died, it had already stopped moving for several hours, coming to rest in the green hills of the Shenandoah Valley.

Ben arrived in the Valley around dusk of some afternoon. He guided the Packard into a parking space in front of a small mom-and-pop diner. Outside, the air tasted crisp. Someone was cooking pork in a smoker out back. It would be a harsh winter here in the mountains.

In the diner, Ben sat at the counter and ordered only a cup of coffee. The few other people in the place ate in solitary silence, crowded protectively over their plates like prisoners in a prison cafeteria.

"Anything besides coffee?" a middle-aged waitress asked him after he'd finished half the cup. "Charlie makes one hell of an omelet."

"An omelet for dinner?"

"Sure," the waitress said. "Why not?"

Why not, indeed. "Okay," he said. "Sounds good."

She looked him over. "You new in town?"

"Just got in now."

"Looking for work?"

"Maybe." He finished his coffee and the waitress refilled his cup. "You folks been having problems with bats lately?" he asked.

"You some kind of exterminator?"

"Something like that," he said.

She shrugged then looked instantly miserable. After a moment, she said, "I'll go tell Charlie to put on an omelet for you."

"Thanks."

She hurried away, as if his question about bats had troubled her.

He brought his coffee to his lips, sipped it. It was hot, strong, and good.

A few stools away, a burly man with a gray beard and a hunting vest cleared his throat and said, "You say something about bats, buddy?"

Outside, the sun began to set.

ACKNOWLEDGEMENTS

Thanks to Daniel Carpenter and all the other fine folks at Titan Books for finding this creepy story delightful enough to set it loose once more into the world.

RONALD MALFI
February 21, 2024
Annapolis, Maryland

ABOUT THE AUTHOR

Ronald Malfi is the award-winning author of several horror novels and thrillers, including the bestseller *Come with Me*, published by Titan Books in 2021. He is the recipient of two Independent Publisher Book Awards, the Beverly Hills Book Award, the Vincent Preis Horror Award, the Benjamin Franklin Award, and his novel *Floating Staircase* was a finalist for the Bram Stoker Award®. He lives with his family along the Chesapeake Bay, and when he's not writing, he's performing in the rock band VEER.

ronaldmalfi.com
@RonaldMalfi